To my friends and family, who have supported me through all this insanity, but especially to my husband. You are my partner, my friend, and my love.

ISBN-13:
epub 979-8-9902243-0-8
paperback 979-8-9902243-1-5

Printed in the United States of America

Contents

Chapter 1: A Way Out

I eased the front door closed, stupidly holding my breath as I crept in. Like that would make me any quieter. Glass clinked in the kitchen, and my shoulders dropped. Mom. She must have gotten up while I was outside fetching the mail. Seven was early for her. She normally slept till noon. It was a good move on her part. I couldn't get to my bedroom without passing her. So much for my grand plan. In one last ditch attempt, I slipped the couple of envelopes that might not be trash into my pocket and left the rest, hoping she'd believe that was all.

When I walked in, she was standing at the sink. Her robe, a tacky thing that barely went down to her knees and was supposed to look like a kimono, hung open. She hadn't even taken time to do anything with her hair, which hung in badly bleached knots down her back.

Without looking at me, she put the coffee pot under the tap with one hand and held out the other. "You're up early, Addie. Oh, you got the mail. Good. Hand it over."

Like she hadn't known what I was up to. She was playing the game as much as I was. I slapped the pile of bills and credit card advertisements into her waiting palm. Still not facing me, she thumbed through the envelopes. She slowly turned to look at me. Her robe flapped open, revealing that she was wearing nothing underneath, and I repressed a shudder. Her eyes narrowed, and the smudged makeup that ringed them made her look like an aging raccoon.

I feigned innocence. "What?"

"You didn't get anything else today?" It was an accusation, not a question. She knew I was hiding something, but without frisking me she couldn't find out for sure. At least I didn't have to worry about that. Mom had always been hesitant to touch me.

I bit my lip to keep from snapping at her. It would only start another fight, and that wouldn't solve anything. It never did.

"Nope." I folded my hands in front of me and smiled as pleasantly as I could manage. "Guess I'll just have to try again tomorrow."

"I don't know why you bother." Mom dropped the mail down on the counter, where it disappeared among the clutter of useless kitchen gadgets and unwashed dishes. Finally, she gave up on the illusion of civility. "Even if you did get in, college classes are all online these days. You don't have a computer."

"You won't let me have a computer. Or a phone." Bitterness dripped from my words, partially driven by self-disgust. Damn it, I promised myself I wouldn't do this. Ever since she found out I'd been applying to colleges, my mother had been harassing me about it. It was one flimsy, nonsensical excuse after another to draw me into a fight, and I took the bait every time.

"If how you keep a kitchen is any indication, you aren't ready for the kind of responsibility that comes with electronics, much less college." Mom snatched the pot out of the sink and dumped the water into the coffee maker, splashing it everywhere before she started pawing through an overcrowded cabinet for the actual coffee. "Besides, they cost money, Missy, in case you've forgotten."

"No, I haven't." Temper rose like acid in my stomach, but I swallowed it down. If she had it her way, I would be stuck at home with her forever. I ignored the shot about the housekeeping. Either I got yelled at for not cleaning, or I got yelled at for not cleaning correctly. It was an argument even more pointless than the one we were having. "But I also remember my English teacher trying to give me a used laptop, and Loren offered me her old phone when she upgraded."

Mom scoffed. "You know, Addie, you need to learn that things cost more than their initial price. You have to pay for the data plan, and for the electricity to run it. Baby, we've had this discussion before."

"Yeah, I know." I didn't bother telling her that the library had free Wi-Fi and would let me charge a phone. The librarians liked me and had offered me a summer job

6

shelving books. It wouldn't have been a lot, but it could have paid for a plan. That meant a lot to me. They were the reason I wanted a degree in library science.

Mom was right about one thing. We'd had this fight before. Nothing new would come of having it again, because it wasn't about electricity. It wasn't about a phone. It was about control.

I pinched the bridge of my nose and closed my eyes like I had a headache. I didn't, but years of training made my mother ease up on me a little if she thought I did. She didn't actually want to risk me having a fit.

The accident I'd had on my eighth birthday had caused some kind of permanent damage to my brain. I had regular headaches, and sometimes things would get so bad I'd have seizures. If there was a name for what I had, I didn't know it. Mom refused to take me to a doctor. She said she didn't believe in them. Instead, she would fake notes for me and make me lie to teachers. Nearly a decade later, the symptoms were less frequent but still present.

Mom was weird about my fits. She desperately tried to avoid triggering them, but she also seemed to know more about them than she let on. More than once, she'd mentioned that a doctor couldn't help. When I'd ask her why, she'd refused to answer, and it would start another argument. Fighting with me was her solution to everything. I was just so sick of it.

"I'm going to take a shower." I walked towards my room, done with the conversation. "Maybe it will help my head."

"Do you want some coffee?" Mom asked, more friendly now that she thought she had won.

"Yeah, I'll drink it later. Thanks." I disappeared around the corner, grateful I didn't have to hide my expression. Maybe I was overusing the headache excuse lately. That could get me into trouble if she caught on, but it was the best tool I had.

When I got to my room, I closed the door and threw my book bag in front of it. I'd never had a lock, and the bag wouldn't stop my mother if she really wanted to get in, but it would buy me a second if she tried to open the door unannounced.

My room was decent-sized, but mostly empty except for my twin bed and a small dresser. Mom didn't like to buy me things, always saying we didn't have the money. Not that it stopped her from buying the next "as seen on TV" gadget we'd never use or new clothes to make her feel young and desirable. I'd always suspected that part of it was so that when she searched my room, there would be less places for me to hide things.

I plopped down on my bed and pulled the folded mail out of my pocket for sorting. Two credit card offers, a coupon for an oil change for a car I didn't own, and a hand-addressed envelope from Pit and Castle Legal Associates. Most likely, it was an advertisement for a class action suit that had nothing to do with me. Or it was a scam.

I tore it open and found a business card and a letter.

"Miss Adeline Gardener,

Greetings from the offices of Pit and Castle. My name is Redmond Castle. I am contacting you regarding the inheritance due to you being handled by our firm."

My first thought was that my grandmother had died and left me something, but I immediately dismissed that. Grandma was too cantankerous to die and was going to live forever in her hate. I hadn't seen her since my Dad left, and she had kicked us out of her house. Grandma was a bitch.

"The terms of this inheritance dictate that it will pass to you on your eighteenth birthday, July 19th, of this year. At that time, you will be able to sign the forms accepting possession of the estates of Isaac Heart."

I didn't know the name, but a familiar needle of pain pricked behind my eyes and twisted my stomach. Sometimes when I tried to recall those missing years before the accident, or something caused me to almost remember, it would trigger one of my fits. First came the headaches, then if I continued to press, it could work into a full-blown seizure. Eyes closed, I made myself breathe and count.

One. My breath was shallow and a little shaky. Two. I forced my lungs to fully expand despite their protest. Three. Increased oxygen eased the pain.

Carefully folding the letter, I put it back in the envelope and slid the business card under the cover of my library book. I needed another bookmark anyway.

I finally went to take that shower. Physical activity helped me not to think, giving my broken brain a chance to relax before I took another run at the letter. The hot water pouring over my head was a relief, and I reveled in one of life's truly uncomplicated moments.

When I got out, I used the hair dryer while I looked at myself in the mirror.

I had the urge to give in to my best friend and let her bleach and straighten my hair. Mom would go ballistic, but that was part of the appeal. Loren had a talent for ticking people off. Especially my mother. It was one of the reasons we were friends.

Loren had adopted me our freshman year of high school. She had this gravitational personality that meant once you were there, you never really left her orbit.

I tried to picture myself as a blonde, but couldn't. My hair was long, black, and slightly wavy. While it was my favorite feature, Loren was constantly assuring me that it would be better if I changed it. The story of my life: I would be so much better if I wasn't me. I left my self-pity in the bathroom. It was stupid and self-defeating.I fell back on my bed, where I picked up the paper and tried again. My head was fine until I hit the name of Isaac Heart. That was okay. I'd learned from previous experience that sometimes, I could desensitize myself through repetition to whatever was causing a fit. This felt like one of those times.

There were no dollar amounts specified, but the rest of the letter hinted that the sum of the inheritance was substantial. There was even a house and some land. This was almost certainly a scam. Some new version of the Nigerian prince, or something like that. Probably hundreds of people had received copies with their names filled in like form letters.

Three things stopped me from pitching it in the trash. First, it was too personalized, handwritten with details like my upcoming birthday. Second, the ache in my head hinted that I had heard of Isaac Heart sometime before my accident. Third, was hope. If the letter was legitimate, then I had my own place and some money. I would be free.

It wouldn't hurt to contact Redmond Castle, I supposed. Unless this was one of those scams that charged you a thousand bucks a call. Possible, but unlikely. Mom wouldn't like it, especially if it was for real. She wouldn't trust me to 'share' the money with her. No way I could call from the house phone, so I'd have to go somewhere else.

Once school had ended, I'd lost my best excuse for leaving the house. My backup of needing to go to the library was getting thin, but I figured today was a good day to use it. I threw on the first clean T-shirt and jeans I could find and stuffed the letter into my pocket, grabbing my book and bag on the way out.

As I walked past the kitchen, I hoped against hope that Mom would be distracted and not question my trek to the front door. When did I ever get that lucky?

"And where do you think you're going?"

"Library." I held up the book. "I finished this one last night."

"Didn't you just get that thing?" She narrowed her eyes, trying to psychically divine any wrongdoing. My mother did this every time I went to the library. She would love to forbid me to go, but couldn't quite bring herself to be the only mother who told her daughter not to read.

"Two days ago," I nodded, "but it was an awesome mystery. Couldn't put it down."

"Uh-huh." Mouth crinkled up on one side, Mom hesitated but finally relented with an unhappy sigh. "Alright, but I want you home early. No later than two, do you understand me? You don't need to spend all day at the library, reading. You can read at home."

I deserved brownie points for not mouthing off. With a nod, I side-stepped my mother to head out the door. She stood on the stoop, robe finally tied, watching me walk down the street until I turned the corner. As soon as I was sure I was out of sight, I looped around behind my house to head to Loren's.

A block away from my house, I thought something streaked across the road and disappeared over a fence. I froze as I argued with myself for just a second. It could have been a cat. It looked awfully big to be a cat. It was probably nothing.

I'd thought I'd seen things before. Mom had even been with me the first time it had happened. I'd been eight or nine. When I'd told her, she'd insisted that it was just my imagination. As she angrily dragged me home, she told me that anything else I saw was just my damaged brain making me paranoid. It had to be my paranoia. What else could it have been?

When I arrived at Loren's house I readied my thousand-watt smile and knocked. Mrs. Tyson was always happy to see me. She opened the door, dressed for the office with hair and makeup all perfectly done, elegant as always. Her immaculately manicured nails were long and painted rose pink. They did look a little like talons, but that was cool. Seemingly startled, but pleased, she reached out to hug me.

I wasted a moment wishing that she was my mom as I squeezed her back. "Hi, Mrs. Tyson."

"Addie, sweetie, I didn't know you were coming. Is everything okay? I'm pretty sure Loren wasn't expecting you, considering she's still in bed." She rolled her eyes. Getting her daughter out of bed usually required either bribery or excavation equipment.

"Everything is fine, Ma'am. I just need to borrow your internet, if that's alright." The smell of bacon wafted out the door and my stomach rumbled. Right, I hadn't eaten yet. I hadn't even gotten the coffee Mom had made.

Loren's mother rolled her eyes again. She thought Mom's tech embargo was stupid. I'd never mentioned that

11

my mother had a cell phone. The hypocrisy might have made Mrs. Tyson lose her temper.

"Of course, you can. You're staying for breakfast too, and don't you try to tell me that you aren't hungry. I can hear your stomach from here. Go on inside and wake up my lazy daughter. I'll have food on the table by the time you get her up."

Mrs. Tyson was a lawyer, which meant that you argued with her at your peril. With a grin of gratitude, I scooted past her through the door and jogged to Loren's room. A caution sign on the door sported the silhouette of a horned horse doing the limbo. It declared this point a 'demented unicorn x-ing.' I rapped my knuckles sharply on the wood and called out, "Hey, Lore! Get up, there's breakfast."

A thud was the only response I got, so I let myself in. Loren's room was in one of the cleaner phases of its cycle of chaos, except for the pile of blankets next to the bed that I assumed contained my best friend. I flicked on the lights and the pink and black mass of covers began to undulate like an opening cocoon. I grabbed the most obvious corner I could see, pulling it up to reveal a face scrunched up like a mole against the sun.

"Nooo..." Loren made a piteous noise. "Turn the light off."

"Nope." I nudged the mountain of blankets with cheerful malice. "You have to get up unless you want me to steal all your bacon."

She froze in mid-action of re-covering her face and turned a suddenly sharp and wakeful eye on me. "Bitch, do not touch my bacon."

I skipped a half-step toward the door and laughed. "If you don't move your ass, I'm going to eat it all."

With surly grumbles, Loren began to struggle out of her wrapping. "What are you doing here? Other than eating my breakfast. Again."

"I need to borrow your computer, and maybe your phone." I pulled the envelope out of my back pocket and waved it at her. "I got a letter from a lawyer that says I inherited some stuff from a guy I've never heard of. I want to check it out."

"Have Mom look at it." Loren waved a hand dismissively, extricating herself from the last of the covers.

"Is she that kind of lawyer?" I asked. I would not make fun of my friend for her rainbow pajamas. It would give her license to mock me later. "I thought she did divorces and stuff."

"I don't know." Loren shrugged. "Ask her anyway. Maybe she knows these guys."

"No harm in it, I guess." I studied the envelope again. I didn't glean any new insights. Oh well.

After a few moments of throwing clothes out of their drawers, she gave up on finding something to wear and led the way out of her room, still rocking her jammies. Mrs. Tyson frowned when she saw her daughter still not dressed but decided not to pick that fight. Not while I was there, at least. Instead, she set plates down in front of us. I had to choke back a laugh when I saw I had been given an obviously larger portion of bacon.

I passed the letter across the table, asking, "Ma'am? Would you take a look at this for me, please? It's from a guy saying he's a lawyer, and that I just inherited a bunch of money. I figure it's a scam, but I'd appreciate it if you'd look."

She took the envelope and pulled it out to read. With astounding speed, her eyes danced through the letter. One corner of her mouth scrunched up. "Well it doesn't look like it passed through a translation program, so that's good. The legal language looks fine, but property and inheritance aren't my fields. I don't know this firm, but they're not local, so that's not odd. Tell you what, let me call a friend of mine who might know more about them. You girls sit here and eat, I'll be right back."

Mrs. Tyson left the room, staring at the paper like it contained a riddle she was trying to solve. I wished her more luck than I had.

13

Chapter 2: Unknown Benefactor

Loren contentedly piled everything on her plate onto a piece of toast, then soaked the whole mess with ketchup. Shaking the nearly empty bottle to get the last drops, she said, "See? Mom's got this. What do you get if it's legit?"

"A house and some money." I picked up a slice of bacon and nibbled. "But it's nothing. I mean, the long-lost relative thing doesn't really happen."

"Does it say he's a relative?" Slapping another piece of toast on her breakfast mess, she took a happy bite out of her monster sandwich. Somehow, she didn't end up covered in it.

"No, and that makes it even weirder. Maybe the name sounds familiar? It gives me headaches." Loren was one of the few people who knew everything. My paranoia, my theory about how my fits were tied to my lost memories, all of it. She believed me. Possibly the only person who'd ever had. Yet another reason we were friends.

Loren set her sandwich down, her eyes filled with wonder and speculation. "Addie, what if he's your father?"

I wrinkled my nose and ate some more bacon. "What do you mean? You know I haven't heard from Dad in years."

"No, no. Hear me out." Loren held her hands up like she was framing the name of a Broadway play. "This guy is your biological father! Your mom had an affair. The jerk you think is your dad left because he found out when you had a blood test at the hospital. You know, after your accident."

"Except I never went to the hospital," I pointed out with my half-eaten piece of toast. "He didn't leave until over a year later, anyways."

"So maybe they were trying to work things out and failed." Loren's hands moved in ecstatic circles. "Addie, it just makes too much sense. Think of the possi–"

"Possibility of what? That there was someone out there who was related to me that actually gave a damn?

That even if there was, it doesn't matter anymore, because now they're dead and all I get is a consolation prize?" The vitriol in my voice took me by surprise. I really wished I would think more before I opened my stupid mouth.

"Ouch." Loren winced. She had the same problem with verbal diarrhea that I did. "Sorry, Add, I didn't think that one through. Forgive me?"

I sighed heavily. "Always. I owe you an apology too. It just hit me sideways, you know?"

"Yeah." She quickly stuffed her mouth with another bite of sandwich. We just ate for a few minutes in silence until the quiet eased into something more companionable.

Mrs. Tyson came out of her office, holding her cell phone in one hand and the letter in the other. She seemed bemused as she handed me the piece of paper. "Well, according to my friend, Pit and Castle are a legitimate firm. They mostly do property stuff in that area. For the last four years, they've bought up all the businesses and land they could get their hands on. The number she had for them matched the one on the letter. So, yeah, give them a call. Feel free to use our phone if you don't want to... bother your mother."

I had to smile at Mrs. Tyson's obvious disapproval of Mom. "Thanks."

"Now, don't agree to anything just yet. Just get some more information. If you have any questions about what they tell you, wait till I get home. I'll look over it for you. I've got to get to work now, but feel free to stay as long as you want." Mrs. Tyson fetched her purse from a kitchen counter and slipped her phone into it.

"Can we have money for pizza?" Loren asked.

"No." She gave her daughter a look that said she was not amused. "Lunch was going to be leftover breakfast whenever you woke up, but you two finished that off. There's plenty of stuff for sandwiches. You'll be fine."

Loren sighed dramatically but didn't argue. Instead, she laid an arm on the table and rested her head on it, giving her mother a lamenting look. "Okay, Mom. We'll make do without. Have a good day at work. We'll be here.

Fording the legal waters of Addie's inheritance. Alone. Without pizza."

Mrs. Tyson frowned and pointed a warning finger. "That's enough young lady. Now Addie, you go ahead and call Castle, but talk to me before you agree to anything, okay?"

"Yes Ma'am," I said, cheerfully. When Loren's mother was out the door, my best friend turned to me with a wicked grin.

"You know what this means, right?" Loren looked like she was a cat that had spied a particularly fat canary. I always got a sinking feeling when she got that smile.

I scooped up a forkful of eggs and sighed. "No, but I bet you are going to tell me."

"Damn straight." She grabbed my hands and shook them. My fork tumbled onto the plate with a clatter. "Add, this is freedom. If you have a house, we can go live there together. Roommates! I'll get a job and pay half the bills. We will be completely on our own!"

I bit my lip. "Yeah, but Mom is never going to let me--"

"She can't stop you," Loren mock-whispered. "You're going to be eighteen in what, a week?"

"Ten days," I corrected, purely for contrariness's sake.

"Fine." Loren rolled her eyes. She looked a lot like her mother when she did that. "In ten days, you are going to become a legal adult and your mother can't tell you to do shit. Once you've got a house and some money, you never have to deal with that woman again. You are free and I can go with you. I can finally get out from under my mom's thumb."

"Hey, your mom is awesome." I pointed a finger at Loren. "I would kill to have your mother."

She grimaced but nodded. "Yeah, okay, Mom's great, but we are driving each other crazy. I do love her, but we would get along so much better if I didn't have to live in the same house as her."

16

Inclining my head in agreement, I picked up my fork and started eating again. Loren would never admit it, but most of the problem between her and her mother was that they were too much alike. Both were strong-willed and sure of what they wanted. Neither liked losing and saw every argument as a fight to the death. Still, they were super close. It made me envious.

Through the rest of breakfast, Loren pontificated on possible plans. I hadn't said yes to her living with me, but honestly, there was little point in her asking. She was too good of a friend to say no to. As soon as she was finished, she dragged me off to her bedroom to look at the house online. Searching the address brought up nothing on any of the real estate sites, so we had to resort to a satellite image.

"This has to be a mistake," I said, looking at the sprawling mansion and property. "No one would leave anything like that to me."

"I'm telling ya," Loren smirked, "it's your long-lost bio-dad. He was a millionaire, and he left you all of his money."

"Stop, please." I held up a hand. "It's some kind of mix-up. Either this isn't the right address, or I'm not the right person, or--"

"It's okay to have a little hope, Add." Though spoken softly, Loren's interruption cut through my words. "And believe it or not, karmically, you're due a little luck."

"Maybe, I don't know." I didn't believe in luck, or karma, or whatever. Good things didn't happen to good people any more than they did to evil ones. My 'bad luck' was just the result of actions, mine and my mother's, and strings of events we put into motion. I wasn't owed anything, but Loren was right about one thing; I was afraid to hope. Maybe because I hadn't earned it, I couldn't trust anything that just fell into my lap.

I checked the address again. It matched the one on the paper. She must have read my mind because she smacked her cell phone into my hand. "You know, there is a surefire way to find out."

The camera on the pearl pink rectangle in my hand glared at me accusatorially. "Not calling would make me a coward, wouldn't it?"

In answer, Loren took the phone back and dialed the number off the page. With a smirk, she hit call and shoved it back at me. I scrambled to hang up, but at the beginning of the second ring, someone picked up, ready or not.

"Red Castle speaking." The voice was aged and a bit tired.

"Oh, um, Mr. Castle. Hi. This is Adeline Gardener. You sent me a letter--" I began in a rush, unsure of what to say next. He burst out in a jolly laugh like a grandfather whose grandkids have unexpectedly shown up at his door.

"Miss Gardener! I am delighted to hear from you. I'm assuming you have questions about your inheritance." He sounded so happy to talk to me, it forced me to smile.

"Um, yeah." I swatted at Loren who was trying to sneak her hand between my face and the phone, presumably to hit the speaker button. "There's a lot of things that don't make sense."

"Well, my dear, feel free to ask anything you like. The inheritance doesn't officially fall to you until your eighteenth birthday, but I'd like to get everything set up for you before then." On the other end of the phone, there was the sound of shuffling paper.

"Um, okay." Damn it. I was saying 'um' way too much. I gathered myself and got down to business. "Are you sure you have the right person? I've never heard of Isaac Heart before today."

"You are Adeline Susanna Gardener, daughter of Michael and Sarah Gardener, correct?" When Castle brought up my middle name, I winced. I had been named for my grandmother on my dad's side and would never forgive anyone for that.

"Well, yes, but, I mean... there has to be some kind of mistake. I don't know Isaac Heart." My assertion was weak in the presence of my full name. It was like an invocation. The likelihood of someone having the same name and parents as me was slim to none.

18

"Be that as it may, it is meant for you." Castle's tone was warm, but chiding, like I was being silly.

"Well, how about the address? I think I have the wrong one." I glanced again at the mansion and small national park's worth of property on the computer screen.

"Oh, I do apologize," he said. "11 Hill Road? In Green Briar, Texas?"

"This can't be right. I mean, it matches what I have, but there has to be some kind of mistake." I scrambled for any explanation, while out of the corner of my eye, I watched Loren rolling around on her bed like she was in pain, dying of curiosity. "The property I am looking at is huge. Why would someone I've never met give me... all this? Did Isaac Heart, I don't know, like, leave an explanation? A note maybe?"

"I'm sorry to say, no." Castle sighed. "Look, my dear, I know that this is hardly normal, and I do understand your trepidation. All this sounds very suspicious, I'm sure."

"It does sound a little like the beginning of a horror novel," I admitted.

A chuckle rolled over the phone. "That it does, but I assure you, legally, it is all strictly on the up and up."

"Are you sure the house isn't haunted or anything?" I hated how desperate my tone was. There was just nothing in my life that could lead to this kind of thing happening to me.

"Not to my knowledge. I've spent quite a lot of time in that house, dealing with the renovations, and the most sinister thing I have witnessed is contractor price gouging. How about you come down here and take a look at the papers and property? You can see everything in person. See that it's real."

"Um, well, I don't know. I'll have to, uh, look at my schedule." That sounded lame, even to me. Loren confirmed this by giving me a disgusted look.

Mr. Castle was kind enough not to notice. "Of course. Whatever is most convenient for you. Feel free to call me, any time, and we can set something up. Now, are there any other questions I can answer for you?"

"That's it for now. Thanks for talking to me, Mr. Castle." I was rubbing at the back of my neck so hard it was sore. Stupid nervous habit.

"Call me Red, my dear. I hope to hear from you soon." He waited for my mumbled, generally affirmative reply before hanging up. I closed my eyes and hung my head back in relief.

"You are such a wuss." Loren snickered.

"Shut up," I said, very much aware that I was, in fact, a wuss.

My friend sprung up from the bed and flounced across the room to grab me by the shoulders. Only half in jest, she lightly shook me. "So, what did he say?"

"Other than confirming most everything we read in the letter, not a lot." I pushed her away, so I could get to my feet and pace. "He doesn't know who Isaac Heart is, or why he willed everything to me. According to him, everything is legit, but-"

"But why would he lie?" Loren threw up her hands in exasperation. "It's not like you have any money to steal. This lawyer knew a lot about you. He probably knows you don't have five dollars to your name."

Rubbing my current poverty in my face was both effective in making a point and irksome. "I don't know. Maybe it's like a human trafficking thing."

Face and posture going slack in disbelief, Loren said, "Really? The only things you have going for you are the facts that you're a virgin, and you look like Wednesday Addams. I'm not sure there's a huge market for that."

"I hate you," I told her, flatly. My resemblance to the black-haired junior psycho had been commented on many times before.

"Yeah." She smiled dopily for a moment, then her face slid into a concerned frown. "You know I'm just screwing with you, right? There's nothing wrong with the way you look."

"Sure, I know." I reached over to bring her in for a hug. "And I know, I'm being a coward, but you know what they say about things that seem too good to be true."

"That sounds dangerously close to superstition," Loren purred, wagging a finger at me. "And we all know that believing in superstition is a gateway to believing in luck."

Rather than validating my best friend's totally legitimate point, I picked up a stuffed pink alien from her desk and threw it at her. Small plush toys are not exactly aerodynamic, and it veered to the left. Loren laughed raucously as it flopped on the sheets next to her.

I pouted a little before saying, "I said I'd talk to your mom before agreeing to anything."

"So, text her!" Loren pointed to her phone, still in my hands. "The sooner she hears about all this, the sooner she can tell you that you are being an idiot and to call that lawyer back so that you can go get eyes on that fabulous new mansion of yours. This is your chance, Add! Don't blow it because you're scared of being happy."

Sighing, I nodded. Loren was right and I knew it. I sent Mrs. Tyson a series of texts explaining what I had learned, and Red Castle's desire to meet up. It was a lot of typing that merited a short response back, telling me to wait before calling again, because she wanted to check some things out first.

Grateful for the delay, I asked Loren, "So what do you want to do? I don't have to be back home until after lunch."

"I don't know. What do you want to do?" Most people said that line automatically, unwilling to express a desire that would be contrary to someone else's. Loren did not have this problem. If she wanted something, she would just tell you.

Thinking hard for a moment, I glanced at the computer out of the corner of my eye and got an idea. There was a chance it was a mistake, and I was setting myself up for a fit, but... When pain is constant in your life, you begin to lose your fear of it. It still hurts, but it's just something you accept. "Feel up to doing a little more research?"

"You betcha."

Chapter 3: The Secrets That Hurt

We searched for more about the house, the town, and the firm of Pit and Castle. What we found on the latter two was mostly mundane. Green Briar was small and scenic, claiming lots of parks and green areas. The main industry appeared to be tourism, since there were a surprising number of shops that advertised on the city's social media, and had almost no crime. Other than a very boring website, there was nothing much on the law firm.

Mainly, we looked for anything about Isaac Heart. We did a search on him, but he didn't have any kind of social media presence. There were men with that name, but none of them had ever lived in the area or were wealthy enough to leave me that kind of money.

The house... well, we found one thing on the house in the archives of the local paper's website. According to the article, a seventeen-year-old named Monica Gardener had disappeared from that address about three months before my eighth birthday. The last people who had seen her were my parents, residents of the house at the time.

The name rang in my head like a bell. My skull felt like it was constricting around my brain. Whimpering, I put my hands to my temples and stood up, wobbling a little.

"What? What's up?" Loren jumped up next to me, her hands hovering helplessly. "Is it one of your fits? Do I need to call 911?"

"No, no." I waved her away, staggering to the bathroom. I lied to my friend to keep her from overreacting. She knew about my fits, but I made sure she never saw them. "My allergies are just bothering me. I'll be right back."

The bathroom was just a short way down the hall. I locked myself in and splashed water on my face. With every breath, I counted and fought to regain control. I was in there for about twenty minutes. Loren had to know I wasn't okay, but she didn't press. When I finally walked back to her room, she was at the desk, quietly reading something on the monitor.

She hesitated before asking, "Feeling better?"

"Yeah, yeah. I'm good." I sat down on the bed. "Well, this was at least fruitful."

"I guess. We know your folks used to live in that house, and you had a... sister?"

"Nah." Shaking my head, I focused on not letting the fit well up again. "Mom would've had to have been, what, twelve when she had her? I mean, she maybe could have been Dad's alone, but I think it's more likely she's a cousin or something. Dad does have an older brother, but they stopped speaking for some reason before I lost my memory. Maybe it had to do with Mon... her."

My brain started twisting again and my stomach followed. This girl seemed to be a trigger that I couldn't just ignore or dull my sensitivities against. If my parents had lived there, presumably so did I. There had to be some hints in the house of what happened to me, but the past was dangerous, and could bring more pain. Was chasing this rabbit a good idea? The siren's call of answers was far greater than the fear. Bracing myself with a deep breath, I nodded. The risk was worth it.

I looked Loren in the eyes. "Okay, assuming your mom doesn't come up with a reason for me not to, I'm going to go see the house and talk to the lawyer."

"I don't know, Addie. This might not be such a good idea. With you getting one of your attacks and whatever happened to your cousin..." Loren licked her lips. "Something's off. It really is starting to feel, I don't know, like something out of a horror movie."

"Maybe," I agreed, pinching the bridge of my nose. "I'm going to be careful, but I also have to pursue this. There are a lot of secrets in my family. Too many things that don't make sense. This is my chance to dig and find out what's going on. Worst case scenario, I get nothing and I'm no worse off than I am now. One step better than that, and I can sell the house, take all the money and start a new life. But, Lore, I have to know."

"Yeah," she said, shoulders slumped in resignation. "Whenever you're ready to go, let me know, I'll go with you."

"You don't have to–" I started but was stopped by her glare.

"The hell I don't," Loren growled. "I'm not about to let you walk into whatever this is without backup. Even if I wanted to, my mom would kick my ass. Besides, how did you think you were going to get there? You can't drive and you have no money."

"I didn't say I had a fully formulated plan," I grumbled. Secretly, I was glad she wanted to come. Things would be so much better with someone to watch my back.

"Uh huh," Loren said, ever the skeptic. "Besides, I want to see this place too. You already said I can come stay with you. No take backsies just because it's a mansion."

"Are you kidding?" I snorted. "You have to come live with me now. That place is huge. I'd get lost in there the first day. You have to be there in case I go missing. You can call for the search party."

"Yeah," she mused, tapping her lip. "You know, it's a good thing you're going to be rich. I bet the electricity bill on that place is obscene."

"Yeah," I echoed. I looked back at the satellite image of the house and its property. "Hey, it looks like there's another, much smaller house on the land. Maybe it would be better to live there?"

For the rest of the morning, Loren and I made plans for living alone in our own private mansion. Some were silly, like setting up a paintball park inside the house. Some were actually something to consider, like staying in the guest house. It was smaller, but still a good size, and we could set up the main house as some kind of hotel. By the time I had to leave, I was feeling cautiously optimistic. I had somewhere to go, and my mother couldn't control me anymore.

I finally realized something Loren had been telling me for months. I was turning eighteen and I could leave anytime I wanted. Even if the inheritance thing didn't pan out, I didn't have to stay. I could beg to crash at Loren's house until I got a job and saved some money. It was... empowering. It made facing the next few days until my birthday much easier.

When I got home, Mom was in a much better mood, doing her daily yoga in the living room. She'd finally gotten dressed, wearing an expensive spandex leotard that was a size too small. She'd put her hair up in a high ponytail and redid her makeup. She always said that the ponytail made her look younger. It didn't. As I walked by her on my way to my bedroom, Mom waved me over. I sat on the couch, and she stood facing me with her hands on her hips.

"What's up?" I asked, wondering why she wanted to talk. She generally didn't speak to me at all unless she was mad at me.

"So, I've been thinking. You've been acting a lot more mature lately. I think you might finally be ready to get a job." Mom looked as if she were bestowing the moon to me, and I guess to her, she was. Allowing me the freedom of money and an excuse to be out from under her thumb was a huge concession from her. She made a big deal about tapping her chin and thinking about what she was saying. "Now, it will have to be something you can walk to. I don't have time to ferry you around. Once we find out what you can get, we'll figure out what you need to pay in rent."

My face fell into a glower. It wasn't that I was against the idea, but Mom didn't need the money any more than she didn't have the time to pick me up. She only worked fifteen hours a week at a little boutique in town that a friend of hers owned. What she made was just mad money. The house payment and everything else came from the settlement.

Mom and I had never spoken about it, but I assumed the settlement she mentioned from time to time was something she and Dad had arranged when he left. Something like child support... Oh. That was it. I was about to turn eighteen, so I guessed the payments were about to stop. Any and all altruism was sucked out of Mom's declaration.

I straightened up, looking my mother in the eye, "I already have plans, Mom."

She snorted. "Yes, I know. You're going off to college. And how are you going to pay for that, huh? I won't help you waste your money like that. Have you even been accepted?"

"No." I struggled to keep my tone level. "But I had a new opportunity present itself today."

"And what kind of 'opportunity' would that be?" Mom emphasized her sarcasm with air quotes.

"My inheritance." Every ounce of my self-control was going towards not grinding my teeth. I was going to be the adult in this, dammit.

"What inheritance?" Mom crossed her arms and sneered. "My family is dirt poor and your father's mother wouldn't touch me with a ten-foot pole, much less you."

We had lived with my grandmother briefly when I was younger. We moved in, supposedly so she could help watch me after my accident. That had been a bad year for everyone. Dad left and his mother had kicked us out. It had taken me several years to understand that his leaving and Grandma evicting us was not my fault. I didn't think that Mom had ever accepted that.

"Isaac Heart." The words were clipped as I said them. The instant draining of color from my mother's face was both satisfying and curious.

"Where did you hear that name?" she whispered.

I pulled the letter out of my pocket. "I got this in the mail. It says when I turn eighteen, I inherit his house, his money, everything."

"No no no no." Mom moved to sit next to me on the couch, wringing her hands. "You can't do that. You can't go back to that place."

"So, we did live there," I murmured to myself. I narrowed my eyes and directed my full attention at my mother. "Who is Isaac Heart?"

"He's a bad, horrible man, baby. You can't trust anything he says." She fell silent for a moment, putting her fingertips over her mouth and tears started to brim in her eyes. "You're my daughter, and I forbid that you have anything to do with him and those freaks of his."

My eyebrows shot up. "Freaks?"

"They are bad, scary people and you shouldn't be around them. Not again. We were lucky to get you out of there the first time." Once my mother started babbling, it was very hard to get her to stop. I tried to put a hand on hers to calm her, and she jumped at the contact. She always pulled away from me, but that was excessive. Whatever was going on, she was spooked.

"Okay, Mom. Take a breath." I took several exaggerated breaths for example. "Now, this time, avoiding pronouns, tell me who you are talking about. Who are the bad people?"

"I... I can't tell you, but you have to believe me that they are horrible." My mother was starting to hiccup and my concern turned into something very close to hatred.

I knew my mom. She only hiccupped when she was fake crying. I had actually been worried about the manipulative bitch. Throughout my entire childhood, my mother had controlled me with crocodile tears. Well, I was done with that, and I was done with her.

As I bent down to pick up the letter, which had fallen on the floor, my mother snatched it away. I bared my teeth at her. "Give that back."

"No!" Mom jumped up and ran. For just a moment, I gawked, unable to believe the silliness of what had just happened. By the time I had rallied and followed her, she had fled into her bedroom and locked herself in.

Wrapping hard on her door, I yelled, "Give that back! It belongs to me. Mom? Mom!"

Pressing my ear to the door, I listened closely. There was silence, except for the neighbor's dog barking madly. The noise was way too loud, like she had the sliding glass door open in her room that led to…

I tore back down the hallway to the living room and flung myself through the door to the backyard. Sure enough, Mom was back there, standing over our never used grill. There was a bottle of lighter fluid at her feet, and she was fighting with the long-handled lighter. After a moment my mother finally managed to ignite the accelerant-soaked paper. It went up in an acrid-smelling little fireball and Mom crowed with victory.

I stared at her triumphant grin in pure bafflement. "What the actual hell? What do you think that even accomplished?"

"The letter's gone, so now you can't go." She pointed a finger at me. "Now you have to stay here and be my daughter like you were always supposed to be."

"Always supposed to..." I trailed off, not comprehending the statement she had just made. It had finally happened. My mother had gone insane. "What the hell are you talking about? Are you saying I'm not your kid?"

"No." Mom's head whipped back and forth. There was a manic gleam in her eyes that kind of scared me. "Never like you were supposed to be. Never like I was promised. You were always strange, never like me. You weren't the baby they swore I would get!"

The grill had already burned out its content, so when I kicked it over, only ash scattered across the porch. Mom jumped and stared at me in disbelief. I met her eyes and glared. "If you think I'm so defective, if you really never wanted me, why won't you let me go?"

"Because I paid for you!" She made a motion like she was throwing something at me while she shrieked. "I did everything they asked me to! I gave birth to you! I was promised a child that was mine, and you were theirs! Well, they can't have you, because I did my part. You are going to stay here. You don't get to go off and live happily ever after without me."

"Who are they?" My hands flexed as I fought for every inch of calm I had.

"It doesn't matter," Mom insisted while she wiped her face. "You aren't going to see them ever again, because they can't have you back."

It was at that point I realized that there was no talking to my mother. She was either legitimately crazy, a possibility I had visited before, or she was making something up in an attempt to manipulate me. It didn't matter. I was done. Mom had even admitted that the reason she couldn't let me go was that she couldn't let me be happy when she was miserable.

I had planned on staying until my birthday, but screw that. I didn't want to put up with her crap anymore, and I didn't have to. Scary though it was, I was ready to leave.

"I'm going to my room," I said. Mom must have taken that as a surrender because she grinned and strutted past me to her bedroom.

"Pick up the grill and clean it before you go in. You made a mess out here." My mother was smug, but I didn't talk back.

Keeping my head down and my fists clenched, I waited until she had gone back inside before moving. I did not clean up the grill. Instead, I went to my room and with a little effort, slid my dresser a few inches so that it partially blocked the door. This wouldn't keep Mom out forever, but it would buy me some time, in case she came to look for me too soon.

Packing everything that mattered to me didn't take long, and I had to get everything out. If I left anything behind, my mother would destroy it. She'd done it before. A couple of changes of clothes and a few odds and ends took up most of my one duffle bag. I also shoved the library book with Red's card inside.

It was a kind of sad moment, looking at my life in a not-quite-full duffle bag. I was starting over again. Not having a lot of my sucky, previous life with me seemed fitting.

I opened my window, popped the screen out, and stepped out onto the front lawn. I walked away from the house I had spent the last nine years in, and I didn't have the urge to look back.

Chapter 4: Home Again

We started our road trip at about five a.m., intending to meet the lawyer at the hotel early in the afternoon. Loren drove since I didn't have a license, and it was her car. We were a little behind because we had stopped at a gas station for breakfast and ended up staying longer than we intended. Loren had spent way too long flirting with the cute cashier. We made up for a lot of lost time due to her lead foot.

As we were approaching the city limits, Loren and I were making a game of betting on worst-case scenarios. Bouncing in her seat, hands still on the wheel, she belted out, "It's going to be a trap-filled murder house, where this Isaac guy is alive and luring in young women to play his sick, twisted games."

I wrinkled my nose. "I'm sticking with 'haunted house that is going to kill us in a weird, coincidental way and then keep our souls for all eternity'."

"Yeah, but why is the house haunted? You can't just go with a generic, 'Oh, it's haunted', you have to say why."

"I don't know. Someone died there. That's how a house gets haunted, right?"

"Oh, gawd! You have no imagination."

"Okay, scrap the ghost thing." I rolled my eyes. "The house is possessed by a demon. Isaac Heart was a devil worshiper, and he wants me to carry on his dark work."

Loren took her hands off the wheel for just a moment to applaud. "See? That wasn't so hard."

"You are taking this way too seriously. It'll just be a rundown mess that I'll need to sell."

"I bet it's all rotting," Loren's eyes darted to me with a devilish grin, "and filled with spiders."

I shuddered. "No. No spiders. Red said he was renovating the place, so it should be clean. No spiders."

"Or maybe it will be like a haunted house, all dark and creepy with boogiemen hiding under the stairs." She wiggled her fingers at me as she laughed.

It felt like a spike was driven into my temple. I covered my eyes with my hands and took a deep breath. I hated that word. Boogieman.

"You are such a chicken."

My best friend loved to tease me about my fear of arachnids. I fought back. "Yeah, since I'm going to have all this money, I'm going to pay clowns to wake you up on your next birthday."

"Ugh," Loren groaned. "Touché."

The town was as movie perfect as the website promised. Lots of trees and clean streets. A small elementary school made of sunny yellow brick was fenced in by a metal bar fence painted a dull red. Non-fit-inducing memories tickled at the back of my head and I broke into a grin.

"Hey, I think I went there." I tapped the window to draw Loren's attention.

She perked up with curiosity. "I thought you didn't remember anything before you moved. Does this mean your memories are coming back?"

"Maybe." I shrugged. "Hopefully. From everything I've heard, familiar surroundings can trigger people to recall things after getting amnesia."

"I don't know. What if it's like, trauma-induced? Maybe your parents ax murdered your cousin and you saw it." Loren stole a moment from looking for the hotel to glance at me. "Are you sure you'd want to remember? I mean, I would, but do you?"

The idea that my fits were a result of some past ordeal had crossed my mind. If whatever had happened was so bad that it caused me that kind of damage, did I really want to know?

If I was smart, the answer would be no. Chasing after brain-frying childhood trauma didn't sound like a good idea. Then again, maybe the best thing was to grab what scared me and drag it out into the light. See if it was as bad as I thought it was. I could always hire a therapist with all the new money I was supposed to get to help me hash things out. Also, only a few favorite teachers had ever accused me of being smart.

"Yeah. I want to know."

"I think it's always better to-- holy shit they have valet parking!" Loren did a double take as we came up to the hotel. It was a grand building with every piece of molding and potted plant designed to imply money. "This place has got to be pricey. Are you sure the lawyer is paying for this? I'm pretty sure this isn't the kind of 'emergency' Mom meant when she gave me the emergency credit card."

"Mr. Castle said that the room and all our meals at the hotel are being covered by the firm." I'd called the lawyer again after I had gotten to Loren's house. When I'd told him I wanted to come early, he'd been ecstatic. At Mrs. Tyson's suggestion, I'd asked for a cash advance from my inheritance so I'd have some spending money. It felt ungrateful, and I was certain he'd say no. I'd nearly fallen out of my seat when he'd said it would be waiting for me when I got to the hotel.

We pulled up in Loren's sensible sedan, but the valet didn't treat us any differently from the man who got out of the expensive, angry-looking supercar in front of us. Inside, it was more of the same. It was like my name unlocked the royal treatment. Our bags were immediately whisked away to our room and the concierge showed us to the restaurant where Red Castle was already waiting.

As we approached the table, the older man was poring over his phone. He was twig thin under a well-fitted gray suit. Wisps of white hair stuck out at odd angles from underneath a shockingly scarlet fedora. When he looked up, I saw he had a large nose, eyebrows that, while obviously trimmed, could double as wings, and wide, brown eyes that had a slight yellow cast to the whites. His face lit up when he saw me, his thin-lipped mouth splitting into a truly epic grin that showed off deep laugh lines. He was small, only coming about to my jaw when he stood. The massive energy that radiated off of him when he surged forward to shake my hand was not something I was expecting. Neither was the strength in his willowy fingers.

"Miss Gardener! I am Red Castle. I'm thrilled to meet you. How was your journey? Who is your friend?"

"Um, yeah. The trip was long but good. This is Loren Tyson. She drove." Involuntarily, the corners of my lips turned up. The lawyer was just so vivacious and happy to see me that he pulled me along in his excitement.

"Well, Miss Tyson, thank you so much for getting Miss Gardener here." He extended a long-fingered hand for her to shake while giving her a grin equal to the one he gave me.

She hesitated before taking the lawyer's hand. With visible effort, she plastered on a shallow smile and said cooly, "No problem."

Castle's grin wilted slightly and his eyes narrowed. A full awkward second went by, then the lawyer pulled a chair away from the table to offer it to me. The concierge did the same for Loren, and we both sat.

I didn't know about my friend, but I felt the 'holding the chair' thing was a little weird. I wasn't sure at what point my butt was supposed to end up in the seat. She didn't seem to struggle, but that didn't mean anything. Loren had mad faking-it skills. With a flourish, the waiter placed a basket of marbled bread and a dish of herb-infused butter, then disappeared.

"Thanks for meeting me on such short notice, Mr. Castle."

"Please, Miss Gardener, call me Red." The lawyer cocked his head to the side like a curious bird, making me laugh just a little.

"Well, call me Addie, then." My hand crept up to my neck again. "So, where do we start?"

The waiter handed us both menus while Loren watched Red like he was going to bite her.

"Since you've had such a long trip, I thought we'd get lunch. Get whatever you like. All of this is on the firm."

I looked over at Loren, who shrugged. She was normally boisterous and on the verge of being overly friendly. I couldn't figure out a way to covertly ask her what was going on, so I just silently looked over the menu.

I took a chance and ordered Surf n' Turf with steak and lobster. Trying to be subtle, I glanced at Red to see if he flinched over the price, but he didn't even notice. Loren got steak and fries and the lawyer got the largest cut of meat they had, as rare as they were willing to prepare it.

As the waiter left, Red leaned on the table, hands steepled. "While I wasn't expecting you this soon, I am very glad you came. I have personally been overseeing the care of the house and a few modernizations that we thought you might want implemented."

"The house does have like, electricity and everything, right?" The word modernization made me nervous. "I mean, it looked pretty old from the aerial photo we saw."

"Parts of the house are quite old," Red admitted with a nod, "But they were moved from other locations to be put together with the new construction a little less than twenty years ago. I can assure you that the house has all modern amenities. The renovations I was overseeing were related to the phone and internet. It took a little doing, but the entire house and the guest house have Wi-Fi."

"Oh, cool. So it's like move-in ready?" I asked hopefully. Even if I decided to sell the house, it would be nice to have a place to live and not have to rely so much on Pit and Castle's charity.

"Yes, but I do have to caution you; you shouldn't move in until the house legally passes into your possession." Before I could panic, Red held up a hand. "And don't worry about accommodations. The firm is more than happy to cover everything. The hotel room and its amenities are yours as long as you like. No worrying about the expense, either. You are our most important account. This is the least we can do."

"Alright. Cool." I was awkwardly grateful and hopeful that this might actually be as good as it sounded. Loren was still uncharacteristically quiet, and it worried me. It was bothering me enough that I didn't care if what I was doing was obvious. I had to find out what her problem was.

I excused myself to the bathroom and thought I'd have to drop a hint for Loren to follow. This proved unnecessary since the second I moved to leave she said, "Yeah, me too."

She obviously wanted to talk to me as well, because she hurried after. Once we were inside with the door closed, we turned to each other and both started in at once.

"What is wrong with you?" I kept my voice low so people wouldn't overhear. "You haven't said a single word!"

"Why are you still talking to this freak?" Loren whispered urgently. "Just being in the same room as him is making my skin crawl. He's got pointy teeth for Christ's sake!"

"What? What do you even mean?" I was startled into speaking at normal volume. "Red's a sweetheart. He's like the grandfather I never had."

"He. Has. Pointy. Teeth." Loren gave strong emphasis to every single word.

"Well," I considered this for a moment before admitting, "Maybe a little. Why does it matter? Maybe he has a condition or something. He's nice and seems like he genuinely wants to help me."

"I think he genuinely wants to eat you." She crossed her arms in the universal sign of not being amused and glared at me in a way that was very reminiscent of her mother. "Your grandpa has great big teeth and might be the big bad wolf."

"I have no idea what you are talking about." I threw up my hands in frustration. "I like Red. He's happy and funny and... I feel like I can trust him, Lore."

"Yeah, well he's setting off all my alarm bells." Loren put a hand on my shoulder and looked me square in the eyes. "You are the least trusting person I have ever met, Add. I know I have been telling you for years to open up and give people a chance, but this would be the absolute worst time to start listening to me."

I bit my lip and rubbed the back of my neck, considering my friend's words. Normally, our places would be reversed, and she would be dragging me into some crazy situation against my better judgment. Most real trouble I had ever found myself in was because of her. I had the temptation to make her go along with it for justice's sake. Despite that, I didn't want to ignore her instincts.

I took a deep breath. "So, what do you want to do?"

After a long pause, Loren said, "I don't want to say we should just go. I mean, this is your chance. Besides, even if he is a creeper, he might not be dangerous. After all, he's ancient. We just... We just gotta be careful, that's all."

"I agree. We'll keep check-ins with your mom, and we'll look after each other. Just promise me one thing?"

"What?" Loren cocked her head to one side, reminding me of Red earlier.

"Try to keep an open mind. I've got a good feeling about him." I folded my hands together and pleaded with a smile. "You told me it was okay to hope and, well, I'm hoping."

She blew out through her lips like a horse, then smirked. "You listen to me at the absolute worst times."

"Ready to go back?" I asked, laughing at Loren's pain. It's what any good friend would do.

Our timing was pretty good. Just as we were walking up, the waiters were setting down our food. If the smell was anything to go by, we were in for an amazing meal. Red stood as we came to sit and executed a little half-bow.

I smiled at the waiter who put down my plate. "This looks wonderful."

"Thank you. Please enjoy." He beamed, then disappeared with the rest of his compatriots.

"Thanks for lunch, Mr. Castle," Loren said as pleasantly as she could manage.

He raised an eyebrow in surprise, inclined his head and said, "You are very welcome, and please, call me Red. I only go by Mr. Castle when a judge orders me to."

This made us smile. The mood at the table became significantly lighter. Everyone dug into their respective dishes and from the noises she was making, my friend was savoring lunch as much as I was. We all focused on our own food.

I'd never had lobster before. It was good, but it was mostly a vehicle for the butter, which was saturated with garlic and lemon. Both Loren's and mine's steak had a beautiful char on the outside and exploded with flavor with every bite. When I did glance at Red, I saw that his steak was as rare as promised, oozing scarlet juices as he sliced into it.

After we finished, the plates were quickly whisked away. Red brought a briefcase onto the table that contained a tall stack of papers. He selected a fat envelope from the top and handed it to me. "First things first, here is the cash advance you asked for. There's five thousand dollars in assorted bills and a card for you to charge what you need. If you require anything else, please, don't hesitate to ask."

My hand froze on the envelope as I took it and gulped. Loren's eyes looked like they were about to bug out of her head. "Okay, that was significantly more than I was expecting. Are you sure—"

Red raised a hand to halt my objections. "Trust me, my dear, on your account this amount is inconsequential. Money is not something you will need to worry about ever again."

"How much money are we talking about?" Loren looked like she was about to have some kind of aneurysm.

"Well, that makes an excellent place to start as we look over the paperwork." Pulling out a clipped sheaf of papers, Red spread them out in front of me and started pointing out figures. I was at a loss for words.

Loren was not. "That is a metric shit ton of money."

"Well put." He chuckled. "As you can see, there's a good reason for us to take care of Addie. And this is just the actual cash assets. There are properties and businesses as well."

My best friend stared at me in wonder as Red showed me lists of things I was soon to own. "You are rich."

"Apparently so." My head swam. "And all this, along with the house, is mine?"

"On your birthday, yes," he said.

"But why?" I blurted out. "Who was Isaac Heart, and why would he leave me anything?"

"I'm afraid I can't say." My lawyer shrugged apologetically. "I was not with the firm when this arrangement was made. Mr. Pit was the one originally handling your affairs, and he is currently out of town taking care of some business."

"Can't you call him or email him or something?" Loren asked.

"He's a bit out-of-pocket, but should be here in time for your birthday."

"So, I just have to wait till then to find out why all this is happening?" I frowned. "Is there anything I can do now?"

"If you want, we can tour the property tomorrow. Take a look, pick out a room, that sort of thing."

"I am curious what the inside of that house is like," Loren admitted.

"Okay." I sighed. "We can look at the house, then we can just hang out in town for a few days. We're staying in a ritzy hotel and have a boatload of cash; it's not exactly a hardship."

"That's the spirit!" Red cheered. "Make sure to have a little fun. It's going to be your birthday soon."

Considering I'd never had a good birthday, I was looking forward to having a week-long celebration with my best friend. It was the greatest present I'd ever been given. I glanced at Loren who rolled her eyes, but grinned all the same.

"Well, I guess I can stick around, spend your money and keep you company," she said, pretending to pout. "But only because I am your friend."

"Well, that's settled then." Red drummed his gnarled old hands on the table. "The only thing left is dessert and any questions you might have."

"They do have tiramisu," Loren mused, tapping her bottom lip.

"You ate like half a cow. I don't want to hear you complain about your stomach later," I teased. This had happened before on trips to restaurants.

"Fine, spoil sport." She rolled her eyes. "We'll split it, then."

I didn't like tiramisu. The one time I had it, it tasted like boozy lard. I nodded anyway. A possibly psychic waiter appeared, knowing that we wanted dessert. He assured us that everything was delicious as he took our order. More likely, he was just an excellent server and had overheard us.

While we waited, I asked Red about the businesses and properties, but he assured me that they practically ran themselves. I wouldn't need to be involved with anything if I didn't want to be. There was nothing else I could think of to ask without running it all by Loren's mom. After lunch, I planned on sending her pictures of all the documents Red was leaving me with. The only other question I had, I didn't expect an answer to.

"Red?" I asked. His eyebrow raised in acknowledgment. "I am pretty sure my family lived in that house ten years ago. Do you know why we left?"

"Again, this was before I joined the firm, and perhaps is a question better posed to Mr. Pit. The best I can say, the decision was mostly made by your parents after an incident that caused injury to you. They wanted to raise you in a more... normal situation." Red waved his hands in the air as he searched for the word 'normal'. The inflection he gave was that it wasn't a good thing at all. I had to admit that if what my mother and I had been through over the last decade together was normal, I was with him. Normal sucked.

"So Mom and Dad never owned the house, right?"

Red shook his head. "No. I can say that definitely. The house has always been in Mr. Heart's name. Paperwork was put in place shortly after you were born for the house to be transferred to you when you reached majority. Your parents were only allowed occupancy of the house while you were under their care. A stipend was paid to them, in addition to lodgings in the house. When you turn eighteen, they lose any and all rights to anything, and everything."

"Wait, are they getting that money now?" My eyes narrowed.

Red glanced at a piece of paper. "Yes. Currently, the whole sum goes to your mother."

"Does it have anything in there about my dad?" Unreasonable anger bubbled up.

He shuffled through his paperwork a moment longer this time before answering. "I'm afraid I don't have any current information on your father. Would you like me to find out?"

"No, I just thought... I just thought that he was the one who had been sending Mom money. Nice to know he doesn't even care that much." Bitterness dripped off my words. I was mad, not only at my dad, but at myself because now Red was sitting there shifting uncomfortably. Even Loren was quiet, just putting a reassuring hand on my back. Our psychic waiter came to the rescue, choosing the perfect time to bring dessert to the table on two small plates.

To stop my foot from fitting in there any further, I jammed a spoonful of tiramisu into my mouth. A short laugh erupted from me as I said, "You know, this is fantastic."

Loren took a bite from her plate. Eyes snapping wide, she said, "Oh my god. That is amazing!"

Things became more comfortable as we gushed about the dessert. When the laughing and the sugar had calmed me down, Red said, hesitantly, "I'm sorry things have been...unpleasant."

"Don't worry about it." I held up a hand to stop him from further apologies. "My drama is not your problem. And you know what? You have given me the best birthday gift ever. I have a chance to start a new life, and I am going to make it great. No old baggage. Well, maybe Loren."

There was only a moment of stunned silence before she squawked in outrage and punched me in the arm. I laughed and Red chuckled appreciatively. After we finished, he handed me a folder with papers to peruse at my leisure and told us that he would be back at nine the next morning to take us to look at the house. He also made sure we knew we could call him if we needed anything.

As soon as Red was out of sight, Loren and I ran giggling to the elevator to go see our room.

Chapter 5: The Smaller the Town, The More the Coincidences

Loren and I decided to go up to the room for a bit and rest. The elevator walls were completely covered in mirrors. The hotel must have a guy whose only job was to run in there every few minutes and clean the glass, because there wasn't a single smudge on it. While the initial idea of a mirrored box was cool, standing inside it was a little uncomfortable with billions of mes staring at each other. I pushed the button for the eleventh floor and it began a smooth assent.

Leaning into me, Loren whispered, "Is it just me or is this elevator the creepiest thing about this whole trip?"

"You're not wrong." I stuck my tongue out and watched my reflections pay me back in kind. "Does this mean you don't think Red is as scary as you did?"

"No, he's not as bad as I first thought, just weird. Maybe the pointy teeth thing is something he did to make himself more intimidating in court."

"It would work." I curled two fingers in front of my mouth to indicate fangs. "Vampire lawyer."

Loren scoffed. "Yeah, well, he's still weird."

The elevator gave a pleasant ding and the little reflective rectangle next to the button panel lit up. I waved the card I'd gotten at check-in. One polite beep and a green light later, the doors opened to a hotel room that would do a movie star proud. There was a sitting area with a huge TV, a full kitchen, a bar, and a dining room with a table that could sit six. The entire wall across from the elevator was windows lined by a balcony. I didn't like the colors of the suite, all flat grays and neutral tones, but I had to admit they were nicely done.

We wandered around like kids entering an amusement park, and wordlessly split up to explore. My friend headed towards the balcony and I went to open the doors going off the main room. Two were identical bedrooms with huge beds and on-suite bathrooms with jacuzzi tubs. The third was a half bath that was still bigger than my bathroom back home.

"Come look at this!" Loren called and I joined her. The town was even more idyllic from altitude, and I was about to comment when I looked straight down. The view wasn't why she had summoned me. Directly below us, a van was stopped at the light with a very bright and intricate, fully detailed, naked lady painted on the roof.

I burst out laughing. "That is awesome."

"I know." Loren grinned at me. She sighed as the light turned green and the van drove away. She turned to lean against the balcony railing. "So, I figure after you send all the documents to Mom, we can chill for a bit. When you feel like it, we can go for a walk to check out the area, and catch dinner."

"Sounds good." I held out my hand and Loren slapped her phone into it.

It took me about a half hour to take pictures of every single document and send it out. Mrs. Tyson sent a note back that she'd have a friend of hers look over everything and get back to me tomorrow. While I was adulting, Loren spent a little while people-watching from the balcony, then channel surfing on the giant TV.

When I had finished all my stuff, I collapsed onto the couch and said, "So, what do you think? Want to go exploring?"

"Well, there's nothing on, so, yeah. Let's go." Loren clicked the remote and the screen went black. She practically bounced off of the cushions in her race to the elevator. I followed at a slower pace, and we took the highly reflective ride down to the lobby. We didn't have a destination, so picked a direction and took off. There were boutiques of every description.

In one, Loren convinced me to buy a cute little black dress. I got to test the validity of the card, since it was not cheap. It took us just a ridiculous amount of time to make it down the street, but in the candle shop near the end of the road, our progress stopped.

There were some very lovely artisan candles in all shapes and fragrances, but sniffing wax was not the hold-up. The tall, long-haired guy with perfect dimples and nothing but smiles behind the counter was the hold-up. He was a couple of years older than us, and admittedly charming, giving almost sensuous descriptions of candle scents to Loren. She was literally twirling her hair while staring into his eyes.

I was feeling like a third wheel, so I murmured, "Hey, Lore? If you're going to hang here, I'm going to continue exploring. I'll catch back up with you at the hotel, okay?"

"Yeah, sure." Loren didn't even look at me. I pushed the bag with my dress into her hand, and she grabbed it without comment.

I wandered away from the main drag of town and ended up in front of the elementary school I'd seen earlier. The metal fence was warm as I ran my hand over it, walking the length of the playground. The bright blue swings were familiar. I was fairly certain that once upon a time there had been a jungle gym shaped like a spider over the sandbox. I'd cried when one of the other kids had thrown my backpack under it, and I'd been afraid to get it. Excitement of finding something I could remember without pain warred with sadness stirred by impressions of jeering children and isolation. I hadn't been happy there.

I felt like I was being watched. That was nothing new, but I hadn't noticed the feeling since getting into town. It had been a nice break. I closed my eyes and pinched the bridge of my nose to try to stave off the threatening headache and faint paranoia. While I didn't think I was close to a fit, I didn't want to tempt it.

I was about to turn and start the walk back to the hotel when someone cleared their throat. Startled, I whipped my head towards the sound and saw a plump older woman with badly dyed red hair. She was clutching a tote that was bright pink, and spattered with old paint. I recognized the bag before the woman.

"Mrs. Manning," I said, the name coming out before I fully associated it with a person. "You're still teaching."

"Oh, you're one of my old students." She put a hand to her chest and smiled. "I was wondering why you were just standing there. Are you okay?"

"Um, yeah. I'm fine. Just a headache," I said. "But how are you doing?"

"Oh, I'm dandy." She hefted the old tote. "Getting ready to come back after a year off. Mr. Manning died and it took me a little while to get myself back together."

"Oh, I'm so sorry. I think I remember him coming to class one day. He was a policeman, right?" The impression I got was of a man equally round as the woman before me, with an impressive repertoire of dad jokes and a truly epic walrus mustache. Surprisingly, there was no twinge of headache.

Mrs. Manning nodded. "He only got to enjoy his retirement a few months before his heart gave out. I'd planned on retiring myself, but I missed it too much to stay away. I had to see my kids. But enough about me. Forgive me honey, but you'll have to jog my memory."

"Adeline Gardener." I smiled wanly. "I was in your class ten years ago and left shortly after the school year ended."

"Addie!" My old teacher burst out and gave me a hug, which I awkwardly returned. "I do remember you. We all worried when you disappeared, but no one could find out where you'd gone. What happened?"

I shrugged. "It's kind of complicated, but there was an accident and my parents took me away from here. I'm only just now moving back. I haven't decided if I'm staying yet."

"No one..." Mrs. Manning moved a hand towards me, but hesitated before putting it on my shoulder. "No one hurt you, did they?"

Cocking my head to one side I said, "No. Why? Do you have a reason to think someone was hurting me?"

"Well..." The teacher let her hand drop, and she took a deep breath. "It's just that you were such a withdrawn child and some things you said about your home life... they were worrying."

"What did I say?" I took a step forward, trying to reign in my urge to grab and shake her for more information. This was a link to my past. Maybe she could help me figure out what happened.

"You were very secretive, but occasionally you'd say something disturbing." The plump woman tilted her head and looked at me with pity. "You talked about monsters and men who could change their faces and having seen people die. I thought maybe it was some kind of cry for help, so I called in your parents. Did you know that? That they came in for a conference?"

I shook my head. Either I never knew, or I had forgotten it like most everything else from my early childhood. A sinking sensation was settling in my stomach. "No. My parents don't... didn't talk to me much."

"It wasn't a good meeting," Mrs. Manning tutted sadly. "Your mother was very high-strung and just fretted that you might not be doing well in school. Your father was uncommunicative and got defensive any time I tried to bring up issues at home. I didn't think he was violent but then you disappeared and… are you sure he didn't hurt you, honey?"

Oh, what to say when I didn't have a real answer? After a long moment, I smiled and told her what she needed to hear to not feel bad. Her guilt wouldn't help either of us. "No. Dad didn't hurt me. I just had an accident, was all."

"Oh, well, I am sorry about that." She did sound sympathetic, but also relieved. That was good. Whatever happened wasn't her fault. Probably. I would love to know whose fault it was.

"Yeah well, it is what it is." I bit my lip and then forced one more smile before making my escape. "Look, I've got to meet a friend at the hotel. It's been great seeing you again, Mrs. Manning."

"You too, honey." With a little wave, she turned around and walked towards the entrance of the school. "Take care."

I halfheartedly waived as I walked away myself. Maybe if I had held on, tried a little harder, I could have gotten more from her. The trouble was, I couldn't ask for more without explaining that I didn't remember.

My mother had trained me to hide my symptoms. She'd told me that if I tried to tell anyone that they would send me off to the loony bin. I'd believed her because Grandma had said several times that I should be institutionalized. I'd tried to tell some friends about the things I'd forgotten, or the things I'd seen, but they thought I was just saying it for attention. Loren was the only person who'd ever believed me. Even now, I still had problems talking about it.

I couldn't help but hang my head as I trudged back to the hotel. I had a scant handful of answers to a whole barrel full of questions. It wasn't right, and it wasn't fair, and I could cry about it all I wanted, and that wouldn't change anything. My lip started to tremble, and I had to stop and take a breath for composure.

Squawks and fluttering in a yard nearby drew my attention. Two birds were locked in mortal combat over a french fry. A crow protected its treasure by hunching over it with wings partially unfurled. A mockingbird repeatedly dived-bombed the crow, who started cawing loudly in protest. The crow was much larger than the mockingbird, but under the constant barrage, couldn't get off the ground. Unable to help myself, I laughed. Both birds startled, causing them to fly away and abandon the French fry. With an angry trill, the mockingbird flew off, but the crow didn't go far. It landed on a nearby fence. The second the mockingbird was out of sight, the crow swept down and snatched up the fry.

"Enjoy your dinner." I threw a little salute to the victor. For no particular reason, I'd always had a soft spot for crows. I resumed my walk to the hotel and felt a little better. It was a reminder that I shouldn't take things too seriously. Nothing else in the world did. The past didn't matter, I had a good future to look forward to.

Chapter 6: A Friend in High Places

Loren ambushed me in the hotel room, pouncing on me in her excitement. "Where have you been?"

"I went for a walk. Saw my old school. Met an old teacher." I shrugged. "It was kind of cool. How long have you been waiting?"

"Only about ten minutes," she admitted, eyes full of mischief. "I spent all the time after you left talking to Sean."

"The guy from the candle shop?"

"Yes." She grinned dopily and twisted back and forth like a shy little girl. "He's really sweet, and he is big into history and stuff. He knows, like, everything about everything in the store."

"You want to date a nerd." Yeah, I thought it was awesome, but I had to give her a little hell.

"There's nothing wrong with that!" Loren squawked. "He's a hot, smart guy. He's the holy grail of men. Don't hate on me because you're jealous."

"I am happy for you, Lore." I patted her on the shoulder. "Did you get his number or something?"

"Oh, better than that." The smile she gave scared me a little. "Tomorrow night you are going out with me and Sean. We'll be meeting up with a few of his friends."

"No. Oh, no. Oh, no no no." I shook a finger at her. "We have the tour of the house in the morning, and who knows how long that's going to take? We're going to be tired—"

Loren held up a hand for silence, oozing smugness. "No excuses. You are going to put on that new, fantastic dress you bought, you are going to come out with me, and you are going to meet some people. Add, this is a new town and a chance for a new life. You said it yourself. It would be a good start to get to know some people. You're like my sister, and I love you, but you need other friends than just me."

For a second I considered arguing, for contrariness's sake, but that was pointless. She was right, so, with a heavy sigh, I surrendered. "Alright. I'll try."

Loren hugged me and said, "As a reward, instead of me dragging you out tonight, we will be ordering room service."

"You're just doing this because you've never been in a hotel that had room service," I teased. She shrugged, then sashayed her way to the table where the phone and the menu were stashed. I shook my head. "Get me whatever. I'm going to take a shower."

When I got out, I felt better for dumping hot water on my head. The free hotel shampoo was more expensive than the stuff I bought at home, and my hair was ridiculously shiny and bouncy. I felt spoiled, even though I didn't care for the lobster pizza we picked at while watching TV. Loren took her own shower a couple of hours later. I wasn't ready to sleep but didn't feel like going out. Instead, I decided to explore the hotel.

The more I rode in the mirrored elevator, the more I hated it. It made me feel like I was trapped in an alternate dimension. The only sign that I wasn't far more alone with myself than I was comfortable with, was the panel of buttons and the key reader. Each button was still reflective, just gold tinted instead of silver. They were labeled G through R, with twelve floors in between. G was the ground floor. R was probably the roof.

When I got to the first floor, I wandered aimlessly. There was a pool and a gym. One die-hard cycler who looked like he was trying to outrun the devil on a stationary bike was in residence. I didn't eat much of dinner and was hungry again, but the restaurant had just closed. No matter where I looked, I couldn't find a snack machine. For a hotel that had everything, it was a strange omission.

As I passed by the front desk again, I approached the attendant. She wasn't much older than me with a very jaunty ponytail. She grinned, looking genuinely happy to help. I read her nameplate, which said Heather, while she chirped, "Can I do anything for you, Ma'am?"

"Is there like a snack machine around here somewhere?" I asked hopefully.

"There's one in the staff area, I could grab you something from there, but if you're hungry, the kitchen could make you something." From beneath the counter, Heather produced a disposable copy of the room service menu and handed it to me.

"Wow. They're still open? It's like nine at night." I glanced at the gold numeral clock on the wall behind the desk.

"The kitchen is always open for our special guests." The girl winked. "There's a secret menu that has some things that are always available."

"Well, I don't know how special I am, but I think the guy paying for the room counts." I laughed and put my elbows on the counter. "But, I've got to admit, you've got me intrigued. What's on the secret menu?"

"There are a few of the owner's favorites that we always have to be ready to make," Heather said. "We have a bacon cheeseburger, coconut shrimp, and cheeseburger pizza."

"Your hotel owner has phenomenal taste," I assured her, licking my lips. "Those are my favorites too."

"I have been told that Mr. Heart is quite the connoisseur. If you tell me what you want, I'll have the kitchen whip it up and deliver it to your room."

I did a double-take. "You don't mean Isaac Heart, do you?"

"Yes. Do you know him?" Heather tilted her head to the side.

"More I know of him." I rubbed the back of my neck. "I inherited a house from him. It's why I'm in town. Who owns the hotel now that he's gone?"

"Mr. Heart isn't dead." The girl's nose wrinkled. "He sent instructions just this morning to get his suite ready for his annual visit. Who told you that he'd died?"

"Well, no one, I guess. I was just told that he left me some things. I guess that you don't have to be dead to leave someone something." I puzzled over this for a moment. How could Red not know that this guy was alive?

Maybe this was a misunderstanding. "Hey, is he, like a junior or something? Like he's named after his dad?"

She leaned over the counter and spoke low and conspiratorial. "You know, I'd bet he is. Mr. Wright, my manager, said he worked for Mr. Heart for forty years before he was brought in to manage this hotel. I've worked here for about a year, and I've seen the owner. There's no way he's any older than twenty-five. "

If Isaac Heart had a son, shouldn't he inherit everything? Maybe they were estranged. Either way, I needed to talk to him, but it didn't sound like Red knew anything about him. I had an idea. "Hey, you guys must have a way of contacting him, right?"

"I suppose Mr. Write does." Heather shrugged. "I could ask him about it if you want."

"Yeah, please do." I nodded rapidly. "Tell him that Adeline Gardener would like to talk."

"Alright, I'll pass it along." She moved to her computer and with fingers that fairly flew, she typed something in. "Do you still want something from the kitchen?"

"Oh, I forgot." I considered for a moment. "Can I have a bacon cheeseburger with fries, please?"

"Of course." She clicked away at her keyboard. "It'll be up in your room in a few minutes and I will talk to the manager personally about your request."

"Thanks, Heather." I drummed my hands a couple times on the counter and gave her a parting smile. I was so excited to tell Loren what I'd found that I didn't even mind the creepy elevator.

When I got back to the room, my friend was lounging on the couch, watching a cooking show. I chuckled, "Nothing else to watch, huh?"

"No." She rolled her eyes. "This is legit interesting. It's on how to make bread from scratch."

"You don't bake," I pointed out.

"I might start. Your new place definitely has a kitchen, and one of us will have to learn." Loren crossed her arms.

"I can cook, you know." I bounced a little on my heels, pretending to be angry. "I was the one who made that cake for your last birthday."

"Out of a mix." She smirked.

"You know what? See if I ever bake for you again." I moved to the couch and chucked a pillow at her. "I did have something cool to tell you, but I don't think I'm going to now."

"Oh come on. You know you're terrible at keeping secrets. Tell me!" She used my own weapon against me, and whapped me in the shoulder.

I repeated my conversation with the desk clerk. Loren was so excited she started bouncing. She grabbed my hands and held them together in front of her.

"Addie, this is going to be epic! He must be coming into town to meet with you. He's your half-brother or something and–"

"Loren, will you stop with this already?" I pleaded, pulling my hands out of hers. "I don't know what's going on, but this guy isn't my brother. I'm not looking for family, I just want to find out why this is happening."

The room bell rang, and I perked up. "Oh. My burger!"

Loren's eyes narrowed as she roused a little from her pout. "You ordered room service? I thought the kitchen would be closed."

"Nope. It's open only to the most important customers. They even have a super secret menu." I walked to the door with a little skip. "I mean, they don't just let anyone order off it, you know, like you."

Loren stuck her tongue out at me while I pressed the button to open the door. A young man brought my food on a tray with a silver dome and set it on the table. He lifted it to reveal the prettiest burger I had ever seen and retreated before I could even think to offer him a tip.

Wafting amazing fumes back at my friend, I asked, "Do you want some?"

Loren sighed heavily as she rose from the couch. "No, but I demand a few french fries."

53

The burger was exactly how I liked it and the fries were thin and crunchy with powdered herbs on them. Loren became more and more distracted as we sat. Eventually, she threw down the fry she was nibbling.

"Your lawyer didn't say anything about Isaac Heart having a son."

My head dropped. "He may not have thought it was important."

"How is this not important?" She threw up her hands. "If nothing else- if nothing else, this guy may want to come for his dad's money."

"Red would tell me if it was an issue, but I'll ask him about it tomorrow."

"What if he doesn't tell you the truth?" She crossed her arms.

"I'm getting in touch with Isaac Junior. We'll figure this out one way or another. Just let me handle it, okay?" Loren's lips pursed. I knew that look and pointed a finger at her. "No confronting Red without talking to me, even if you think it's for my own good. Promise?"

She let out a deep, controlled breath. "Fine. I'll behave."

"Thank you." We went back to eating, and the talk turned to more pleasant chit-chat.

When I went to bed, I was tentatively excited about seeing the house, and the prospect of talking to the mysterious Isaac Heart. Eventually, I managed to close my eyes, only to open them again around one a.m.

I was no stranger to nightmares and had them constantly for a couple of years after my accident. Usually, I just took a few deep breaths before going back to sleep. Sometimes, like tonight, I couldn't.

I tried to read for a while, but couldn't make myself concentrate. After I snuck into the living room to watch TV, I realized I wasn't at home and didn't need to sneak, so I felt a little silly. It was just habit. Thankfully, there was no one there to see me. Not that it helped. There was nothing but infomercials on at that hour, and they were more annoying than restful.

It was already tomorrow. The day was going to be busy, and I needed to sleep. Either the long ride had messed with me, the strange room was too unfamiliar, or I was just too excited. It was probably a little of each. I wanted to move, so I went to the balcony and looked out into the night. It was beautifully dark and dotted with lights. Only the brightest stars were visible through the city's glow.

A faint illumination shone above the thirteenth floor. That was the highest story, so any light would have to be from the roof. I craned my neck, trying to see something beyond the balcony above me. The delicious scent of honeysuckle came very faintly over the air. Was there a rooftop garden?

There had been that button on the elevator labeled 'R'. Would I be allowed on the roof? A walk usually cleared my head, so I decided to give it a try. The worst that would happen was that a polite staff member would ask me nicely to go away. I took the time to put on real pants instead of pajama bottoms and pushed the button to summon the elevator.

It was less than appealing, standing in a mirror box, being forced to look at myself at one a.m. While I had remembered pants, I had forgotten to brush my hair. I looked horrible, and the two-story ride seemed to last forever. My reflections had the audacity to stick their tongues out at me when I did the same.

When the elevator opened, there was a little foyer painted a plain cream color and a narrow but long table against the far wall. The room looked incredibly bare next to the opulence of the rest of the hotel. To the left, there were a set of glass doors.

A gentle push let me out into the roof garden. The smell of honeysuckle was much stronger here. Every wall in the place was covered in thick vines and unopened honey-white buds studded the green. There were islands of planter boxes with roses and some kind of small yellow and red flowers. Some of them had leaves that were purple or red. There was a decent-sized fountain in the center, but

55

it was currently dry and was partially disassembled with tools left at its base.

Off to one side was a large gazebo clothed in honeysuckle with bits of white shingle peeking out. Wooden benches sat in a circle and the side facing the edge of the roof gave a brilliant view of the city. Little white fairy lights were woven through the foliage and latticework, but weren't currently on.

And it was oh, so achingly familiar.

I should have turned around right then. That kind of familiarity invited fits. Inevitably, my curiosity won and I walked into the gazebo. Like submerging in water, pressure started to build around my head. It was a bad sign. Impressions of bright colors and loud bangs like the Fourth of July ghosted around me. A light switch was nestled unobtrusively onto one of the supports. Under a compulsion that was just my masochistic need to know, I walked to the post and flickcd on the lights. They glittered to life and I remembered ball gowns and fireworks and a man in a tuxedo.

The fit took me so hard that my legs buckled, and convulsions wracked my body.

It was only five or six minutes that I lay on the floor of the gazebo, but it felt longer. I forced myself through the routine I learned from long years of practice. Each deep breath was a struggle as I made my mind go quiet, ignoring the pain and just thinking of nothing. Slowly, the agony eased, and my body started to relax. I became aware that someone was stroking my hair and talking to me, telling me I was alright.

Without opening my eyes I asked, "Hey, could you turn out the lights?"

A high and raspy feminine voice said, "Um, yeah, sure."

The petting stopped and I heard rapid, soft steps across the wooden floor. There was a click and I relaxed a little more. Hesitantly, I opened my eyes to a slight figure in a gray hoodie and tightly belted baggy jeans. She stood awkwardly by the light switch, hands in her pockets and face hidden under her hood. She twitched and gave the impression of barely contained motion. Was that because she had just watched me having an attack, or something else?

"Thanks." I gingerly pushed myself up.

The girl in the hoodie made an aborted step forward, thin and frail-looking hands hesitating in the air, opening and closing ineffectually. "Are you sure you should be getting up? Maybe I should, I don't know, call somebody?"

"No, no." I held up a hand and shook my head. "I have a condition, and there's nothing anyone could do. I just had an episode, but it's passed now. The best thing for me is to get back to my room and rest."

"Should I carry you or something?" The girl was practically dancing on her toes with worry. I looked at her small frame and delicate hands with skepticism.

"I'm okay. Although I wouldn't say no to some help up?" I extended a hand with a smile, intending just to make her feel better.

Hoodie still low, not letting me see much more than a pointed chin and a small mouth, my savior darted forward, and locked my hand and elbow in a surprisingly strong grip. I had thought I would have to brace against the floor to get up, and just use her hand as a balance point, but as I put a little pressure on her, I might as well have been holding onto an iron railing. She was absolutely steady. The girl didn't let go until she was certain that I was stable, then she jumped back like a startled rabbit.

"Are you sure you're okay?" Hoodie girl was dancing on her toes again. "Maybe I should see you back to your room."

"No, really. I'm fine. I'm just a short ride down the elevator. Thanks for all your help, though." My head ached when I smiled. I needed to leave before I started thinking about what had set me off in the first place.

I got about halfway to the foyer before I remembered my manners. When I turned back to introduce myself to my odd new friend, there was no one there. Stunned, I swept my gaze over the roof. "Hello?"

No answer. I was about to walk back to the gazebo, but stopped. There wasn't anywhere anyone could hide, and I didn't want to tempt my luck by going back to the cause of my fit. I turned on my heel and almost ran back to the elevator. I pressed the button for my floor so hard I was worried that I'd break it.

When I got to the room, I tried to go back to sleep. The unease over the disappearing girl dimmed with distance and exhaustion. I probably hadn't seen what I thought I saw, anyway. No need to mention it to Loren, since I couldn't tell her anything without mentioning the fit. I didn't want to make her worry.

And she thought I couldn't keep a secret. I was always keeping secrets.

Chapter 7: Haunted

Far too early for my liking, Loren came bouncing into my bedroom. She grabbed a pillow and beat me repeatedly with it until I groaned, "I'm awake."

"Good. Get up. This hotel is supposed to have a world-class breakfast buffet. I want to see what a world-class breakfast buffet looks like. You have to get up now if we are going to have time to enjoy it before Red, the vampiric wonder lawyer, gets here." Loren poked me the entire time she was talking until she finally harassed me into sitting up. I felt like someone had beaten me with a baseball bat. It was always like that after a fit.

"Fine. Get out, and I'll get dressed." I pushed her away and she smirked.

"Okay, but if you aren't out in fifteen minutes, I'm assuming you've gone back to sleep, and I will be coming back with a glass of water to pour over your head." Loren only chuckled at my glare, because she knew that I knew that she would absolutely do it.

The door slammed shut, and I painfully pushed myself out of bed and staggered to the bathroom. Doing my business and splashing some water on my face made me feel a little closer to human. I put on the only other clean clothes I had, another pair of jeans and a long tee-shirt that usually was a nightshirt. I was going to have to do some laundry and go shopping.

A lot of preparation time was dedicated to coaxing my hair into a reasonable facsimile of a neat ponytail. It was a rat's nest after my rough night. My remaining two minutes I used to stretch out, in the hopes that Loren wouldn't notice how sore I was. As promised, my punctual friend burst in at the fifteen-minute mark, water glass in hand. I was bent over, almost able to touch my toes again.

"Oh. You're up. I don't need this, then." She set the water on a table and pouted. I was not sorry to ruin her fun.

"Okay. I met your absurd deadline. Let's go get your world-class waffles, or whatever they have." I flicked

Loren's hair on my way to the elevator. She took it all in good cheer and flounced after me with the disgusting energy of someone who had enjoyed a decent night's sleep.

The breakfast buffet was as grand as advertised. After a couple of over-easy duck eggs on homemade rye toast and an amazing cappuccino, my outlook on the day vastly improved. Loren stuffed herself with every type of pastry they had, most of which I did sneak a bite of.

When she was done, she leaned back with a sigh and said, "You know, this trip has not been good for myself control. I'm going to have to use the hotel gym tomorrow."

"We could go swimming," I offered.

"I didn't bring a bathing suit, and neither did you."

"We don't have any workout clothes either. I'm going to have to go shopping anyway. I'll buy us what we need."

"Have I mentioned that you are the best friend ever?" Loren grinned and glanced at her phone. She squeaked. "It's a quarter after nine. We gotta go."

Red was waiting for us in the lobby. He wore a charcoal-colored suit, but the same crimson fedora. It made him very easy to see across the room. For just a second, I thought he was deep in conversation with a slight figure in a gray hoodie, but then an employee with a full baggage cart passed between us. When Red was visible again, he was alone and looking at us with a smile.

"Ah, Addie. Loren. How are you both doing? Feeling alright this morning?" His eyes fell on me, filled with concern.

Suspicion reared. Did he know about last night? Was he associated with the girl in the hoodie? I shook my head to knock loose the wary thoughts. He probably just saw the circles under my eyes, and the girl... It didn't matter. By this point, I was half convinced that I dreamed the girl.

"I just didn't sleep well. You know, first night in a new place." I said.

"The tour can wait if you'd like to rest today. We have all week." They were both watching me for an answer. Red radiated low-grade worry, but Loren looked calm and curious as to what I would do. I wasn't used to people letting me make decisions.

Since I wasn't going to let my condition get in the way of my new life, I turned my smile up to eleven and said, "I really am fine. Let's go see the house."

No one argued with me, and Red ushered us out to a big, black, expensive town car. He held the door for us while Loren and I scooted into the back seat. It was nice fawn leather, and extremely comfortable.

Loren shifted around while mouthing the word 'damn' at me. She seemed to share my assessment. Red got into the driver's seat and the car purred to life. As we traveled through the town, he played tour guide. He pointed out a curiosities shop that was run by a friend of his, and he promised to take me in later. There was a café that he swore was the best in the world and a tailor that he highly recommended.

As we left the main roads and headed out through the residential areas, Red talked about the quality of the neighborhood. He pointed out an idyllic park that backed a strand of trees that was part of the land I was getting. It acted as a barrier between the road I lived on and any other houses. Mine was the only house on Hill Drive. We crossed a low bridge that spanned a creek onto my new street, and a little way up, I spied the driveway to the house.

The part of the property that touched the street was guarded by a red stone wall. The gate was open and two wing-like structures of black iron ushered us down a straight, white cement drive. It ran about a hundred yards and was lined with white flowering trees and old fashion style lamp posts. The house lay at the end, like a sleeping dragon, massive and intimidating. It sprawled out behind the pale brick front, a few spires jutted above the roof, and you could just see the peak of a great glass dome. Double white columns book ended the door and two tall and narrow windows. The effect was not unlike eyes and a mouth.

The driveway made a loop in front of the door and wrapped around the house. Red pulled around the circle so that the passenger side was facing the stoop. He started walking around the car, probably to hold the door for me. I opened it on my own and got out. Seeing that, Red stopped and took a step back with a nod and a patient smile.

Loren scooted out behind me. She whistled at the pure scope of the house. "You could fit every person I've ever met in here and have enough room that they would rarely have to see each other."

"And I'm betting the house is even bigger than you realize." Red's grin was extraordinarily toothy and I did take note that his teeth were quite pointy. I supposed that someone could consider that creepy but kittens had sharp teeth. In fact, Red reminded me a lot of a playful kitten.

I sprinted up the steps with Loren following at a slower pace. Red fished through his pockets. At the top step, I looked at the door with its lion's head knocker and expected a twang of memory, but there was nothing. It was cool looking, but it was just a door. The handle had elaborate flowers molded all over it and I reached out to feel them on a whim. My fingers just barely pressed on the leaver and it pushed down, clicked, and silently swung open.

"That's odd. I'll have to have a word with the contractors about locking up when they're finished." Red didn't sound particularly upset. Instead, he disappeared into the darkness of the front room. "Hang on a second. I'll go find the light switch."

Loren and I looked at each other, and she shrugged. There was just enough sunlight from the doorway and windows to see a rich and dark wood floor, a large, open room and the sweeping stairs that led into darkness.

I took a deep breath and stepped inside. The lights came up as my foot crossed the threshold, and Red turned towards us. Perhaps it was my imagination that he wasn't quite close enough to the wall to have flicked the switch. I didn't have much time to think about it though, because the room took my breath away.

The walls stretched up at least to the third story and a vaulted ceiling sported a huge and glittering chandelier that would make the Phantom of the Opera jealous. The wallpaper was a soft cream color, but there was some kind of thin and delicate gold pattern weaving through it. The vast wooden staircase had an honest to god red carpet going up it and led up to the second story, before splitting like butterfly wings to a walkway on the third.

Through archways, I could see sitting rooms that could belong to any gentleman from the early twentieth century. One of them had a black princess-style rotary phone on a desk that I loved. I hugged my arms around myself, feeling small, but oddly happy.

I asked, "Is this really mine?"

"Well, in a few more days, but yes, my dear. It is." Red put a hand on my shoulder and asked in a playful tone, "I take it you like it?"

"It's absolutely perfect," I whispered.

"This place is totally haunted," Loren said flatly.

"There are no ghosts," he chided.

"How do you know? This place just feels heavy. Like it's watching you. Has anyone ever died here? I'm pretty sure you have to disclose that." My friend glared at the walls each in turn like she expected them to start bleeding at any moment.

"If I was a realtor, maybe, but I'm a lawyer. I don't have to disclose anything." Red's arms crossed, but he still seemed amused. "That being said, not as far as I know."

"Come on, Loren. This place is amazing. It feels homey." I patted her back as I wandered into the nearest room. I ran my hands over the brown leather furniture. One of the coffee tables had a glass insert in the middle that had a chip in one corner. Caressing the smooth surface, I got the vague impression that I might have been responsible for the damage. I couldn't quite remember why. Thankfully, no headache ensued.

Chapter 8: Only Half Remembered

"What would you like to see first?" Red rubbed his hands together. "I'll admit, I don't know the entire house, but I have a fairly good grasp of the general layout."

"Bet the first thing she wants to see is the library." Loren smirked.

"Not necessarily." I crossed my arms defensively, then I gave up and admitted it. "But yes, if there's a library, I'd like to see it."

"If there's a library, she says." Red scoffed to hide a smile and rolled his eyes. "What would make you believe that a house like this wouldn't have a library? There are several, as a matter of fact. At least I am assuming there are more than just the two I've found. Rooms are a bit like mice here. If you see one, there are bound to be more. I'll take you to the biggest one if you'd follow me?"

Red led us down a hallway that branched off the main room beside the staircase. The labyrinthine series of halls we went through after that was nearly impossible to remember. On our way, the lawyer pointed out such sites as a lavish office with a vault that would be the envy of some banks, and an honest-to-god ballroom. The library was as tall as the main hall, if not taller, and I bet it had entrances on all floors.

Once, on a trip with Loren and her mom, I had seen one of the big city municipal libraries. It hadn't been this big. I asked, "How many are there? Books, I mean."

"Afraid I don't know." Red dipped his head and smiled wryly. "I always meant to get an appraisal and inventory done, but the original man I had to do it had a conflict of schedule. With all the hullabaloo of getting the gardens back in order, that kind of fell by the wayside."

"Oh, don't worry. Addie will find out all on her own." Loren gave me a long look. "You know, it's a good thing you keep me around. Otherwise, someday someone would find your skeleton curled up on a pile of books, dead because you refused to leave this room."

"You're not wrong," I said lightly as I moved to pull out a leather-bound volume of who knew what.

Loren smacked my hand. "None of that. If you start book surfing, we'll waste the whole day here. When the house is yours, then you can browse to your heart's content. Now, let's go look at something else."

I gave my loudest, most put-upon sigh. "Fine. Red, any suggestions?"

"Right this way, ladies." Again he took us into the maze of a house. I made a silent promise to the library to spend some quality time with it later.

Everything I could ever want in a house was here and oh, so much more. There was an Olympic-sized swimming pool complete with diving board, nearby hot tub big enough for ten people, and a sauna. The game room had a billiards table, darts, pinball and a couple of old-style arcade games.

I did waste a few minutes dying a lot at Mrs. Pac-Man. I wondered who CRW was that had all the top scores. A small private movie theater, complete with popcorn machine had just enough seats for me and my nine closest friends, which I didn't have at the moment. Next to that was an area like a pizza parlor. The tables were low enough for children, and one entire wall was lined with ski ball games and automated basketball hoops. A whole corner of the room was dedicated to a mammoth ball pit.

Loren met my eyes, and we had a moment of pure understanding. With whoops and cheers, we ran side by side and cannonballed into the ball pit. This could have ended badly, but fortunately, it was deep enough. It was as glorious as I thought it would be. Red put a hand on his mouth as he leaned on the door frame. He stifled a laugh as my friend and I tried to wade out of the pit, all the time tripping over unseen balls and giggling like idiots.

"Do you wish to resume the tour, or would you like to spend some more time here?" Red's amusement was palpable.

"No, no. We're good." I pulled myself out by a rail on the side that was probably there for just that reason. "I just had to do that, or my inner five-year-old would never forgive me."

"Understandable." He waved a hand towards the door. "Let us continue."

The dining room had the longest table I'd ever seen. I'd bet the kitchen was bigger than the one for the hotel and had a walk-in fridge as well as a normal one. Copper pots and pans hung from a rack above an island. Splashes of color painted shapes along the far wall, cast from a line of high and narrow stained-glass windows. There was a doorway that led to a breakfast nook, which looked over a freshly planted plot. I was no gardener, pun not intended, but I thought they were herbs.

"Is this the garden that you were talking about needing replanting?" I asked, looking at the neat rows of small plants.

"One of them." Red glanced over my shoulder. "There are many gardens, and they've been mostly untouched for the last ten years. Except for the rose garden. I had to have the edibles garden redone, it's just past the hedge there. The ponds for the water garden needed quite a bit of love."

"How many are there?" Loren asked.

"A lot." Red sighed, a put-upon look on his face.

"Why didn't the rose garden need work?" The fact bugged me like a seed in my teeth.

He shrugged, studying the windows. "From what the people I hired told me, it was especially well-designed. It only needed some trimming."

This was strange, but not even close to the strangest thing I had dealt with that day, so I let it go. Instead, I just followed as Red left the kitchen, wondering what he would show us next.

Loren asked, "Is there a bathroom anywhere around here?"

Red froze. His eyes settled in the middle distance while his hands ticked back and forth and he mumbled under his breath. I realized with relief that he was running through the hallways in his head, trying to comply with Loren's request. "I believe there's one this way. Follow me, please."

Two turns later, Red stopped at a door and directed Loren with a sweeping arm. "That should be a servant's lounge and there is a bathroom on the right-hand side."

My friend disappeared into the room. I braced myself and took advantage of Loren's absence. "So, did you know that Isaac Heart had a son?"

Red twitched, then raised one of his giant eyebrows. "I hadn't heard that, no."

"Yeah, well, it turns out that he owns the hotel that I'm staying in." I crossed my arms while I searched his face.

His eyes widened and he spread his arms in a shrug. "I'm sorry Addie. As I said, Mr. Pit is the one who originally managed your account, and he never mentioned a son to me. As soon as he's available, I will ask him about this situation, but I promise you, I will not let this affect your inheritance."

My mouth scrunched to one side as I glared at him, but Red looked so earnest that I uncrossed my arms and sighed. "Mr. Pit sure is putting a lot of crap on you."

Red burst out laughing. "Now, if that isn't the unvarnished truth, I don't know what is."

Down the hallway, a door opened and a much-relieved Loren came out. I smiled at her. "Want to find the gym?"

"Sure," she said, and we acted like good little ducklings in a row as Red led us on.

The corridor he led us down overlooked the front lawn. There was a nagging of familiarity again, then we crossed a short hall that led to a plain pair of double doors. I froze in place to stare at them. It took my companions a moment to realize I wasn't following them anymore. Loren got to me first.

"What is it?" Red moved to my side.

"Well, I believe I used to live here, now." My stomach was sinking. Tears started to well. "That was my parents' suite."

"What, like an apartment?" Loren asked.

"Yeah. It's all self-contained." I leaned against the corner, letting it dig into my shoulder. "They lived here to be isolated from the rest of the house. I don't remember why, but I do know I wasn't allowed in.

"Sometimes, I would crouch right here, wanting to see them but afraid to knock. I heard Mom and Dad fighting once. It was about me. My father was convinced that I wasn't his. He was screaming at my mother, saying it was all her fault. She just cried. I'm beginning to think that some of my memory loss wasn't the accident. Maybe, I just didn't want to remember."

Everyone was quiet for a few seconds before Loren grabbed my arm. "Tell you what, it's lunchtime and I'm hungry again. We can always do more house touring later. Hey, Red? How about we go to that coffee shop in town? I bet they have something tasty to snack on."

"Absolutely. We're not far from the front door." He started walking and Loren pulled me so that I was between them. He leaned in to whisper to me in a mischievous tone, "If it would make you feel any better, I could hit your dad in the head with my club."

"You have a club?" I asked.

"A golf club. It's specially made, though."

I laughed in spite of myself.

Chapter 9: Into the Woods

Red wasn't wrong about the coffee shop. It was amazing. I had a slice of chocolate cream cake and some kind of dark, sweet beverage so caffeinated it could have doubled as a horse stimulant. Having self-medicated with food, I felt stupidly better. The guy behind the counter had recommended everything. He had a light Italian accent and was very handsome. Loren mimed fanning herself when he wasn't looking and that lifted my spirit as well.

By the time Red dropped us off at the hotel, I was feeling much more myself. Maybe better than my normal self. A little catharsis may have been exactly what I needed. When we got back to the suite, I crashed onto the couch and sprawled out in my best impersonation of a dead body.

Leaning over me, Loren said, "You know if you want to catch a nap before you have to get ready for tonight, you have time."

"You're still making me go out?" I groaned.

"Don't give me that. You need this." My friend wagged a finger at me like a scolding mother. Like her scolding mother. Because I didn't have a death wish, I didn't point out the similarity. "Go be an introvert for a couple of hours. Or sleep. Or whatever you want to do. You are going to go out and make some friends tonight, damn it, if I have to drag you around the entire night."

I was tired, so I did try to nap. I dozed for about a half an hour, then I went to take a shower. While I washed my hair, I pondered.

Even if I did decide to sell the house, which was something to consider because I just didn't need anything that big, I wanted to stay in it for a while. One, it was a beautiful house, and I loved it. I couldn't wait to see more of it. Two, there were bits and pieces of who I was before the accident in there, scattered like objects in a scavenger hunt. If I found them, maybe I could reclaim some of myself.

When I got out of the shower, Loren was waiting to pounce on me, ready to make me up for the night. I decided that it would just be easier to surrender, so I submitted to her ministrations. She did my hair and makeup, and I slithered into my new dress. Gazing at my reflection in the mirror, I could agree the results weren't too shabby.

I presented myself for inspection and said, "So, am I ready to go out and play, Mom?"

"You'll do." She sighed. "I wish you would let me doll you up more often."

"Um, no." I rolled my eyes. "I am sticking by my rule that you get to make me up on special occasions. This barely counts. I don't have the patience to do this all the time."

"Fine, heathen." Loren stalked off to go get herself ready. I waited in the living room, watching TV.

When she came out of her room sporting a little beaded dress, I raised an eyebrow at her. "Why did you pack that?"

"In case an opportunity for socialization occurred." She put her hands on her hips. "And you know what? It happened, so shut up."

I held up my hands in surrender, and we called to have Loren's car brought around. We went down in the stupid mirrored elevator, which I was beginning to hate, and had my friend's little sensible sedan presented to us at the front door like it was a Maserati. I could get used to the luxury.

With GPS assistance, we found the restaurant we were supposed to meet Sean the candle man at. It was a pub-themed restaurant, with a blue swan rearing up in neon over the door. It was a bit tacky, but that made it fun. Loren's date was already at a table with a half dozen other people. One stood out with a short red mohawk rising like a parrot's crest from his otherwise bald head. Loren led our approach and greeted her date with a shy smile.

Sean rose and hugged her before nodding at me. We were introduced around and admittedly, the only one that stuck with me was Nigel, the guy with the mohawk. We ordered food and I listened to people joke and play around. Loren absorbed into the group with ease, laughing and teasing. I envied her.

No one noticed that I wasn't talking. I ate my fish and chips while listening to everyone drone on. It was actually quite pleasant, like watching characters on TV rather than being there myself. At any rate, Loren was having a good time, and that had been my entire goal for the evening.

Eventually, the pub filled up, and the noise became so cacophonous that we couldn't hear each other. It was Nigel who suggested that we leave, and head to the park. Neither Loren nor I knew where they meant, but Sean offered to ride with us to show us where to go. He jumped into the car with us, while everyone else loaded into an old van. As we were leaving, I recognized the style of the paintings on its side. Nigel was the one driving, and this was so fitting because I was pretty sure that it was the same van I had seen from my balcony. The one with the naked lady.

All the way to the park, Loren and Sean gabbed about a fantasy book. For once, my friend didn't try to drag me into the conversation. She was too busy flirting. When we did arrive, I was pleasantly surprised that I knew where we were. This was the little park down through the woods from my new house. It was a little juvenile to be hanging out in a playground after dark, but I had never done it before. Maybe it would be fun. I took a seat on a swing while the others perched around various bits of equipment.

They talked and joked and I just listened. While I got the impression I was welcome to join in, no one sought me out. It was nice, up close people watching. At one point, most of them broke into a chase when Guy-A-Whose-Name-I-Couldn't-Remember stole Guy-B-Whose-Name-I-Couldn't-Remember's hat, and almost everyone was trying to get it back. A girl in a pair of heavily slashed jeans and a t-shirt so faded I couldn't read it sat on the swing next to me.

Even though I didn't feel like participating any more than I already was, I knew Loren was right. With a fresh start, I had to be willing to put myself out there. At the very least I needed to attempt to converse. I smiled experimentally at the girl whose jeans had more holes than material. "Hey."

She seemed surprised, but happy enough to talk. "Hey. You're Addie, right?"

"Yeah." I scrunched my face up in embarrassment. "I'm sorry. I don't remember your name."

"It's okay." She waved it off with a hand that sported a hefty silver snake ring. "Sean kind of rushed through the introductions. I'm Crystal."

"Nice to meet you." I nodded towards the hunt that was still on. "You don't feel like playing?"

"Nah. I've been playing with my kid all day. I'm tired." She spared them a withering glance. "He's seven, and they're acting just like him. So, what brings you two to our scenic, yet boring little town?"

"I inherited a house in the area. Loren's just here for moral support. And to give me a ride." My friend was currently racing after the stolen hat with everyone else. Acting childish or not, she was having a good time. Looking Crystal over, I wondered how old she was. She seemed the same age as the majority of the group, maybe a couple of years older than me. She must have had her son awfully young.

"Ah, I'm sorry." Crystal sounded more curious than apologetic as she rocked a little on the swing. "Who died, if you don't mind me asking?"

"I'm not sure anyone did." I searched for the words. "Everything was set up so that it legally passes to me on my eighteenth birthday."

"Oh, so like a trust, then." She nodded. "Where's the house?"

"About a mile that way." I pointed through the trees.

"Holy shit, you own the haunted Gardener Mansion?" Crystal stood up still clutching the chains of her swing. Her expression was perhaps best defined as devilishly delighted. "What's it like inside? Have you ever seen a ghost?"

"Well, I don't own it yet." I was a little startled at the energy of her response. "I only got to see it today. Really, it's just a cool, big house. It's not that old. Why? Do you know something about it?"

"Are you kidding? Gardener Mansion is like, the local legend." Crystal let go of the chains and stood in front of me, leaning over and chopping her arms wildly as she spoke. It looked like she was pitching a movie. "When I was a kid there were a bunch of people who lived there. They were all weird and rarely went into town. Neighbors said they sometimes heard strange noises and saw eerie things. There was a little girl too. She was younger than me but in the same school. I never met her, but she was supposed to be bizarre."

Crystal plopped back into the swing seat, but leaned in, eyes glittering with excitement. I wasn't sure how I felt about being described as bizarre. The story wasn't done though. "One day, there was this girl staying there, babysitting the kid. The babysitter brought her boyfriend over, and they both disappeared. There was a city-wide hunt to find them. The parents made a plea on TV for someone to find their daughter. Everyone in town joined the search, everyone but the people in the house where she disappeared. Maybe the family who lived there killed them. Or, maybe they themselves fell victim to whatever haunts that house because a few months later, they disappeared too. Ever since, the house has been empty. Until you, that is, so I'd be careful when you walk through those halls. You never know what may be walking with you."

"Jesus, Crys, don't scare the girl away already." The voice made me jump and I whipped around to see Nigel standing behind us.

"Oh come on." Crystal rolled her eyes. "She's moving into the Gardener house. I have to let her know what she's up against."

"You're going to live in the Gardener house?" Nigel dipped his head skeptically, making him look more like a parrot.

"Yeah," I said, a little sore about the scare he'd given me. "And the story doesn't work quite as well as you think. The Gardeners didn't disappear."

"What happened to them then?" Crystal pouted.

"We moved about ten hours away to go live with my grandmother." I raised an eyebrow at both of them, feeling a little smug at their total surprise. "Hi, I'm Adeline Gardener. You know me as the bizarre girl a few years younger than you."

"Holy shit!" She broke into a broad grin. "Really?"

"Yeah, really." I shrugged. Despite having the end of her story ruined, Crystal was nothing but excited. "I can't tell you what happened to the babysitter, though. I don't know."

"That is so cool." She stood again, and moved in front of me with hands clasped, bouncing on her toes. "Can you show us the house?"

"Not yet." I rubbed the back of my neck. "It isn't officially mine for a few days. I don't have keys."

"Yeah, but we can go look at the outside, right? They aren't going to charge you with trespassing if the house is going to be yours." Nigel cracked a mean grin, and I started to dislike him. I didn't like pushy people. Except Loren. She'd earned that right.

"Yeah, but we wouldn't be able to see much. Just the outside and the gardens. Maybe in a few days..." I flailed at excuses, feeling helpless. I didn't want to take Crystal and everyone to the house.

Sean skidded to a halt in front of us, panting. "What's up?"

"Addie was going to show us around the Gardener House," Nigel said.

"I didn't say that." I frowned at him.

"What? Seriously? That would be awesome." Sean perked up, and the rest of the group stopped the chase to listen.

"What would be awesome?" the hat thief asked.

"Going to check out the Gardener House. Addie has an in," Sean told his friends, arms waving with excitement.

"Are you sure, Add?" Loren, also breathless, raised an eyebrow. "Do you even have a way in?"

"No. I'm not taking anyone anywhere." I clenched my fists and my voice rose. "And I wish people would stop putting words in my mouth."

"Hey, no one is putting words in your mouth." Nigel put his hands up, but was still smiling. The conflict seemed to delight him. "You just said you could show us the outside of the house. If that's all you want to do, that's fine."

"I don't want to show you anything, and I never said I would. Stop pushing me." I bared teeth as I spoke, but he was undeterred.

"Oh, come on, please?" Crystal begged. "I've always wanted to look at that house up close."

"And you promised her she could." Nigel blinked his eyes in mock innocence. "Crystal doesn't get to go out too often, so it would be a shitty thing to promise her, and then not deliver."

"Nigel, come on," Sean said, exasperated. "It sounds like she did no such thing. Why do you always have to be an asshole?"

"Hey, I'm just trying to get my girl what she wants." Nigel smirked as he went to put an arm around Crystal's shoulder. She pushed him away.

"I am not your girl." The young mother crossed her arms, using a tone that made my inner five-year-old freeze. "Do not make me kick your ass."

Hat-thief-guy raised his hand. "I would love to see the Gardener Mansion. I hear it has a hedge maze."

"It might be fun, Add, and I'm sure your lawyer wouldn't mind." Loren, I think, was trying to defuse the situation, but I was done being told what to do.

"No. I'm not taking anyone over there." I shook my head furiously. "And I think I'm ready to head back to the hotel."

Loren frowned and grabbed my arm as she walked away from the group. No one else noticed us as Crystal and Nigel were getting into a bigger fight. Everyone ringed them as they took sides. Pulling me to face her, she said, "What's up?"

"I don't like being pushed around. If I wanted that, I would have stayed at home with Mom." I took a step back, wrapping my arms around my stomach.

"Then don't let one jerk stop you from having fun." She reached out to grab my arm again. "Now come on. You can tell Mohawk-head to go screw himself, and then we can get on with the evening."

"You're having fun, Lore. I'm not." I took another step out of her reach. "These aren't my people. This isn't my thing. You're right that I need to put myself out there and meet new people, but these aren't them. I think I need to find my own friends."

Loren let her hand drop, hurt covering her face. "Okay. Fine. But I'm not ready to go yet."

"Fair enough." I took another step back. I looked at the growing distance between us, and wondered if it was symbolic. Loren and I had never made much sense as friends, despite her being the only real one I had. "I'm going to wait over by the car."

She looked a little lost for a moment before her eyes hardened. "Do what you want. I'll be over that way when I feel like leaving. It may be awhile."

"Fine." I turned on my heel and walked back to the car. To give due credit to my self-control, I didn't look back at her until I was close enough to touch the hood. Then I did take a covert glance over my shoulder. I needn't have bothered trying to hide it. Loren was talking happily to her date, although it looked like the rest of the group was still egging on the argument between Crystal and Nigel.

Even though I had no right to, I felt abandoned. This was supposed to be my chance, my glorious rebirth. That was me being selfish though. Other people's lives didn't stop because I was trying to start mine over. I would apologize to her later. For now, I didn't want to bother her.

The car was locked, and I didn't have keys. There was a bench I could wait on, but it was in plain view of Loren's new friends. It would make me feel pathetic to be seen sitting there alone. Instead, I wandered to the tree line and stared out into the shadow-painted woods. The moon was bright, almost full, and it gave everything a film noir ambiance. The gardens around the house would look amazing. Was it hypocritical to go there by myself after making such a big deal about not wanting to take the others?

The argument had broken up, and the group was all playing on the climbing equipment, except for Crystal, who was back on the swing. They were all doing their own thing, so I was going to do mine. Besides, I was under no obligation to let them on my property. Or, rather, my soon-to-be property. Relatively sure I could cross less than a mile of woods without getting lost, I stepped off the manicured lawn of the park.

I had never been the outdoorsy type. I mean, I liked trees and bunnies as much as the next person, but my experience was limited. This being my first excursion into anything resembling wilderness, it wasn't bad. The occasional tree root or hole was easy enough to avoid with the light that filtered down through the thick leaves. Mosquitoes buzzed by my ear, but didn't bite. Even the pungent smell of green plants and decaying leaves wasn't unpleasant.

I took my time, enjoying the unfamiliar noises of creaking cicadas and one lonely owl, but eventually I cleared the tree line. I wasn't far off from the front gate. The driveway looked longer than the walk through the woods, but that was an illusion facilitated by the trees that lined it. The electric lamps on either side cast pools of gold amidst the silver light of the moon. I was falling even more in love with the house.

Red had definitely locked the front door when we left, so I didn't bother trying it. Instead, I followed the leg of the driveway that curled around the house. The path led to a little parking lot right near the herb garden. There was a checkerboard of wide paths allowing access to any portion of the garden and the kitchen door. The part that was visible from the breakfast nook was an uninterrupted swath of new baby plants.

I knew I should start heading back. It had to be almost eleven, and it was a long walk back to Loren's car, but... on a whim, I grabbed the doorknob. It turned and opened into the shadowy short hall that led to the kitchen. As I leaned in to look, the lights came on and I jumped back with a squeak. I laughed and shook my head. Red had said that the house had undergone renovations. The lights were just motion activated, that was all. Although, my lawyer did need to have that talk with his contractors about locking doors behind them.

If I left now, by the time I got back to the park, Loren should be ready to go. The urge to continue into the house for a little exploration on my own was strong. Since my friend had blown me off, making her wait didn't feel unwarranted. Feeling a little petty, I set out into the house. I wasn't sure where I was going, but I was having real fun for the first time tonight.

Chapter 10: Strange Strangers

There was still quite a bit of the first floor I hadn't seen yet, but when I found some stairs I took them. I glanced in a couple of rooms on the second story. There were some open areas, offices, a room with a chalkboard and desks, and one with nothing but a piano, but nothing all that interesting. I continued up to the third floor, but that's where the staircase stopped. If I wanted to go further, I'd have to find another way. I wandered hallways that rivaled my swanky hotel with gold and cream wallpaper and elegant gold light fixtures. Occasionally, I'd open a random door for fun.

It was predominately bedrooms. They were all easily three times as large as my room back home, not including a huge walk-in closet and bathroom. Most of them were blandly decorated with a neutral color palette. A few of them were different. One was done up in a kind of renaissance-looking style, all elaborate gold and royal shades of blue and purple. The bed was the most elaborately carved thing I had ever seen and was honestly ugly. Another room was more tastefully decorated in soft grays and peacock greens. Under a broad window was a huge writing desk made of pale gray wood. A handful of things were placed on its surface. Curious, I stopped to take a closer look.

Amongst stationary and various brick-a-brack, there was a photograph of me as a little kid. I was sitting on a tire swing, grinning at the camera. My breath hitched as I picked it up and stared. Mom didn't have any pictures of me before the accident. I must have been about six years old and looked genuinely happy. Who was I looking at that made me smile like that? Who would have a photo of me in their room?

Thinking about it too hard made a headache start to build, so I set the picture down in the middle of the desk and just left. I didn't bother to close the door. If I was in danger of having a fit, it was stupid to be here alone. I retraced my way back to the stairwell, and just as I put my hand on the railing, agitated words echoed from below. I stopped breathing as I froze and listened.

"... And if this is some kind of joke that you've concocted, then I swear to you, I will make you pay. Call me when you get this, bird, or I am coming to find you." Stomping footsteps accompanied the voice that was growing closer.

I had a couple of options. Technically, I wasn't supposed to be in the house but if Red found out I was here, I wouldn't get in that much trouble. Whoever it was probably worked for him, and came to check that the doors were locked. They'd seen that the lights were on and came to investigate. He would find me, and call the lawyer to confirm who I was. Even if Red was mad, nothing would come of it. It was the wise option.

Unfortunately, I panicked.

I turned on my heel and sprinted down the hall. The room with the photo was still open, so I stepped inside and quietly closed the door behind me. I flicked the light off and crept to the closet, covering my mouth to muffle my suddenly loud breath. There was no reason for him to come into this particular room looking for me. It would be fine.

When the door to the room opened and the switch clicked, my heart nearly stopped. As I stared in horror at the light cutting a little slice out of the darkness from under the closet door, the man continued to rant. "Damn it, why isn't anyone answering their phones? Someone has to be out... What the hell?"

The man was silent for a moment, but I heard a few more steps across the floor. My stomach was doing flips, but when he spoke again, it felt like all my insides froze solid. "I know you're in here. Come out now and I won't call the police."

There was no point in staying in the closet. I didn't know how he knew I was there, but he did. Hopefully, if I just came out like he said I could explain, and he would at least find the situation funny. Slowly getting to my feet, I took a deep breath and opened the door, giving him a meek, "Hi."

The man standing in front of me with his hands on his hips was stunningly handsome. At some point during the day, he must have been immaculately groomed, but he looked a little ragged now. His charcoal gray suit was expensive, but the slacks were wrinkled, and his lavender shirt lacked a tie and was untucked under the jacket. Black hair stood up at odd angles, but not like it was on purpose. He had the strangest, most beautiful eyes I had ever seen. They were a dark brown, but glittering in his irises like chips of garnets were little flecks of red. My breath hitched.

"Hi." The man mimicked me with a touch of sarcasm. He seemed a lot less impressed with me than I was with him. He took a couple of steps forwards as his eyes scanned me from head to foot. It made me extremely self-conscious. "Who are you, and what are you doing here?"

"Um," I ground my toe on the floor, feeling like a stupid, naughty little kid. "I, uh, was just exploring the house. I know I'm not supposed to be here, but if you just call Red-"

"How did you even get in here?" The gorgeous man interrupted, crossing his arms.

"The kitchen door was open. Apparently, the contractors left several doors unlocked the last time they were in." I tried to tell him to contact Red again, but he cut me off.

"I haven't hired any contractors," he said.

"That's what I'm trying to tell you. Red did. He brought me by today for a tour of the house, and we found the front door unlocked." I nearly face-palmed when I realized what was causing part of the problem. "I'm the one who's inheriting the house next week. I'm Adeline Gardner."

Too quick to see, his hand lashed out and grabbed me at the elbow. My heart raced, partly from fear of violence and partly from an almost electric sensation when he touched my skin. That was... attraction? Something more. Something strange. He leaned in, the garnet flecks in his eyes almost glowing with intensity as he searched my face.

"You're Addie?" he asked. The pressure of his hand was firm, but not painful.

"Yes." I licked my suddenly dry lips.

"No. Addie died ten years ago." There was a rasp to his voice, a raw pain. Like a flipped switch, his entire demeanor changed. The grip on my arm became a light, delicate touch, stroking my elbow. He smiled mischievously and my stomach fluttered. I wanted to smile back. "Tell me, who put you up to this? It was a mean thing to do, but I'm not mad. Please, who told you to pose as Addie?"

Pain stabbed through my head and his charm evaporated. My hands clenched as fascination was replaced with rage. He was handsome, sure, but who was he to think he could use his... his... my knees nearly buckled as my skull felt like it was constricting my brain. Something he was doing was bringing on a fit. I put my hands on his shoulders and pushed with everything I had. He didn't move, but I stumbled backward, so I took the opportunity to run.

I got as far as opening the door and was about to take off into the hall when I heard, "No, no, no. Wait! Please wait. I'm sorry. I didn't mean to scare you."

"You didn't scare me, you pissed me off." I couldn't explain why I stopped. Maybe because I wasn't exactly sure how to get out of the house. Maybe because there was something very familiar about this guy, even though I couldn't say what. "Don't ever touch me like that again."

"Absolutely." He nodded vigorously. "Once again, I apologize. Please, if you are Addie, could you tell me where you've been for the last ten years? I knew her... you."

I shifted, now more uncomfortable than alarmed. Was this someone that I knew? He was a few years older than me, but young enough to be a childhood friend, maybe. I rubbed the back of my neck. "There was an accident. I... I lost my memory, or some of it, anyway. My parents took me away and I haven't been back since. I didn't know that this place existed until a few days ago when a lawyer contacted me about it."

"What do you remember? Do you recognize anything about me?" He was almost pleading. Tension sang through his body as he leaned forward, and stared into my eyes.

"Maybe a little? Were we friends when we were kids? No." I answered my own question. With the throbbing pain in my head came an echo from my fit last night. "Something about fireworks on the roof of the hotel?"

He took a half step towards me, hand partially raised like he wanted to touch me, but he stopped. Perhaps he was afraid I would bolt. I might have. "That night at my hotel was something only Addie knew about. I took her to see the New Year's Eve fireworks, but I wasn't supposed to have her out that late."

I couldn't handle whatever memory was trying to push its way to the surface. I needed to focus on something else. 'My hotel'.

"Wait, you're Isaac Heart?" I asked.

He raised an eyebrow. "You know that name?"

"Only as the one on all the paperwork Red showed me." I shrugged and studied him for a moment. "Your dad was the one who left me the house, right?"

"That is a complicated question." Isaac chuckled wryly. "But who's this Red you keep mentioning? I don't know him."

"Redmond Castle, with Pitt and Castle, the law firm handling all the paperwork on the estate? They've been making sure Mom got the money from the allowance all these years and contacted me about coming down to look at the house."

"The money to your parents was cut off after you d... disappeared. They should have only gotten anything while they were taking care of you, then it would all transfer to you..." I could watch dots connecting in Isaac's head. "Something isn't right. This Red has to be one of us. But how does he connect to your disappearance?"

"One of who?" I asked, eyes narrowing.

Isaac ignored me, still pontificating to himself. "The memory loss could be easily explained. You were a child, you couldn't defend yourself properly yet. From there, with your parents' help, it wouldn't have been hard to kidnap you."

I threw my hands up. "What are you talking about?"

"Your parents had wanted out of the bargain for years. They would have been easily obtainable accomplices. Bringing you back here would be risky, but if you didn't know us, and felt indebted to him..." For the first time in a minute, he seemed to actually see me. "You really are Addie."

"Yeah." I shrugged, feeling lost. "So, if you would explain what's going on, I would appreciate it."

"Yes. I think a very long talk is in order." Relief, pain, hope, and a dozen other expressions flickered across Isaac's face. He took another step forward and asked in a shaking voice, "I promise I'll tell you everything, but, please, can I hold you for just a minute?"

I took a step back into the hall. "I'm sorry, but I don't know you. It's a little weird."

"It's fine," Isaac said, but his face fell. "That was too much to ask."

"It's fine," I repeated his words, a little strained. "But what's going on? Who kidnapped me? Who is 'us'? You are a little too fast and loose with the pronouns."

Isaac choked out a laugh. "You could never remember that for your English test. Pronouns. We had to make up a rhyme for it. You were a rhyme fanatic."

"I don't like rhymes," I mumbled, thinking back to my first year after the accident. "They used to give me headaches. Not anymore, but... they did."

"They give you headaches?" Isaac said, incredulous.

"Yes!" I snapped, the old wound stinging. There had been so many years of people not believing me, mocking me, sneering at me, and all I had been able to do was bear it. When I'd cried in my room at night, Mom had told me it was my fault for being different. I was an adult now. I didn't have to put up with it anymore. "Weird things give me headaches, and can sometimes cause seizures. I am not making it up. I do not fake them. Understand?"

"Yes." Isaac raised his hands in surrender. "Once again, I apologize. Please, I didn't mean to be disrespectful. I'll explain, but where to start?"

"Start with who you are to me. That's a good place." I took a deep breath to help calm myself and I looked Isaac in the eyes, willing him to just tell me.

"I, uh, used to take care of you when you were a kid." He rubbed the back of his neck, and the gesture was as familiar as looking into a mirror.

"What, like a babysitter?" It was my turn to be skeptical.

He shrugged. "Part babysitter, part tutor. I was whatever you needed me to be."

I snorted. "You're what, five, six years older than me? How could you have looked after me? You what? Helped me with my homework?"

He chuckled dryly. "I am older than I look, believe me. I originally was just supposed to look after your money, but after you were born... I took care of you when you were a baby. As you grew your parents pulled away, and I was your friend. I held you when you were scared or sad. Yes, I helped you with your homework. I took you places on the weekends. We went to the zoo a lot. You loved the tigers."

A nagging feeling at the back of my head said he wasn't wrong. There was a shadow of someone there, a caretaker, a parental figure that wasn't a parent. Someone had been there, but trying to picture anyone in particular started a warning ache behind my eyes. I held up a hand. "Wait."

Isaac stopped, head tilted in curiosity. "What is it?"

"The headaches, they sometimes happen when I try to remember." I pressed my palms to my closed eyes, using a slight pressure to ease the pain while I counted. "What you're saying, it feels familiar, but it hurts. I've had too many close calls and one full-on fit this week. It gets stronger the more I push it in a short period. I can't take much more right now."

"Sounds like a curse." Isaac's eyes narrowed.

"It is," I said. "I've never been to a doctor for it. I looked, but I can't find anything online that totally matches it. Maybe now that I'm out of my Mom's house, I'll go to see a specialist. Or a shrink."

"Perhaps." He considered a moment before shrugging. "Ask another question. One that I can answer without hurting you."

I thought it over, appreciating his consideration. Finally, I asked, "How did you know I was here?"

Isaac burst out with a little half laugh. "I didn't. I knew you were in town, because of the message you left at the hotel, but they said you were out. I was coming to get something out of my old room and you were here."

"This is your room?" I asked, unable to believe the coincidence. When he nodded, my lip curled and I crossed my arms in disgust of my luck. "Okay, I moved the picture, so that's how you knew I'd been in here, but how did you know I was still in here?"

"Again, I didn't. I tried calling out just in case. A friend of mine always said that if you act like you know someone is there and they are, you look amazingly sharp. If you do it and there's no one there, then no one is there to see you looking stupid."

"Now I feel stupid," I grumbled.

"Don't." His smile was kind. It lacked the pure... sexiness of before, but it was still nice. "It's just a damn good trick."

I nodded, still a little embarrassed. "So, you don't know Red at all?"

"I don't, and I wanted to ask you more about him." Isaac lost his humor and his interest became sharp. "Tell me, what's he like?"

"Um, old, short, skinny, but stronger than he looks. Surprisingly energetic for his age." I rubbed the back of my neck again, trying to think of anything relevant. "He seems like a good guy. I can't see him having to do with anything sinister. Mischievous, yeah, but not mean. He almost always has a cat with a canary grin, he even has sharp teeth. Oh, and he always wears a red fedora. Cheesy, but it works for him."

"A red fedora?" Isaac's nostrils flared and his eyes widened. "Red Castle. Pit and Castle. That's what you said the firm was called, right? Is the other partner named Tom or Thomas? Tommy, maybe?"

"Um, I think so. Redmond Castle and Thomas Pit." I hadn't remembered the partner's first name until Isaac said it. "Why? Do you know him?"

"I know of him," he said. "And I think I know what's going on now. I'm all the more terrified for it, but I at least know what we're up against. I have to contact the others and come up with a strategy to protect you from Tommy and his minions. Fortunately, we have some time. Anyone who is your enemy shouldn't be able to get into the house."

"Well, doesn't that prove that Red isn't an enemy, or whatever? He gave me a tour of the house earlier today, or yesterday, I guess." My brain hitched as it absorbed something Isaac had said. "What do you mean my enemies can't get in? How does that work?"

As I reminded him about the lawyer being in the house, panic filled Isaac's eyes. He moved towards me again. "Later. We have to go now."

"What? No." I backed farther into the hallway. The fear and determination were visible in every step Isaac took. I didn't know what he was planning, but I wanted no part of it.

"Addie, if the Red Cap can get in, then it's almost certain that Tommy can as well. We aren't safe here. Now, come with me. I'll take us somewhere he can't find us." He was almost to the door now and was reaching out a hand, palm up like he expected me to take it.

Isaac had taken on a kind of crazed quality, and I didn't want to go wherever he was taking me. I lunged forward, grabbed the door handle, and slammed it shut. I held on tight as he tried to turn it from the other side, pleading through the door.

"I wish I could lock this thing from the outside," I whimpered. There was a click and the knob stopped moving in my hands. On the other side of the door, Isaac must have kicked it, because it jumped in its frame. I didn't understand why the lock had engaged, but it had, so I took the advantage and ran for the stairs.

Sounds of crashing egged me on. I was moving as fast as I could, but I'd only reached the first step when the loudest crash yet echoed through the hall. Isaac called, clear as a bell, "Addie! Addie, wait damn it! I'm not going to hurt you!"

I didn't wait. Not this time. I pushed as hard as I could, nearly tripping down the stairs. It felt clumsy and slow, making circles downward, but I just couldn't get down any faster. When I heard the regular thumping above me, I spared a glance up to see Isaac hitting the stairs at a frightening speed. He yelled, "Addie!"

At the same time, someone screamed. It was a high, reedy, female voice that was almost familiar. "Get the hell away from her!"

Surprised, I tried to turn mid-step. The toes of my right foot somehow hooked across the opposite ankle. For just a moment, with my arms flung out to the side, I almost managed to keep my balance. I looked up and I saw Isaac looking down. I had that moment of slow time people always seem to experience when something bad is about to happen.

He was opposite of me in the stairwell, just one turn above. His eyes snapped wide, seeing I was about to fall. He vaulted the railing and launched toward me. I arched backward, breath catching in my throat as I tried to scream.

Isaac slammed into me, midair. His right arm cinched around my waist and his left extended as if to catch us before we hit the stairs. I winced, waiting for his arm to crunch as it took the weight of both of us. His fingers flicked, like he was shooing a fly, and the world opened up beneath us like a curtain being pulled aside.

We fell into a sky the color of apricots. I looked up and there was no sign of the house or the hole we'd fallen through. My head whipped around and saw that we were fast approaching the ground, a field with high grass that was a purple shade of gray. I opened my mouth to scream, but a strange feeling overwhelmed me. As we plummeted, somewhere I felt a pair of eyes open and even though they were far away, I knew they could see me.

I might have had a fit then. I wasn't sure, because as a huge wave of pain and terror hit me, I blacked out. Or maybe it was just me hitting the ground.

Chapter 11: The Curse

I woke up. That was a welcome surprise. Less so were the padded cuffs that bound my wrists to the arms of a heavy wooden chair, that would have looked more at home in a dining room.

Instead of my new black dress, I was wearing a huge blue tee shirt that went almost to my knees, clinging to my damp skin. My hair was clammy and cold against my neck. The scent of chlorine was faint, but present. Thankfully, I could feel that all my underwear was in place, even if they were uncomfortably moist. Gross.

I jerked against the cuffs, but all I got for my trouble was a nausea-inducing throb in my head. Everything hurt. It must have been the mother of all fits when we'd fallen... It was best not to think about it. My head was so tender that another fit seemed imminent. Even the one on the roof of the hotel hadn't made me black out like that. That scared me more than I wanted to admit.

The room was small, and every surface was covered in blackboards. Symbols drawn in white chalk made elaborate rings around my chair. I moaned and closed my eyes. Whatever they were, they made the pain surge, and I struggled to swallow down bile.

There was the soft creak of a door opening behind me. Isaac's voice was shaky with relief. "Oh good. You're awake. How are you feeling?"

"I've been better." I glared at Isaac as he crept into my field of vision. He'd changed into a pair of jeans and a tight-fitting gray tee shirt, and his hair was messy like it had been dried in a hurry. There were so many questions to ask, but the first one to fight its way out of my mouth was, "Why am I wet?"

Isaac winced and rubbed the back of his neck. "I'm really sorry about that, but we were falling and I thought it might be better to land in the pool."

The shirt I was wearing meant that he had changed my clothes. He'd seen me in my underwear at the very least. I would love to rip him a new one over that, but I didn't think it was the best idea to start an argument with my kidnapper. Despite my anger, I wondered where the shirt came from. It was too big for Isaac.

"How long was I out? Where are we?" I didn't look at the markings on the floor but did note that he had a book and a stick of chalk with him.

"You've been out for a little over an hour. We're in the casting room of my safe house. I'm not the best magician, but I have to try to break your curse. Normally, I'd wait for the Sidhe to do something this complicated, but Addie..." Isaac took a step towards me, a hand raised as if to touch my face, but he pulled up short and dropped his arm back to his side. "I saw you convulsing after I took you through the Betwixt. Whatever Tommy did to you, it's a frightening bit of magic. We can't wait."

I'd never had a single word hurt me as bad as 'Betwixt'. Spots danced in front of my eyes, and I focused on breathing. The name he'd said, if it was a name, was almost like an appetizer of pain. Less dangerous than the word Betwixt, but agonizing all the same. I tried to rub my eyes, but the cuffs stopped me.

"What the hell is with these?" I yanked hard against my restraints.

"I wish they weren't necessary Addie, but I can't have you running away while I'm trying to get this curse off you. It's delicate work, and I'm already worried about performing this. The Sidhe could do it so much safer. He understands your magic better than anyone else."

"Who is She? He? The name's familiar."

"Oh, so him you remember." Isaac chuckled bitterly. "It's pronounced 'She' but it's spelled S-i-d-h-e. He's the original magician lord from under the hill. It's the reason he was chosen as your tutor. Unfortunately, he isn't answering my calls. He's always hard to get a hold of this time of year. I guess we all mourn in our own way."

Again I tried to lift a hand to my eyes and made a disgusted noise when I couldn't. Isaac shook his head. "I know it's not optimal, but it's the best I can do. I even used the most comfortable pair I had."

91

With a sinking feeling, I began to suspect why he had padded cuffs on hand. I gulped. "How do you know they're comfortable?"

He huffed a little, like a laugh almost made its way out. "I've employed them a few times. They aren't my thing, but some girls really get into them. For when I'm the one wearing them, I like to make sure they're not onerous."

I closed my eyes and whimpered. "Eww."

This time, Isaac laughed. "Don't worry, I clean them well every time I use them."

I opened my eyes to glare at him. "You chained me up with sex toys."

"For the thousandth time, I'm sorry. If it wasn't absolutely necessary, I would let you out." He held up his hands in surrender and changed the subject. "But I'm curious. You don't appear to remember magic, so why haven't you said anything about the curse I'm trying to break?"

I kicked a foot out toward him. Not because I had any hope of hitting him, but because it was the best act of defiance I had at the moment. Spitting at him wasn't an option, since I'd probably just hit myself. "Because it's crazy. You're crazy. There's no such thing as curses."

"You think so?" Isaac raised an eyebrow. "I would show you some magic, but I'm afraid it would trigger another seizure. It's fine if you don't believe for now. I'll get this thing broken, then you should have your memory back. After that, we can talk."

Isaac ignored me while he redirected his attention to the floor. He drew with the chalk, but paused often to consult the book. When I called his name, his eyes flicked up the first couple of times, but after that he ignored me. I was reduced to just watching him work because I couldn't study what he was writing on the floor, and there was nothing else to look at.

Whatever he was doing, the chill in my stomach told me it wasn't a good idea. I had to keep him talking. "Why did you think I died?"

Ink paused, then didn't look at me as he answered. "Because I was told you did by someone I trusted. It wasn't just that I took his word for it, either. I looked. If you were here in this world, I should have been able to find you. This curse is ridiculously strong and intricate. Not even the Sidhe felt it. I know it doesn't mean anything to you right now, with me a stranger, but I need you to know something. I did not abandon you. If I had any inkling that you were out there, I would have found you. Please believe that."

He still wouldn't look at me, but I felt Isaac's sincerity. It dimmed my anger infinitesimally. He was still nuts. "Look, I may not accept a lot of what you're saying, but for what it's worth, I don't think you abandoned me."

He turned his head just enough to smile at me, sadly, before resuming his work. "Thank you."

I had an idea. It was stupid, but it was the best I had at the moment. "Look, you said you'd rather wait until your friend was here to do this, right? I want to talk to you. Contact him, un-cuff me, and we can wait together for him to get here. I promise not to try to run away."

"Unfortunately, we don't have that kind of time." Isaac crawled on his hands and knees, still drawing. "Tommy and his ilk are out looking for you. I've left messages for the Sidhe. I even sent one directly to his home. Who knows when he'll get them? There's no way I can fight the Bloody Bones, so my best option is to evade. Without your memory, you have no reason to trust me. Running would be just too difficult."

"Talk to me! I could trust you if you talked to me."

Slapping a hand against the floor, Isaac spared a moment of work to glare at me. "About what? Everything I say about the truth or your past hurts you. You were unconscious when we landed in the pool. You didn't see the way you convulsed. Even asleep you whimpered in pain. I watch your eyes tighten every time I mention something familiar. When you were a little girl, you did the same thing whenever you had a headache. I don't want to hurt you anymore, Addie. I don't want to scare you. This is the only way, and it has to be done now."

Isaac stood up, dusting off his hands. Taking one last look at the book, he mouthed a few things, maybe memorizing them, and then tossed it away. I shouldn't have been worried. There was no such thing as magic. At the same time, I had seen a purple field as I fell through an orange sky. Heart in my throat, I watched as he took a place inside the circle, and began to speak.

Nothing he said was in English. It was some smooth, flowing tongue. I didn't understand the language, but the more he spoke, the more I could almost comprehend what he was saying. I had guessed that my head would start hurting at some point, but I was unprepared for the sickening vertigo that accompanied the pain. The world tilted and dilated as Isaac's words turned into a child's rhyme that almost made sense. I wanted to beg him to stop, but couldn't pull myself together enough to speak.

Anguish, fear, and confusion wrapped around my mind like a fist and then dragged me down into darkness. I could no longer see the world around me, just the empty void inside my head. I was sinking but suddenly stopped.

It was like I hit a wall. A black tide was crushing me against it. I screamed as the wall bowed under the pressure before shattering, flinging me into free fall. Like Alice down the rabbit hole, I floated down. Fragments of my memories hung around me like sparkling stars, just out of reach. Consciousness slipped away, but I lost the pain somewhere before the nothingness claimed me.

Chapter 12: Awaken

I rolled over with a groan and buried my face in a fluffy pillow that smelled like lavender. This was the second time I'd passed out from something Ink had done. Once again, I didn't know where I was, but I wasn't chained up with sex toys, so I took the win.

My eyes snapped open. Ink. His name was Isaac. Why had I called him Ink?

And where the hell was I?

A cotton candy pink canopy that matched the sheets stretched over me. I sat up and looked around. The sudden movement reminded me that I had suffered two of the worst fits I had ever experienced in rapid succession. My muscles screamed, and my head was still tender. The room wasn't helping. It wasn't giving me a fit, but there was a niggling, strained sensation like something was trying to bust out of my skull.

My eyes were suffering. This room was pink. Every shade of pink imaginable, and some that weren't. Disgustingly, childishly, monotonously...

Flash

***

"Pink!" I shrieked, then giggled. My friends winced. Ink crouched in front of me. Today he'd made his skin really tanned, his hair pale blond, and his eyes bright blue. The long top was tied back in a ponytail, making him look like a surfer boy. I liked that if you looked carefully at his eyes, the crimson flecks that were always there made them look purple. No matter how he changed his face, his eyes always had that little bit of red.

He put a hand on my arm. I clutched my stuffed tiger and grinned at him. "Are you sure, Addie? You can have any color you want. You could have lots of colors—"

"All pink!" I slapped Tiger against my leg, then brought him up to stick his ear into my mouth.

Almost everyone looked pained, but Ink looked back with a shrug. "Well, the princess has spoken. Make the room pink."

***

I blinked. What was that? My head had lit up like a camera flash. A piece of my memory had broken loose and played in front of my eyes like a movie.

This was my room. I had wanted it painted like this; decorated like a Disney Princess's lair. Impossibly, the man from my memory had been Isaac... or Ink? I was pretty sure that wasn't his real name either, but it was closer.

Once I got past the pink assault, the room was actually kinda cool. It was huge, with tall archways that gave glimpses of other rooms. When I slipped out of bed, my bare feet hit the silky fibers of a thick carpet. I was wearing my sleep clothes that I'd left at the hotel. Someone had dressed me and brushed out my hair. I should have been bothered, but I was dry and comfortable. Everything was still creepy, but it did a lot to mitigate my unease. Taking a moment to stretch greatly increased my mobility, and I padded out to do a little recon on my old room. Hopefully, I could find out how I got there.

The room I woke up in was the bedroom area, complete with princess style four-poster bed and a window seat full of cushions. There was also a small bookshelf off to one side filled with books that were advanced for an eight-year-old. To the right was an alcove that had a plain wall with a poster of a tiger, but inside there were two doors. The left led to a spacious bathroom with a separate shower and deep, inset bath. On the right was a walk-in closet bigger than my room back home. It was stocked with clothes for a little girl who still loved, but was starting to age out of her obsession with, pink.

The rest of the areas were divided by archways into a media room, a study room, and a playroom. All the electronics looked brand new, and I wondered if it was Red's doing. If so, I would have to thank him for the enormous TV, sound system, new computer, and every gaming console known to man. The playroom housed dolls, stuffed animals, a shelf of board games, and a doll house that came up to my waist.

Besides a huge round table which had my bags from the hotel on it and a bookshelf, the studying area contained the only other door. That had to be the way out, unless exiting required magic, which I wasn't ruling out. I opened the door and nearly tripped over Red. He was sitting against the wall, his hands folded over his stomach and his hat pulled down over his eyes. As I struggled to regain my balance, Red lifted his head.

"Addie, my dear, you have no idea how happy I am to see you awake." He almost exploded to his feet and scooped me up into a hug. I patted his back, but gently tried to push away. I had never been much of a hugger. He let me go, but stayed close. "Are you feeling alright? Can I get you anything?"

"Some aspirin or something would be great. I feel like I fell down the stairs." I raised an eyebrow as Red whipped out a phone and started texting. "Speaking of which, I'm assuming that you know I was briefly kidnapped, and was hoping that you knew how I got back here."

"Yes, and yes." Red shoved his phone back in his pocket. "I am so sorry that you had to go through that ordeal, my dear. We tried to stop your abduction, but we got there too late. Mr. Pit was able to find and rescue you."

"What happened to Ink?" I asked, walking slowly forward. Each step made my muscles complain, even though I'd stretched. This appeared to be some kind of sitting room. I plopped into a large, cushioned chair and looked to Red, who was hovering behind me like he was afraid I would fall.

"Who?" he asked, fidgeting.

Of course, Red would have no way of knowing who I was talking about. "My kidnapper, Isaac Heart. What happened to him?"

"Ah, well, before I answer that, I need to ask." Red's long fingers twined and untwined. A nervous gesture. "What do you remember?"

"About what? The kidnapping?" I rubbed the back of my neck. "Most of it, except getting and leaving there. I passed out during those bits. Why?"

"Not about that." Red sighed, looking painfully uncomfortable. "Do you remember anything from your childhood, before you lost your memory?"

I narrowed my eyes. "You know about what he did."

Red spoke very quickly, waving in a soothing gesture. "I wasn't there. Mr. Pit was the one who retrieved you and—"

"That wasn't a question. It was an accusation." I crossed my arms. "You know Ink did something to my memory."

"I do." With a sigh, Red lowered himself slowly onto the nearest couch, looking old for the first time. "Mr. Pit set me to find out the extent of the damage he did, or the success he achieved."

"So you're admitting the curse is real. This whole magic thing is real," I said, again, not asking.

"Yes." Red's lips pressed tight together, then he continued. "Magic is real. I haven't lied to you, but I have, well, kept things from you. Not to harm you, but because revealing them to you would cause you harm."

"Look, I understand and I'm not mad. Okay, I'm a little mad. I don't blame you though, considering just seeing magic hit me so hard it knocked me out. Something's changed though. What Ink, Isaac did... well, I don't know what he did. I had that feeling of familiarity in the bedroom. Usually, that would have been followed at minimum by a headache, but this time I remembered something." I stood up and started to pace. Excitement made my words come quickly. "It was like a flashback or something. I remember being a little kid and wanting to paint my room pink. I mean, it's a horrible color, and if I'm going to stay in there it has to go, but I do remember it. I couldn't have been more than four or five. Do you have any idea what that's like?"

Red chuckled at my enthusiasm. "My own childhood was nothing to write home about. There are certainly parts of it I would wish to forget, so I can't say I completely understand. I am happy you're pleased, but Addie, I need to know if you remember anything else."

I strained, but nothing came. "No. I mean, we're here talking about magic and I'm fine, so that's good. My head still hurts a little, but that's just residual, I think."

"I brought aspirin." A new voice made me turn. The girl in the hoodie from the hotel walked in, bearing a small white bottle and a glass of water. She grinned shyly at me, and in the well-lit room I could see her clearly. Her long face was narrow and her mouth was small. Her eyes didn't make me jump, but only because by the time my brain registered that they were totally black, no iris or whites, I had already accepted it and decided this was not my biggest problem at the moment.

She set the water and aspirin down on the little side table next to me. "Hi. I'm Rat. Sorry I couldn't introduce myself before. I wasn't supposed to talk to you."

"Yeah, thanks for your help, by the way." I fought with the childproof cap for a second before pouring out a couple of pills and popping them with a quick drink of water.

"I wasn't much help," Rat said bitterly. "I couldn't stop that Incubus trash from taking you."

Incubus. That was Ink's real name. My brain finally caught up to the rest of what she said. "You were calling from the top of the stairs."

"For all the good it did." Rat's lip curled in disgust. "I wasn't close enough. I didn't know he was in the house. I didn't know he could get into the house. Someone told me that your enemies couldn't enter."

"I gave you all the information I had," Red snapped, then ran a hand over his face. "Something is wrong. As far as I knew the curse should have stopped him from recognizing her even if they were face to face. Still, I

99

shouldn't have put her up in the Incubus's hotel, but damn it, he wasn't supposed to be in town. What I want to know is, why was he here to begin with?"

"Um," I raised my hand, feeling sheepish. "That one is on me. I found out that Isaac Heart owned the hotel. You kept saying that you didn't know anything, so I asked them to contact him. I didn't mention it because you were acting a little suspicious. Loren said- oh my god, I forgot about her."

"Relax." Rat waved it off. "Red had me leave a note for her. It said that you were going to stay the night here. I put it in your room last night when I got your stuff. I copied your handwriting from the paperwork on the table. Did a good job, too."

My stomach sank. Our fight was bad enough that Loren might believe it. "She's not going to buy that forever."

"You can call her after we get things sorted out." Red sighed and rubbed his temples. "I can't blame you for contacting the Incubus. It's not like I was telling you everything. Although, I would like to point out that I never said I knew nothing about him, I said I had never met him. At no point did I actually lie to you."

"You know what, I will give you that." I held up a warning finger. "But there is such a thing as a lie of omission. Remember that for the future, okay?"

Red shook his head but smiled. "Very well, my dear."

"As for Ink being here, he came to get some things from his old room. I don't think he's my enemy. He was just as surprised that you were allowed in the house. Yeah, he did kidnap me, but he said he was doing it to protect me from you and Mr. Pit. Why would he assume that you were going to hurt me? " I looked back and forth between Red and Rat.

"I knew that the Incubus was associated with you as a child, but I didn't know that he lived here. Tommy neglected to mention that, and it explains why he was allowed in." Red bit his lip, deep in thought. I noticed he didn't answer my question. Another one on the pile.

"Tell me two things. Why does Ink think you are my enemy, and is he hurt?" Holding Red's eyes with mine, I let him know that I wasn't letting this go.

With a heavy sigh and a sour look, he said, "Alright. I think these are questions that should be answered by our dear Mr. Pit himself."

"Way to go passing the buck." Rat snickered.

"I am of the opinion that if a man is going to call himself king, he should be ready to shoulder the hard decisions. Aren't you?" Red grinned at Rat, and it was just a little mean and very full of teeth. When he turned to me, the smile shifted to one that was much softer, but I couldn't help but notice that his eyes were a little too wide and tension sang through his shoulders. "If you'll come with me, I'll take you to him."

I shifted uncomfortably. "You're spooked. Is Mr. Pit dangerous?"

Rat snorted, but Red was surprised. "No! Well, not to you, anyway. He would literally die before he allowed harm to come to you, much less cause any himself. Besides, I would never lead you into any danger. That is the complete and unfiltered truth. Do you believe me?"

My trust seemed important to Red. I had only known him for a couple of days, but I wanted, needed, someone I could count on. Honestly, I was way out of my depth, and Red had my best interest at heart. At least, I hoped so. Nodding, I said, "Lead the way."

Hopping to his feet, Red took me down the hall to a set of double doors. They were huge, like they were made for something larger than a human. Even if they were big, they were just doors. My stomach shouldn't have been turning into a freezing lump like it was. I was hoping to just walk by, but Red stopped right beside them. He held a hand out, indicating that I should take the handle.

I gulped. "You aren't going in first?"

"He's afraid the boss will be pissed at him. He's going to stand behind you in the hope that Tommy won't risk hitting you to get at him." Rat stood by Red, arms crossed and smirking.

He bared his teeth at her. "You failed just as much as I have."

Rat snorted. "What? I'm hiding behind her too. I'm just willing to admit it."

In unison, Red and I shot her a dirty look. I asked, "Are you guys in any danger?"

He said no, but Rat said yes. They locked eyes, having a silent argument until I stepped between them. "Oh, heck no. Do not shut me out of this. I am not going to let him hurt you."

"He's angry, but he won't actually injure us," Red assured me.

"Tommy needs us. He won't take us out of commission. He's got a lot of plates to juggle. Though, he can't let us get away without some punishment. Maybe a little smacking around," Rat said.

"Over my dead body," I hissed. "I don't care who he is, he's not raising a hand to either of you."

"Make sure you tell him that." She smiled playfully, like this was all a joke. "Then we'll probably be fine."

"Will you shut up?" Red sounded weary, like he had to ask, but knew she wouldn't. "You're setting her up for a fight with Tommy before she even meets him."

Rat shrugged. "What? She said no more omission or misdirection. I'm trying to do what she said."

"I'm with her." I hitched a thumb at her while looking at Red. "No hiding things from me, for what's supposedly my own good. That's a stupid idea. I mean it."

He heaved a sigh. "Very well. But please, keep in mind, everything we've done for you, everything we've done to protect you, was at Tommy's behest."

"Why are you trying to sell him?" Rat's words stepped on the edge of Red's. "You two are always half a step away from killing each other."

"Because she's irrevocably tied to him, and I don't want her to be stuck for the rest of her life with someone she hates." For the first time since I'd met him, Red stood up perfectly straight, no hunching, crooked stances or posing. "And despite the fact that sometimes, most of the time, I think he's being a stupid ass, Tommy's still my sworn king. I will not intentionally sour his relationship with his liege."

I gave him an annoyed look. "You aren't going to explain any of what you just said, are you?"

Unable to remain serious any longer, the corner of Red's mouth quirked, and he winked. "No, I won't. Now, go ask Tommy. He can answer all your questions. It won't be as bad as you're expecting, I promise."

In a moment of self-realization, I had to admit that I was stalling. Something about the doors scared me and I didn't want to open them. Steeling myself, I reached out and...

Flash

***

I pushed the door open, sneaking in on socked feet. Without windows, the only light in the room came from the hall behind me. Everywhere there were shelves at weird angles, towers of boxes and large, old cabinets. Plenty of places to hide and plenty of places to seek.

Just a few steps inside, the door slammed behind me. Absolute darkness closed in, and I listened hard. A big taloned hand seized me gently around the waist and lifted me up to a pair of glowing red eyes.

"No fair!" I pouted, but giggled anyway.
***

My breath hitched as I tried to swallow the fear that was choking me. As a little kid, I had been delighted, but as an adult I was terrified. What the hell had I just seen?

Chapter 13: What You Do Know Can Hurt You

My hesitation didn't total more than a second or two, but it was enough to prompt Rat to say, "Go on. Red is right about one thing, Tommy would never hurt you. It will be fine."

"Yeah, sure." The air in my lungs felt heavy and hard to move. Should I tell them what I just saw? Was the thing with red eyes waiting for me on the other side of the door? Maybe I should say something, but I was afraid that my courage would fail, and I would run back to my room if I delayed. I turned the handle and stepped inside. After all, I was supposed to be asking my questions to Mr. Pit.

It was not the same room from my memory. Or rather, it was, but now there was light from a series of softly glowing sconces placed randomly around the oddly angled, worn gray walls. Those were new. A large, modern-style bed sat over to the farthest side of the room, made up with ruby and white linens. On a posh, scarlet leather sectional that dominated the middle of the room sat a man. He waited calmly, but his presence took up more space than the couch.

I advanced, grateful to hear Red and Rat following me as Mr. Pit rose from his seat. He was massive, tall with a wide frame. His head and face were clean-shaven and muscles moved clearly under his well-cut, midnight-black suit. While I supposed he could be called handsome, it was in the same way a tiger was handsome. An imposing aura hung around him. It was like I was daring to disturb a king, but when I approached he bowed to me.

"Miss Gardner. It's an absolute pleasure." He said, voice rich, resounding, and kinda made me think of Shere Khan. He looked me in the eyes, and I was relieved that his were a normal chocolate brown, not red.

"Mr. Pit." I forced a smile. "I'm told you're the man who can answer all my questions."

"Please, call me Tommy. I don't know if I can answer all your questions, but I'll do what I can." He glanced at the two behind me. "You can go."

"I want them to stay," I blurted out. Tommy raised an eyebrow but nodded.

"As you like." With a sweep of his hand, he ushered me over to the couches. Red and Rat book ended the door, staying in the room as I'd asked, but giving us space. As I sat, Tommy stood in front of me, hands clasped in front of him, like a soldier at attention. "Now, I need to establish how badly the curse was broken. How do you feel?"

I licked my lips. "My head doesn't hurt when I think about my past. That's something, but it's not like I regained my memory. Except..."

"Except?" Tommy's voice was too deep for his chest, but the tone was kind.

"When I woke up, and again just before I opened the door, I had a... I don't know. A flashback? First I remember wanting to paint my room pink when I was little. Then, I remembered going into this room. Someone else used to live here, didn't they? Someone with glowing red eyes?" I searched his face for answers.

Tommy closed his eyes for a moment, expression smoothing out, like he was trying to conceal his emotions. "Yes, but I wouldn't worry. He's out of the picture. It's unfortunate that your memory hasn't completely returned, but not unexpected. That idiot tried to undo the curse on his own. He botched it, and now we'll need a true expert to figure out exactly how badly."

"You're talking about Ink, I mean, the Incubus, right?" I asked, and Tommy nodded. "Red told me that you were the one who found me and brought me back. I don't think he'd have let me go without a fight. What happened?"

Tommy tilted his head to the side. "I wouldn't really call it a fight. The Incubus isn't much of a warrior, and he was unprepared. He was badly injured, but alive when I left. Why? Did you want him dead?"

105

"No!" It came out more of a squawk than a yell. "I don't want him hurt at all. Is he going to be okay? Can we send someone to help him?"

Tommy seemed more confused by this than anything. "I could, but I doubt the Incubus would stay in a compromised den. He'll have scampered off somewhere to heal. Why would you want to, though? You said yourself, you don't remember him, and he stole you away."

"I do a little," I said, defensively crossing my arms. "I know he took care of me as a child. Yeah, he kidnapped me, but he was trying to save me. He thought you were the one who was going to hurt me. Why is that?"

With a deep sigh, Tommy asked, "May I sit?"

"It's your room." I shrugged.

"It's your house," he countered. I wasn't at all sure about that, but I had bigger things to worry about for the moment.

"Fine. Sit." I pointed at the spot on the couch farthest away from me. My lips were pressed tightly together, and my breath was short with a rising temper. "Tell me why Ink would think you're a danger to me."

Obediently, Tommy sat where I directed and offered an apologetic smile. Not a convincing apology, but at least it was an effort. "I've made you angry. Let me make amends. Rat? Go check on the Incubus. Find help if he needs it."

"A joy to serve." Rat's voice dripped with sarcasm. With a flippant salute, she left.

"Now, to answer your question, I'll have to give you some background. Quite a lot of it." Tommy sighed and rubbed a hand over his face. "Admittedly, I wasn't prepared for this talk. I had a plan to have the curse broken properly on your birthday. Things would have been easier if you had regained your memory. There's a literal world to fill you in on."

"So, start at the beginning," I urged.

"If you like. We have to begin with the Accords." Tommy wrinkled his nose thoughtfully.

"If you go that far back, we'll be here all day." Red scoffed from the door. "We'll have plenty of time to go over the full history of the fae later. Give her the abridged version."

Tommy glowered. "Very well. A couple of millennia ago, to avoid conflict with humans, the fae created the Betwixt. This was the Second Accord. It was a flawed creation, and about two centuries ago it became known that it was failing. Our artificial realm couldn't survive without a connection to the world from which it was cleaved."

"It was going to collapse. We had to do something or return to the mortal world full-time. No one wanted to do that." Rat leaned against the door frame while twining and untwining her fingers. I narrowed my eyes. Hadn't she left already?

"I am the one telling this story if you would let me finish," Tommy said. "In order to keep our world alive a Third Accord was reached."

"And what's an Accord in this context?" I asked.

Red answered. "It's a powerful magical work that a majority of the fae consent to lend their power to."

Tommy shot him a glare and Red mimed zipping his lips.

"Anyway," Tommy grumbled, tearing his gaze away from the smaller man. "The Third Accord created you, a child born of two mortal parents with a soul patched together from a bit of every living being in the Betwixt."

Rat held up a finger as she interrupted. "That makes you both fully human and fully fae. There are a lot of perks in that. Supposedly, you'll live as long as any of the fae whose souls you share survive."

"I think I'm fully confused."

"It would be less confusing if everyone would stop interrupting. Now if you two would please SHUT UP!" Tommy roared. Everyone winced. He turned his attention back to me and dipped his head. "I apologize for having to yell."

People were apologizing to me a lot lately. It might have been appropriate, but I was getting tired of hearing it. "It's fine. So, do my parents know about this or... what?"

"They do. I don't know all the details of the original deal, but your parents were unable to conceive on their own. To be able to have a child of their own flesh and blood, they agreed to let the fae use our magic to help them. They were allowed to live here and paid a stipend, in exchange your chosen caretakers had unfettered access to you."

I sighed and my gaze fell to the dull gray wood of the floor. Unfortunately, I could totally see my parents turning to black magic to have a kid rather than adopting. Especially if there was money involved. "Okay, I'm a magical bridge between two worlds. That's weird, but I can handle that. I guess."

"You are more than that." Tommy grew insistent, and I looked up at him in surprise. "Great Works rarely have completely predictable effects. You are no exception. When all the souls of the fae were joined together, they created something more than the sum of their parts. You are not just a fae. You are a Queen. One with the kind of power only spoken of in our oldest stories."

"How does that even work?" I raised a skeptical eyebrow.

"If I may, Tommy? I think I have a good analogy," Red said. Tommy mulled that over for a moment, then nodded sharply. Tipping his hat to the larger man, Red continued. "Think of it less like the Queen of England, and more like a queen bee. You have a bit of each of our souls, our magic, inside of you. Every fae is naturally drawn to you. We want to protect you like you were our kin, which by some definitions you are. It gives you a limited type of control over us, and allows you to access our power."

I rubbed the back of my neck while I processed that information. I wasn't a queenly sort of person. Honestly, I wasn't even a people sort of person. Unless I had hidden depths that I hadn't guessed at, I was in way over my head. Then again, last night I had discovered magic.

Impossible was a word that didn't have a lot of meaning right now.

"Your old court, the people who took care of you before, had plans to raise you up to be a true Queen that would rule over the fae. They thought that you could bring us together as a race like the royalty of legend. They were teaching you here in this house," Tommy said.

"So what happened? Ink said something about a curse that took my memory. He thought you had something to do with it." I dragged my attention back to the conversation.

"Objectively, I could see why he would." Tommy took a deep breath. "Again, our knowledge of the situation is incomplete. One of your original courtiers, your Guardian, betrayed you. He recruited your parents to take you and hide you away, then cursed you to forget everything in your life related to the fae. The part I know for certain is that after the curse was cast, but before it completely took hold, you managed to escape. You found me and obtained my services as a Champion.

"I defeated the one who betrayed you but was unable to stop the spell. Lacking a better plan, I went through with your Guardian's plot and had your parents take you away. I needed to keep you safe while I tried to find a way to break the curse safely. It took years, but we finally found a solution. We were going to remove it on your birthday, ten years to the day from when it was set. It would have been at its weakest, and easier to remove."

I swallowed hard. "So my parents, they, um, they knew what was going to happen to me?"

Tommy nodded. "They were surprisingly ignorant of details, but they knew that they would be leaving and that you were supposed to have your memory altered to not remember your court. It was part of the deal they cut with your Guardian. They were very eager to have fae influence cut out of your life so you could have a normal childhood."

My fists clenched. Not only had my parents known about all of this, they had helped plan the worst thing that ever happened to me. They'd done it just so they could have a 'normal' daughter. And... I wasn't surprised. My shoulders drooped and my hands relaxed. Mom and Dad were assholes who didn't care about me. It was nothing I didn't already know. I had to let it go. I had to focus on the subject at hand. "You... you defeated him? So, is he like... dead?"

"If only. He isn't that easy to kill, but you don't need to worry. He's gone to stone." At my look of confusion, Tommy said, "It's like a magical coma where a fae is turned into a statue as a defense mechanism. Those who go to stone rarely awaken, so you are safe from your Guardian."

"Comforting, I guess." I rubbed the back of my neck. There was something itching in my head, something I almost remembered. Squaring my shoulders, I took a deep breath to rally myself. "I get why you couldn't tell me what was going on until the curse was broken. It just would have caused a fit. But what are we going to do now?"

"Since you acquired my services, I've been looking after your interests. I had plans for after your memory returned, but now I am unsure how to proceed. The next step will have to be getting some of my own magic workers here to check and see what can be done about your condition. If it cannot be fixed, well, I suppose then it will depend on what you want to do. It is your life after all." Tommy was studying me intently enough to be uncomfortable.

"How did I acquire your services? Do I pay you? I mean, I have money, or will have money." I was babbling a little, but in my defense, I was trying to think and absorb at the same time.

"No, you don't pay me." Tommy frowned, seemingly reluctant to explain. "You... helped me and I am in your debt."

"What did I do to help you that is worth all this?"

His nose wrinkled in distaste, but finally admitted, "You brought me from stone."

Flash

110

Chapter 14: The Quarry

***

I ran as fast as I could. The magic stuck to me like tar, and I didn't know how to get it off. The longer it stayed the more it closed around me, constricting, suffocating, hurting. When the landscape suddenly changed, it dropped me into a different Realm of the Betwixt. I didn't notice until I nearly ran into the giant stone Dragon that marked the beginning of the Quarry.

Even laying down, the Dragon towered above me. The ancient beast was curled in on itself like a wounded dog. Its head was almost directly in front of me, its remaining eye staring on, sightless in stone. The other was impaled by a spear, the tip buried somewhere deep inside the petrified brain. Before the beak-like nose sat a plaque. The words on it were carved so long ago that I could barely read them. Buggy had told me that the language it was written in no longer mattered. None were left who could use the incantation.

The thought of my Guardian and his betrayal made me cry. My hands shook as I swiped at the tears. I stifled the pain and started to run again, fleeing further into the Quarry. I was running out of time. The spell was spreading, and jumping Territories wouldn't hide me long.

Before either my Guardian or the spell got me, I had to find help. I wanted Ink, but in the Betwixt, I didn't know how to call him. I didn't know how to contact any of my friends here. The only thing I could think of was to try magic.

I didn't know any spells for this. Sidhe had always grumbled about how little time he'd had to teach me. I could only do some basic things. Summoning, locating, or anything like that was way beyond me. Still, someone had once told me that since all fae power was in my nature, my magic was mostly instinct. It couldn't hurt to try.

Closing my eyes, I focused on my power. It was a deep, dark well of a thing and I gathered as much of it as I could, concentrating hard. I need help, I thought. I need someone to help me. My hands clenched and shook from the effort. I willed with everything I had, needing, wanting, praying, and then the feeling of power burst. In its place was a compulsion to go somewhere nearby.

I had done... something. I started running again, following the demands of my spell. Sidhe would be so proud.

Most of the Quarry was nicely aligned like a cemetery trying to conserve space. Creatures locked away in petrified sleep made orderly rows of macabre statues, each frozen in their dying pose. A hedgehog man with an ax lodged in his stomach lined up with a long, slender figure with a crooked face who held a jeweled cup.

The Quarry was a graveyard, of sorts. The fae were very hard to kill and sometimes, if they were strong enough, they could go to stone. When that happened, they ended up in the Quarry, where they would rest until something woke them up.

The spell led me to a hill, and I stopped at its base. Only one statue stood at its apex. Was it alone because it had done something really bad or really good? It was weird and wrong, and I didn't like it.

The call to the lone figure was strong, almost like a voice emanated from it. I couldn't make out words, although I was sure I could if I knew how. It was full of emotions; fear, anger, dread, and panic. Loneliness and longing were nearly lost in the storm, but they were there, too.

I crept up the hill to get a better look at the lone statue. It was something like a man, but almost ten feet tall. He might have been taller than that, it was hard to tell because he was hunched over. He was curled up around a spot low on his huge chest, face turned up and slightly away from me. The look was enough to make me cringe, full of rage and dagger teeth, and maybe a touch of betrayal and fear. I could feel it in the mass of emotions he was using to reach out to me now. He was so scared.

The more I listened to him, the more details I got. He was terrified. He was disappearing. I suddenly understood something about going to stone; it would protect you from damage, but it was dangerous. The self inside was fragile, and it took a certain strength to remain. With enough time, it faded away and all that remained was stone. The oldest creatures here were empty shells. It was possible to reanimate them, the flesh would move again, but it wouldn't be them. They would be someone new.

He had been there a long time. He was strong, but he was losing the battle. I felt for him, but I didn't know how to help him. Bringing someone from stone was something I had never even heard my tutors talk about.

I would come back for him later, I tried to promise. I would come back for all of them later and save who I could.

He understood, and his fear spiked. He couldn't wait. The push to wake up and grab onto my spell was the last of his strength. In a few minutes, he would be gone. He was desperate. He was begging. He would be my Champion. He would help me, protect me, serve me, slay my enemies, anything I wanted, just, please, please, please don't let him slip away. His life was in my hands.

I stared up at the creature, looking into angry, sad, stone eyes, feeling his terror. This was a bad idea. I didn't know who he was or why he was there. He could have been a monster so horrible that the rest of the Betwixt had sent him to stone and stood him alone on the hill. It was just as likely that someone could have placed him there in a place of honor and love. That was dangerous too.

Once upon a time, Buggy told me that when it came to right and wrong, there was only one gauge; could you look at yourself in the mirror each morning? If I left him here to die, could I live with it?

No, I couldn't. Besides, I needed a protector and here in the Quarry, they were in short supply. I was desperate and so was he. Magic, my magic anyway, was mostly instinct. My instinct was to save him. Maybe it would save me too.

I felt him slipping away as I climbed his frozen form to get a closer look at his large stone face. I didn't know how to do this, and didn't have time to figure it out. What would my tutor say? Magic was mostly instinct. What did my instinct say?

When I was a little younger, Ink had brought me a book of Grimm's Fairy Tales. They had been wonderfully different from the books my mother bought me. I had a slight disdain for most kid stories, where the monsters were weak and stupid and everything was solved by some guy kissing some girl he barely knew. The kiss, however, was something both story types had in common.

Supposedly, it was true love's first kiss that made the magic work, but I didn't believe that. I had asked Sidhe about it once, and he thought it silly too, but he had said there might be something to it. He said it wasn't about love. The act could be representative of a promise, a commitment to the other person.

A kiss was just a kiss, but there was power in a contract.

I was scared and hurting and running for my life, but I couldn't help it. I laughed. Putting my hands on either side of his face I leaned forward to touch his cold, hard lips with mine. A kiss from the princess to break the spell.

Stone cracked. The noise was sharp and almost melodic, like a sledgehammer ringing on concrete. I jerked back and fell, hitting the ground hard. Fissures were forming all over the creature and from those cracks, he bled. Wounds opened across his back and legs and belly. I scrambled backward.

Oh god. I'd done something wrong.

The hand that had hovered half open suddenly clenched, stone screaming like grinding metal. More blood splashed on the ground, followed by shards of rock. The skin beneath was raw and red, still bleeding. His arm wrenched back above his head and stone and blood went flying. His eyes opened and I could see brown irises and bloodshot whites. The rest of the change went quickly as he straightened up, shedding his prison skin.

He let out a roar made by huge lungs feeling air for the first time in centuries. The sound was wordless, but I was still inside his head, or he was inside mine. I couldn't tell anymore. A mental howl echoed into the forever sunless Betwixt.

Tommy Raw Head and Bloody Bones was loose!

I knew that name.

Whimpering, I fought my way to my feet and began to back down the hill, staring at what I had released. Once upon a time, Buggy had told me about a creature so fierce, so cruel, that all the fae had banded together to try to kill it. It had been the King of the Boogies and lord of the Marrow Pit, one of the darkest, most dangerous corners of the Betwixt. Tommy Raw Head and freaking Bloody Bones.

He was about ten feet tall, and his skin was red and corded with the huge muscles beneath. It looked like they were bare to the air, but a longer look revealed that it was just skin. It wasn't still bleeding or anything. Atop his head, a bone cap protruded like the armor of a dinosaur. He grinned at me with his huge, sharp teeth, and chuckled so deep, it sounded like a purr.

What had I done?

***

Chapter 15: Setting Boundaries

Fear seized my chest. This man was Tommy Raw Head and Bloody Bones, a monster among monsters. I sprung to my feet and backed towards the door so fast I nearly tripped.

Tommy stood and held up a hand. "Addie, wait, please. Did something come back to you?"

"I remember the Quarry," I said, voice shaking. "I remember k-kissing you to bring you back from stone. You were–"

"Frightening? A monster?" Tommy supplied, not succeeding in hiding annoyance behind levity. "Yes, I am terrifying to humans."

"Just to humans. Right." Red scoffed and I whirled to face him. I had forgotten he was there and was nearly to where he leaned against the door frame. He gave me a soft smile for encouragement. "It's alright, Addie. Don't be afraid."

"He's right. There's no need to fear me," Tommy said, snapping my attention back to him. "I am your Champion, and beholden to you. I couldn't hurt you if I wanted to."

Taking another step back, I asked, "Do you want to?"

The question seemed to confuse him. "No. I would never."

Red put a comforting hand on my back. "It's alright. Come on. Sit back down."

I let myself be led back to the couch. A part of my mind was annoyingly pointing out that the white-haired lawyer I had decided to trust, was most likely no more human than the man in front of me. Tommy was a giant skinless monster. Who knew what Red was. I sat back down, took a deep breath and counted. It didn't matter. I needed something to hold onto in all this, and my gut said that was him. I was going with it.

"So, can you change the way you look like Ink does?" I asked Tommy, willing myself not to flinch as he cautiously approached.

Red made his way back to the door but shot me a thumbs-up. Tommy resumed his original place in front of me, standing with hands clasped. When he spoke, there was an element of uncertainty that made him seem less the imposing king, and more just a man in an awkward situation.

"Not like the Incubus. I did not have a human seeming until recently. It occurred to me during the last ten years that as your Champion, I might need to look a little more comely at times, so I acquired one."

"He's very vain of it, too." Red smirked. "He made a big deal about being pretty for you."

Annoyance and embarrassment flashed across Tommy's face. The effect was ironically humanizing. Red winked, making me think that was on purpose.

Not looking over at the other man, Tommy's voice deepened as he said, "Silence."

Annoyed, awkward Tommy was much easier to deal with than cold, regal Tommy. Falsely contrite Red's head dropped in a comical semblance of shame. That did a lot for my morale.

"Sorry. I'm just trying to raise her spirits a bit. She's had a bad day, and it is my job to look after her."

"Not the best fact to remind me of, since you failed at it." Tommy turned slowly to look at Red. "I did not enjoy having to rescue my lady when she was supposed to be under your care."

"Well if you care for Addie as much as you claim, perhaps you should have bothered to give us more accurate information." Red's mood swung. He broke into a very different grin, one that gave the impression he might bite. "I do seem to remember you saying that the house was Addie's ultimate protection. Something about how no enemy of hers could get in. Funny, I don't recall any mention of the fact that the Incubus had lived here, and would be able to come and go as he pleased."

"He was a part of her original court, you dolt." Tommy's foot slammed down like a stallion stomping in displeasure. "Any of them can come and go as they please."

"If I had known that, I would've never arranged for her to stay here! What were you thinking? Why didn't you tell me this place is inherently insecure?" Anger made Red's voice go high and reedy, clashing with Tommy's resonant rumble.

"I assumed you had a certain level of competence. You said you could handle Addie's care while in town, that it wasn't any different from what you were doing for the past ten years. No one could have predicted that the curse would fail, but I would have thought you would check out all other possible risks. If you don't want to put the effort in, I can find someone who will." Tommy growled, his arms spreading out and back. It reminded me of an animal raising its hackles to look bigger. He didn't need it.

"Don't you dare question my devotion to Addie!" Red made my name an inhuman shriek.

As Tommy took a threatening step forward, I leaped out of my seat and grabbed onto his arm. He turned to me with a snarl, and Red lurched towards us like he was coming to my defense. I was expecting Tommy to yell, or even strike me, but all he did was stare, breathing hard.

Emboldened, I moved my face towards his and bit off each word. "Cut. That. Out."

Tommy still stood rigid and angry, but he immediately stopped growling, and didn't try to pull away. "Red is my subject, Addie. I have to discipline him. Not only is he talking back, he failed me."

"And whose fault is that?" I threw down Tommy's arm and walked around to stand between him and Red. Pointing at the frail-looking man, but glaring at Tommy, I said, "You claim to be his king or boss or whatever, so what he does is your responsibility. You gave him a job to do and then didn't give him all the information. His supposed failure was because you failed first. This is all on you. You're the one who didn't protect me."

Tommy took a sharp, deep breath to yell, then he thought better of it. He exhaled slowly, and said more calmly, "I know, and I can only apologize."

Now Tommy wouldn't look me in the eye. He was honestly ashamed. My mouth scrunched to one side. While I believed he was sorry, he had been more than willing to pass the blame on to Red. Maybe the lawyer had snapped a little, but he had also been right. I was so tired, I couldn't keep up any level of actual anger.

Sighing, I stepped up close to Tommy and whispered in an attempt to keep Red from hearing, "Look, I do get it. Well, no, I'm not going to lie, I don't completely get it. I know you're Red's king, and positions of authority require you to maintain discipline. That much I do understand, but does any part of your position require you to be an asshole? I'm asking because I don't know."

Apparently, Red could hear me, because he snorted. When Tommy's glare started to stray to the other man, I moved to intercept his attention.

As desired, he looked back at me and said, "I am king of the Boogies. We are those cast away and rejected. The ugliest and most violent. If I did not display the same level of aggression as my subjects, they wouldn't respect or obey me."

"There's a difference between aggression, and being petty." I didn't bother to keep quiet since it was evident that at least one person in the room had super hearing. "You say you're my Champion, right? Well, that means that your actions reflect me, so I expect better from you."

"I am the king of the Boogies, we are–" Tommy began again.

With a backbone I had somehow acquired in the last couple minutes, I shouted, "I don't care if you are the king of the island of misfit toys! I'm not saying you have to be nice, but treat your people with a little respect, and own up to it when you're the one who screws up."

Ineffectual anger flickered over Tommy's face. A part of my brain was letting me know that I was being very stupid. He was three times my size before he turned into a giant red monster, but somehow I was getting away with it. He closed his eyes, and in all likelihood, was counting to ten.

When he looked at me again, he seemed to have calmed down. "And if I am respectful and they do not reciprocate?"

"Then you can kick their ass," I said, looking back at Red. "This means you too, you know."

"I have always endeavored to treat others the way I am treated," he said with a playful incline of his head.

"Well, great. That's settled, then." I slapped the side of my leg. "I am sure we have a lot more to talk about, but I need a moment. And food. Breakfast? What time is it anyway?"

Tommy pulled a slender red phone out of his coat pocket and tapped the side. "A little after ten in the morning."

I sighed. "I should call Loren. Even with the note and the fight we had, she'll want to talk to me."

"Your friend contacted me earlier this morning," Red said. "I told her that you were still asleep."

"I'm surprised that held her off this long." I rubbed the back of my neck, just like Ink had the night before. Huh. So that's where I learned it. "If I don't talk to her soon, she's going to come up here, demanding an explanation."

"If I may suggest," Tommy put up a hand. "If you care about this friend of yours, you might want to get her out of the way. The Incubus will almost definitely tell the rest of your old court that you are alive, and they will come for you. I will fight them, but it is a lot harder to protect two people than one. Because your friend is human, the Incubus could use his gifts to ensnare her mind. She could be turned against us, and I can't guarantee that she wouldn't get hurt in the crossfire."

"Also, unless you want to explain the existence of magic to Loren right now, she can't be here," Red added. "It would be hard to hide it from her since fights between the fae tend to be flashy."

"Why does there have to be a fight at all?" I flipped my hands around in frustration. "Why can't we just talk to my old court? I'm still a little weirded out about this whole me being raised to be a queen thing, by the way."

"Your previous Guardian, who was part of your old court, was the one who stole away your memory." Tommy shook his head. "We have no idea who else among them might have been involved."

"Ink wasn't," I murmured.

"I believe that." My Champion snorted and fiddled with something on his phone. "If he had been in on the plan, he wouldn't have bungled things so badly when he kidnapped you."

"Don't be a jerk." I said it reflexively, but honestly, it was hard to defend Ink. He had been a little stupid. "And what are you doing?"

"You said you were hungry. I'm arranging for breakfast. Is there anything in particular that you would like?" He raised an eyebrow at me, and I couldn't decide if he was messing with me, or if his consideration was sincere. I went with the assumption that he was trying to be nice.

"I don't know. Anything with eggs. I'm in an egg kind of mood." I shrugged, then remembered to practice what I preach. "And thank you."

Tommy stopped tapping on his phone and put it away. "You are welcome. I am your Champion, and that means that I serve you, whatever you need."

I paused. "I know we made a deal when I was a child. I mean, sort of, but you aren't actually forced to be here, are you?"

Letting out a long breath, Tommy said, "Forced? That's not an applicable term in this situation. I gave you my oath that if you helped me, I would be your Champion, well knowing that this was a lifelong position. You fulfilled your end of the bargain, I have to fulfill mine. Whether I want to or not."

"Do you want to?" I asked for the second time.

121

A long moment passed while Tommy looked at me, appraisingly. "Maybe."

"Well, that's not definitive but I appreciate the honesty." I sighed. "I don't want to lie to Loren."

"I know what you said about lies of omission before—" Red began hesitantly.

"It's still lying." I frowned at him, but couldn't keep it up. He wasn't wrong, and I hated it. It made me feel like a hypocrite. "If she gets hurt because somebody messed with her head, I'd never forgive myself. On the other hand, if I send her away to protect her, she'll never forgive me."

"She's a good friend." Red patted me on the back. "I have no doubt that she'll yell a bit, but she'll let it go in the end. Besides, you aren't exiling her. We just need some time to secure the home front, and then you can bring her right back."

"Well, here's hoping." A thought occurred to me, and I paused. "Is Loren going to be safe if she leaves? What if Ink follows her? What if she meets another fae?"

"That's highly unlikely." Red shook his head. "The fae rarely venture into the human world, and I made sure there were none around the area where you lived. For extra safety, I'll wait to call back the security I left there. As for the Incubus, I doubt he knows about Loren. The sooner she leaves, the better."

I rolled my shoulders, trying to loosen up. "Okay. I'm going to ask her to go home. I just need a phone."

Red took his out, made a few swipes across the screen, and handed it to me with Loren's number already selected. "Use mine."

Readying myself, I gave a wan smile. "I'm going to the other room to face the firing squad. You two play nice while I'm gone."

It was a relief to be out of the strange room. I was significantly less stressed outside of it. What had my old Guardian done to me that just being in his room made me afraid? Fortunately, I didn't see myself going into Tommy's bedroom much. He was my Champion, but while I didn't think he hated me, I didn't think he liked me either.

Tommy was, oddly, emotionally delicate. I was certain that he was a tough-as-nails king, but because of his oath, I guessed he couldn't bully me. It made him unsure and defensive. Shaking my head as I let myself back into my bedroom, I focused on the battle at hand. I hit the call button and waited.

Chapter 16: Well-Intentioned Hypocrisy

Loren picked up on the first ring. "Where is she, you creep?"

Even though I remembered that this was Red's phone, and she thought she was yelling at him, I still winced. "It's me, Lore."

"Where the hell have you been?" she shrieked. "You said you were going to wait by the car, and then you freaking disappeared. Jesus, Addie, I thought you'd been kidnapped or something. Then, all I get is a stupid note. Were you that pissed off?"

To my credit, I did not laugh. Quickly, I got serious and let fly with my half-cocked, not thought-through story. "I'm sorry. I was an asshole. I was mad and went for a walk through the woods. The house is just on the other side from where we were. I met Red while he was making sure everything was locked up, and he offered to let me stay overnight. I am really, really sorry."

"Yeah, well I was really, really worried. You could have called me last night, you jerk." Loren groaned into the phone. "And after that huge deal you made, you just went to the house anyway. What the hell was all the fuss about then?"

"I am not obligated to entertain your new friends." My lip curled. "I didn't, and still don't, appreciate you pushing me into it. That's why I left."

She was quiet for a moment. "You're right. I didn't take your side, and I should have. I don't blame you for being angry. That was still a dick move, though."

I took a deep breath. "Yeah. I was being a brat. Forgive me?"

"Always. So, now we've both admitted to being idiots and are all good." Mirth crept back into my friend's voice, and a weight lifted off me. "What have you been doing all morning? You never sleep this late."

This was the part I had been dreading, so I thought up a lie, and thought it up quick. "I was super exhausted. Red showed up with breakfast and we looked around the house some more. I found my old bedroom. It's amazing, but it's totally pink from ceiling to floor."

"I can't wait to see it." I could hear Loren's smile. She had refused to relinquish her love of pink with age.

"About that," I rubbed the back of my neck. Thankfully, over the phone, Loren wouldn't be able to see my face and know instantly that I was lying. "The next few days are going to be busy. Mr. Pit came back early and we're trying to get a jump on the paperwork. There's going to be a lot."

"That's cool. You can take care of business, and I'll bum around. I can use that pool and hang out with Sean." She sounded delighted by the prospect.

"Loren–" I tried to interrupt.

"Don't worry." She laughed. "I won't bring him over."

"That 's not what I'm worried about." I hesitated, then inspiration struck. "I need your help."

"Yeah, what's up? Is something wrong?"

As I spoke I was very aware of the fact that I was going to hell, but I wanted to keep my friend safe. "I need you to go back home and get something for me. When I left, I didn't think this was going to work, and, well, I always assumed I was coming back."

"Why can't Mom just mail it?" Loren asked.

"Two reasons. One, it's at my mom's house and if your mother asks for it, she's not going to be able to get it. You know the trick to jimmy my window and can just go in and take it. Two, you're going to need to go back anyway. You have to get your stuff so you can move in." I took a pleading note, feeling like scum. "Please, Lore? I left my set of Jane Austen novels in the closet. If it hits my birthday and I haven't come home yet, Mom is going to know that I'm never coming back. She'll throw them away or burn them or something."

"You don't even like Jane Austen. Why would you want those?"

"Because they're the only things my dad ever gave me." I closed my eyes, thinking that if Loren wanted to punch me in the nose when she found out I was lying, I was going to let her.

Immediately her voice softened. "Addie, he doesn't matter. He's the world's biggest asshole. He's–"

"I know. I know." I didn't have to fake the misery in my voice. "It's stupid, but would you do it?"

"Of course I will. But keep in mind, if your mom catches me and I go to jail for breaking and entering, you're paying the bail."

"Absolutely. I'll deploy my vampire lawyer and everything." I nodded, even though she couldn't see me. "Thanks, Lore. You are a lifesaver."

"Yeah, yeah." I could almost hear the eye roll. "I'll leave after lunch. If I'm going to get all my stuff together, it may be like three days before I can get back. Are you going to be alright here on your own? You can't drive."

"Red's offered to play chauffeur." I tried to sound dismissive. "It turns out that I am their biggest account. I'm pretty sure he'd pick up my dry cleaning if I asked him to."

"Well, okay, but you'll let me know if anything is wrong?" My best friend was behaving like a mother hen, and it was funny. Not that I had the nerve to say anything about it.

"Sure," I lied. "Now, I gotta go. There's paperwork that needs explaining, so I know what I'm signing."

"Alright. Be thinking on what you want to do for your birthday. We'll do anything you want. I mean it this time. If you want to sit at home, drinking tea and reading, then by god, break out the Asimov and earl gray." Loren sounded so earnest it was a struggle not to laugh. She had made this promise for the last couple years but had yet to be able to resist sneaking me out to some social event that she deemed good for me.

I expected no different this year, but I humored her. "I'll think of something. After all, I have my own ball pit now."

"Oh, my god yes!" Loren shrieked, delighted, then sobered a little. "No offense meant, but you had a freaking weird childhood."

"None taken, and I am in total agreement." The pressure of having to lie was fading, but the uneasy sensation in my stomach was settling in for a nice long stay. "Be safe on your drive."

"Sure." There was a pause, then she asked, "Are you really okay, Add? You sound stressed."

Relief washed over me as I got to be somewhat honest. "This trip has just dredged up a lot of old memories, but I'm managing. Tell you what, when you get back we'll have a long talk and I'll dish everything. I'll get us an entire gallon of chocolate brownie ice cream."

"It's a deal. See you in a few days." Loren laughed.

"See you," I said. The line went dead. When I closed my eyes to rub them, someone cleared their throat behind me. I whirled around to face Rat, who was standing in the open doorway. "You scared me."

"Sorry." Rat's grin was unsympathetic. Her demeanor changed, her head ducking and her voice softening, when she said, "If the books are important, I can get them quicker."

"Mom can burn them for all I care. There was a reason they were gathering dust in the closet. I have a moral objection to throwing away books, or I'd have done it myself." The fact that Rat was here finally clicked. "Are you getting ready to go check on Ink?"

"Already been." She shrugged. "It was like Tommy said. The Incubus was gone. Probably out there screwing someone to heal."

I froze. "What?"

Rat rolled her eyes. "Kids these days. Haven't you ever read anything about the Incubus?"

"The only stuff I've heard about incubuses is what friends have told me from TV and stuff. Reading about that kind of thing literally gave me a headache." I glowered at her and went to sit at the round table. "I didn't even know until you just said something that 'Incubus' wasn't just his name."

"Damn, you have a lot of ground to cover." With two graceful strides, Rat jumped up onto the table and sat cross-legged in front of me. Expertly ignoring the dirty look I gave her, she elaborated. "First of all, it's incubi, not incubuses. Secondly, it's Incubus, not Incubi. There's only one. Human stories paint it like there are entire races of people who are actually one of a kind. Part is because the fae travel fast. It's easy to appear to be in multiple places at once. Part is because it makes for a better story. Or they want to blame us for something we didn't do."

"So all the stories of incubi seducing women..."

"Were your friend 'Ink'. Or the woman was getting busy with the next-door neighbor and just blamed it on him." Rat drummed her fingers on the table behind her. "What there are multiples of, are members of a classification. Tommy is the king of the boogies. Boogie isn't a race or species. They're just a group that identifies together. In this case, they're inhuman looking, generally disagreeable, and always predatory. Red. Red is an example of a boogie. Your Incubus is what is generally classified as a vampire. Although some don't like the term. Associations and all that. They haven't come up with a better one, though, so that's what we use."

So, Red was a boogie, not a vampire. It was something I'd have to tell Loren once I could. "Aren't you a Boogie?"

She swung her head back and forth like a pendulum. "I mean, you might could call me one. Most people don't like me. I could never manage a hundred percent to pass for human. And I'll eat whatever I damn well please. The fact that I live in the Marrow Pit might cinch it for some people, but I'm a shapeshifter."

"What's the Marrow Pit?" I'd heard it referenced a few times now.

"It's just a Territory in the Betwixt. Tommy holds the land. The Boogies inhabit that land. Thus, Tommy is king of the Boogies." Rat sighed as she wiggled her legs around so that she was kneeling. "I stay there because I like it. This makes him my liege. Even though I am not a Boogie. I'd say you should tour it but humans tend to die there. Even before they get eaten by someone. The air is toxic."

"Sounds lovely." I wrinkled my nose.

"It's not too bad." She squirmed back down to sit cross-legged. "If you can ignore the miasma. And the resident monsters. And the masses of corpses that you find all over the place."

I snorted, but couldn't tell if she was joking or not. Instead, I retreated to an earlier part of the conversation. "So, does Ink really, um, feed on sex? Heal from it?"

"It's well-known." Rat bit her lip and drummed her fingers again. "Then again, just because it's well-known, doesn't mean it's true. I suggest you ask him the next time you see him."

"Yeah." Leaning back in my chair, I tilted my head back to look at the ceiling. It was white. I had thought it had been a pale shade of pink before, but I hadn't looked at it closely. "I'm not sure I'll be seeing him any time soon. It sounds like Tommy hurt him pretty bad. He may not want to come around."

"Oh, I wouldn't worry about that." Rat's face came into view, blocking out everything else. "He had the audacity to snatch you right out from under Tommy Raw Head and Bloody Bones. Do you think he'd give up that easy?"

"I don't know him enough to say." I scooted back to get out from under Rat's face. She stayed where she was, crouched at the edge of the table, peering at me curiously. "I mean, yeah he went through a lot of trouble, but I barely remember him. He doesn't know me either. I'm not the little girl he knew ten years ago. It's a lot of time for a person to change."

Rat shrugged, then lay down on her side. "Not so long as you might think. It's all a matter of perspective. When you've lived as long as some of us, a decade is no time at all. Although, any amount of time can be long, if you're hurting."

I stood up and rubbed the back of my neck. I wasn't sure what to say to that, so I redirected the conversation. "So, how old are you anyway?"

With a big stretch, she hopped down from the table. "Now, you're a girl. You should know what a rude question that could be."

My 'someone is screwing with me' sense was tingling. Being friends with Loren over the years had finely honed it. "Is it a rude question?"

"You're quick. I like that. No, but it is a fruitless one. " Rat pushed her hood back with a laugh, revealing short, shaggy brown hair and thin-skinned, pointy ears. "Some people have the time and patience to figure out how old they are. I just don't care."

"Fair enough." I shrugged.

She leaned back against the table, drumming her fingers against the side. "It gets confusing, living in two different realms. Time doesn't always move at the same rate. That, and the occasional change of calendar that humans insist on now and then. It just gets too hard to keep track of. By your standards, I'm really old."

"Time moves differently?" I paused. That was a simple statement that raised a lot of possibilities. It made my head hurt, and it was almost nice to have an honest headache for once.

Rat's pocket buzzed and she pulled a small, old-style flip phone from her hoodie. She opened it and perused the screen as she spoke. "It's not like a big thing. As the Betwixt separated from the human world, time got wonky. It was never much. No more than a day ahead or behind at the worst of it. After you were born, it started stabilizing again. It should have gotten worse after you died, but when it didn't, no one noticed. It must have been part of the curse."

Something on her screen caused Rat to make a happy squeak worthy of her namesake. "Breakfast is here. We can go get it downstairs. Or Red can bring it to us here. Either way, he needs his phone back."

I had to think for a moment before remembering that I had left it on the table. "Let me go change, then we can go down to the kitchen. Assuming you know the way. I would get us lost."

"I can find it." Rat hopped back up onto the table to wait. I grabbed my clothes before heading to the bathroom. Someone had washed them. Yet one more mystery.

I threw on a pair of jeans and a shirt, thinking I was going to have to go shopping soon. The shoes and dress I had been wearing out with Loren were gone. That made me more than a little grumpy, but there was nothing to be done about it. My sneakers had been left at the hotel, so had made the trip here with the rest of my clothes. Thus armored, I went out to seek my breakfast. Rat, who had been laying on the table like a reclining nymph, hopped up, and we were on our way.

Chapter 17: Courting Shadows

Walking with Rat was an interesting experience. She would scamper several feet ahead, then wait. It was like she only had two speeds of movement, ridiculously fast, and almost still. Every so often, as we passed halls or open doors, she'd stopped talking. Her nose would quiver like she smelled something, then she picked the conversation up like nothing had happened.

"So, you can change into a rat?" I asked as we descended to the first floor.

"I can. Quite frequently, I do." Rat raced ahead of me to go stand at the base of the stairs. By that time I had learned not to try to keep up with her and took them at my own pace.

When I got closer, I asked, "Is Rat like a nickname or something?"

"Yes and no." For a moment, she kept perfect step with me. "See, no fae gives people their real name. True Names have power and can be used against you. We have aliases that we give out. Some fae will pick a name and stick to it forever. Most of us like to change it up now and again. It's quite fashionable right now to go by your human-given name."

I raised an eyebrow. "I've never met a human whose actual name was Rat."

"No." Her lips pinched in a sour expression, and she waved one hand dismissively. "I meant, like your mythological name. Like Incubus and Red for Red Cap. In my case, my animal name."

"Ink goes by Isaac Heart."

"What you put on the paperwork doesn't mean anything. You have to change those out every what? Fifty, sixty years at minimum? I don't deal a lot with formal human society. I have two I alternate between. The last time I used one was to sign a petition to bring back a TV show."

"What was it?" I asked.

"Firefly." Rat ran ahead again and did a little jig as she pointed down a hallway. "Found it!"

"I meant the name." I was glad that we were finally there. Living in this house was going to drastically increase my step count per day.

"Oh. Marie Stahlbaum, I think." She tilted her head to one side. "Yeah, I think that was the one."

"That sounds familiar," I mused. We entered the kitchen. Red and Tommy were already there. The smaller man was standing next to the island, putting a piece of pie on a plate.

"It's from the Nutcracker." Rat rushed ahead to press her fingertips to the counter and stare greedily at the food. When she noticed there was only one plate, her nostrils flared. "What? None for me? I haven't eaten yet either."

"It's for Addie." Red scolded with a wagging finger. "There is more in the refrigerator but it's up to her whether or not you can have it. The coffee is brewing. You can have some of that."

Finally, I caught up again and offered Red's phone back. He took it with a little nod. Rat was looking at me with big, black puppy dog eyes. "Of course, you can have some."

With her signature squeak, Rat swept across the room to the fridge. She grabbed the pie container and hopped up to sit on the nearest countertop. Tommy swiped the air with a growl, and she dropped back onto the floor.

"Addie, he's being mean to me." She whined like a child, but the look in her eyes was pure calculated mischief. There was barely controlled murderous rage smoldering on Tommy's face.

"Actually, I'm with him on this one." I pointed a finger at her. "Stay off the counters. It's not sanitary."

Rat pouted, but winked at me.

Tommy looked somewhat mollified and pushed away from the wall. "Well, I have to take my leave. It's been a long night, and I haven't slept yet. You two will watch over Addie."

Red held up an objecting finger. "I have to go as well. Not only do I have actual legal matters to attend to about the estate, but someone has to get some food in the house."

"You're a real lawyer?" I raised an eyebrow.

"Yes, I am." Red crossed his arms. "I told you, I didn't lie to you. Tommy needed someone to handle the human legal side of things. I already had a couple of human degrees, so I decided to take that on as well. I passed the bar and everything."

Holding up my hands in surrender, I said, "Okay, I was just asking. With everything going on, I can't take anything for granted."

Tommy snorted. "Yes, well, Rat will keep an eye on you until he gets back. She isn't to leave your side." He glared at her. "Stay inside. Addie, your old court may be able to get in, but the house still offers protection from any others. The Incubus knows you are alive, but we don't know who he's told. There are guards outside, but they won't come in unless there is no other option. I trust them to kill anyone who makes an attempt on you or the house, but they aren't the most savory of characters. I'm not even sure some of them are housebroken."

My Champion started for the door, but paused. "I'll be asleep in my room upstairs. If you need me, Addie, call."

Without waiting for a reply, Tommy left, head ducked. Red chuckled and I looked at him. "What?"

"Tommy's just starting to appreciate some... aspects of being your Champion, that's all." Red smirked as he headed for the door to the garden.

"But he's been my Champion for ten years."

Red just shook his head and walked out the back door.

Rat moved in front of me, and I jumped at the sudden amount of face in my field of vision. "I think it's just that he hasn't been personally involved until now."

"I think you're both laughing at me," I grumbled.

"Less you and more Tommy." Rat hopped up on the counter again, saw the look I shot her, and got back down. "He can be a little stodgy. It's fun to see him off kilter."

I took a bite of my pie while I considered her answer, and whether or not she was mocking me. It was a delicious, savory morsel, full of meat, tomatoes, and eggs like I'd asked for. "This is fantastic."

"Yeah. It came from the coffee shop in town. I think the guy who owns it delivered. He's one of us, by the by." Rat put down her meal, the entire pie minus my piece, and took down a couple of mugs. "Do you want anything in it?"

"I take a little coffee in my cream and sugar." I smiled.

Rat fished through a plastic bag that contained all the drink fixings. Offhandedly she said, "I've only met the guy once, but I'm impressed. His cooking is superb. And he's incredibly hot."

I ducked my head and giggled shyly. "I agree on all points."

There was a crash from the garden, and Rat looked as surprised as I was. I moved to look out the breakfast nook window. She was by my side instantly, putting a hand on my shoulder. "Addie, you're not supposed to go outside."

"I wasn't going to, but what was that noise?" Even when I leaned to look past her and catch a glimpse out of the window, I couldn't see anything out of the ordinary.

"I don't know. It might be the Incubus trying to draw you out." Rat held an arm out to bar me from the door like I might make a dash for it while she cocked her head, listening.

"Red just went out there, do you think something could have happened?" A second, louder crash made me jump. Rat bared her teeth, and they looked significantly more rat-like than they had been a minute before. What was cute on a small rodent was much more intimidating on a human-sized being.

"Red's left by now." Hair rising like hackles, she jumped and screeched when a third crash came from the garden. "What are the guards doing out there?"

Rat was growing more and more agitated. I put a hand on her shoulder. "Look, let's just sit down and–"

There was a fourth crash and she snarled, arms spread and hands crooked like she was going to take a swipe at an invisible enemy. A shudder ran up her spine and she pushed me back towards the center of the kitchen. "You stay right there. Don't move from this spot. I am going to take a look. I will be right back."

"Rat–" I reached after her, but in a blur, she was gone.

There was a clack and thump behind me. I whirled. A man crouched on the floor and behind him, one of the narrow, stained-glass windows had swung down. It was too small for a human to get through, but as he looked up at me with all black eyes, like Rat's, I knew he wasn't human at all.

He stood, and his shaggy, blue-black hair flopped in his face. With a little shake of his head to get it out of the way, he grinned at me, but it didn't reach his eyes. He was on the tall side of average, with a long, straight nose, large, hooded eyes and very light brown skin. A crow's head done in artistic swirls of gray and white stood out starkly on his black tee shirt.

"She is a horrible bodyguard, isn't she?" he asked, playfully nodding at the back door. "Then again, you'd expect Boogies to be. They're wolves, not sheepdogs."

"Who are you?" I asked, backing towards the interior door.

Holding up his hands in a sign of surrender, the new arrival chuckled, "Hey, it's alright. I'm here to protect you, too. My name is Crow."

Flash

***

136

The parking lot was brightly lit, making it an island in the darkness. I watched the moths hovering around the light I stood under. I wanted to be good and wait where I was told, but I was getting bored.

There were noises from around the side of the building where Crow had gone with the man. At first, there had been silence, then crying. Now, the man was pleading.

Crow might scold me later, but he didn't hold with rules either. He'd understand. I crept close to hear what was being said.

"Please! I won't do it again, I swear. You know my word is good, Jack." A slight tremble made a lie of the man's upbeat and friendly tone.

"Stop whining. You're disgusting, but you could at least die with a little dignity." Crow's voice dripped with loathing.

"No! Please, my wife and kids–" The man started to stammer.

Crow cut him off. "Will never have to know what a monster you are, and how much better off they are without you. Goodbye, Johnny."

There was a swish and a thud. I risked a peek around the corner. The man was crumpled on the ground, his head about a foot from his body. I screamed.

***

My stomach clenched. This wasn't one of Tommy's people. Crow was someone I had known before, maybe one of my old court. Why he was here, I could only guess. I kept an eye on him, facing him as he sauntered across the room to stand a little closer to me. It didn't escape me that he was standing between me and the door to the outside.

Faking nonchalance, I walked over to the stove. As I poured I counted my breaths, trying to calm the nervous tremor. "Okay then. You want some coffee?"

"Sure," he said like nothing was wrong. "Your name is Addie, right? You used to live here ten years ago?"

"Yeah, I mean, I don't remember it, because of the curse." I grabbed the bag with the sugar and cream, hoping if I stalled long enough, Rat would return. I gave him a shaky smile. "You want anything in it?"

"Nah. I like it black." I handed him the mug and he took a sip. "That's good."

"Yep." I doctored my own coffee, not looking at the man behind me. Should I buy more time or scream for help?

Crow made that decision for me. He put a hand on my shoulder. "You recognized me. Not right away, but you did. Let's not play games here. We don't have the time. Addie, sweetheart, we all thought you were dead."

I turned to face him. He was standing very close to me, his black eyes searching mine. My heart fluttered and I could feel his body heat, inches from my chest. Hands vice-gripped on the counter, I tried to answer, but my throat locked. He must have seen my fear, because he took a step back, giving me room to breathe. His eyes changed, the black receding so that they looked normal human brown.

Crow cocked his head to the side like the bird I suspected he was. He gave me a warm smile and held up a hand. "Hey. Hey. It's okay. It's just me. I'm not going to hurt you. I'd never hurt you. You do remember me, right?"

I gulped. "My Guardian, Buggy, or whatever his name was, stole my memory with magic. The only thing I remember about you was that you beheaded a man in an alleyway when I was six. I saw his head rolling on the ground."

"Ah. This is going to make things more difficult." Crow took one more step back, eyes cast down to the floor while he bit his lip. He thought for a second then said, "Addie, I know you don't have a lot of reason to trust me at the moment, but I really need you to. My little distraction won't hold the Rat for much longer. If you don't have your memory, you have no idea how much danger we're in at the moment. I don't know what all you know about him, but Tommy Raw Head and Bloody Bones is here, and he is the monster all other monsters are afraid of. I need you to come with me, please."

He held out a hand, but I shook my head. "I have no way of knowing if you were in on the plot to steal my memory. Not to mention the fact that you beheaded a guy right in front of me. If you want me to believe that you're the good guy, wait here with me. I'll make sure Tommy doesn't do anything rash. Come on, we can figure out things together."

"I'm sure he's been very careful around you to make you think that would work." Fingers curling into a fist, he sighed. "I am sorry about this Addie, but I swear it's the best I can do in the situation."

Crow was fast, but I was already holding the coffee pot. As he was lunging to grab me, I chucked it at him, and he caught a face full of scorching liquid. I fled for the door into the house. Screaming, I ran out of the kitchen into the hall.

"Tommy!"

I tried to take as many twists and turns as possible, but I had no clue where I was going. As I took a corner so fast that my feet nearly went out from under me, I panted, "I need somewhere to hide."

I picked a door, desperately hoping Crow would think I had passed it by. There was a short, broad length of stairs going down. I slammed the door behind me and leaped to the floor below. When I hit the ground I stumbled, but I managed to stay up and kept running.

It was some kind of wine cellar. Racks of green and blue glass bottles stood like bejeweled wooden soldiers in straight rows. They gave way to giant casks of who-knew-what in a room like a small warehouse. I raced to the end of the row. Maybe I could crouch behind the last row of barrels. It wasn't great but it was better than nothing. It was too bad that having found myself in a situation where there was magic freaking everywhere, I didn't have any to help me hide.

Flash

***

Crow put a hand on my shoulder. "You see, the trick to an excellent game of hide-and-seek is to up the stakes. If you want to beat your Guardian, you'll have to use magic."

"Sidhe said I'll have to learn the theory and stuff before I can do any actual spells." I pouted.

"Well, Sidhe is stupid, and I'm going to teach you how to hide so well I couldn't find you." He bopped me on the nose, and I giggled.

"Does it have a rhyme?" I bounced with excitement.

"What?" Crow laughed, scooping me up so that he could look me in the eye.

"That's how spells work, right? I saw it in a movie. You speak in rhyme to make it a spell. You know, 'mirror mirror on the wall' like that." I waved my arms around as I explained.

"You know, why not?" Crow placed me on the ground and crouched down next to me. "You see, the best hiders in the world are shadows. You can look right at them and still don't see them. Not really. They can hide you too, but to do that, you have to court them."

"What's courting?" I asked, eyes wide in wonder over learning such secrets.

Crow stirred his hand in the air, searching for words. "You know, sweet-talking. That thing you do when you bat your eyelashes at all of us to make us do whatever you want. You have to court the shadows to get them to let you in."

He pulled me close again and sat me against his knee. "All you have to do is look into the darkness and think real hard about it parting for you to let you into their world. Are you doing it?"

I nodded hard. "Yes!"

"Well, you just keep that in your mind, and whisper the secret words." Crow put his mouth next to my ear and hissed, "Shadow, shadow, on the wall, make me hidden, make me small."

Suddenly, he rocked backward on his heels and I squealed in delight as he pulled me into the shadows.

***

My breath caught. I knew a spell to hide, and the one seeking was the one who taught it to me. Staring at the pool of shadows in the corner I contemplated it, wondering if I dared. The sound of the door opening was followed by Crow's voice calling, "Addie, damn it, please don't run. We don't have time for this."

Out of options and time, I prayed as I threw myself forward, "Shadow, shadow, on the wall, make me hidden, make me small."

It was peaceful in the shadows. When I hit the floor, it was slow, like I was falling through water, and I had enough time to turn and land on my back. The world swam with pale colors and I could still hear him coming, but it sounded far away.

"Addie, please, come out," Crow called as he walked to the edge of the row I was hiding on. He looked in my direction, and I held my breath for a moment. There was no way he could not see me as clearly as I could see him. I pushed myself into a sitting position and stared up at the man who was looking all around the floor like he couldn't find me. He did know I was there, he just couldn't pinpoint me.

"I have to say, I'm impressed that you've managed this after ten years," he said. Too much white showed in his eyes. "But Addie, search your memory. Look for me. I'm your friend and always have been. I would never, ever do anything to hurt you or let you come to harm, so please come out. Let me get you out of here."

He took a step closer, toe to toe with me. I thought about the man who had taught me how to play a better game of hide-and-seek. The feelings in that memory had been very clear. I had loved and trusted him, but that was a child's view. Young me had trusted the creature with the red eyes that glowed in the darkness, too.

Crow closed his eyes, but still moved his head back and forth, searching. He spoke softly and it came out barely a whisper. "You know how I found you? When you were little, hide-and-seek was your favorite game. You'd ask the house to hide you, but it's a house, and not very smart. It always took you here. I know you're hiding in the shadows, just like I taught you, but please, come out. The spell I spun to keep the Bloody Bones from finding us is wearing thin, and he'll be here soon. I won't leave you, but when he finds me he will kill me."

If this was a ploy, it was a good one, because it stabbed me in the heart. I couldn't let Tommy hurt him. Intense concentration on his face, Crow reached into the shadows just to the side of me. Like reaching into water, his arm distended and seemed to grow longer but when it broke into the space where I was, it appeared normal. Eyes still closed, he waited for me to take his trembling hand. I believed he was afraid, and couldn't just leave him like that.

Pushing through the thick world of the shadows, I took Crow's hand, and his eyes snapped open. Relief filled his face. As he stood up, he pulled me with him, and the shadow world fell away like a shower of silk scarves. It was a good thing we were in a dim and quiet room, because the sudden lights and cacophonous sound of the world outside was jarring. Without meaning to, I whimpered and collapsed against Crow's chest in an effort to hide my eyes. He petted my back and made soothing noises.

"Yeah, next time don't try that on your own with no preparation. You're lucky I was here to pull you out. You could have gotten hurt." He pushed me upright by my shoulders and started to say something, then a funny look ghosted across his face. He stared at me like he was seeing me for the first time. "You're so tall, and so much more beautiful than I thought you would be."

"Um, thanks?" I winced, half at the sound of my voice, half at Crow's words.

He shook his head. "Sorry, I didn't mean it like that. Anyway, we've got to go now."

"No. Look, Tommy's on my side. He's my Champion. I bound him to me when I was a kid and–"

I barely saw the blur of red that sped into the room and grabbed for me. So fast I didn't have time to be dizzy, Crow spun us out of reach. His arm extended to fling me away, the momentum sending me twirling into a barrel. Gasping, I clung to the wood to keep from falling.

Tommy stood before us, but he was no longer a man. The giant, bloody-looking creature I'd seen in my memory clenched enormous fists, his armored head nearly brushing the high ceiling. He growled so loud and low it felt like a train passing nearby.

Crow moved between us, his legs braced and his eyes level with Tommy's waist. Feathers appeared in his hair as he pulled a katana from thin air like he was drawing it from a sheath. "Run, Addie! Go to Ink at the hotel. I'll buy you as much time as I can."

"Why would she run?" Tommy's chuckle was like a rock slide thundering down a mountain. "Once I kill you, she'll be perfectly safe."

Chapter 18: Compromise

Tommy exploded forward and crashed into Crow. The katana arched through the air in a silver blur, slicing toward my Champion's shoulder. A massive red fist collided with Crow's forearm. His sword flew out of his hand and skittered across the floor.

The shapeshifter gave a strangled cry as Tommy's other hand wrapped around his throat. With a triumphant roar, Tommy rushed to the wall and slammed him against it. Crow's head hit the brick with a crack and his hands clawed at scarlet fingers.

"Don't kill him!" I ran towards the fray. Tommy continued to hold Crow as his feet kicked and his face started to turn purple. "Put him down!"

"If I do, he'll get away." Tommy leaned into him, grinning jaws too close to Crow's face. The flesh of his neck was bowing beneath my Champion's grip.

"Put him down, Tommy. I mean it!" While I had no illusions about being able to force Tommy to let go, I had to do something. I leaped up to seize his elbow. It was like grabbing onto a pull-up bar. Instead of his arm coming down, I hung with my feet inches off the floor. Even though his skin looked like raw, bloody muscle, it was firm, dry, and fever warm.

Tommy's face contorted in surprise. For a full two seconds, we just stared at each other. He lowered his arm enough for my feet to touch the floor and opened his hand. Crow dropped bonelessly to the ground. He spared Tommy a disgusted look as he lay gasping, and grasped at his throat.

I went to check on him, but Tommy put a hand over mine, trapping me against his elbow. "I let him go because you told me, but don't get too close. He could still snatch you."

"If he was going to, he would have done it when he spun me out of the way of your first grab. I don't think he wants to hurt me any more than Ink did. If we can just talk, I bet I could get things straightened out." I'd been looking at Tommy's still oddly human eyes, but a motion to my side caught my attention. Crow was giving a thumbs up above his head while he clutched his neck. "See? Let me check on him."

"The shapeshifter will be fine" Tommy's hand still pinned mine. His voice was strange, like he was trying to sound harsh, but ended up having a soft note. "I won't kill him, but I have to insist you stay behind me."

I nodded and slowly pulled my hand out from under my Champion's. "Crow, are you okay?"

"Oh," he wheezed. "I am just great. Someday I might even be able to breathe again."

"If you want to continue breathing, don't move." Tommy stepped to block me from Crow's view.

"That is not a problem." With a relieved croak, he lay prone on the floor. Peering around Tommy's arm, I could see black and purple swaths across the shapeshifter's neck. Crow turned his head to give me a wan smile. "I have to admit, I'm impressed that you tamed the beast. I never thought the Bloody Bones would play lapdog to anyone."

Tommy snarled, but turned his attention from the man on the ground when the door opened. A filthy and injured Rat stumbled through, panting and eyes wide. She attempted a smile, but didn't quite succeed. "So, um, I guess you discovered that we have an intruder."

"You think?" Crow tried to laugh and coughed instead.

"Not helping," I said. He waved a hand in the air, signifying nothing that I could interpret. In any case, he shut up, so that was an improvement. "Rat, are you okay?"

"She's fine." Tommy's eyes narrowed at her. "For the moment."

"There were giant stick golems in the garden!" Rat whimpered and pointed behind her. "Me and the others had to take them down and–"

"And you were supposed to keep Addie safe. You should have never left her side to even know what was out

145

there. That is why I stationed people outside." Tommy took a step towards Rat.

I grabbed his arm again and pulled him to a stop while Rat cringed against a rack of wine. "Come on. Rat tried her best."

"She left you to get kidnapped. Again. This is the second time she's failed me in the same damn way. I can't let this pass." He pointed at the hunched form against the bottle covered wall, looking dumbfounded that I was stopping him. Again.

"Does she have any training as a bodyguard?" I asked, remembering Crow's comment earlier.

Head tilting in surprise, Tommy said, "Well… no."

"Then why do you keep expecting her to know how to do a job you know she wasn't trained for?" I tugged at his wrist, and he turned to face me. "We've talked about this."

With a heavy sigh, Tommy relaxed. His voice was strained with the effort of being reasonable. "She's not skilled as a guard, but I gave her explicit orders. She doesn't need training to do what she's told."

He had me there. Rat was a skittish creature, and a bad bodyguard, but I liked her. I wasn't about to let Tommy punish her for not being able to do a job she wasn't suited for. I needed to protect her, so I fudged the truth a little. "Red had just left, and I was worried. Rat went outside to check on him to keep me from getting myself into trouble. You told her to take care of me, and she was doing her best. The fault is mine, so if you have a problem with it we'll talk, but don't take it out on her."

Tommy seemed conflicted, glancing first at Rat, and then at Crow, who was watching us, still flat on the floor. What calculations were going through his head, I didn't know, but at last he nodded. "We will speak later. Rat! Go get something to restrain him with."

"Good dog, Tommy," Crow rasped, head raised and eyes challenging. "You would never know from your past performance how obedient you can be."

Before my Champion had a chance to respond, I grasped his arm more firmly, under no illusion that I could

146

stop him if he didn't allow it. Through clenched teeth, I told Crow, "If you keep mouthing off, I'm going to assume that you feel well enough to hold your own. The next time you do it, I'm giving Tommy a free kick."

"It's alright, Addie." There was a surprising smugness to my Champion's voice. I glanced up, to see him grinning wickedly at Crow. "The fact that all setbacks aside, I am taking infinitely better care of you than he ever did is bound to rub him the wrong way. After all, when I lost you, I got you back."

Rage filled Crow's features and Tommy chuckled. I snarled, all too aware that I had the least impressive set of teeth in the room. "That's enough! The next one of you that tries to pick a fight, I get a free kick on both of you. I'm going to contract it out to Rat to make sure it's hard enough for you to feel it, and I will tell her what sensitive area to place it in!"

By the time I finished that sentence, I was out of breath and panting. Rat, who had scampered out when Tommy had ordered her to look for restraints, chose that moment to return. She looked like I had just told her Christmas had come early. Slow horror crept over Tommy's face and Crow made a kind of choking noise before he said, "You know, it would almost be worth it to watch you take out a hit on the Boogie king's balls."

"No, it wouldn't." Rat licked her lips with a hunger on her face that made me very uncomfortable.

"I said almost, didn't I?"

"Rat, just tie him up. If he tries to shapeshift to get out of it, break his feathered neck." Tommy sounded tired, and I sympathized. Heavy rope in hand, Rat almost skipped to go bind their captive. She was less than gentle about it, and I should have told her off, but I didn't. Rat didn't do any appreciable damage, and I felt like I had pressed myself too far by standing between a giant red monster, and a couple of shapeshifters.

"Since we have the Crow secured, I will station Rat here to keep an eye on him." Tommy shot her a dirty look.

"She will not leave him alone. Someone will be sent to relieve her in a bit. I shall return you to your room."

"Can we stop to pick up my food? I haven't gotten a chance to eat." My stomach was growling. It didn't care that I had more important things to do than feed it. Besides, I owed my Champion a talk.

Crow cleared his throat. "I have a request."

"Denied," Tommy responded automatically.

"God, at least hear what he's asking." I rolled my eyes.

"I'd listen to her." A crooked smile crossed Crow's face.

"I don't have much of a choice. Speak."

"I will only agree to remain captive here if you let me talk to Addie alone." Crow's eyes bored into Tommy's. "You've heard the stories. You know how hard it would be to keep me if I don't want to stay. If you do not give me what I want, I will escape and will rally Addie's old court along with every ally I've ever had. We will descend on you in mass. You might win or you might not. Either way, it's a fight I think you'd like to avoid."

"If you think I am willing to give in to threats–" Tommy's fists clenched so hard his bare chest and arms trembled. It was only just then that I noticed his state of dress, no shirt with a pair of tightly fitted sweatpants. I didn't know whether he had changed clothes once he had gone upstairs, or if he had the Hulk-like ability to retain his pants no matter his form.

Crow inclined his head, the closest he could come to a bow while tied up. "I'm sorry, that was a bad way to start, but I spoke the truth. If I can't speak to Addie, I've no reason to stay. What are you willing to give me so that I can justify remaining a prisoner?"

Was this overly bendy line Crow's attempt at manipulation? Maybe he started demanding at first, so now that he was being reasonable, Tommy would feel obligated to make concessions. Maybe he was up to something different. I was out of my depths in this kind of game.

"What do you need to tell her that you cannot say in front of us?" Tommy's large, warm hand slid back over mine. I hadn't let go of his arm, afraid of what he might do. It was a protective gesture that reminded me how tiny my hands were compared to his. God, he was big.

Crow noticed the move as well, and for some reason, it made his eyes narrow. "Oh, it's not that you can't hear it. I plan on trying to convince her that you were the one that cursed her ten years ago and that even now you are manipulating her. I just don't trust you not to interrupt and let me say my piece."

"Why would I let you try to turn Addie against me?" Tommy snorted.

"Because I have a compelling argument, and if you don't let her hear it, she's always going to wonder why. It would plant a seed of doubt, and you can't afford that, can you, Bloody Bones?" Though still rough, Crow's voice sounded better. He raised an eyebrow at my Champion. "Could you let her hear me out? Do you trust her enough yet, to hear me without your voice there invading? Could she ever trust you if you don't? What does your eternity look like, Bloody Bones, if your liege looks at you in suspicion? Will it turn to hate? Will it end again with you alone on a hill, locked in stone and friendless?"

The echo of Tommy's fear and pain from my memory was still fresh in my mind. For all it had happened ten years ago, it felt like it could have been yesterday. Now, like then, my heart ached for him. Pulling myself in front of Tommy, I told him in no uncertain terms, "I won't let that happen. You're my Champion. You take care of me, and I take care of you. If I have anything to do with it, you will never end up back on that hill."

He studied me a long moment before he answered Crow's question. "It's not her I don't trust. As you said before, you are a legendary trickster. Without being watched, I can't know you won't grab her and flee."

"If she doesn't want to go, that would be hard." Crow bit his lip in thought. "Perhaps a compromise? I suggest you leave the Rat here to watch, and you can stand outside the door. You could easily come back in if you were called for. I am no threat while bound."

"You don't think the Rat would cause the same problem I would?" Tommy looked at Rat, who seemed disappointed she wasn't going to get to kick someone.

"I think she dislikes me only a little more than she dislikes you. If Addie wants to hear what I have to say, I'm betting she'll let her." Crow's glance at Rat was met by a shrug.

"If he tries anything, I'll tear his head off," Rat said, pleasantly. "One of those toys he left in the garden tossed me into a thorn hedge. I feel I have sufficient motivation to correct him with extreme prejudice."

We all believed her without discussion. Tommy pondered this a moment then said to Rat, "This is your last chance. I will be right outside the door, and if anything happens, you will call. If this goes amiss you will be removed from this detail and returned to the Pit. You, Crow, I want your oath that you will not take Addie from this room."

"I won't do anything she doesn't want me to do." His mouth curled into a crooked smirk.

"Don't say it like that." I wrinkled my nose. "You make it sound creepy."

Crow's eyebrows shot up. "Really? It sounded creepy?"

"Like in a sex offender way." Rat put a hand over her mouth like she was hiding her laugh.

It was hard to tell with the splotchy colors on his face left over from his run-in with the wall, but I thought Crow blushed. "That was not my intention. Let me clarify; I swear I will not try to abduct Addie from this room."

Tommy chuckled at Crow's discomfort. "As much as I hate to admit it, you are well-known to be a creature of your word. Between that and the fact that if you do break your oath and kidnap her, I can summon the Wyld Hunt. I feel comfortable with our arrangement. Addie, if you want me at all, just call."

There'd been a strange pressure to the air when Crow said 'I swear', and the name 'Wyld Hunt' made my skin crawl. A memory nagged at me, but didn't manifest like the rest of my flashbacks. I clasped my hands around my elbows to keep from squirming.

With a slight bow, Tommy left, leaning forward and turning sideways to ease through the door. The motion was surprisingly smooth. Rat watched him go in vague bemusement. She met my eyes and shrugged. I assumed she was as confused as I was about him suddenly being cool with everything, and echoed the motion. At least I wasn't the only one who didn't know what was going on.

Chapter 19: Through Another's Eyes

I turned back to Crow. "So, what was so important?"

"Well, to make my argument make sense you need a little background." He cleared his throat. His voice was almost back to normal, but there was still a harsh burr from the damage. The marks on his neck had turned from purple and black, to green and brown. "How much do you remember?"

"There were a bunch of people who took care of me that called themselves my court. My Guardian cast a spell on me to make me forget everything. Whatever he was planning was screwed up when I woke Tommy from stone, and he was defeated. Tommy is my Champion now. That's pretty much the whole of what I know."

Crow nodded. "Most of that is true, and I'm sure, after everything I've seen, that he is indeed your Champion. The Bloody Bones is too prideful and hot-tempered to let you get away with everything you've done today. Not if you weren't his liege. But you have been misled on one point."

"And what's that?" I crossed my arms.

"Tommy was the one who cursed you." When I went to object, Crow jerked inside his bounds. Rat surged forward, then relaxed when he stopped moving. I realized, as he stared in disgust at the rope, he had tried to lift his hand to talk and forgotten he couldn't.

"I was already cursed when I found Tommy." I went to take a step closer, but Rat cleared her throat in warning. I stopped. "That's why I woke him up. I brought him back from stone in exchange for him swearing to be my Champion and defend me."

"That can't be right, Addie." Crow shook his head vehemently. "Your Guardian was sworn to protect you and would have died before hurting you. Even if he wanted to, he couldn't with the oath he swore. Between him and Tommy, the Bloody Bones is the only known oathbreaker."

"You say that like it's a bigger deal than just breaking a promise."

"There's no such thing as just a broken promise," Rat interjected, uncharacteristically serious. "That's something you should get out of your head right now. Humans can make or break promises with impunity. Fae live and die by their word. Literally. If you become forsworn, the Wyld Hunt will kill you."

"What's the Wyld Hunt?" I asked. The term was so familiar, but still didn't trigger a flash.

"A group of warriors led by the Huntsman. They can be summoned to punish oath breakers. Everyone fears them." The very idea of them made Rat shiver.

"And Tommy doesn't," Crow said. "It's well-known that he broke his oath to the last king he served, and killed him. The Hunt was called, but they refused to ride. They feared the Bloody Bones, and would not stand against him. Those fae who couldn't bare the injustice banded together to kill him themselves. Even then, they couldn't manage to finish him off. That's how he ended up on that hill."

"If they were so scared of him, why didn't they just break the statue?" I couldn't believe that Tommy would betray someone. He seemed like he would be honorable to a fault.

"You can't destroy a fae gone to stone. It's a protected magical state." Crow sighed, then sagged against the rope. "I've also only heard of someone returning from it a handful of times. You were untrained in magic and a kid. There was no way you could have brought him back. I don't know how Tommy got free, but I think he was the one who sent your Guardian to stone, abducted you, and messed with your memory."

"No, making him my Champion is one of the few things I actually remember." It was my turn to shake my head.

"And do you think that's a coincidence?" Crow's lips curled in frustration as he squirmed against the ropes again. "He removed almost all of your memories. Do you think it would be any harder to plant one? That he's your Champion is obvious, but I don't know how it came about, and I'm not sure what the end game is. Maybe he intends to use you as a tool to conquer the Betwixt."

"So, you're saying I can't trust anything I remember?" I narrowed my eyes at him.

"Yes." The look on his face was sympathetic, but I don't think he understood how frustrated I was getting. "That's why the Incubus and I were trying to get you away from here. We wanted to see if we could get you somewhere safe and try to fix your memory. Admittedly, the Incubus screwed up. He's impulsive. Always has been."

"I have two memories of you." I searched his eyes for the truth. "In one, you teach me that trick with the shadows. In the other, you cut a man's head off in a parking lot, right in front of me. Are either of those true?"

Crow winced. "Both. Although, I would like to point out in my defense, the man was a child molester. He was going to hurt you."

"Why was I alone with him to begin with?" I suspected part of the answer.

The ropes creaked a little as he squirmed, and stared at the floor. "I might have brought you to an illegal poker game with some business associates of mine. You wanted to learn how to play. I was talking with one of them, and Johnnie led you away. I took care of it, though. You were never in any danger."

"And you say Tommy is the one I should be worried about?" I snorted and Rat laughed.

Leaning over him, she gloated. "Are you done yet? You can't say anything that is going to make a bit of–"

Crow exploded forward in a flurry of feathers and darkness. Rat bared her teeth and tried to grab him, but her hand passed right through. He reformed into a man right in front of her, face contorted in pain. One of his hands flung out, and silvery dust appeared in the air, scattering over her face. She froze, still as stone. He grabbed me around the waist and pulled me close. I tilted my head back to scream for Tommy, and Crow clapped his hand over my mouth while he made desperate shushing noises.

I bit him. He barely seemed to notice as he held me tight and whispered in my ear. "I'm not going to hurt you, but I need to tell you something without either of them listening. I need to let the spell muffling our voices go before Tommy notices it, and the powder paralyzing the Rat will only last a few minutes. I have to be tied up by then or I don't think even you can stop your Champion from killing me. Will you listen? Please?"

Glaring at him, I nodded. He put his hand down hesitantly, and when I didn't scream he stepped away. I could still feel residual heat from being pushed against him and was very aware that even though he didn't seem as strong as Tommy, he was still a lot stronger than me. Too bad punching him would be useless.

I did it anyway. His head barely ticked with the impact and my knuckles stung like anything, but I felt better. "Okay, now I'm listening."

"I deserved that," he admitted. "Look, I know you have even less reason to trust me at this point than you do the Bloody Bones, but listen. He's using you. I know it, and I can prove it."

"So, prove it," I challenged.

"I'm betting once you leave here, Tommy will want to talk to me. Find out who all knows you're here, things like that. Once we're alone, I can get him talking about the truth." Crow's voice was low and urgent as his hands hovered by my shoulders like he wanted to touch me. "I have a spell that will allow you to see what I see and hear what I hear. If you'll let me cast it, I can show you the real Tommy."

"You're going to get him to monologue?" I raised a skeptical eyebrow. Behind Crow, Rat was like a statue. It was highly unnerving. I'd never seen her be still for that long.

"Be obnoxious enough, and it's amazing what you can get people to say. I'm tricky, Addie. Even the boogie king admits it. Please? We're running out of time." His eyes were completely black again, and as alien as that looked, I could still read the pleading in them.

I needed to make some hard decisions. Crow was right on one account, I had been trusting too easily. My gut said that I could believe my Champion, but I felt the same for the man in front of me. I didn't see how they both could be right. So far, Tommy had better credit for his actions, but maybe this should be a case of trust, but verify. "Okay. What do I do?"

He reached out. "Give me your hand."

I did, unsure where this was going. He took hold of my wrist and turned my palm up. In one smooth motion, he pulled a small folding knife out of his pocket, flicked it open, and slashed it across the tip of my index finger. I gasped and tried to pull away. It didn't really hurt, the cut was so shallow and the blade was so sharp, but a drop of blood welled up on my skin.

Crow shot me a quick smile that failed to be reassuring. He pulled my hand close to his face and said, "It's okay."

"What..." I started to ask, but my breath hitched when he dipped his head, taking my bleeding finger into his mouth. For the most uncomfortable three seconds of my life, he sucked on it while I looked on in embarrassment.

Sliding my finger out from between his lips, he murmured, "By the bloody binding ties, seeing secrets with my eyes, seamless souls no more apart, mind to mind and heart-to-heart."

Only then did he release my hand. I pulled it back and cradled it against my chest protectively. The cut was so small, it was almost closed. There was a strange thickness to the air. It reminded me of the feeling I had when Ink had been trying to remove my curse. Minus the pain. "What the hell was that?"

"The spell," he said. There was a glazed look in his eyes that cleared up in a moment. "Now, I need you to focus on the magic around you. Do you feel it?"

"I guess." I rubbed the back of my neck. "Next time you're going to do that, warn me."

"Noted, but, please, Addie, concentrate." He glanced at the still frozen Rat. "We are running out of time."

I closed my eyes and focused. The feeling was there, thick and tangible, I just didn't know what to do with it. "Okay, I feel it. Now what?"

"Good." Crow touched my hands. "Now, it's like focusing on one particular sense. Keep your eyes close, but try to see. My eyes are open, and you can use them."

Taking a deep breath, I stared at the back of my eyelids so hard it started to hurt. Finally, I felt the magic tugging, and I tried to follow. It faded just as I felt I was getting somewhere. Exasperated, I blinked and had a moment of the strangest vertigo. I realized not only had I not actually blinked, but had changed views so I was looking at myself.

Looking at yourself in the mirror is not the same as looking at yourself through another's eyes. For one, Crow was a little taller than me, so the angle was different. I could hear my breathing, through both Crow's ears and my own. As his skin touched mine, I was also feeling my hands through the tips of his fingers. It was doing everything he said it would do, but so much more.

Crow was thinking how much, standing there with my eyes closed, face scrunched in concentration, that I looked like my childhood self. It was obvious that I was as stubborn as always, and that was good. Inconvenient, but good. It meant that I would not be easily manipulated by the Bloody Bones and his goons.

I realized Crow had no idea I could hear his thoughts. This was not supposed to be part of the spell. Somehow, I had gotten more. Was this one of the elements that made me more than other fae? I listened, hoping to find out more than he was willing to tell me.

I could taste the faint copper of my blood on his tongue.

He worried. Worried that he wouldn't be able to protect me from Tommy. He wasn't sure if there was a power in the Betwixt that could protect me from that monster.

It was laughable that he had told me he would hold off the boogie. The only hope had been if he could make the Bloody Bones angry enough to take his time. It didn't matter right now, anyway. Crow knew I wouldn't run unless he could make me see the truth. If the spell worked at all.

"It's working," I said, blinking hard. There had been a brief moment of confusion as I was seeing out of both pairs of eyes, but it only took a second to push back Crow's sight. The connection was still there, though, and it was distracting. It reminded me a little of the kind of empathic telepathy or whatever Tommy and I had shared in the Quarry. "How long does this last? It's weird."

Crow smiled, thinking that I was cute when I was puzzled. "An hour at most. Now, that powder is going to wear off the Rat soon. I need to be back in that chair and restrained when she wakes. Quick now, redo my bindings."

He sat, and I did my best to replicate the knots that Rat had tied. As I cinched them tight, Crow grunted. It wasn't that I was hurting him, but it was rather uncomfortable. All he could think about was that if this didn't work, and he couldn't get Tommy to reveal his intentions, he would have failed me. Again.

Once he was secured, I leaned down to look him in the eye. "Are you okay?"

"I'm fine Addie." Crow smiled, glad that I still felt some sort of connection with him. His eyes flickered down and saw that my t-shirt gaped a little. It was impossible not to notice that I had grown up. For just a second, when I rapidly stood up, he was both grateful and regretful, and felt very uncomfortable about his feelings. He desperately hoped I had moved because I had realized time was short, and not because I had seen him looking down my shirt.

Trying to cover, Crow said, "Quick now, back to where you were before I froze her."

I repositioned myself behind Rat, followed by about five seconds of awkward silence. When she resumed moving, she was confused. Everything was where it was supposed to be, like nothing had happened. Whipping around to look at me she saw my best approximation of mild concern. I wasn't a great actress.

"Are you okay?" I asked.

She shook her head. "Yeah. I'm fine. Look, are we done?"

"I guess." I didn't know what else to say, wiping my sweaty palms against my legs. Thankfully, Rat missed the gesture while she was glaring at Crow.

He smiled sadly. "Don't forget about me, and keep an ear out. You never know what that Champion of yours is going to do."

Rat snorted at him, but I nodded, understanding his meaning. As I turned to walk away, I watched myself leave through Crow's eyes.

Chapter 20: Fun House

Tommy leaned against the wall just outside the door. The first thing I noticed was that he was back to his human form and wearing the same suit as earlier. I was sure that he hadn't gone upstairs to change. He had either left it in the hall, or there was some kind of clothes-changing magic involved. Having watched Crow whatever the hell he had done when he escaped his bonds, that was most likely. After all, he hadn't been naked when he reformed. Thank God.

The second thing I noticed was that this was not the same hallway I had entered the cellar through. That one had been wood paneling halfway up the wall, then honey-white paint the rest of the way. This was all wood.

Tommy must have seen the baffled look on my face. "What's wrong?"

I shook my head. "I don't know. Maybe I'm confused. I wasn't exactly paying a lot of attention while I was running, but I don't remember the hallway looking like this."

"I am impressed with how far you managed to flee before the Crow caught up with you. If you didn't notice some details in your haste, I wouldn't be surprised." Tommy smiled. If it was supposed to be reassuring, he needed practice.

"That I got any distance at all was probably due to the fact that he was busy. I bet doing whatever he did to keep you away was distracting. By the way, how did you know to come and get me?"

Pride peeked through Tommy's smile. "I am your Champion. When you call for me, I hear you, no matter where you are."

"Oh." I blinked. I guessed I shouldn't have been surprised. After all, back in the Quarry, Tommy and I had shared some kind of deep connection. And, you know, magic. "Well, that's useful."

"Yes." He held out his arm like I was supposed to take it. "Shall we get your breakfast? Red is waiting in the kitchen for you. I will hand you off to him, and then I have business to attend."

Through the spell that was still functioning at the back of my mind, I felt Crow being tormented by Rat. She was telling him all the awful things she was going to do with him as soon as I would let her. He didn't care and was just resting. His healing was coming along fine, but Tommy's assault had been rough on him. And he worried about me.

"Is this business involving the man tied up in my wine cellar?" I asked, not taking his arm.

"It is." Tommy sighed and dropped it back at his side. "What's the problem?"

"Nothing, I just want to make sure you aren't going to hurt him," I said.

"If he gives me no reason to, I won't. I understand that he is dear to you, Addie. I will act accordingly."

Automatically, I started to protest that Crow wasn't dear to me, but stopped because that wasn't true. Even though I didn't have more than a couple of memories of him, some feelings from my childhood must have remained. I nodded and inclined my head, so he'd lead the way. Not long into our walk, I realized that I had no idea where we were. "Okay, this is weird. I may have gotten confused during the run, but there is no way I came through here. Where are we? Are we anywhere near the kitchen?"

Tommy raised an eyebrow. "Quite a ways. As I said, I was impressed with how far you had gotten. Maybe it was some trick of the Crow's magic?"

"Maybe." I pressed my lips together, thinking hard. "I mean, he said that I would always hide in that spot when I was a kid. That seems an odd thing to say if he was the one who got me to that room. Or maybe it isn't. I don't know. I need to go back to the kitchen and retrace my steps. Maybe there's like, weird portal doors that are like shortcuts around the house. That's a thing, right?"

He chuckled. "Magic is involved. Anything is possible"

"Let me check something before we go to the kitchen." I tried a door at random. There was that nagging feeling of something almost remembered, and it opened onto the kitchen, where Red leaned against the island while drinking coffee and playing with his phone. He started as the door opened, bafflement on his face. I looked over my shoulder, to find my Champion standing there, as perplexed as I was.

"Any ideas what just happened?" I asked him.

He thought for a moment. "Go through the door. I want to try an experiment."

"What's going on?" Red asked, the beginnings of concern in his voice.

Tommy followed me inside the kitchen and stepped to one side to allow the lawyer to see into the hallway. "Do you recognize where that is?"

"Not immediately." Red stood side by side with him. "But it is most definitely not the pantry, which was what was there a moment ago. Are you going to explain this, or am I going to have to wait?"

"You'll have to wait." Tommy closed the door, waited about three seconds, then opened it again. It was a long, narrow room with sparsely stocked shelves. Turning back at me, he commanded, "Addie, I want you to state that you want to go to your room, then open the door."

I had an inkling of where Tommy was going with this, so I obeyed. "I want to go to my room."

I opened the door and there it was. More confusing, it was considerably less pink. The furniture still ran high to Disney Princess, but long swaths of the walls had turned white, like they had drunk in the color. Earlier, I had expressed that if I was going to stay in that room, the princess colors would have to go. I looked back. "I think the house is listening to me."

"I think you are right." Tommy rubbed his chin while he considered. "This has real possibility. And I have to say, I approve of the changes to your room."

"This works out well, actually." Slipping his phone back into his pocket, Red grabbed a plate with my breakfast in one hand and two cups of coffee by their handles in the other. He walked so smoothly that he didn't look to be in danger of dropping anything. In the back of my head, Crow's annoyance at Rat refusing to shut up made me irritable too. "We can take this back to your room and be a little more comfortable."

"Neither of you seems upset by this. You don't even seem that surprised." I looked between them, and Tommy shrugged. Red shrugged as well, but it was infinitely more impressive due to him holding hot beverages.

Red led the way into my room. "There's something you should learn, Addie. Where magic is involved, some things are improbable, but very few are impossible. This is especially true of you. No one knows what you're capable of. This house was created by some of the same people who wove the spells for the Accord, just for you. I wouldn't be surprised what it could do."

My Champion gave a little half-bow. "Don't worry. I have been listening, and won't hurt the Crow. Go on, I will come to see you when I have finished talking to him."

"Okay." The double vision was getting more distracting by the moment, so my parting smile as I shut the door was a little weak. With a heavy sigh, I dropped into a chair by the round table. "Sorry if I pulled you away from your errands."

Red blew out through his lips like a horse. "Don't apologize. You are the most important thing. Besides, I had just enough time to drop off the document. While you eat, I'll make arrangements for groceries."

"Sounds good." I picked up my fork while my lawyer went about lawyering. Somehow, the breakfast pie was still crispy and warm, but not like it had been microwaved. I was willing to attribute it to some kind of magic and leave it at that.

Red resumed texting on his phone, and I ate. The ensuing quiet was useful. It allowed me to focus on Crow's senses. Rat had gotten tired of harassing him and was sitting on top of a cask, picking at a crack in the wood. Behind his back, Crow rubbed something between his thumb and forefinger. It was a small object shaped like a coin. When I concentrated, I could feel that one side was rough, and the other was almost glassy smooth, but I couldn't tell what it was.

His thoughts told me. It was a small pottery Christmas ornament. On one side, a generic-looking teddy bear was shallowly stamped, on the other, my name was scratched into it. I had made a handful of them one year at school and given them to a select number of my court. He had kept it, all those years and wished he had time to show me.

Ten years of mourning had dulled the pain for him, but now all the wounds were bleeding anew. On top of that, there was the danger of losing me again. If he could get Tommy to tip his hand, just maybe he could figure out how to get me to run away with him.

That was no good, because no matter how far he ran, the boogie was my Champion and would find me. Unless Crow could manage to kill him… and it was no use.

Even if the Bloody Bones were using me, I would be better off with him. The boogie could at least take care of me, and would probably treat me well enough. Depression settled over Crow, who closed his eyes against it, and I wished I could comfort him.

I would later, but now I waited. Fortunately, Tommy moved quickly, and I didn't have to wait long.

Chapter 21: Baiting Confessions

No one heard the Bloody Bones unless he wanted you to, but Crow felt his presence. He didn't recognize the tall, bald man who walked through the door but knew it was Tommy. With a rough bark, the boogie ordered the shapeshifter to go stand in the hall and she scampered to obey. It was still the Bloody Bones under that strange skin, but it was unexpectedly disconcerting. He had never seen the king of the Marrow Pit try to look mortal before.

"That's a new look for you, isn't it?" Crow cleared his throat. It was still a little sore, but would be fine soon.

"If I'm expected to be in court, I thought I should dress a little more appropriately. A human skin for a human queen." Tommy's voice was tinged with bitterness. No, the old boogie wouldn't like being confined to such a frail-looking body. Crow was betting the form was unfamiliar. That could prove useful.

"The status of Addie's humanity has always been a subject of hot debate." Crow tilted his head, trying to read Tommy's face. It was much easier to see the nuances of these newer, less practiced expressions. "Honestly, Bloody Bones, I thought you swore you would never bend a knee to a king again. Not after what happened to the last one."

Tommy puffed, eyes narrowed. "For one, I never made an oath. Secondly, I serve a Queen, not a king. A Pixie's length of difference, I'm sure, but one all the same. Finally, no matter what magic made her, the girl has spent over half her life being merely human. Whatever she might have become before her Guardian's interference, she is just a girl now, stepping into a whole new world that she only knows from shattered memories. This would not be the case, I would like to point out, if your comrade hadn't interfered. I had a plan to fix everything."

"You'll forgive me if I don't believe the new, benevolent you." Crow smirked as he leaned as far forward as he could against his bonds.

"It's not benevolence. I am Addie's Champion, and I must act in her best interest. It is just the bargain we made.

She brought me back from stone, and now I serve her." Tommy leaned against the wall to glare at Crow.

"Oh, come now. It's not like you haven't ever betrayed a liege before."

Rage contorted the boogie's face. The Bloody Bones roared so loud the wine bottles rattled in their racks, and he charged the bound man. He stopped with his nose an inch from Crow's, his teeth gaped in a snarl that wanted to bite. The shapeshifter didn't flinch, but it took a good deal of his will.

"You don't know what you're talking about! You are ignorant. You all are." Tommy's lips pulled back in a grin too wide for a human, and Crow was acutely aware of the boogie's powerful jaws. "And how dare you question my loyalty? You, her original court, were the ones who failed her. Whatever curse that was put on her, it was no simple thing. It would have taken months of preparation, and multiple castings to establish a base to make something that elaborate work. And none of you noticed anything."

"We trusted her Guardian." Crow's back stiffened, and his fists clenched tight, making them twist in their bonds. "I have only your word that he wasn't sent to stone while trying to protect Addie from you."

"Are you really going to pretend that you can't sense the bond between us? I am her Champion, bought and paid for with a life debt. Even she couldn't release me from my obligation." Tommy smiled, but it wasn't a happy expression.

Crow couldn't deny it, but that didn't mean he liked it. There was no way to know the boogie's intentions, or why he had kept me hidden for the last ten years. But he had to admit that Tommy was not responsible for the curse. Damn it.

Before he could think about it, the words escaped his mouth, "Why didn't you call us?"

"What?" Tommy was caught off guard and laughed at the question.

"If you meant her well, and you saved her from her Guardian, then why didn't you contact her court?" Crow hoped that the Bloody Bones would speak the truth. He had no reason not to. After all, the bastard had a reputation for honesty, as long as it was the brutal kind.

"Why would I?" Tommy's face turned upwards, his eyes closed and expression pained. "I had just been brought back to the world after two hundred years to serve a mistress who was under attack by a particularly horrific curse and one of the few monsters I fear. I didn't know who the rest of this court was, but I couldn't assume that they weren't traitors as well.

"I was alone without allies, caring for an injured charge. She was the most important creature among the living fae, but everyone thought she was dead. Because I had no idea how to care for a child, I followed the plan her Guardian had set out. I am no nursemaid, and it was a way to keep her unknown to the rest of the Betwixt. It meant safety for her while she was at the mercy of the spell, and unable to defend herself. I needed to find out if there were other traitors among her court, and I needed allies I could trust. For the last decade, I have consolidated my power. Not for me, but for her."

Tommy's breath was heavy, and tension sang through his shoulders. This human form of his was easier to read than his boogie form. He was angry, though whether with Crow or the situation it was hard to say.

"So you're saying that you have no designs on using her to conquer the Betwixt?" It was impossible. Crow couldn't reconcile the idea of Tommy Raw Head and Bloody Bones not being the villain.

"My only goal is to serve." The boogie king didn't seem to like speaking the truth any more than Crow liked hearing it. This complicated things. "If it is Addie's will to stay here, in this town, enjoying her luxuries forever, then I will ensure her comfort. If she wishes to rule, I will bring both worlds to their knees for her pleasure. Believe me, I would much prefer the former. It would be easier to protect her, and I have tried to conquer the Betwixt before. The whole endeavor brought me nothing but misery."

"Did you care nothing for our heartache?" Crow closed his eyes, just feeling the cold twisting sensation in his chest. He knew the answer, but he needed to hear it, needed me to hear it. "Our queen was dead, and we mourned her."

A deep chuckle peeled through the stark room. It made the shapeshifter shudder.

"Why should I?" Tommy asked.

"Because we mattered to her." Crow's voice cracked, and tears edged his eyes as he opened them to glare at the boogie. Too much water behind a battered dam. The words conveyed a plea to me, through his own ears. They had been important to me, even if I couldn't remember them. He had been important to me.

"Maybe back then." Tommy nodded, cruelty creeping into his smile. "Not anymore. Your presence during the span of her curse would have only caused her pain. Any interference now would bring about, at a minimum, confusion. I don't intend to kill you. It would upset Addie. Best you walk away from this, Crow. Best for her."

Tommy's words echoing Crow's thoughts cut my old friend deeply. Swallowing hard, he said, "For you to make that offer, you must believe I wouldn't hurt Addie. Otherwise, you would never let me go."

"Purposely hurt her?" Tommy shook his head. "No. Cause her harm through more well-intentioned idiotsy, like what the Incubus did? Yes."

Crow couldn't deny that Ink had been stupid. If he was being perfectly honest, the fact that one of my only memories of him was of that unfortunate run-in with the mobster pedophile was a bit telling of his own lack of sense sometimes. He had experienced a lapse in judgment that night by letting me out of his sight. I should have been fine in a room full of men who knew his reputation and had children of their own, but then he'd found Johnnie leading me out to his car. Compounding his earlier mistake, he had lost his temper and left me alone again to punish the man who had dared to lay a hand on me.

I had only been about six. The sight of a decapitation had frightened me. Of course, it had. I had been a child, and he had known better. Dropping his gaze from Tommy, he looked at the cold gray stone floor. Maybe he should leave me alone, but... But Crow was not that selfless.

He brought his eyes up again, meeting Tommy's curious gaze. "I believe that you are doing your best for her. I won't seek to take her away, and I will speak to the others of the court so that there are no more misunderstandings. That being said, I will not leave her. If she asks me to, I'll go, but not until then. Will you try to keep me from her? Your people are not trained to protect. I am. You want to keep her safe? Use me."

"Are you asking to serve me?" The boogie's head rocked back as he laughed.

"I'm suggesting that you don't prevent me from serving her." Crow took a deep breath. "I believe that her Guardian betrayed her. To be honest with you, and myself, I suspected that he was up to something even before she disappeared. When we found his message that Addie had been murdered, and he had gone to find the killer, something wasn't right. On some level, we knew it, but the spell stopped us from exploring it. Curse or not, I did fail her all those years ago by not seeing the danger. I will not fail her now."

For a long, quiet moment my Champion watched Crow. "I shouldn't trust you."

"That's fine. I definitely don't trust you." Crow sagged against the ropes. "It's entirely possible that you are a better liar than I give you credit for. But... I think we need each other, because, as you said, this kind of intricate spellwork would have taken months to pull off. It was beyond her Guardian's capabilities. There had to be another actor. Now that I don't have the curse hampering me, I can help you find them."

"You think I didn't come to the same conclusion and haven't been looking this last decade?" Tommy huffed.

"I believe you have. No one can scour the darkness like a boogie, but maybe you need someone who can work in the light. I have a lot of connections and information about her Guardian that you may not have." Crow forced a smile. "If nothing else, look at it this way; you'll have a trained guard watching her so you and your people can get things done. I am not expecting peace, but could we at least manage a truce? For Addie's sake?"

My Champion chuckled humorlessly. "I suppose it is best. Maybe you will be able to deal with her. Since I've brought her back into this life, she has been... demanding."

Crow laughed, but he meant it. "Now that is the Addie I know. Including that everyone will play nice or else. Don't worry. She grows on you. In no time at all, you'll wonder how you ever lived without her. So, can I get up now?"

Tommy rolled his eyes. "Very well. I'll untie you."

With a flourish of hands that I couldn't follow even using his eyes, Crow slipped the bonds and stood up. Theatrically, he rubbed his wrists, despite the fact they didn't hurt. I wasn't that good at knots. "Oh, I've got it. Thank you though."

"You are an ass," Tommy said flatly.

"Aren't we all? Now, if you don't mind, I'd like to get back to Addie." Crow started walking towards the door. "And I would like to bring in the Incubus and the Sidhe. After I have fully informed them of what's going on, of course."

"The Sidhe, I understand and agree with. While irritating, he is almost as good a mage as he thinks he is. Why would you invite the Incubus, though? It was his brash actions that caused Addie's current memory issues." Tommy drummed his fingers on his crossed arms as he frowned with contempt.

The boogie wasn't wrong, and it grated. Crow held up his thumb and two fingers, folding them down as he counted. "Three reasons. One, while he screwed up, he believed that he was doing the best thing in the situation. According to him, the curse was causing her to have some kind of seizures. He panicked, but he would never hurt Addie on purpose. This leads me to two. The Incubus is another pair of eyes to keep on her, and he would fight more fiercely than you would believe to protect her. Third, I don't want to have to spend the energy trying to keep him away. Do you?"

"Point taken." Tommy led the way out of the cellar. "Contact them both then. Maybe the Sidhe will have some input on how to secure the house against unwelcome visitors. He helped build the house, as I understand it."

"Oh, I can help you there." Crow grinned when my Champion scoffed. "Almost all the defenses in the house are keyed to Addie. The house, while not actually intelligent, can follow instructions as long as they aren't complicated. All she has to do is tell it that no one enters unless expressly allowed."

"It's that simple?" Tommy raised an eyebrow.

"It is that simple." When they saw Rat on the other side of the door, Tommy sent her to patrol outside. They continued down the hall in sulky silence, and I directed my attention back to my actual location.

Chapter 22: Don't Know Any Better

The entire time I had been slowly eating my breakfast, Red had been texting on his phone and then making a call to someone named Lar. He arranged for groceries and meals for the next week or so. I figured that Tommy and Crow would be a few minutes getting to us, so I took the opportunity to ask something while they were still absent. The lawyer hung up his phone and smiled at me.

"Red? Earlier, Crow said something about Tommy being an oathbreaker..." The second I said the word the smile fell from Red's face, and he held up a hand to stop me. I complied but looked at him expectantly.

He pursed his lips for a moment before answering, "The story itself is not mine to tell, but I will say this much; Tommy is not an oathbreaker. For anything else, you'd have to ask him. Fair enough?"

I nodded and gestured at my plate by way of changing the conversation, "This is from the coffee shop in town, right? I have a feeling that I am going to be spending a lot of money there."

Red chuckled, like at some private joke. "Perhaps. You never know what the future holds."

I headed to the media room to settle down and watch some TV while I waited for Tommy and Crow. Someone knew my propensity for quirky British detective shows, because I had streaming channels full of them. I pointed at the listings, "Who checked out my preferences?"

Red shrugged. "We always had an eye on you. Someone noted it."

Looking at my hands in my lap I asked, "So you know everything that happened at home? With my mom?"

There was enough of a silence that I looked up to see him casting me a guilty look. "We would have stepped in if there had been any danger. Maybe we shouldn't have left you with your mother. I knew you were unhappy there sometimes, but the only other solution would have been to find you some kind of foster family. It couldn't have been a fae, either, because we couldn't risk you having regular fits. In hindsight, I wish I had. But with what I knew at the time… you were already destabilized by the curse, and then by your father deciding to leave rather than live with our terms... I did the best I could, and it wasn't enough. I'm sorry."

"That's o…" I began, but then my brain caught up with me. "Wait, what do you mean, live with your terms? Did you have something to do with my father leaving?"

Red shrugged. "Only tangentially. Do you remember the night before you left your grandmother's house?"

"A little." I squirmed uncomfortably. "That day Grandma and I got into a fight because she thought I'd faked a fit to get out of school. I thought she was going to hit me but Mom grabbed me and ran. They all argued after that, but I had to go to my room, so I didn't hear the details. When I woke up in the morning, Dad was gone and Grandma said we couldn't live there without him, so we packed up. We stayed at a hotel for a couple of days, waiting for him, but he never showed."

"The fight that night was about whether or not your grandmother was allowed to hit you. Your father insisted that his mother needed to be able to discipline you, since they were staying in her house. Your mom, idiot though she is, at least knew better. We would not allow that. I approached your parents myself and told them that I would not suffer a hand to be raised to you. They either had to control your grandmother, or leave the house.

"Your mother decided to get out and take the accommodations I set up. Your father left on his own, at the time I thought to clear his head. He had inherited your grandmother's temper after all." Red sounded sympathetic and regretful at the same time. "He returned to her house a few hours later. When I confronted him, he said he wanted nothing more to do with us or our arrangements. He lived there for about a year before moving to another city, where we stopped keeping track of him."

"God, my dad is a dick." I crossed my arms and tried to sink into the couch.

"Yes, but you have plenty of people who care for you, Addie. Never forget that." Red reached over to squeeze my hand and I smiled wanly at him.

The others took their time getting to my room. As I quietly watched TV, Crow's thoughts and feelings began to fade. By the time he and Tommy knocked on my door, I was alone in my head. When they walked in, I froze. How was I supposed to react since I shouldn't know Crow was coming? I was a horrible liar, so how did I pull this off? My heart was thudding in my mouth, and I was afraid it was going to fall out if I tried to talk.

"It's alright, Addie, we've reached an agreement. He will stay and help arrange your protection. There's a plan to secure the house but you need to implement it," Tommy said while Crow stood behind him, holding his hands in front of him in a bodyguard pose and trying not to smile.

Tommy gave me a list of people to allow in. I very strongly considered telling him about the spell and that I knew everything. If he found out later, he would be angry, but I didn't want Rat to get into more trouble. Crow didn't say anything either.

"House? Please stop everyone from getting inside except for Loren, Tommy, Red, Rat, Crow, Ink, Sidhe and the Knocker. Thank you." It felt a little silly, but considering that I could go anywhere I wanted in the house by saying it and opening a door, I was willing to believe it would work. I thanked the house, just in case it could appreciate it, and everyone in the room looked at me like I had done something adorable. I glared back.

"I'm surprised you didn't object to us calling in the Knocker," said Red.

Crow shrugged, then turned his attention to Tommy, head cocked to the side. "I've found him a clever and pleasant fellow, but I do wonder why invite him, specifically? From what I've heard, the Hag is the end all in curses."

"I would love to have the Hag consult, but that will have to wait until I feel it would be safe to take Addie into the Bone Swamp. The old crone will not leave her home,

174

even on my order." Tommy's voice brimmed with long-suffering agitation.

Crow snorted. "I don't feel safe going into the Bone Swamp."

"No one does. That's why she lives there," Red said dryly.

"The Knocker has expressed willingness to answer my summons, though he is not strictly speaking a boogie. Also, while his main works are centered in enchantments, he is one of the most brilliant technical magicians I've ever seen." Tommy paused for a moment, considering. "And I suppose he is a likable and trustworthy sort. I feel comfortable having him around Addie."

"Alright then." Crow collapsed on the couch next to me. "The Sidhe and Incubus should be here by tomorrow. So, what does everyone want to do till then?"

"I have to get in touch with the Knocker, but he cannot be reached by conventional means. I'll send the Rat to get him." Tommy rubbed a hand across his face. "Then after that, I may try to finally get some sleep. Red, stay with Addie. I am sure the Crow won't attempt to kidnap her again, but I'd feel better if you were with her."

He waved a hand in acknowledgment. "Right."

"No comment about having the Sidhe around?" Tommy raised an eyebrow. Red shook his head.

"I've no problem with him. We've only ever met each other in passing, and we both hate his brother. Who knows. Maybe we'll bond over mutual disgust."

"Why do you keep calling people 'the whatever'?" It had been low-key bugging me all day.

"It's just a formality." Red looked up and waved his hand like he was searching for a word. "I'd compare it to saying mister. You refer to someone as 'the' as a sign of respect unless you are very familiar with them, or if you're addressing them directly."

"It's the closest Red gets to actual respect." Tommy chuckled, then turned to me with a bow. "If you need me, all you need to do is call."

"I know." I smiled and put a hand on his arm. This seemed to fluster him and he retreated from the room.

Crow put a hand over his mouth, but I could hear the smile in his voice. "And you are going to have him wrapped around your little finger in no time."

"Will not," I said, not willing to admit to myself how much like a little kid I sounded.

"What about you, bird?" Red asked, the words more teasing than offended.

"Oh, I've been under her spell for years." Crow put a hand over his heart and fluttered his eyelashes at me. "There's very little I wouldn't do for her."

"How about being quiet?" I grumbled.

"Well, that's one of the few things I can't do. Sorry, Addie." Pretending to look sad, he dropped his head and Red laughed. I huffed and went back to watching my show.

Chapter 23: The Garden They Built

None of the experts would arrive until after nightfall, so I had some time to kill. Just relaxing in my room and watching TV was an option, but the sun sparkled warmly through the window. It was a shame to stay inside.

"I don't suppose there's a safe way for us to take a look at the gardens? I haven't gotten a chance to see them yet."

"I don't see why not." Crow looked at Red. "I mean, with the Incubus brought in officially, there's no one coming after her. Between you, me, and whatever nasties Tommy has around the house, she should be perfectly safe. What do you think?"

"It shouldn't be a problem." Red brightened. "I would love to show off my renovations."

"Awesome." I got up, and they followed me to the door. I ignored them when they chuckled at me for whispering for the house to please take me to the kitchen. It didn't matter if they made fun of me, I wasn't going to be rude to the magic house. With my head held high, I opened the door. I was stupidly proud of that trick, even though the house did all the work. We stepped outside, and I beamed at them. "So, which way?"

Red took the lead. He led us into a carefully planned and tended world of flora. I was far more delighted than I had any right to be over these gardens that were officially mine.

There was an 'edible' garden, where everything produced something you could eat, as well as being decorative. The predominant colors were green and the yellow of various blooms, but there were hints of blues, purples, whites and reds as well. Beyond that was a water garden, and a hedge maze that I left for later. There was a walled-in garden, like from one of my favorite books as a child, and a field that was just full of wildflowers.

I didn't know a lot about plants, but I was pretty sure most of these flowers weren't supposed to bloom at the same time. Yet more evidence of magic, but this was an excellent example. It felt like a real fairy tale. I had to resist the urge to run to each new type of flower to smell it.

Across the wildflower field, I could see that the road, probably the same one that went around the garage, led to a pleasant looking one story house. Pointing to it, I asked, "What's that?"

Red glanced at it. "The guest house. In case you want to put someone up, but don't want to have them inside your stronghold, I suppose."

"It was built to house any relatives of Addie's who came to visit. It shielded them from anything strange under the guise of giving them some privacy." Crow frowned at the building. "Your uncle and his family stayed there for a while, before your cousin... disappeared with a boy."

The rumors Crystal had told me echoed through my mind, agitating the nagging feeling that there was something there I needed to remember. "So, I didn't just imagine the hesitation in your voice just now, did I?"

"No." Crow sighed. "Your Guardian was the one who told us that she had run off, but... let's just say we weren't all convinced. Don't get me wrong, the girl was an idiot who was dating an even bigger idiot. She'd been pulled in by the police a couple of times for shoplifting and trespassing while following the lead of her boyfriend. Her father didn't like the boy, and she did tend to make it out like hers was some great, tragic love story. Running away was within character."

"So, what makes you think she didn't run away?" Red asked, seeming only vaguely interested.

"Nothing in the way of hard evidence," Crow waved a dismissive hand. "She was an extremely materialistic person and there were a handful of things she left behind. She didn't steal anything on her way out, either. Addie didn't like her cousin, but the morning after the disappearance, she was distraught and couldn't tell us why. We questioned her Guardian, but he was less than helpful on the matter."

Flash

***

"Go back to bed, Addie," Ink said solemnly. He was looking Buggy dead in the eyes, rage seething from his very posture. I sniffled, head thick and wooly from crying, and trudged to my door, dragging my stuffed tiger behind me. Once inside, I closed the door and slipped into the shadows, knowing that they wouldn't be able to tell if I was eavesdropping. I snuggled Tiger on my lap as I listened in. He was still damp from his bath, and he made my nightgown wet too.

Ink had asked me what had happened, and got upset when I wouldn't tell him. My stomach still felt sick, and I was shaking, but I couldn't tell anyone why, because... I couldn't remember.

"Are you going to pick a fight with me, Incubus?" From his voice, I bet Buggy was sneering.

"Only if I have to," Ink said, bravely, "but you are going to tell me what happened. Why is Addie crying?"

"She fell and scraped her knee. It happens sometimes." My Guardian made it sound like it was no big deal.

"And that's how blood got on her toy as well, I suppose?" Anger made Ink's words hard.

"As you say." Buggy sounded bored.

"And I'm sure this has nothing to do with the fact that no one can find her cousin anywhere, does it?" Ink's voice was getting softer, harder to hear.

"What are you insinuating?" My Guardian's growl rumbled through the shadows. I whimpered and hugged Tiger tight.

"You son of a bitch!" Ink burst out. "You got rid of her so that you wouldn't have to hide anymore. Is her body rotting in the Marrow Pit as we speak? Is that why Addie was crying?"

"I don't answer to you, so you might want to watch your wagging tongue. If I see too much of it, I might feel compelled to rip it out."

179

There was a pause, then Ink said, "No, you don't. One day though, you will have to answer to her, and if she is half as fierce as I expect her to be, it better be good."

It was Buggy's turn to pause, then he sounded sad. "That may very well be, but when she has grown, if she decides that I have wronged her, that will be between Adeline and myself. You will have no part of it."

There was nothing but silence then. Silence, and my grief in the shadows. I had never felt so helpless, and no magic I knew or friend I could call on could fix it.

***

"I'm pretty sure he killed her," I whispered, more to myself than them.

"Do you remember it?" Now Red sounded interested.

"Not the thing itself." I shook my head. "An argument between Ink and my Guardian afterward. The things I remember, they aren't like normal memories. They're like little fragments of time that come back when something prompts me. It doesn't happen all the time. It's a little like my fits used to be, only minus the pain."

"Are you alright?" Crow touched my arm. Unexpected, the contact made me jump, but I gave him a smile for reassurance. He pulled me into a hug, and after a second I relaxed into it while he stroked my back. "It's going to be okay. We'll get this straightened out, and I will be with you every step of the way."

"Thanks," I mumbled against his shoulder, then pulled away. "That helps."

"I know something that will help too," Red said, and gestured for me to follow.

Curious, I walked after him. Crow stayed at my back like a friendly ghost, and we crossed through a brick archway into the most amazing rose garden I had ever seen. There were raised beds that had every type and color that roses came in, and the smell of them was sweet and thick enough to taste. The crowning glory was a wall, covered in roses that changed shades from white at the top, to almost black at the bottom, with every shade of red in between.

"Roses are my favorite." I stepped forward to caress a bloom that was a delicate peach color.

Crow snatched me around the waist and spun me behind his back. The shapeshifter drew the same sword I had seen before from nowhere and was facing the wall, ready to fight. I peeked past his shoulder and saw what he was guarding against.

Clinging to the garden wall was something like a man, if you crossed him with a lizard and an angler fish, then dragged him through hell. He clung tight against the wall with long, inhuman toes that dug into the golden brick. A heavy coat that may have been white once upon a time hung on his massive form and a squat and battered gray top hat perched on his head in defiance of gravity. Craning his neck at an impossible angle, the man on the wall looked up at me with glowing red eyes and a grin full of needle-sharp teeth in a face that was too wide. My fingers dug into Crow's shoulders and I gasped.

"Oh, don't mind him. That's just Jack." Red waved off Crow's concern. "He's a coward, but Tommy has him keeping watch back here in the gardens. None better than him for skulking about. Nimble bastard, too."

Crow's eyes narrowed. "Wait, you mean Spring-Heeled Jack? As I remember it, he's rumored to be a little too fond of young women."

"He's toothless." The irony of Red's statement made me nearly choke on a laugh. Jack did not appreciate it. The grin slipped from his face and his teeth bowed out in a whistling hiss. Dollops of drool dropped from the corners of his mouth. "Don't pay him any mind. He's here as a pair of eyes, nothing more."

"I thought Spring-Heeled Jack was a serial killer in Victorian London." A smattering of fictional references ran through my head. Being an extensive reader had its advantages.

"Yes and no," Red said, giving a disapproving eye to the monster on the wall who was beginning to writhe like

181

an angry cobra. "Our clumsy malingerer there was spotted once while stalking a woman one night. He usually hunts dogs and cats, but he got bold on that occasion. When he tried to grab her, someone saw him and shouted. Just like that, he took off like a scolded puppy. The woman got a good look at him, and word of his visage spread. After that, several ne'er-do-wells dressed up like the infamous Spring-Heeled Jack to hide their own misdeeds. I don't think he's had the nerve to come within a dozen feet of a human since."

"Why is he staring at us, then?" I asked, softly. Jack's appearance was unsettling enough, but his eyes were very similar to my old Guardian's, and it made me intensely uncomfortable.

In a slithering motion, he climbed along the wall towards us, glowing eyes fixed on me. I stopped breathing for a second and tried to make myself small behind Crow's back. His mussels were like rocks beneath my hands.

"Why wouldn't I want a look at my new queen?" Jack's voice was high and scratchy, like an insect's buzz.

"You can look without being seen." Red crossed his arms. "Now scurry off like the cockroach you are."

"You are not my king." Jack slapped his hand against the wall and his long fingernails clattered against the brick.

"I speak for him in this case, and you know that. So, go!" Red took a menacing step forward, hands curled into fists. Jack made an angry noise somewhere between a trill and a screech and scampered to crouch on top of the wall.

The initial shock over Jack's appearance had faded, so I tried to move around Crow to address him. My self-proclaimed bodyguard put an arm out to prevent me from getting past, and his expression told me in no uncertain terms that I would not get any nearer. Fine. It felt a little less than dignified to speak from behind someone, but I wasn't willing to argue about it.

"What is it exactly you want?" I stared into those disturbing red eyes.

His grin returned, but curled so that his teeth bent out again. "I just wanted to meet you."

"Well, Jack, I'm Addie. Pleased to make your acquaintance." I forced a smile of my own.

"I want to touch you," he squealed. With speed that was no longer surprising at this point, he slithered down the wall. Before he even got more than a couple of yards across the ground toward me, Red intercepted him and arced a graceful kick at his head.

Jack changed direction with ease to miss the strike and ended up back where he started. He whined like a spoiled child, "I want to touch her! Let me touch her! Addie, let me touch you!"

"No," I said, hiding behind Crow again.

As Jack threw a tantrum, thrashing and beating his fists on the brick, I began to wonder if he maybe had some sort of developmental issue. He was so oddly childlike, but he was a child who had the ability to pull someone's head off. "You're mean! You're a bitch! You're not my queen! I hate you! I'll kill you! Let me touch you or I'll kill you!"

"And that is enough of that." Red took off his suit jacket and handed it to Crow. The shapeshifter let his sword drop to the side and took the coat with an amused expression. Stalking towards the hissing and shrieking boogie, Red began to roll up his sleeves. When Jack jumped down the other side of the wall and out of sight, the slight framed lawyer vaulted the same wall, barely touching it to follow him.

Crow chuckled. "So, that's taken care of."

"Um, is Jack okay? He seems off." I looked after them, mouth scrunched.

"In a moment he won't be." Seeing my expression, Crow cleared his throat and tried to look serious. "No, none of the Knucklebones' children are what you would call completely functional. Tommy's the closest, and he has issues aplenty."

"Who's Knucklebones?" I asked.

"Johnny Knucklebones. King of the Marrow Pit before Tommy and, well, I guess the term would be foster father, to several of the creatures that live there now. The old strangler has a soft spot for hard-luck human kids, but a lot of hard luck kids aren't the most mentally stable. The process that he used to make them a fae... well, let's just say it isn't kind."

"Wait, Tommy was once human? Humans can turn into fae? How does that even happen?"

"In the order you asked; allegedly, yes, and it depends." Crow considered. "I suppose he could have been some orphan fae that the Knucklebones adopted, but it's unlikely. If you want to know more about it, I suggest asking the man himself."

I added this to the list of questions for once I got to know Tommy a little better. What I did ask was, "What turns someone into a boogie?"

"There is no method of changing a human that consistently makes them any particular type of fae. Mind you, I've never heard of the Knucklebones' approach producing anything but boogies. I don't know every detail, " Crow admitted as he plucked the rose I had been about to touch before, deftly ran his fingers down the stem to strip the thorns and placed it behind my ear. "But I know it includes long periods of isolation, pain, some kind of brutal training, and the culmination is murder ending with the consumption of human flesh."

"Oh, God." I recoiled. "I thought you said the Knucklebones liked these kids. That sounds horrible."

"A lot of people don't think that pain and harm are the same thing." Crow weighed his words for a moment. "The Knucklebones thinks he's helping these children. They escape a bad life into one where they have power and can defend themselves, so it must be better. Is he right? You'd have to ask them. Jack is damaged, no one disputes that. It might have been kinder to leave him in the life he had, or even just kill him, but what's done is done."

"I feel sorry for him," I looked at the wall the broken boogie had disappeared over.

"Yeah." The shapeshifter sighed, following my gaze. "Me too."

Red walked back through the archway, looking none the worse for wear. Straightening his cuffs, he reached out for his coat, which Crow handed back wordlessly. "Well, now that I've given him a little reminder of the pecking order, we can continue the tour. And I know that look on your face, Addie. No, I didn't hurt him. I just shook him around a bit. He's such a coward, it's all I needed to do."

"Oh, okay. Cool." It was strange that someone I had only known for a couple of days knew me that well. Then again, I had been very vocal about my stance on unnecessarily beating people up.

Crow's pocket dinged, and he pulled out a razor-thin smartphone. Glancing at the screen, he said, "The Incubus has arrived early, so if you want to go and meet him, he's in the front hall."

"Do you think he's mad at me?" I asked, remembering that Tommy had hurt him badly during my 'rescue'.

"You? No. At everyone else in the house including me? Definitely." Crow pouted in feigned disappointment, then shook his head. "No matter what, he never could stay angry at you."

"Well, let's go talk to him, then." I smiled, but I didn't feel it. When we got back to the kitchen, I didn't use my trick to shortcut us to the front of the house. I followed Red and took the slow way, thinking over what I was going to say.

When we got there, Rat and Tommy were standing before an obviously agitated Ink. Back to being dressed in a neat suit, the Incubus was face to face with my Champion but tried to keep an eye on Rat, who was circling around like a velociraptor.

"I came to see Addie. The Crow said she was here and wanted to see me, or was that just a trap?" Ink snarled.

"It's not." I walked into the hall. Ink started to rush toward me, but my Champion moved in front of him.

I was about to object when Tommy said, "I will let you pass, but remember you are not to try to take her again. The results would be more... severe than last time."

185

"I wonder if she really understands how brutal you are. Maybe I shouldn't have healed myself all the way. Let her see what you did to me."

"Are you okay now?" I ducked around Tommy. "I know you were just trying to help me before, and I'm sorry you got hurt."

"I'm fine," Ink assured me.

"Ink, this has all been a misunderstanding. Tommy hasn't been hurting me, he saved me. The curse you tried to lift was put on me by Buggy, not the boogies." I stopped as Ink was staring at me in a way very like wonder. "What?"

"You called me by my old nickname. No one has done that since the night you disappeared." He shook his head like he was clearing it of cobwebs. "I know now that Tommy was not involved in the curse, even though he did take you away from us. Crow has explained the current truce. I don't like it, but I'll abide by it."

"Good thing, because I am with her, permanently." My Champion smiled rather nastily.

"Will you two stop, please?" I was about two seconds away from begging. Or yelling. Or something. "There's nothing to fight about."

Tommy inclined his head. Ink glared at him, but did the same.

Suddenly, Ink stepped forward and hugged me tightly. Surprised for a second, I made myself relax and hugged him back. He didn't let go until I pulled away, but he didn't fight me when I did. Crow smiled crookedly, but everyone else looked vaguely disapproving.

"So, you remember me now, right?" Ink's eyes darted around my face.

"A little." I shrugged, feeling a bit helpless.

"That's fine." Ink was so eager he was almost manic. It was strange. Viewed through my childhood memories, he had seemed so cool and mature. Through adult eyes, he came off as young, somehow. "The Sidhe will be here tomorrow, and he can fix it."

"That's the hope," Tommy's voice still had a bur of irritation. Then again, we did keep waking him up. "Of course, nothing is certain."

Before the tension I felt rising off of Ink came to a head, I decided to try to de-escalate. "Either way, we'll find out tomorrow. And even if I don't get all my memories back, I can make new ones. It's inconvenient, not life-ending. So let's get some coffee and we can catch up. From what everyone was saying, there's nothing to be done until the experts get here anyway."

Looks were exchanged and nonverbal agreements were reached. Tommy excused himself again, hopefully to get that nap he'd been chasing. The rest of us made our way to the kitchen.

Chapter 24: Phone Home

As we all settled down in the kitchen, Red's phone buzzed. He glanced at it, then offered it to me. Loren's number showed on the screen.

"I'd better take that." I sighed and took it from him. "I'm just going out into the hallway, if you guys don't mind."

"Just don't wander far, my dear." Red chuckled. "We have precious little to converse about without you here. We might just start fighting for something to do."

Sparing him a frown, I went out into the hall and answered, "Hey, Lore."

"Awesome. I thought I'd have to talk to the creepy lawyer again."

"He's not... that creepy." I had to amend my statement. I liked Red and felt comfortable around him, but Loren's feelings weren't unjustified. What, with him not being human and all.

"He's pretty creepy. Anyway, I just got home. Anything going on there?" I didn't want to lie to my best friend again... And it occurred to me I didn't have to. I sent her away because I didn't want to risk Ink doing something to turn her against me, but that was no longer an issue. I could tell her everything, and it was safe for her to come back. Unfortunately, revealing the supernatural wasn't an easy thing to do over the phone.

"Um, yeah. A lot has happened. Most of it good. I've reconnected with some old friends, and I've found things out about when I used to live here." I gauged carefully what I said next. "There are some cool things I need to tell you when you get back, but you won't believe me if I don't show you."

"What? Weirder than the fact that you inherited a fortune out of nowhere?"

"Oh, worlds."

She was quiet for a few seconds. "Is everything okay?"

I rubbed the back of my neck. "Everything is fine, good even. It just requires some explanation. Trust me?"

"That's a big ask." Loren didn't sound happy about it.

"Yeah, but it's worth it, I promise. It's practically magical. When you get here, I'll tell you everything, and you're going to love it."

"Okay, I'll trust you this time." She sighed. "I'll get my stuff together along with those books you wanted. Mom isn't thrilled that I left you there on your own, but she agreed that me staying with you for at least the summer is a good idea."

"Hey, you are welcome to stay as long as you want. And don't worry about the books. I don't really need them." I would wait until Loren got back to tell her that my little quest for her was just an excuse to get her out of the house. Fingers crossed that proving the existence of magic would cancel out any rage she had.

"Oh no, you made a big deal about them, you're getting your books."

My shoulders slumped in acceptance. "Yes ma'am."

"Okay, so I'll get things together and see you in three days. Does that work for you?"

"Works for me."

"And you'll check in every day to let me know you're alright?" God, Loren sounded so much like her mother sometimes.

I rolled my eyes. "Yes."

"Okay, be careful."

"Bye." I tapped the end button, and some of the guilt in my stomach lifted a little.

"Is that a good idea?" Red asked as I re-entered the room. Oh, right. Super hearing. Had everyone heard that? Ink looked confused, so maybe not him. At least I wasn't the only one.

"Telling Loren everything? She's my best friend." I shook my head. "I need to tell her, and she deserves to know."

"Well, I hope she's resilient. She'll need to be if she's going to hang around with us." Crow leaned back in his chair at the little kitchen table.

"She'll be fine. Loren's stronger than I am," I said.

189

"You don't give yourself enough credit." Red was busying himself with the coffee pot.

"You've always been extremely strong," Ink said. He was seated at the table, having an unfriendly staring contest with Rat.

"You don't know me." I dropped into one of the chairs. "I was a little kid when you last saw me and a lot can happen in ten years."

"I've only known you for a few days and I think you're plenty brave. Not many people would have the guts to stand directly between Tommy and his prey." Rat tapped her fingertips on the table.

"You stood up to the Bloody Bones?" Ink raised his eyebrows, managing to look both impressed and unhappy.

"I was pretty sure he wouldn't hurt me." I looked at the table to avoid everyone's eyes.

"Pretty sure?" The volume of Ink's voice rose, and I glanced up to see the brown in his irises drown in scarlet.

"Let it go, man. It's already done." Crow put a hand on his shoulder and winked at me. "She thought she could get him to spare my ass, and it turns out she was right."

"It figures that you would be the one to lead her into doing something dangerous." Ink glared at the shapeshifter with narrowed eyes. "You always did like getting her into trouble."

Crow removed his hand and frowned. "You know, I asked for you to be brought back in. I'm already beginning to regret it."

"Stop it, everyone! Stop being stupid." I slapped the table.

"That might be impossible." Rat snickered, and didn't acknowledge when Ink glared at her. Crow shrugged, impervious to the insult.

"I know things aren't ideal right now. Everyone's stressed out. Hell, I'm stressed out, but things are never going to normalize if we're picking at each other. Please stop, for my sake."

Crow put up his hands. "I'll play nice."

I nodded, then looked at Ink. He stared at his hands for almost a full minute before he looked me in the eye. It wasn't a challenge, more like a calculation. Finally, he let out a breath and his shoulders slumped.

"Alright. I'm sorry. From now on I'll try not to start things." As he rubbed the back of his neck, I had a nagging feeling that he wasn't completely sincere. Oh, I thought that he thought he meant it, but he didn't seem committed. There was a chance I was wrong. After all, I didn't really know him.

"Coffee's ready," Red said. His bushy eyebrows were arched in quiet amusement. At least one of us was having a good time.

"Let's take it to my room. I want to watch some comfort TV and I don't trust you lot without me." I stalked over to the counter and began doctoring my coffee with short, angry movements.

"So, what are you into watching these days?" He tried to sound casual, but Ink's voice was stiff. Points for trying, anyway. "I don't imagine you're into cartoons anymore."

"Depends on the cartoon, but right now I'm into British detective shows."

Crow wrinkled his nose. "Well, that's, um, quirky."

"Screw you," I said, flatly. I'd been teased enough about my television choices by Loren. "I like it and it's what we're watching."

"So, this is at least how things used to be." Ink sounded amused. That was good. Maybe it was the echoes of an eight-year-old me, but I hated seeing him unhappy.

While they got their drinks, I went to the door and whispered, "House, please take me to the bedroom."

Crow laughed. When I glared at him, he shrugged. "What? It's cute when you're polite to inanimate objects."

Not pouting was an effort. "Yeah, well I'm not entirely sure it's inanimate, so I'd rather be safe than sorry. Also, am I the only one here without super hearing?"

Knowing looks were exchanged and Rat smacked her lips. "Pretty much."

"Excuse me, my hearing is human normal." Ink frowned at her. "Not everyone is a boogie or a shapeshifter. You don't know what I can do."

"Yeah, but I do, and I distinctly remember your senses being almost as good as mine." Crow crossed his arms.

Ink smirked. "Your arrogance strikes again. The Sidhe made me a charm for enhanced senses. We both used them, and you never noticed."

Crow's mouth opened, then closed. He smiled and shook his head. "I hate to admit it, but you got me. What else were you faking?"

"Not half as much as you were, Bird." Ink's jab was playful. There was the ghost of a friendship there.

"Hey, I was more honest with all of you than I am most people." Crow pouted, then laughed at the incredulity on Ink's face.

"And how honest have you been with me?" I asked, hands on my hips. My assumption was not a lot, but I didn't hold it against him. Crow gave the impression that he lied like he breathed, and couldn't stop doing one any more than the other.

"Any lies I've ever told you were either for your protection or amusement." He made an X over his chest. "Cross my heart."

"Well, I believe that you believe that." I rolled my eyes and opened the door. My bedroom was waiting and I stalked in to put on my current favorite show. It was an odd couple detective agency of a lady chemist from a noble English family and an ex-Texas Ranger solving murders in London. My friends followed me in and settled down to watch.

Five minutes into the episode Crow said, "So the father did it."

"Have you seen this before?" Red raised an eyebrow.

"No, but it's obvious that he did it." The shapeshifter slurped his coffee with his little finger sticking out in mockery of the main character. "Are they all this easy to solve?"

"Well, yes," I admitted, "but you don't watch it for the mysteries. You watch it for the character development."

"They'll misunderstand each other for a few episodes until they kiss, and then they'll be a couple. It's not exactly complex, and it's been done a million times." Ink at least had the grace to sound apologetic about teasing me.

I pressed my lips together. "Okay, fine. We'll watch something else so you leave my poor show alone. How about a movie?"

"Oh, something with explosions." Rat nodded her head.

I sighed. "Mindless violence it is."

She cheered.

Chapter 25: The Ignoble Death of Spring-Heeled Jack

Someone was yelling. I shot up in bed, half panicked while I whipped my head back and forth, looking for the source. It took me a moment to figure out through the haze that the shouting was outside my room.

After watching the movie, I laid down for a nap. It had been light out at the time, but was dark now. I must have been more tired than I thought. The shouting was getting louder. I scrambled out of bed to stop whoever it was from killing each other. Red and a tall blond man with shoulders like a draft horse were arguing. Tommy turned to look at me as I emerged from my room. He was leaning against the wall right by the door. The other two men just kept quarreling.

I stood next to Tommy and bit my lip. Things hadn't escalated to physical violence, so I was hesitant to butt in, especially with a stranger involved.

"Did they wake you, Addie?" My Champion asked in a soft voice that carried surprisingly well over the din.

"Yeah, but it's fine." I said that, because that's what you're supposed to say. In actuality, I was grumpy. This had better be about something important. And who was this new guy? Was this Sidhe or the Knocker? "What's up?"

Instead of answering, Tommy raised his chin to draw my attention back to the arguing pair. I took the cue and stopped to listen.

"She doesn't need to see!" The blond man bellowed. His voice, while not as deep as Tommy's, was still low and rich. "You don't think she has enough to deal with right now? You were the ones going on about how you had her security covered, so why don't you do your job and take care of it?"

"Jack may not have been much of a fighter, but he was still a boogie. Anything that could have taken him out that easily, that brutally, is a credible threat. She's not a little girl anymore, Incubus. She needs to see so she understands." Red spoke through clenched teeth, his lips pulled back in a snarl.

My eyebrows shot up. Until that point, I hadn't even considered that the tall, blond man was Ink. Technically, I knew he could change his face and voice, but this was beyond that. It was a jarring reminder that I wasn't playing with humans.

I turned back to Tommy. "Someone took out Spring-heeled Jack? As in, killed him?"

He nodded. "A little over an hour ago, all the guards alerted to some kind of disturbance in the gardens. When they got there, they discovered Jack's body and a lot of damage to the surrounding area."

A knot started to swell in my throat, making it difficult to swallow. "I was under the impression that boogies are hard to kill."

"They are. Whatever killed him was large, strong, and has a capacity for violence like one of us."

"So, it was another boogie?" I was unsure whether to hope for this or not. Jack had been a horrible character. Maybe he had enemies that had caught up to him. Maybe whoever killed him wasn't a threat to me. So far, all the supposed threats against me had been misunderstandings, but everyone was so sure that I needed protecting. It could be just their paranoia rubbing off, but I was worried.

"It's possible," Tommy said with a sigh. "We don't know what did it yet. I'm certain that whatever happened, it wasn't one of mine. My court knows I protect this place, and I don't think anyone hated Jack enough to risk my wrath to attack him."

"What else could kill a boogie?" I rubbed the back of my neck, not sure what answer would make the situation less scary, but hoping, nonetheless.

Tommy's reply didn't help. "One as weak as Jack? There are a multitude of things. The pure scale of the destruction in the garden speaks of something with a large physique, but those same results could be accomplished

195

by magic. Boogies are a force within the Betwixt, but we aren't the only ones."

The shouting was growing in volume. Red was insisting that I needed to see the scene to understand the danger, so I could make decisions. Ink loomed over him, yelling that I shouldn't have to see it. He kept reiterating that I was still young and didn't need to be bothered with such gruesome details, and they could take care of it for me. Neither of them seemed to have noticed that I was in the room.

"We should stop them before they start hitting each other," I said. Now, I had no idea how to accomplish that, but we needed to come up with something.

"Oh, I don't know. A throw-down between the Incubus and the Red Cap might be quite a site to see. Their fighting styles are so different, and the situation so unique, I honestly don't know who would win." Tommy's voice was mild and amused. He turned to me with a grin, but the expression slipped a little when he saw that I wasn't smiling.

"Not funny." I crossed my arms. I didn't know what to do about this, but I had a Tommy, so I might as well use him. "Now seriously, we need to break these two up. Help me."

My Champion raised an eyebrow. "You wish to stop the fight?"

"Yes," I said, impatiently.

He cocked his head to the side and considered for a moment. He took a step forward, paused, looked at me with a thoughtful frown, then leaned against the wall again. With a heavy sigh, he said, "You should do it. They will both listen to you. If I do it, things would escalate."

"How?" I asked. My hands flexed by my side in frustration.

"Just try. You can do it. I'm here to back you up if you need me."

I opened my mouth to snap at him for not being helpful, then paused. Why couldn't I just stop it? It wasn't like I hadn't stepped into a bigger fight between Tommy and Crow earlier. This wasn't nearly as stupid a thing to do.

I took a deep breath. "Hey!"

They didn't react to me. My eyes narrowed and my face grew hot. I didn't like being ignored. Rallying, I stalked over to the two men, wedged myself between them, put a hand on each of their chests and shoved. Neither one moved far, but it succeeded in getting their attention.

Red's eyes widened, and he turned to me with a mouth opened wide, as if ready to bite. He saw me then, because his shoulders slumped and his face relaxed. Ink took a half step to regain his lost ground then he stopped when Tommy let out a low, rumbling growl. I decided to take this less as interference and more as support.

"Addie, what are you doing?" Ink scolded, like I was a misbehaving child.

"Stopping you two from doing something stupid. I said no more fighting earlier, and I meant it. And stop treating me like a kid. If there's something I need to see, then I'll see it." I crossed my arms for emphasis and glanced back at Red, who surprisingly was behaving himself.

"I wasn't trying to step on your toes, Addie, but you shouldn't have to deal with this. It's a grisly business, and we are here to take care of the unpleasant things for you." Ink clasped my shoulder, but dropped his hand when I glared at him. Red opened his mouth to engage in the conversation again, but I put up a hand.

"This isn't an unpleasant thing. This is a life. I may not have liked Jack, but he was here because Tommy asked him to help protect me. That means, not only does this involve me directly as a possible threat, I owe it to him to make sure we catch whoever did it." I hadn't intended that last part. It just felt right, so I went with it.

"I understand this is serious, Addie." Ink made soothing motions with his hands. It wasn't working. "I'm just saying that we can take care of it for you. Really, you've been through enough the last few days. You don't need any more nightmare fuel. Now go back to bed and–"

197

I remembered my flashback from earlier, where again Ink had insisted that I go to bed while the grownups talked. Fear and sadness lingered like an aftertaste in my mind. I burst out, "I am not a little girl anymore, and I will not be sent to my room like a child! I'm an adult who can take control of my own life, and you will treat me like that. Now, take me to see Jack."

"B–but–" Ink stammered.

"No!" I chopped my hand through the air. "This is happening, and that's that."

As I turned, I saw Red giving a smug grin to Ink, and I pointed a finger at him. "Would you please not antagonize him? You're going to make him do something stupid."

"I don't make anyone do anything." Red sniffed, offended.

"Force, no. Goad into, yes. Look, I'm not asking any of you to be perfect. I know it's probably impossible, but I am asking you to be better. For my sake. Please," I said.

Conflicting emotions chased across Red's face but finally settled on resignation. "Alright, Addie. For you."

"Thank you. I've just got to throw on my shoes," I inclined my head, then I turned to look at my Champion.

Tommy was staring at me in a way that was half impressed, half amused. As I passed him, he murmured, "Shutting up Red. Now that's something I've never managed. Well done."

Until I was sure whether I appreciated that comment or not, I decided to ignore it. As I ran back into the room to put on my sneakers, I realized that I had just had an argument about wanting to go outside to look at a corpse. Apparently, this was my life now. I shook the thought off because it wasn't useful, and marched out to face a crime scene.

Neither Ink nor Red was waiting for me when I emerged. Only Tommy was in his expected place, still leaning against the wall. Suspiciously, I asked, "Where are Tweedledee and Tweedledum?"

"I sent them to go get some lights so you can see what's going on. Your night vision is probably not as good as ours." Pushing away from the wall, there was an awkward moment where I thought he was going to offer me his arm like a lady at a dance. Instead, he moved in front of me to usher me on to the main hallway off my sitting room.

Briefly, I considered using my trick to just open a door and appear somewhere downstairs, but I was in no hurry. Screw Ink and his assertions that I couldn't handle this, but I had been brave the last few days. It wasn't dragging my feet too much, not rushing to look at a dead body in the middle of the night. Still, the walk was far too short. That was either because someone who knew where they were going was leading, or because I didn't want to arrive.

Discordantly, it was a beautiful night. We walked across the gardens in silence, but the crickets were singing at full volume. They didn't care that there'd been a murder. The moon was gibbous and unobstructed, bathing everything in a faint, silver light and discoloring all the plants. Even at night, the flowers were still in bloom.

Tommy worried too much. There was plenty of light.

My heart was swelling and trying to crawl up my throat. Tommy's walk was slowing a little and I felt we must be getting close to the body. There were fragments of broken brick on the walkway. We made the turn that should have brought us to the wall of red roses but...

There was no wall. There was nothing but a crater filled with rubble, shredded bits of foliage, and the occasional jut of brickwork, scarred by claw marks so wide it would have taken both my hands to cover them. In the middle of it all was a flattened mass covered in a piece of material that looked like once upon a time it might have been white.

It took me a moment to realize that this was the wall of red roses. Rather, what was left of it. Tears welled up as I mourned the poor flowers. They had been so beautiful, so carefully tended, and so well-loved. I had no memory of them from my childhood. They and I had no past together that I knew of, but I had liked them. Not younger me, but me as I was now. I had thought about putting in an alcove with a bench off to one side where I could come out to read.

It was one of those idyllic plans that would never have happened. The weather would have been too hot, or too cold, or too wet. Maybe there would have been too many bugs. Maybe I would have only ever done it once, on one perfect day, then never again. That choice was now taken away from me, because even if the wall could be rebuilt and the roses re-planted, it would never be the same. My eyes drifted to the pile... no, the body in the middle of all the destruction.

I hadn't liked Jack. I'd been disgusted and a little frightened, but then again, I hadn't really known him. Maybe he had just been too broken to communicate effectively. Maybe it was hard to give a good first impression when you are being forced to play bodyguard to some stupid girl you'd never met before by people who loathed you, and you were just a child in the body of a monster.

It occurred to me that I might not be upset about roses.

Ugly, yellow, artificial light sliced through the night, killing my night vision. I had to blink several times before my eyes started to adjust. The greater detail and colors I could see now were not a kindness; the brown of the smashed brick, the deep greens of the shredded plants, and all the rose petals strewn around, still in all the shades of red from almost white to almost black. In the too-harsh light, the roses from the middle weren't blood-red. At least, they weren't boogie-blood red. Not dark enough.

Red was the one illuminating the carnage. I wasn't sure what he was holding, but it looked like some kind of electronic cannon. Looking at him, because I wasn't quite ready to look at... Jack, I asked, "What is that? The world's biggest flashlight?"

"Basically." Red's shrug caused the beam to bob over the scene, making shadows slither among the debris. "The Incubus is looking for something a little more stable. I thought this would be a good start. Oh, Tommy, I ran into the Crow. He's combing through the woods looking for signs of our intruder."

"Murderer," I said, dully. My stomach felt cold.

"Beg your pardon, Addie dear?" Red asked, tilting his head in that way that didn't seem quite human sometimes. The light swayed again, splashing amber across Jack's coat.

"An intruder is someone who sneaks into a place and steals something, or breaks something, or spray paints dicks on walls or some shit like that. This is murder." My voice was getting louder, starting to tremble.

"Are you alright, Addie?" Tommy's eyebrows shot up.

"I know you guys didn't like Jack any more than I did. Hell, you may have hated him. I don't know and I don't care either. He was alive and here doing the job you made him do. Now he's dead. Show a little freaking respect, for the life lost if not the person."

My feelings were fluttering through me like butterflies in a tornado. One thing I was certain of though, is that I was getting mad. Not the fast, flailing anger I usually felt, either. This was something deeper, stiller. It was a cold ball in my stomach, more akin to fear than temper. My hands were clenched so hard they were starting to shake.

To answer Tommy's question to myself, no, I was not okay. I was freaking out and I needed to calm down. I closed my eyes and started to count. Breathe and count. My hands ached as I finally relaxed them. My palms felt bruised.

"I'm sorry, Addie." It was Tommy that spoke, but both he and Red were staring at me, near identical looks of calculation on their faces. "I understand, and we will show a little more reverence. You're right. No matter what we felt for him, a soldier of ours has fallen and we will give the gravity of the situation its due."

"Thank you." The cold in my stomach dulled, but didn't go away. I jerked my head to indicate the body. I wasn't ready to see it, but I probably never would be. So I took the old cliché advice and ripped the Band-Aid off all at once. "Keep the light steady on him, Red."

Picking my way through the brick and vines was harder in the semi-light than it had been in the dark. Tommy hovered behind me like he was waiting to catch me when I inevitably fell, but my balance didn't fail. Finally, I managed to end up next to the bloody mess that had been Spring-Heeled Jack.

It didn't look like a person. It didn't look like much of anything. The closest thing my brain could come up with was that someone had taken a couple of hundred pounds of raw, bone-in beef ribs, tied them up in Jack's clothes, and smashed them thoroughly with a sledgehammer. Add a few dozen buckets of pig's blood straight from the set of Carrie over the entire mess, and that would be about right. The next moment I saw a fragment of his skull nearby. It was part of the eye socket, with bits of flesh smeared with something gray, and maybe that was a bit of scalp and blood-matted hair and oh, hey, that was a tooth...

My stomach contorted and I stumbled backward. Forcing myself to breathe again, I retreated to a remaining section of wall and braced against it. One hand clutched the rough end of a broken brick to keep from falling, while the other slapped over my mouth to keep from throwing up. It was the smell. It was too much. The stench of blood, feces, and roses.

It took a lot of willpower to stand up straight and put my hands by my side. Tommy was hovering next to me, radiating concern. I took a deep breath. Then another. The nausea faded, but I could feel one of those flashback memories pounding at the back of my eyes. Steeling myself, I pushed it away, and was surprised that I could. I couldn't afford the distraction right now.

Taking one more breath, I swallowed hard and said in a voice that sounded a little reedy, even to my ears, "So that's what beaten to a pulp looks like."

Someone started to laugh, but the sound was cut short. Tommy's large hand settled on my back, awkwardly stuck in a motion between a rub and a pat. I'd bet he didn't do a lot of comforting, and wasn't sure which one to supply. "Are you alright?"

"God, Tommy, it... it's so bad. How do you do that?" I turned to face him. The hand that had been on my back dropped away. "I mean, physically, how could someone even do something like that? He's just... just little bits, and the garden... so much destruction. How could someone not hear this? Didn't they hear the walls breaking? Didn't they hear Jack scream?"

"It was over quickly, Addie," Tommy said, softly. "We heard the crash and were here in seconds. The intruder, the killer, was already gone. Jack didn't have time to scream."

"On the plus side, it does mean that he didn't suffer at all. Even if he didn't deserve..." Red hesitated as he saw my face. "Well, it wouldn't have hurt much. Too fast."

I rolled my eyes and said, "Thanks for the self-editing. I know it isn't easy and, as weird as it seems, that does help. Still, Tommy, I need to know. What could do this?"

Embarrassment flooded his face. "I'm sorry to say, Addie, I just don't know. There are clues; the fact that there is no smell other than roses and death, the speed and amount of destruction, and all the trauma shows both blunt and claw damage. It all points in every direction at too many people. We will find out who did this, and they will pay. Don't worry Addie. I won't let them hurt you."

"Can you stop something that could do this?" I gestured at the surrounding ruin.

"I can and I will." The absolute confidence in Tommy's voice was soothing. Not because it sounded like heroics, but because it sounded like simple truth.

"Well, I'm not getting any more sleep tonight," Or ever again, I added to myself with a sigh. "And I don't know anything about CSI to help with any of this. Let's all go to the kitchen and get some coffee. It's going to be a long day."

"You drink a lot of coffee," Red said, probably intending to tease.

"Yeah, I figure I'll develop a caffeine habit now, before I'm old enough to drink. That way I don't become an alcoholic later."

No one laughed. That was okay. It wasn't funny.

Chapter 26: Making a Stand

Tommy, Red, and I went to the kitchen. Rat was there, grinding coffee beans. I wondered if her being there was a coincidence or if someone had called her. We gave each other weak smiles and I went to sit at the table. The outside door opened and Ink and Crow walked in. Neither looked happy, but while Ink was sulking, Crow was grave.

I was debating calling Loren and telling her not to come at all. It was more dangerous than I thought. Unfortunately, that was the fastest way to guarantee she would come straight back. I had a couple of days to figure out how to make things safe enough for her. It would have to do.

"It would have been nice to know that you had already returned to the house before I hauled those flood lights out to the garden." Ink's smile was almost a snarl.

"Ink," I said without heat, but fortunately, the warning was enough. I couldn't deal with him right then, I just didn't have the energy. He dropped his head and chose a bit of empty wall to stand by.

Crow fell into the seat next to me at the little kitchen table. "I surveyed the area around the house. The only movement I saw was your boogies scrambling like ants, so unless it was one of them—"

"It wasn't." Tommy glared at the shapeshifter. Crow shrugged, unaffected by the death stare. I almost missed my magical link with him that let me know what he was thinking. With it, I would know if he was actually unafraid.

My eyebrows furrowed. "You know, he brings up a good point. How do you know it wasn't one of your guys?"

Tommy took a deep breath. He didn't seem happy about the question, but he answered. "I hand-picked the people I have guarding this place. They wouldn't be here if I didn't feel I could trust them to behave to a certain extent. Besides, I don't think that any of them had a grudge against Jack."

"He annoyed everyone. Not enough to kill him, though," Rat said.

"I almost wish it was one of them." Red sighed. "As it is, there are a good number of creatures in the Betwixt that are suspect."

"There are ways to narrow down the search. I have tracking magics—" Crow began, but Tommy interrupted.

"You are an adequate tracker, but whoever killed Jack went straight into the Betwixt. The methods to trace someone across the worlds are not simple, and I haven't heard that you have that level of skill. " Dagger looks were exchanged over the table between them. Only a slight tightness around his eyes betrayed any fear from Crow. Was I the only one who saw it?

"Give me time and I can find anyone, anywhere," Crow said between gritted teeth. "I would have thought that the great Tommy Rawhead and Bloody Bones could say the same."

Tommy sneered. "I could, but unlike you, I am more focused on protecting Addie. Until we can assess whether or not this threat is aimed at her, I do not intend to leave her long enough to go hunting."

"You aren't the only one who can protect her, you know," Ink grumbled.

"Really, Incubus?" Tommy's eyebrows rose in mock surprise. "Because I would love to hear from one who has done her more harm than anyone else in this room. How would you safeguard her?"

"I never hurt her!" Ink slammed his hand against the wall. The red flecks in his eyes sparkled menacingly.

Tommy's low, rumbling chuckle filled the room, but there was no humor in it. "Do you think so? Your little stunt may have cost her memories for good, and you never hurt her?"

As Ink was about to reply, I lost it. I'd had to wake up to deal with a dead body and was in the mood for no one's crap. At the top of my lungs I shouted, "Alright, that's enough! I have had it with all this stupid little infighting bullshit! There's a murderer running around out there, so I'd think you'd all have something more crucial to focus on. No one is the enemy here. I'm not sure why everyone is bickering. Is it some kind of weird, childish fear of favoritism? If so, don't worry. I'm equally pissed at all of you right now. The next person who starts something is getting kicked out on their ass. Understood?"

"How do you plan on doing that, exactly?" Ink turned a stern eye on me. A look I'd seen on plenty of teachers' faces when I was young, saying I was a silly child making silly claims.

"I'll have Tommy do it. I think he'd be more than happy to." I met his garnet glare with mine.

"Absolutely." My Champion crossed his arms.

Crow asked, "And if he's the one who starts it?"

"Then I'll kick him out, personally." I crossed my arms.

"Do you truly think you could?" The boogie grinned. It was an amused, friendly smile, but there was something about it that reminded me that beneath the pleasant human facade, Tommy was a predator. I don't think he meant it as a challenge, but as he met my eyes and studied me, waiting to see what I would say, I took it as one.

In a moment of insanity, I looked into Tommy's eyes and answered him. "Absolutely."

He went quiet and contemplative. No one spoke as we continued our staring contest. Finally, his grin dimmed to an almost demure smile and he dropped his eyes.

There was a gentle nudge at my elbow, and I turned to see Rat, touching me with the back of her hand. She was holding a mug and asked quietly, "Cream and sugar?"

"Um, yeah. I'll get it." I stood up and went to go fix my cup, trying not to think about what I just did.

The silence remained thick for a few more seconds, before Crow said hesitantly, "The magical experts we called should be here anytime now. I know the Sidhe has a way of tracking a killer wherever they go, even across worlds, as long as he has the body. The Knocker surely has similar tricks. I say… I propose that we just keep things secure until they get here."

"That does sound like the best option." Tommy agreed with only a hint of reluctance.

"Okay." I poured milk into my mug, relieved that no one called what may or may not have been a bluff on my part. Even I wasn't sure. "So we wait for the experts. That's great. I'm going to get a snack and go back to my room. Come and get me when they get here."

"Someone should stay with you as a precautionary measure." Tommy rose from his chair.

"Awesome." I couldn't keep the annoyance out of my voice. "Rat, come on."

"Why on earth would you choose to take her with you?" Ink asked, mortified.

"Because she's the only one I'm not pissed at for fighting," I answered sweetly, then turned to Rat. "Come on, we're bringing coffee. Did the groceries get here? Cool. I'm sure there's some kind of portable junk food in here."

Rat grinned widely and scrambled off through the kitchen. She quickly procured a bag of chips and another of sandwich cookies before following me. No one questioned again as I reached the door and quietly mumbled for the house to take me to my bedroom. When I shut it behind Rat and her loot, the ball of tension in my stomach let go a little. Maybe it shouldn't have, but this room felt like it belonged to me, like it was safe.

"You okay?" Rat dumped her armload of goodies on the empty table.

"Yeah, it's just a little much, you know?" I leaned against the door like I could barricade it from the outside world.

"Not really." She leaned over the table and drummed her fingers on the wood while she laughed at me. "I mean, there's a lot to choose from. Are you referring to dealing with the most sexualized predator in the Betwixt acting like a stodgy older brother? Or backing down the King of the Boogies with a look? What about the dead body lying out in the garden?"

I spared her a sour glance. "Yes. All of it. I am so far out of my depth here it's not even funny."

"Oh, I don't know about that." Rat opened the bag of chips and stuffed a few into her mouth. When she spoke again a few fragments flew out and I grimaced. "Sure, you got thrown into the deep end, but you appear to be swimming just fine."

"I have no idea what I'm doing," I reiterated.

With a dramatic sigh, Rat wiped her hands off on her pants. "You are under some strange illusion that someone, hell, anyone does. Come on. I think I saw some consoles in here. We'll find something for two players, so I can kick your ass."

"Are you allowed to beat your queen?" I smiled against my will.

"I am only willing to throw the game if you are willing to admit you had to order me to lose." She smirked with her nose turned up.

"Bring it, Ratty." When I won the first game I couldn't swear that she wasn't letting me win. She said that she wasn't, but I wasn't sure I believed her. The overly sweet sarcasm in her voice convinced me that whether she threw it or not, she was definitely screwing with me.

Chapter 27: Reunions

A couple of hours later there was a soft knock at my door. By then, Rat and I had gotten tired of video games and were playing cards at the round table.

I looked up from my pitiful hand. "Come in."

Red opened the door, just enough to peek through like he was afraid I was going to throw something at him. An hour ago, this might have been the case, but I had calmed down quite a bit. I smiled and put down my cards. He took the invitation and stepped into the room. "I was just coming to tell you that the experts are here, and to ask you to speak alone for a moment."

Rat and I exchanged glances as I weighed the wisdom of it. In the end, her expression gave me no insight and with a sigh, I nodded to her. Gracefully, she rose to her feet like a marionette lifted by strings and left. Red came forward, hesitancy threaded through his posture.

"Besides retrieving you, I came to apologize. You were right, the bickering was inappropriate and I should have known better. We're all feeling insecure right now and it makes us lash out."

"It makes you all stupid," I said a bit more harshly than I intended.

"Well," Red lingered ruefully on that word for a moment. "Lashing out is rarely smart. It rather denotes that one is being illogical and can't think of anything useful to do. I'm sorry. For the better part of ten years, I've looked after you. I watched you grow up, but you never knew me. Finally, we get to meet properly, and I have the chance to introduce you to the life you were always meant to have, then your old court shows up out of nowhere."

"So I was right? All this is about jealousy." I shook my head and crossed my arms as I leaned back in my chair.

"Maybe a little. Well-intentioned or not, the Incubus's bumbling did you harm, and the Crow is an unknown quantity at the best of times. He's the villain of the story more often than he's the hero. You accepted them just as easily as you did me. It grates, and I'm sure it's only worse for Tommy, who shares a connection with you. I imagine it's a similar feeling for your old court when they see you with us. We are boogies of the highest order and most of the Betwixt considers us the biggest villains of all." Red took a tentative step forward and put his hands flat against the table. He closed his eyes and let out a long breath. When he opened them, his shoulders drooped and he smiled wryly. "They only recently discovered you weren't dead. It would be quite a shock. They love you, and it has to be hard to see you with us. I am not unsympathetic, but I'm not good at making peace. For you though, I will find a way."

"Well, um, thank you," I stammered, unsure how to deal with such an honest apology. Neither honesty nor apologies had played a major part in my life. Well, any life that I remembered. "I appreciate it."

Red held out an arm. "Allow me to escort you to the foyer?"

I pushed to my feet and looped my arm through his. "Well, it'll be a short walk."

He rolled his eyes, playfully. "Perhaps for you, my dear, but the house doesn't hear my commands. It took me a good five minutes to get here from the front door, and I move fast."

We both laughed. I asked the house to take us to the foyer and when Red opened it, we came out in a small hallway. I was momentarily confused, as I stepped through to see where the house had taken us. All became clear as I looked to the left and saw the prismatic lights on the cream walls of the foyer a short distance away. Thanking the house, I pulled Red into the hall to head toward the sound of agitated male voices.

Tommy was in what I was coming to think of as his customary pose of leaning against the wall with his arms crossed, not engaging in the argument that was brewing between Ink, Crow, and one of the two newcomers. My two friends stood shoulder to shoulder, so I couldn't see who they were arguing with. The other man in the room was keeping his distance from the fight, but even if he had been standing in the middle of it, he would have been hard to miss.

The thinnest person I had ever seen was off to the right of the squabbling group, watching like they were an interesting documentary on television. His skin was a pale shade of beige and wrinkled like an old potato. I wasn't great at guessing heights, but I was betting he'd have to hunch to get through most door frames. The shape of his head was inhumanly long and narrow, making the small, shabby brown hat that sat on the crown of his head look all the more peculiar. His large, protruding eyes were a gray so pale they almost matched the small, round frames that perched high on the bridge of his crooked nose. He frowned at the arguing trio, which was impressive on a mouth that was far too long for his thin face. Like most of the fae men I had met, his modest brown suit seemed perfectly tailored to him. He hefted a massive, faded carpetbag up and down at the tips of his fingers.

Before I could introduce myself, Tommy spotted me and pulled away from the wall. He took a place by my side, opposite Red. The movement drew the attention of everyone and the argument stopped. The tall man in the brown suit turned his head in a long, fluid motion and smiled. Like everything else he did, it was pleasant, but oddly out of proportion.

The man behind Ink and Crow called my name forlornly in a beautifully smooth voice and pushed through them to the front. I had heard descriptions of people being breathtakingly beautiful, but I had never seen anyone fit that description without the benefits of digital touch-ups.

It was strange. I had seen Ink earlier when he'd used his power on me, but I'd still have to say this man was more beautiful. Not more attractive, but more fascinating. I couldn't point to any one thing, either. By human standards, he was tall. His golden hair was in a long, silken ponytail and his eyes were hypnotically blue. All his features were somehow delicate and masculine at the same time. None of those things were why I couldn't look away, and the fact that I couldn't was suspicious in its own right. Objectively, he wasn't any better looking than any of Ink's faces I'd seen so far, or Crow's, or Tommy's. He was... striking. That was the word. Striking.

Elf struck.

It wasn't a full flash of memory, but the phrase rang in my head like a gong. My gut swam with the strange, electrical feeling that I was learning to associate with magic. Looking at the man anew, I saw the spell radiating from him, and the second I recognized it, it stopped affecting me. While he was still handsome, he wasn't perfect or mesmerizing.

In the moment it took for me to break through whatever spell that was, the new man crossed the room and threw his arms around me. He wasn't hurting me, but I yelped in surprise and tried to push him away. Tommy grabbed the back of his jacket and tried to jerk him off of me. The man tightened his grip on me, and we were both airborne for a moment before he let me drop. I staggered when I hit the ground but managed to keep my feet.

My Champion swung him around so they were face to face. The blond man held up a hand. Emerald green fire dripped from his fingers as he bared his teeth at Tommy. Where flame fell, the floor sizzled and blackened like it had been scarred by acid.

"Stop it," I said, realizing what had happened, and that things were about to get much worse.

They didn't hear me. The blond man made a flame-covered fist and swung it at Tommy's head. My Champion flung him away. With a crunch, he hit the wall and the wood paneling buckled under him. Tommy surged forward. Before the man collapsed to the floor he threw out one of his hands and the green fire launched, hitting the boogie in the shoulder. The fabric of his suit melted and the flesh underneath bubbled and hissed.

Tommy bellowed, a sound that started loud, and grew by exponential decibels as he was forced to take a step back. As his foot lifted and slid through the air I watched him slip into his true form, growing and roaring, fully transformed before he touched the floor again. With surprising ease the blond man rolled to his feet and while one hand maintained the green fire the other reached into his jacket. Tommy streaked forward and slammed into the smaller man, making the wall crack again.

This kept happening. Everyone kept fighting and this time it was cataclysmic. Tommy was hurt, I could smell the sizzling flesh, and I couldn't imagine the other man was much better off. Once again it was over a stupid misunderstanding, a hug I hadn't expected. I had had enough. This was going to stop. Now.

Up until now, I had ended things by yelling and getting in the middle. That wasn't going to work this time. The fight had gone too far. I needed more. From somewhere deep in my mind, the part that I had been afraid to touch for years because of the pain, came a whisper of an idea. Magic was mostly instinct. What did I want to do? I wanted to yell and shove them apart again, but make it stick this time.

With no real clue what I was doing, I reached my hands out straight, palms pressed together. Focusing deep inside on what I wanted, I surprised myself by not yelling, but by quickly pulling my hands apart and calmly saying, "Stop."

The sound of my voice echoed off the walls, thunderous and quiet at the same time. Tommy's feet skidded across the floor as he was shoved halfway across the room by the psychic push, and I held his opponent gently against the wall, his fire extinguished. Both were a little worse for wear but alive, and currently staring at me in shock. At least they seemed uninterested in continuing the fight. I wobbled a little, suddenly exhausted. It felt like an electric current had just passed through my body, taking all my energy with it. The magic was gone as quick as it came.

Forcing myself up straight, I tottered over to the nearest wall to lean against it. I took a deep breath and said in my most reasonable voice, "Now, that's done with. Everyone is going to get medical attention, and then we are going to find one of the sitting rooms and talk. Tommy, it was a misunderstanding so I'm not holding it against you this time. You, sir, are new, and don't know, but there is no infighting. I am not going to tolerate it. Now come on. Let's get you two looked at, wherever we do that."

"I don't need—" my Champion began, anger raw in his voice.

"Do not argue with me right now." I pointed a finger at him, scraping up the energy to be mad from somewhere. "I can smell your shoulder cooking from here, and it's making me queasy. Whatever medical attention looks like for the fae, go get it."

Tommy looked abashed, but I didn't feel bad. He was the one who tried to talk back. The stranger with the carpet bag smiled, one side of his mouth curling, and said softly, "Well done, Hwegen."

Chapter 28: Magicians

Medical attention in this case meant Ink giving the blond man, who turned out to be Sidhe, a once over. Ink had been telling the truth earlier when he'd said he had a little healing ability. He had his hands on Sidhe's cracked ribs when I asked him about helping Tommy afterward.

Ink shook his head. There were no glowing hands or anything flashy while he healed the other man. It was almost disappointing. "I can only help with normal injuries. Sidhe used his balefire, and it's highly magical. The Bloody Bone's own healing abilities will take care of it."

I glanced back at Tommy, who nodded in agreement. The burn did look better, the blistered brown patch on his scarlet skin was already smaller. "So you're going to be okay?"

He rolled his shoulder and winced. "It will be gone in a couple of hours. I can't assume my human form until then, but I am fine. That little trick of his is potent, but not lethal. To me, anyway."

"It does in a pinch." Sidhe's eyes were narrowed as he looked at my Champion with resentment plain on his face. "I apologize for your injury, and I thank you for your restraint. I realize you could have killed me quite easily and chose not to."

I don't think I'd ever heard a less sincere apology in my life, but Tommy accepted it with a gracious nod. They might have said more, but there was a slight pop from Sidhe's chest where he was being healed, and he whipped his head around to glare at Ink.

"Damn it, Incubus! Do you think you could be a little more gentle?" Sidhe slammed his fist against his leg. Rat snickered, but no one paid her any attention.

"There's nothing gentle or rough about it." Ink kept his eyes closed while keeping his hands on Sidhe. "I help your body heal at a faster pace. It can be painful. Deal with it."

"Don't be a pu..." Crow's eyes darted towards me and he corrected himself to, "pansy."

The three started bickering, and I decided to leave them to it. I moved next to Tommy, who was leaning against the wall, arms crossed and brooding like he always did. Familiarity was making it so that his giant form looming beside me was no longer imposing. Glancing up, I registered that despite the fact he was shirtless after changing, he was also wearing the brown sweatpants that he'd been in the last time he shifted form. They made me think of a big red Hulk, and once I saw it, I couldn't let the picture go. It begged the question, "Where do your clothes go when you change forms?"

Tommy seemed surprised at my asking, then considered for a moment before shrugging. "Same place the other thousand pounds of me goes when I make myself look human, I suppose."

"And where's that?" I tilted my head to the side, curious.

Tommy was in mid shrug again, when Sidhe answered, hopping down from the table he had been sitting on. "It's less a place and more that it is converted to magical energy. I taught you that once upon a time but it has been a while, and the Incubus did say you were experiencing some memory loss. Although I am pleased you retained your basics enough to manage that little display earlier. Moving us with raw magic was showy, but effective."

"I hardly remember anything. That back there was guesswork, since most of what I can recall about magic is the phrase 'Magic is mostly instinct.'" I found myself crossing my arms, looking like a lopsided bookend to Tommy.

Sidhe asked, suddenly timid, "You don't remember me at all?"

Even though I wracked it, my brain, ever unreliable, provided nothing. I shrugged as my head drooped. "No. Sorry."

It took him only a moment to rally, and then he extended his hand. "No bother then, we'll just get to meet the first time for a second time. I am the Sidhe. Years ago I was your magic tutor."

I reached out my hand only to have him clasp my fingers and place a light kiss on my knuckles. It was awkward as hell, and I was very glad that it only lasted a moment. If he had tried to make it a lingering thing, I would have felt compelled to pull my hand away. Thankfully, he read my discomfort and let me go. The sheepish grin on his pretty face was kind of endearing and softened the uncomfortable situation.

"Um, nice to meet you, again." I smiled weakly at my own stupid joke. Glancing around the room, I saw frowns on the faces of everyone but the tall stranger, who looked more amused than anything else. Feeling that he might have a better grasp on sanity than anyone else here at the moment, I went over to him to extend my hand. "Hi, if we haven't met before, I'm Addie."

"We haven't." With a soft, rolling chuckle, he reached out and shook. It was a very nice, normal handshake, despite the fact that his fingers were long enough that they could have wrapped around my hand twice. "I am the Knocker."

"Good to meet everyone, I guess. Glad you could come and help with our whole murder problem, so, um thanks for coming." It was times like this that I wished I had paid better attention in speech class. Knocker chuckled dryly.

Sidhe huffed. "If I had been called in earlier–"

"Shut up, will you?" Crow rolled his eyes. "We all know how magically gifted you are. We only knew like a day before you did that Addie was even alive. What could you possibly add to that sentence that wouldn't just be you stroking your ego, or you picking a fight for something beyond our control?"

Sidhe's face contorted and I cut in. "Remember, there's a no fighting rule in effect. Crow, you're not wrong, but don't be an asshole. Now, we have a job to do. Spring-Heeled Jack is dead, and I need your help to find out who killed him."

"My understanding was that we were here to assist you in regaining your memory." The Knocker stroked his chin with long fingers. "I am perfectly willing to help in the investigation, but why would you care about what happened to that particular boogie? If I remember, he was quite reprehensible."

If anyone else had asked any other way, it might have made me mad. Disregard for life seemed to be rampant among these people. This didn't sound like a lack of respect, though. This sounded like a technical question, like he was trying to figure me out. So I answered.

"One, he was murdered literally in my backyard. Two, yeah, he had problems, that doesn't mean he deserved to die, or that he doesn't deserve justice."

"Justice?" The Knocker's tone was almost pitying. "And what kind of justice are you thinking of, Hwegen? We are people of the Betwixt. We have no police, no courts, no prisons. Would you order the killer's death? Be judge, jury, and executioner?"

My stomach dropped. I hadn't really considered what to do when we caught the murderer. If there were no prisons, what were my options? Clearing my throat, I opened my mouth and said whatever came to mind and hoped it was good, because everyone was looking at me. "When we catch him, or her, I guess, he'll get a chance to explain himself. Then, once I have all the information, I'll decide what to do."

That seemed to be at least an acceptable answer, because the Knocker nodded and reached out a long arm to pat my shoulder. "As you like, then. Again, I would be more than happy to help, but I do believe that your Sidhe has magic much more suited than I to track down your killer. May I suggest that he do what he can there, and in the meantime, I will take a preliminary look at this spell on you. I promise I will do nothing without consulting anyone else, but I'd like to get a feel for things."

Sidhe gritted his teeth for a moment, then relaxed, seeming to decide that grace was the best course of action. Nodding, he said, "I can create a blood wisp that can find the killer, but I need someone who has the tracking skills and endurance to chase it. Crow?"

He started to rise from where he was seated at the window, but Red cleared his throat. "If you're looking for the best among us for tracking blood, I would submit that would be me. Does anyone disagree?"

Looks were exchanged, especially between the old court. Eventually, Crow nodded curtly. Sidhe's lips pressed tight before he said, "Very well, follow me."

Sidhe spared me a nod as he walked out briskly, Red following close behind. The Knocker looked around at everyone in the room and rubbed his hands together with a smile.

"Well, now that everything is settled, would you all step outside, please? This will not be particularly invasive, but I have to ask some personal questions that Miss Addie may not want you to hear the answers to."

There was a hesitation, and I thought they were going to protest, but then Crow said, "Alright, but we'll just be in the next room, and we'll check up."

Ink looked sullen, but followed Crow's lead. What surprised me more was that Tommy agreed without question. Then again, he had called in the Knocker.

I looked at Knocker, and I wanted to trust him. He had a calm, competent aura that made me feel like he understood the situation and could fix it. The fact that everyone else was willing to leave me alone with him should have cemented it, but it had been a rough day and I didn't know him.

As Crow and Ink left, I swallowed hard, but as my Champion reached the door, I blurted out, "Hey, Tommy?"

He turned immediately, hairless red eyebrow raised in question. When I didn't say something right away, he asked, "Yes?"

I hesitated again, then just let my mouth go, since it had a better record than my brain today. "Stay close, okay?"

Emotions flickered across Tommy's face, all too fast to read. In a voice too soft for someone with a chest that big, he said, "Always."

Chapter 29: Unbirthday Gift

Tommy had to bend nearly double to slide through the door, but he did it with a supernatural grace. I felt better, knowing that he would be to my rescue in a moment if I needed it. I turned back to the Knocker, who was beginning to pull all sorts of instruments out of his carpet bag. When he tugged out a microscope twice the bag's depth, I concluded he bought his luggage from the same place as Mary Poppins and Felix the Cat.

"So what kind of tests are we talking about here?" I warily approached him as he pulled out a large set of tuning forks.

"Nothing painful, I assure you." He chuckled, and flicked one of the tuning forks so that it hummed. "For the most part, I will ask you some questions. Mind magic, especially when dealing with memory, is delicate work. Not something you want to dive right into. The fact that someone already has complicates things. This shouldn't be any more onerous than a normal doctor's visit."

"Why are you getting all that stuff out, then?" I leaned around him to see inside the bag, but he moved it away with a chiding smile.

"Because, I am looking for something in particular. Aha!" he said, pulling out a small wooden box. With a little flourish, he twirled it in his fingers and held it out for me to see. While it was about as long as my outstretched hand, it seemed much smaller in his palm. It was beautifully carved, with the visage of a young woman in an old-fashioned ballerina outfit, laying with her arms crossed over her chest.

"It's pretty. What is it?" I asked, admiring the pure art of the box.

"A while back, I made this as a present for someone very special." He stroked the carved face with a fond smile.

"It's beautiful," I said, unsure where this was going.

"It is true that we've never met, but we were supposed to." The Knocker's voice took on a calm, soft tone, like someone telling a bedtime story. "Once upon a time, I knew your Guardian, you see. I had thought him a friend of mine. The Sidhe was your magic tutor, but your Guardian approached me about teaching you as well, to give your education a more balanced approach. While the Sidhe is a master of the art of magic, I am a master of the science."

I wrinkled my nose in confusion. "What's the difference?"

The corners of the Knocker's mouth curled up and out in a grin too broad for his face. "Practically? Nothing. Two roads to the same destination, but it would provide you with a different way to think. Your Guardian thought it was important for you to have multiple perspectives, considering the complexity and variety of your magic. We spoke at length about it. At the time, I thought some of the questions asked of me were odd, about possible ways you might develop magically, about containment of your power, should there be a need. I never thought he was up to anything hurtful, Hwegen."

"You've called me that a couple of times now. What does it mean?"

"It's just an old endearment. It means something like 'pet'. You don't mind, do you?" His eyebrow pulled up in mild distress and I had to chuckle.

"No, it's fine. I like it. No one ever had a pet name for me when I was a kid. At least, not that I remember." When the Knocker let out an exaggerated sigh I had to laugh again. He patted my hand, but there was a sadness to the gesture. "What's wrong?"

"I can't help but feel that some of this was my fault. I knew there was something odd about the questions he was asking me." He dropped his gaze to the table and took hold of my hand. It was a familiar gesture that should have been awkward with someone I'd just met, but it wasn't.

"It wasn't your fault."

"Perhaps not. I had intended to ask him about those questions the next time I saw him, but it had only been a few days before your birthday. I had been busy getting ready for your first lesson, and wasn't focusing on much

223

else. My plan was to give your gift to you then, but when the news came of your death it lay abandoned on my shelf. A lot of things got forgotten, in my grief. All those strange questions, shoved aside. I'm sure the curse was part of that. I am normally not easy to distract.

"I look back on those questions now and wonder. The spell needed to lock you away would have been complex. Many factors would have had to be considered, some of which your Guardian and I had just discussed. Seeing you today, hearing what was done to you, I remember all our talks. It reminded me of your present, though." With a courtly bow, he offered the box. "Happy birthday, Addie. I'm only ten years late."

My heart squeezed in my chest. Shyly, I took it and ran my fingers over the carving. My stomach also churned a little, thinking of the betrayal of this Guardian I couldn't remember. I managed to give the Knocker a wry smile. "Nah, you're like days early."

He chortled. "You know, the present is inside."

"Oh." I blushed. Why was I always so awkward? Kindly, the Knocker didn't laugh at me, as I fumbled with the lid until I discovered it slid down. It revealed a perfect little woman. "That is the most beautiful doll I've ever seen."

"A bit more than that." Long, nimble fingers plucked the box from my hands. Setting it down on the table so the little woman's feet were pointed down, he moved his hands away with a flourish and said, "Wake up, my lovely."

The tiny eyes of the doll flew open. With an adorable little hop, she descended out of the box. She stood like a ballerina, hands held in an odd circle in front of her. Her dainty head turned back and forth, as if she were looking to the two of us for direction.

"Dance, my lovely," the Knocker said in a hushed tone. The small figure did just that. With no music, she twirled and leaped, arms sweeping and eyes closed like the dancing was ecstasy.

We both watched her dance in silence. After a minute or so, he said tentatively, "It was originally intended to be a gift for a much younger girl, but I wanted to show you. Of course, I can make you something else—"

"No, no," I hurriedly interrupted. "I love her, she's beautiful. She's the best present I've ever gotten."

I meant it, too. Birthdays before my eighth were nonexistent to me. All the ones after that had been... somewhat stressful. Neither one of my parents had been interested in anything I wanted. It wasn't that I didn't get presents, and it wasn't that I wasn't grateful, but every gift had been chosen by them, calibrated to help turn me into the daughter they wanted. Everything they gave me was accompanied by a lecture on how much I owed them and threats that I should start to behave, even when they couldn't tell me what I'd done wrong.

This was a present, meant not to manipulate, but to please. He'd made it for me, and kept it all these years because he'd been sad he'd never gotten to give it to me. I'd never had to fight so hard to hold back tears in my life. Instead, I gave the Knocker a hug. My head only came up to his mid chest and it made me feel very young.

"Well, ah..." He sounded flustered, but not displeased. Realizing I had been a bit forward, I released him and stepped back, feeling sheepish. He smoothed his suit, but his mouth twitched, fighting a grin. "I'm glad you like it. It's a golem doll, so it doesn't need much maintenance other than to occasionally wipe it down with a damp cloth. It can follow simple commands, although it is just designed to dance. If you wish to return it to the box, just say 'Go to sleep, my lovely,' and she will put herself away."

Sure enough, as soon as Knocker spoke those words, the little ballerina stopped dancing, turned on her heel and walked back to her box. As she stepped in, she did a pirouette, turning to face us while crossing her arms back over her chest and closing her eyes. Once again, she was a perfect, lifeless doll. Tenderly, I picked up the box and carefully put the lid back on.

"Thank you," I said again.

"Think nothing of it." With a grand sweep of his arms, he ushered me toward the couch. "But please, Addie, have a seat. I do need to ask you some questions."

So I sat with him and recounted the last ten years of headaches and fits. I went over what few bits I did remember, and what kind of thoughts had been my worst triggers. For the most part, he patted my hand and looked sympathetic, but occasionally, something I said caused a flicker through his face. It looked something akin to rage, but would quickly disappear. It sounded like I was confirming that the information the Knocker gave was used to craft the curse.

When I finished, he closed his eyes and bowed his head. I reached a hand out, hesitated, then touched his arm. "Are you okay?"

With a deep breath, the Knocker raised his head and smiled. "Of course I am. Do I feel betrayed? Yes. Someone I thought a friend used me to hurt you, but it makes no difference now. He is stone, and done is done. What I can do now is try to fix this tangled mess I, however inadvertently, helped to create."

"How hard is it going to be?" Despite some of the bad I knew could come from getting my memories back, I desperately wanted them. My grandmother hated me, my father had abandoned me, and my mother and I had been stuck in a constant loop of disappointment and resentment for the past ten years. Now, we didn't even have that. For all the annoyance they had caused me thus far, I did believe that my old court had loved me. Knowing that for sure was something I needed, especially right now.

"Fixing things the way Tommy originally intended now that the Incubus has meddled may be nigh on impossible." The Knocker was grimacing and I winced for Ink's sake. He had meant well. "However, that doesn't mean that those memories are forever out of reach. They would come back on their own, eventually I think, but there should be ways to help them along. I will need to look into a safe way to do it. Conferring with the Sidhe should help. He rarely agrees to work with others and can be most frustrating, but he is brilliant. Between the two of us, we should be able to come up with something."

Rubbing my thumb slowly over the lid of my present, I asked, "You said my Guardian was your friend. Do you know why he did it? Why he took my memory away?"

Sighing deeply, the Knocker patted my hand again. "As far-fetched as it seems, I think he was trying to protect you. Many nights he would come to me and rave against the way the others treated you. Oh, they never treated you badly, would have died before they did, but they acted like you were one of us. He was concerned that you were not getting to experience being a human, or a child."

"Do you think he was right?" I couldn't stop seeing the severed head of Johnnie the mobster on the pavement.

"I can't say." The Knocker shrugged. "I only have what anecdotes your Guardian passed on to me. If I were to guess, I would say it isn't without a grain of truth. I know very little of children and how to treat them. I doubt your court had a much better idea."

"And Buggy did?" Unsure how I felt, I wondered how the words sounded as I said them. Bitter and confused, or hurt but earnest? I felt it all.

The Knocker seemed hesitant. His fingers twined around each other in a nervous gesture that I'd seen Rat use. "That… is a more complicated question than I feel we have time to go into at the moment. Suffice to say, he knew more of children than many of the fae."

I was about to ask for clarification on why we didn't have time, but there was a sharp rap at the door. The voice of Sidhe came through, "The hunt is on. May I come in?"

I glanced at the Knocker but he just shrugged. Realizing I wasn't going to get any input from him, I decided to shelf the conversation for later and called, "Come in."

The door opened and Sidhe walked in, brushing at his coat. He smirked, pride written on his face. "The Red Cap is on the hunt. My wisp should bring him to the killer in no time."

"Thank you, Sidhe." I smiled at him, hoping he was right and that Red could find the murderer quickly.

Sidhe asked the Knocker, "Have you gained any ground on our Addie's problem?"

"A bit," he said, eyeing me. "Her memories aren't gone, just buried. I believe that her Guardian always intended for the duration of the curse to be finite. But, unless you have some insight I do not, I don't foresee bringing them back as a whole now that the original framework of the spell is broken. Between the two of us, we should be able to gain her access to them, eventually."

"That may be, but the magic of the mind is a bit of a specialty of mine. Maybe I can find something helpful. Sit up on the table and I will begin my examination." Sidhe patted the table like a doctor trying to persuade a child.

He turned away for a moment and before I could move to where he indicated, Knocker sat on the table and winked at me. When Sidhe turned around he stared at the man on the table, head tilted to the side in bafflement.

"What are you doing?" Sidhe asked as his shoulders dropped.

"Oh, I'm sorry. I thought you were talking to me." Knocker's eyes went improbably wide in mock surprise and I couldn't help but giggle.

Sidhe rolled his eyes. "Yes, very funny, but could you please get down so I can examine Addie?"

Knocker stood up and patted me on the shoulder as I took his place on the table. The weight on my chest lifted a little as he sat on the couch and gave me a thumbs-up. It was an awkward gesture, he looked at the thumb like he wasn't sure he had gotten it right, but it made things a little easier.

I ended up repeating everything over again. After retelling my story so many times, the pain of it was starting to blunt. Therapy can be found in the strangest places. It felt like a standard doctor's appointment, with Sidhe looking into my eyes and feeling behind my jaw, then he patiently waited for me to finish before he nodded, like he had confirmed something to himself.

"Now, this may sting, but I need you to keep looking at me." Sidhe's smile was probably meant to be reassuring, but the words made me nervous. He put a hand on either side of my face and locked onto my gaze. Getting that good a look at his eyes I had to admit, they were stunning. At a distance, they were the color of sapphires, but up close, they were a complex design, like a flower with petals that were interwoven with every shade of blue. They reminded me of the wall of roses, only in another spectrum. The hypnotic color made them almost glow and the brightness stung as I stared into it.

Fighting to keep my eyes open for Sidhe

Flash

***

I fought to keep my eyelids from closing, but the burn of Sidhe's eyes was growing to be too much. Tears welled up as I said, "But I can't!"

"Yes, you can, but it's hard and uncomfortable, so you don't want to. It's not an invalid concern, but it's important to mark the difference. Sadly, you have to bear it in this case." Even as he scolded me, Sidhe released my chin and let me look away.

"But why?" I rubbed my eyes, trying to relieve the sting.

"Because to fight an invasion of the mind, you must first engage." Sidhe put a hand on my back, rubbing it for a moment before using a finger to gently pull my face up, so I would have to meet his gaze again. Sympathetic, but stubborn. That was the Sidhe. "Avoiding direct contact makes it harder to breach your mind, not impossible. Try again. This time, look into my eyes, but do not allow yourself to flinch. Feel for the connection that I am forging. Once you feel it, it's just like any other magic, you can seize it if you have the will enough. Now, turn the tables on me. Come on, we'll make it a competition. Whoever loses makes the winner an ice cream sundae."

***

229

The connection was there. I was more observant than I'd been ten years ago, and I could feel Sidhe starting to comb through my mind. Anger spiked as I realized he was in my head without my permission. He might have meant well, but this whole problem started with people messing around in my brain without asking. I reached out with those muscles of magic that I had recently re-acquired and clumsily grabbed the probe in my head. Sidhe instantly stopped and took a step back, releasing my face.

"Ask before you do that!" I snarled. The second Sidhe ceased, the power disappeared, leaving me metaphysically holding nothing. It felt a bit like I had missed a step on a flight of stairs, jarring myself.

"So sorry, Addie." Sidhe dipped his head in apology. The Knocker covered the bottom half of his face with his hand, probably to hide a smile. "I didn't mean to intrude. It was a thoughtless breach of conduct and I apologize."

Because he just apologized and didn't make any excuses, my ruffled feathers were soothed. "It's alright, I guess. I get it. What were you doing, anyway?"

"In simplified terms, I was looking for remnants of the original spell in your mind."

"Find anything, or do you need to go back in?" I tried hard not to wrinkle my nose in distaste, but I don't think I succeeded. I detested the idea of anyone else messing around in my head. Besides, my eyes hurt, and I was trying to get a headache.

"No, I didn't find anything to the contrary of the Knocker's hypothesis. The curse was very badly broken at the end of its life cycle and has wound around you like an old cobweb. It's all tangled, like there were numerous levels from the spell being cast multiple times. Individual memories can be plucked out with some provocation, but removing the whole spell, well, I don't think it's impossible, but it would take time. Maybe years. I am going to skin that Incubus." Sidhe sounded more exasperated than angry, so I didn't tell him to lay off Ink. Yes, my old friend meant well, but I was beginning to understand just how badly he had wrecked things by being rash. I wasn't mad, just tired.

"If we work together, I think we can come up with some way to start cleaning away the last of the spell." Knocker smiled as he spoke, I think trying to appear especially congenial.

Sidhe did not visibly blanch at the suggestion, but there was a new tension in his shoulders. He glanced at me out of the corner of his eye, then forcibly relaxed. "Alright. I need to retrieve some relevant texts from my home and perhaps some other accouterments. Shall we reconvene here in a couple of days and get to work seeing if we can liberate Addie's mind?"

"Excellent." The Knocker clapped his hands and then rubbed them together. "I always enjoy a challenge and I look forward to working with you."

Sidhe seemed less than thrilled, but he nodded at the Knocker before turning back to me. "I have to say, considering you remember none of our lessons, you handled my mind probe rather well."

I shrugged. "Like I said, occasionally bits and pieces come back to me if something reminds me. On top of that, one of the first things I remembered, something somebody told me, stuck with me and has been serving me pretty well. Magic is mostly instinct. Was that you?"

Sidhe cocked his head to the side, his eyes narrowing. "No. I'm afraid it wasn't."

"Huh, I could have sworn..." I let the words trail off as the thought hit a dead end. I thought I remembered remembering that he told me that. Then again, it was important to keep in mind that I had been a child, and not necessarily a well-adjusted one at that. Just maybe, I was not the most reliable narrator of my own story.

We returned to the front hall, where we were joined by everyone else. Sidhe was talking with Crow and Ink, so I said goodbye to Knocker. He leaned over to hug me, and my head tucked neatly under his chin.

"I should be back mid-morning by the latest, Hwegen, and then we'll see what we can do about what remains of that spell." He tweaked my nose, which made me giggle. I'd never had a grandfather, but I imagined he was what they were supposed to be like. "Maybe I'll bring you another present."

I wrinkled my nose. "You already gave me something. You don't need to get me anything else."

"Yes, but that was a gift for a child. You're a young lady now, so I need to find you something more appropriate." Knocker looked me up and down, appraisingly. "I think I know just the thing, too."

"That's right, your birthday is coming up." Sidhe put a hand on my shoulder and I jumped. I hadn't seen him come up behind me. "We'll have to plan something."

"We should deal with the whole murder in my backyard thing first," I said. There were a few dry chuckles and Sidhe grinned.

"Oh, very well. First, we solve a murder, then we plan a party." Sidhe rolled his eyes, but he never stopped smiling. He held out his arms for a hug.

It wasn't that I disliked Sidhe. It wasn't even that I didn't trust him. I didn't think he'd hurt me, but there was something about him that made me just a little bit wary. Maybe it was the mind probe he'd done without asking, but I felt like he needed to be watched. I hugged him anyway.

"Do you think you could get some sleep?" Tommy asked after Sidhe and the Knocker left. We were all gathered in the kitchen yet again.

"Oh, hell no." I rubbed the back of my neck. I didn't see smooshed boogie every time I closed my eyes, but I was betting my dreams would not be as kind. With a deep sigh, I rolled my head once and opened my eyes. "I am going back to my room to watch my show. Anyone is welcome to come too, but no heckling."

"No heckling, no fighting, no being stupid. You keep asking for impossible things." Crow shook his head, but grinned.

"I will watch without heckling," Tommy said.

"Well, you can join me then." I turned and marched towards the nearest door.

Chapter 30: Stone

"So, why aren't they together?" Tommy asked.

"Because she knows her family wouldn't approve." I rolled my eyes. Supposedly, Tommy had been in the modern world for the ten years since I'd awoken him from stone. He obviously hadn't spent any of it watching television.

"But they already don't approve of her career. Why would this be worse?" Tommy played with the arm of the couch while he concentrated on the show. He'd finally healed enough to revert to human form. He'd taken off his ruined shirt but hadn't bothered to replace it. This led to the rather awkward situation of a shirtless Tommy sitting in my room. No one else seemed to notice, so I tried to ignore it as well.

"She's afraid of getting her heart broken, and she's using her family as an excuse." Ink popped a sandwich cookie in his mouth, then looked mournfully at the bag. "We're out."

"But he clearly cares for her." Tommy pointed at the screen.

"But she can't see that, because humans get foolishly wrapped up in their emotions." Crow sighed. "Besides, if they got together too soon the show would be over."

"We need more snacks." Rat sprang to her feet and trotted towards the door. "I'll get them."

"Here, I'll get the door for you." I got to my feet more slowly, exhaustion was starting to take its toll.

"You just want to do your trick again." Crow smirked at me and I stuck out my tongue. He blew a huge raspberry back.

Laughing, I asked the house to take me to the kitchen, opened the door and froze.

Sidhe, burnt and bloody, was leaning against the wall, his shoulders convulsing as he coughed. Red lay in a motionless heap on the floor next to him, blood starting to pool on the tiles.

I threw back my head and yelled, "Tommy!"

My Champion shoved past me and went immediately to Red. With one arm he picked up the small man and put him on the island for examination. Crow and Ink went to Sidhe, who pushed them away. He was covered in blood and soot, but insisted that he was fine.

"Rat!" Tommy bellowed, and she was instantly by his side. "Rally the outside guards and find out if we're under attack. Go!"

Rat was gone, the door suddenly waving open into the night. Crow closed it behind her. Ink was trying to tend to Sidhe, who kept pushing him away.

"What happened?" I asked Tommy over the table. He only shook his head as he focused on Red. I looked at Sidhe. "What happened?"

He drew the back of his hand across his mouth, which smeared the ash and blood. "I was attacked by the Boogieman."

Flash

***

"That girl at school said you were a bad guy. I had to punch her." I pouted with my arms crossed.

"You didn't have to do anything." Buggy bared his teeth at me, his glowing eyes narrowed in annoyance. "She's a stupid girl. Nothing she could say would hurt me."

"Buggy?" I put a hand on his talon. "You're real name's Boogieman, right?"

He snorted. "More or less. Why?"

"Well, she said you hide under beds and eat children." I smiled up at my Guardian, doubt making my tummy sick. "You'd never do that, right?"

"I can't say I ever remember hiding under a bed." He wasn't looking me in the eye anymore.

I moved to be face-to-face again. "And you don't eat kids, right?"

It took him a full two seconds to answer. "You have nothing to fear from me."
***

Sidhe pulled a handkerchief from his pocket and tried to wipe his hands in vain. His voice was gravelly and stuttered with coughs. "He first attacked the Knocker. The Red Cap somehow figured out that I was next and got to me just in time to warn me to throw up my defenses. They staved off the first attack, but it took both of us to escape and the Red Cap took the brunt of the final assault. I'm sure the bastard was badly injured, but I couldn't manage to kill him. The creature is utterly insane and I'm afraid it's only a matter of time before he makes a move on the house. He wants Addie, and he'll stop at nothing to get her."

I whimpered. The Boogieman. My childhood Guardian had been the real freaking Boogieman. No one else was surprised by this, so everyone knew but me. I guess they thought I knew. Not that it mattered. I couldn't afford to freak out about it now, Sidhe and Red needed me.

"He's back from stone?" Crow asked.

"I thought that was implied when I said he attacked me." Sidhe coughed hard enough that his shoulders shook.

"How do you know he's after Addie?" Ink said.

"Because he told me in a mad rant."

"How did he get free?" Tommy asked, still tending to Red.

"I don't know!" Sidhe snarled. "I can only guess that it had something to do with the curse breaking. Anyway, it doesn't matter. We have to prepare for an attack."

"Wait," I said, forcing my brain to start again. "You said the Knocker was attacked. Wh-where is he? Is he hurt? Do we need to send someone to get him?"

Sidhe laughed bitterly, which sent him into another round of barking coughs. "He's dead, Addie. Your Guardian killed him. The Knocker dealt some damage back, though. That's for sure. It's probably the only reason the Boogieman was slowed down enough for Red to get away. We'd both have died, otherwise."

For me, the world stopped. The stupidest thought fluttered through my head. The Knocker was dead? I had just seen him a few hours ago. My mind scrambled at the idea, unable to grasp it. Latching on to a faint hope, I asked, "Do... Do you mean like, stone? Tommy told me earlier that the fae sometimes go to stone instead of dying."

Sidhe shook his head. "No. I'm afraid he's gone. The Red Cap witnessed it himself."

Sorrow for the dead was violently shoved away in favor of concern for the living. I couldn't save the Knocker, couldn't even process that he was gone yet, but I could save Red. I had to. I turned my attention back to him. The first friend I'd found since leaving home was laying in a bloody mess on the island.

His normally pristine gray suit was covered in swaths of a crimson so dark it was nearly black, and long streaks of mud brown. There was a sickening smell of meat and feces. Tommy pressed a towel tightly against Red's stomach. Years of reading murder/mysteries where the injuries were graphically described let me know that his guts weren't where they were supposed to be.

I grabbed his left hand, because his right one looked crushed. "Oh, god Red, I am so sorry. You got hurt doing this for me. Because of me! Ink, you can fix this, right? Tell me you can fix this!"

"Addie," he winced. "There's nothing I can do. He's too badly injured and no one here is a good enough healer to help him. There's no time to get someone who can. All we can hope is that the injuries aren't enough to prevent him from going to stone, so he can go dormant and heal himself."

"Well, do that, then. Make him go to stone," I insisted. Panic struggled to assert itself like a small creature writhing in my grasp, struggling to get free.

"It doesn't work like that." Crow dropped his head. "Either he will or he won't. There is no forcing it."

"No." It was a simple statement of fact. The Knocker was gone. Jack was gone. I would not lose Red too. I took one breath, then another, counting to reassert the calm. Out loud I said, "You can't bring me into a world of magic and then tell me something is impossible."

"Magic has rules, same as everything else, Addie," Sidhe said.

"Screw the rules!" I snarled. I was angry. Angry was good. So much better than afraid. "You are the ones who keep telling me how powerful I am, how special. Fine, I'm a queen. The queen. Tell me how to fix it!"

"We don't know," Sidhe said, unimpressed by my rage.

Helplessness surged, threatening to usurp my anger. Red was dying and there was nothing I could do. Putting my fists on either side of my head I screamed, knuckles grinding into my temples, smelling the blood on my hands as it got in my hair.

Flash

***

The smell of blood was thick. It was in my hair and on my nightgown and on Tiger. My poor stuffed Tiger. The entire living room of the guest house was splattered in red. My Guardian had taken the bodies with him when he left, but the gore and I were still here. I was supposed to wait there, alone, until he came back.

Should I listen to him? The blood was on his claws, after all. I'd seen people die before, but this… this was so much worse. This was someone I knew. I couldn't do anything when he'd killed her. I'd been so weak. But what could I do now? Nothing. All my friends were out of the house for the week of my cousin's stay and even if I thought Mommy and Daddy could do something, they were at the movies. They probably had their phones turned off. There was nothing I could do but sit there in the blood. After all, they were dead. After someone is dead there's nothing you can do but cry.

***

Red wasn't dead yet. There was still something I could do. There had to be. Magic was mostly instinct. The memory hurt. Not like a full-on fit like I used to have, but a sharp pain rang through my head like a bell, and it came with an odd kind of clarity. There was something there, less memory and more impulse. Maybe, if my instincts were right, there was something I could do.

"Sidhe?" I asked, feeling a calm brought on by a new determination.

He pushed away from the wall, wincing as he limped to my side. I was still resolved, but I felt my expression soften, remembering that he had been attacked as well. "Are you okay?"

Sidhe nodded. "I got away more or less intact. I can't say the same for my home."

I wanted to ask what happened, but there wasn't time, so I got to the point. "The night I lost my memory, I ended up in the Quarry. At the entrance, there was a dragon statue. There was a plaque at his feet with a poem on it. Do you know what I'm talking about?"

Nodding again, my old tutor cleared his throat. "It's an incantation written in the original language of the fae. It's not actually a poem. The old tongue is, I believe the most fitting way to put it, is more psychic than a literal language. It appears in the reader's mind how it is best interpreted by them, and their experience. Anyone can read the words, but no one has figured out how to use them. I know. I've tried."

"So, it's a spell to send someone to stone?" I was almost certain, but I had to ask.

"It is, but Addie," Sidhe hesitated, searching for what to say. "It's not as simple as just speaking the words. You aren't hitting a button to play a song, you are conducting an orchestra. You must control the magic. Maybe if I had time to teach you–"

"Maybe, but you said yourself that you don't know how to use it." I squared my shoulders and moved to stand next to Red's head, staring down at a face that wasn't precisely symmetrical. Something was broken beneath the skin. "Do you think he's going to pull out of this on his own?"

Another hesitation from Sidhe while everyone around the table looked uncomfortable. Except Tommy. He looked ever so angry. "No. No I don't."

"There's nothing to lose from trying, then." With a deep breath, I leaned down to whisper into Red's bloodied ear.

I wondered about my younger self and how I saw the world, because the words I whispered were simple. They were a child's rhyme, meant to convey a story that must have been much more, once upon a time. I steeled myself to try to wield whatever magic I summoned, flexing those nonphysical muscles that I was just starting to learn to use.

"Far too weary, far too old. He's gone to sleep in dark and cold. Forsworn, forsaken, all alone. The dragon now has gone to stone."

Sidhe was wrong. It wasn't hard, or even particularly complex. The words told the story, and offered a way to survive, safely entombed. Red wanted to live, so he followed the spell I wove. I had no clue what I was doing, but acting on instincts seemed to be working.

A soft hissing noise filled the air as Red's body went stiff and stone flowed over his still form like rising water. Tommy cursed and snatched his hands back, although it didn't seem to be spreading past Red's skin as the towel and what remained of his clothes lay unchanged. Grinning at my victory, I looked around at the others, who were all staring at me with varying degrees of a look that said I had grown a second head.

"What?" I was suddenly self-conscious.

"Nothing at all." Crow shook his head. "You just proved that none of us know anything. Especially when it comes to you."

"Oh," I said rather lamely, unsure what to say to that. I elected to just stick to the practical. "So how long does he have to stay like this before he's healed?"

Crow opened his mouth, hesitated, then finally spoke. "Addie, there isn't a set time for this kind of thing.

No one I know of has ever been purposefully sent to stone, unless you count the legend of the Dragon, and he's still stuck as a rock two millennia later. Usually, it's years before someone is brought back, if ever. Sidhe, do you have anything helpful on this?"

He shook his head. "I'm afraid in this case, I am as much in the dark as anyone. There is little information available on the subject, and none of it useful."

"Well, okay," I said, only momentarily put off. Rallying myself, I clapped my hands together and forced a smile. "I've already done this once, it can't be that hard."

Everyone but Tommy turned to look at Sidhe, as if searching for confirmation. Sidhe shrugged, expression sour, like he was wondering why they were asking him. My Champion was looking at me, face soft with wonder. The second he saw me looking back, the boogie's gaze dropped to the floor, embarrassed. What did that mean? I shook my head. That was something to figure out later.

I took deep breaths and counted to calm myself, stopping to dissect everything I'd seen and done. I came to an interesting conclusion. Tommy had drawn me to him because he had a great need. I had followed, because I was likewise, desperate. There was no immediate danger now. While I had kissed my Champion to wake him, that wasn't what did it. The kiss represented a contract, his freedom from stone in exchange for his service. It had felt fitting to use a kiss, a princess to her knight. What would fit here?

Tommy was my Champion, so I didn't need another. Wasn't even sure I could have another. I was pretty sure that the contract, exchanging one binding for another, was what brought him back. I turned to the others and asked the room in general, "Hey guys, in this court thing, what kind of positions are there other than Champion?"

"Why do you ask?" Sidhe asked.

At the same time, Tommy answered me. Perhaps he knew where I was going with this. "There's Steward."

"What does that do?" I'd heard of a room steward, but I didn't know how this related.

"They handle all the day-to-day details of your court. Paperwork, finding the right people for the right job, that kind of thing." Tommy moved to my side. "Red is actually a lawyer and has been handling all your accounts, as well as all the new infrastructure for the house. It would be an ideal position for him."

"No, Addie! Absolutely not!" Ink burst out. Everyone turned. "You can't fill your court with these… Monsters."

"Incubus–" Crow began, his voice measured and calm.

"No!" Ink balled his hands into fists while his eyes turned completely scarlet. "These are boogies! Creatures of nightmares and death! We all agreed when she was a child to keep her away from the worst of us, the bloodthirsty ones, the killers."

"Well, if we are going by body count, don't forget your own dead, Incubus." Tommy rumbled, then sneered. "Besides, seeing who has done the most harm here, I'd say being a monster is a far sight better than being an irrational and impulsive idiot."

"That's enough," I said, not bothering to raise my voice. Meeting Ink's eyes, I said, wearily, "You know, Ink, I have backed you through this entire mess. I have defended your actions and your intentions and I still do believe that you did the best you could, considering the circumstances. That doesn't mean that I am not getting tired of your bullshit. You start most of these fights. I thought you were doing better but you keep coming back to this. You're juvenile and you don't think before you open your mouth. While I appreciate that you are trying to help me, it needs to stop. I am not a child anymore and can make my own decisions. I think… I think you need to leave. Not the house, it's too dangerous, but you need to not be here right now. Just… go to your room."

Ink went rigid, then he sagged, defeated. There was a tremor in his voice as he said, "Alright, Addie. If that's what you want, I'll go."

As he walked past me I grabbed his shoulder to make him look me in the eye. "Hey, we will talk."

Nodding, with the forced stoicism of someone trying very hard not to cry, Ink continued his way out of the kitchen. I was grateful that no one said anything as he left. Shaking my head at the necessity, I turned back to Red. He was still doing an excellent impression of statuary on the island.

It was possible that I was being just as foolish as Ink. Maybe Red needed more time to heal, or I was going to do something to hurt him in my ignorance. Leaving him for a while was an option, since it didn't appear to be hurting him at all. Then again, I didn't know that for certain. Tommy had been fading away when I found him, and yes, that had taken hundreds of years, but Red wasn't as strong as my Champion. It all came down to advice given by some unknown person sometime in my childhood. Magic was mostly instinct. Mine was telling me that I needed to wake him up.

One more time, I leaned over Red, like to whisper in his ear. Instead of speaking, though, I reached out with my mind and power. It wasn't hard to find him, although he seemed a little confused. Understandable, considering. We didn't use words and it wasn't as clear as when Tommy and I had communicated like that, but I conveyed to him the deal I had to offer. Service in my court as the Steward, in exchange for his freedom from stone.

Red hesitated.

I did understand, it was a big commitment, tying himself to me. There were no words but he responded. It wasn't that he didn't want to, it was that he wasn't sure he would be best for the job. He was, after all, disliked by the majority and wasn't known to be the most reliable of characters. I could do much better than him.

No, I thought to him. No I couldn't. He had been taking care of things for me these last ten years, even if I didn't know it. I trusted him. Right now, there weren't many people I could say that about. I needed him. If he wasn't sure that was one thing, but I definitely was.

Very well, then, he agreed.

This wasn't the same as bringing Tommy back, I didn't need a kiss to wake my knight. It didn't feel… thematically correct. What was appropriate for a Steward? A handshake? No, I was thinking of the position, when I should be concentrating on the person.

What had Ink said about him? A ghoul who stalked the battlefields, dining on the dead and soaking his hat in the blood. Red's fedora now lay at the corner of the table, abandoned. Come to think of it, this was the first time I had seen him without it. An idea struck me. Red was the Red Cap. The hat was part of his identity. I looked around and in short order, found what I was looking for; a block of wood housing several kitchen knives.

When I grabbed one, Crow asked, "What are you doing?"

The knife pulled out without the metallic 'shink' noise I always expected thanks to television. Everyone exchanged concerned looks. Except Crow, who just asked, "What's that for?"

"Well," I said, dragging out the word, considering. "The plan is to drip some of my blood onto his hat then put it on his head. If I'm right, it will make a connection with him, then I can make the deal for him to become my Steward. That's reasonable, right?"

Crow looked over at Sidhe, who shrugged. "She knows better than I do. She has more experience on the subject, at least."

"Addie's instinct in magic is impeccable. If she says it will work, it will work," Tommy said, sure in his conviction. If only I had his confidence in me. This felt right, but I didn't know. This was a guess. Not even an educated guess. Oh well. Nothing ventured, nothing gained.

As I laid the blade against my palm, Crow raised a finger. "If I may—"

"I'm doing this. Red is going to be a part of my court. Deal with it." Putting my empty hand on my hip, I flexed my hand around the knife handle and glared at the shapeshifter.

He held his hands up, placatingly. "All I was going to do was make a suggestion. If you're going to cut yourself, don't do it across the hand like that. Every time you go to grab something it will hurt and will take longer to heal."

I blinked. "Oh, yeah. That makes pretty good sense, I guess. I'm not sure how then…"

As I trailed off, Crow came around the island and held his hand out for the knife. "Allow me."

Remembering how the cut he had done in the cellar hadn't hurt, I decided to bow to Crow's expertise and grabbed the back of the blade to hand it to him, handle first. Gently, he took it from me and then led me over to where the hat lay.

"Now how much blood do you need?" he asked, holding the knife above my arm, which he positioned palm down.

I stared at the blade, nervous now that someone else was wielding it. Tommy shifted uneasily, but he didn't say anything. Sidhe was ignoring everyone while he tried to scrub his hands at the sink.

I licked my lips. "I'm not sure. More than a couple drops, but not that much, if you know what I mean?"

Crow nodded. "I believe I get the idea."

To my shame, it took an enormous amount of willpower not to cringe as he lowered the knife. I was forcing deep breaths to calm my nerves, when Crow said, "Do you think Red will be naked when he comes back from stone?"

My eyes snapped up to his. "What?"

The sting was sudden and unexpected. The shapeshifter grinned wickedly. "Oh, nothing. Just distracting you."

I stuck my tongue out at him and he laughed. The shallow cut ran across the back of my arm. Crow released my hand and I moved so that as the blood welled, it trickled on to the fedora. Bright, jaunty red darkened to rich garnet with a liquid sheen. Wound still dripping, I picked up the hat. The material was far too wet for the amount of blood that had fallen, and it felt right.

Closing my eyes, I reached out to Red with my mind. Was he ready to take the deal? He would come back from stone, I would bring him back if he would become my Steward.

He was ready.

I placed the hat on Red's head, then stepped back. Tommy handed me a clean kitchen cloth and I pressed it to my arm, even though the cut was beginning to scab already. Crow knew what he was doing.

Thin rivulets of blood began to flow from the fedora like it was bleeding. They poured down, but instead of hitting the table, they followed the contours of his face and neck like he was the center of gravity. I kept expecting an explosion of stone like there had been with Tommy, but no cracks formed. The blood spread to cover Red in a ruby sheen, before soaking in to turn him the color of clay. For a moment, everything remained static, and he was like a terracotta soldier lying on the table. Then with a crackling noise, the shell changed to the texture of sand and fell away. An unmarred man lay on the table, blinking like the light was startling.

He sat up, causing a poof of brick-colored dust. More poured out of his sleeves, and he stared at it with distaste. "Well, that is something I never care to repeat."

Throwing my arms around Red, I cheered, "You're alive!"

Patting my shoulder, he said, "Yes, yes. Thanks to you, yes, I'm alright. A little dusty and in desperate need of a shower maybe, but I am feeling quite well."

"Well, I am admittedly impressed," Sidhe said.

The sound of running water drew my attention to Crow, who was leaning against the sink, grinning at me while he rinsed the blade he had used.

Tommy clapped a hand on Red's back, saying, "I am glad to have you back, old friend. Welcome to the new court."

The last bit could have been a small jab at the others, but without Ink in the room, the reaction was less severe. Sidhe just rolled his eyes but Crow gave me a cocky grin and asked, "So, since you're taking applications for a new court, I was wondering if I could give you my resume? I assure you, I have plenty of experience and the best of references."

Relief was still coursing through me. It made me a little giddy, so I was able to laugh and ask, "What position would you be applying for, exactly?"

It would not have been nearly as funny when Red, Tommy, and Sidhe all said 'court jester' at the same time, if Crow hadn't said it too.

Chapter 31: Battle Plans

Red went off for a change of clothes and a shower. I offered for Sidhe to do the same, or at least to get his wounds tended, but he insisted it was unnecessary. He preferred to stay while we planned.

Rat reappeared from outside and stood before Tommy with her fingers twining so fast that I almost couldn't follow the motion. "They report that no one's seen anything, including they didn't see the Sidhe and Red come in."

Tommy's fist clenched and his face flushed before he closed his eyes and took a deep breath. As he released it, he opened his hands and responded calmly, "Go back outside and bring anyone who's patrolling the woods in closer. We must be spread too thin. I want everyone watching the house. Her Guardian can't cross a threshold without her permission, but he can get right up to the doors if he's inclined. We need to consolidate."

"We need actual guards." Crow crossed his arms.

"Yes, but unless you can produce some right this moment, what we have is us and a handful of boogies." I could almost feel Tommy putting a stranglehold on his temper. He nodded at Rat, who gave me a quick smile before scampering out again.

"Why can't we just bring everyone inside where they'd be safe? It isn't like the house isn't big enough." My stomach felt cold as I watched Rat go.

"We'd be pinned." Sidhe fought to clear his throat. "I don't like being besieged."

I looked out the big kitchen window, but couldn't see anything but my reflection. "Is she going to be okay?"

"As much as any of us will be." The look on my face must have been awful, because Tommy quickly amended, "Rat is resourceful. She'll be with all the rest of my people, and no one can evade like she can."

It wasn't a big relief, but it was the best I was going to get for the moment. I counted silently while I took a deep breath to calm down again. "So, since no one is actively dying, what do we do now?"

There was only a slight pause before Crow said, "Well, we know who's doing this. That's something we can work with."

"Better than nothing." Tommy trailed a finger through the red dust all over the island, face grim. "But that's not enough. We are going to have to formulate some kind of plan, or knowing that it's the Boogieman isn't going to help."

"Can't you defeat him? You said the night of my birthday you fought him and sent him to stone."

"I did." Tommy rubbed his forehead like he had a headache. "Unfortunately that may be a one-time performance. He has more advantages this time. I would bet that he has the same surge of power I gained when I awoke, and he's mad."

"Like mad angry, or mad crazy?" I asked.

"I can vouch for both," Sidhe said, lip curling as he tried to knock the ash from his shirt. "He knew who I was and what he was doing, but there was no rationale in his actions. He kept talking about needing to protect you and about how the curse needed to be maintained."

"It's not unexpected for him to be crazy. Being in stone for ten years could drive anyone mad." Crow shook his head.

"I was stone for much longer than that and I didn't go insane." Tommy raised his chin a little and crossed his arms.

"Yes, well no one will debate that you're special." Crow sneered, but the taunt lacked bite. My Champion glowered, but said nothing. I guessed that counted as getting along better.

Sidhe coughed again. "Addie's Guardian wasn't of sound mind right before he went to stone. He was paranoid and overprotective."

"And crazy is harder to fight than angry." Crow sighed. "Or at least more difficult to predict."

"If he decides to attack the house we will have trouble." Tommy directed his attention to Sidhe. "You repelled him once, could you do it again?"

"With another house built from sacred stone, a pack of hungry corpses, and a few hundred years of creating layer upon layer of intricate protection spells, almost certainly." Sidhe rolled his eyes. "Beyond that, I'm afraid not. But this house is not without its defenses. We should be safe as long as we stay inside, and that will have to work in the short term. Long-term, we will have to think of something else."

"Tommy, when you beat him last time, how did you do it? Could we maybe replicate it?" I was neither a tactician nor a magician, and felt rather useless.

"Last time, I fought him on open ground where he's weakest, unable to hide. Stealth has ever been his purview. I doubt we could lure him out without great difficulty."

"And I know of no way to duplicate the surge of power you were riding coming from stone into Addie's contract." Sidhe picked at the dirt under his nails in short, jerky movements. "What I felt when the Red Cap was brought was amazing. I can only imagine what it was like to experience it."

Against my expectations, Tommy didn't get angry. Instead, his mouth bunched on one side and he said, "It certainly didn't hurt. In an even fight, without those advantages, I might be able to take him, but it isn't at all certain."

"You said Red got a rush of power when he came from stone. Could he do something?" I asked.

Tommy considered, then shook his head. "No. He's temporarily stronger, but he isn't a match for the Boogieman."

"Taking out the Knocker and Red, then on top of that, tangling with the Sidhe's security, couldn't have been easy on him. He has to be hurt." Crow tapped his lip as he pondered that.

"Injured, angry, and insane. Not a mixture I'd like to test myself against. Not with him. Unless you'd like to take a chance." Tommy raised an eyebrow at the shapeshifter, who shook his head.

"No. It would have to be a hell of a deck stacked in my favor before I would even dream of taking him on and surviving, let alone winning." Crow clenched his hands, then released them with a long sigh.

I went to the pantry. It was well stocked now and well organized, so I quickly found what I was looking for. Walking out with a box in one hand and a jar in the other, I placed them on one of the counters and started taking down mugs. While I fussed, Sidhe was talking.

"So we do not have all the advantages we would like. That's fine. We'll just have to make new ones. If Addie's Guardian does put us under siege, the resources available in the house are plentiful and time is on our side. I have some magical supplies and can work on some kind of weapons. Tommy has a small army at his command. The Crow's experience as a tactician should also not be overlooked, and even the Incubus… Addie, what on earth are you doing?" Sidhe's train of thought was derailed by me shuffling around the kitchen.

"Making tea with honey," I said, lining up the mugs. Just in case Red felt like a cup when he came back from his shower, I got down one for him. "You sound a little hoarse, so I figure your throat is probably sore. None of us would be worse off for something hot and sweet to drink."

Sidhe blinked, taken aback. He put a hand on my shoulder to stop me and spoke softly, so I couldn't hear the rasp in his voice. "You don't have to."

"Yeah, but there's not a lot else I can do at the moment, so I might as well try to take care of what little I can. Right now, that means making tea. Hope you like earl gray." With a shrug, I pulled away to grab the kettle and started filling it at the sink. I didn't notice when the tears came.

"Hey," Crow said, putting a hand over mine. "What's wrong?"

I shook my head. "I'm just tired."

"And that's all?" he asked skeptically, leaning over the counter so that he could look me in the eyes.

Turning away from his gaze, I hugged myself. "No. I guess I'm sad, and scared, and frustrated. That's two people dead now, nearly four, and it's because of me."

"This is not your fault, Addie, even a little," Sidhe insisted. He replaced his hand on my shoulder, and this time I didn't pull away.

"I know, but it is because of me. I just wish there was something I could do. You guys talk about me being a queen someday. I want to be that queen, but I don't know what to do or how to help." A small cut on Sidhe's cheek held my attention. It was the least of his injuries, and wasn't even bleeding, but it was indisputable proof of the harm that had befallen him. Because of me. He'd been hurt, and he'd had to destroy his own home to get away. When he pulled me into a hug, I let him.

"You haven't asked anything of us that we weren't willing to give. Everything, up to and including our lives, is yours." Sidhe murmured in my ear, petting my hair.

"But why?" The words spilled out of my mouth. They'd been wanting to escape every time someone professed loyalty or devotion. "I haven't done anything to earn it. I'm not special. You don't know me. Not grown-up me."

"If it's any help, I have to be here. I'm contractually obligated to take care of you," Tommy said. After a second the corner of his mouth quirked up. Sidhe shot him a dirty look, but I caught the joke and laughed. It knocked me out of my sadness just a little.

"Well, that excuses you," I said. With a deep breath, I pushed away from Sidhe and gave him a grateful, if watery smile. "But the rest of you–"

"The rest of us would do it all for the child we remember, if not for the woman we feel a connection to now," Sidhe interrupted.

"This whole connection thing, I don't know. I mean, I think I feel it too, but is it really worth dying over?" I looked around at each of them, trying to divine reason from their faces.

"You literally have a piece of our soul. Trust me, it makes you pretty important." Crow took his turn at a hug and laughed. "But as far as having done nothing, I wouldn't precisely say that. In the last half hour alone you've broken every rule everyone thought they knew about the stone state. I have made an illustrious career of being a rule-breaker, and even I find that impressive."

My laughter wiped away the last of the crying. "That's not a good enough reason for you to throw in with me like that."

"Maybe in your opinion. I demand a certain amount of rebellion from any authority I follow." Crow stared at me proudly while ignoring the brief look of distaste that Sidhe shot him.

"On top of all that, you're brave and compassionate." Sidhe switched to smiling warmly as he shifted his gaze to me. "I haven't known the new you a day, and I already know you are someone I respect. You may not be leader material yet, but I can see what you are growing into and it is worth protecting."

I couldn't think of a reply, so I just hugged him again, then turned to hug Crow. Both returned the gesture. Hugging Tommy was a lot like hugging a post. Even though he tried to reciprocate, his arms closed over mine, light and stiff, like he was afraid I would break. When I pulled back I apologized. "Sorry, I should have asked. I didn't mean to make you uncomfortable."

"No." My Champion took a step back, face half turned away while looking at me out of the corner of his eye. He was slouching more than I thought was possible, and he still couldn't make himself look short. "It's fine. I don't mind."

Normally I wouldn't accuse someone who could turn into a red giant of being cute, but seeing Tommy shy was adorable. I realized that every time I had touched the boogie he had either frozen or shied, but always seemed to be amicable to the touch. Maybe he hadn't had a lot of affection in his life. Being king of the Boogies wasn't the most cuddly job description, after all.

"Now, I think everyone should get a little rest," Sidhe said. "It takes clear heads to plan and none of us are fresh."

"Yeah." I suppressed a yawn that reared its ugly head when Sidhe mentioned sleep. "That sounds good. Don't start planning without me, okay? I may not be able to add much, but I want to listen in. I figure it's a way to begin learning things, anyway."

"A wise decision," Sidhe agreed, "but first, go get some rest. I don't know about the others, but I plan to do the same."

This was a relief since Sidhe still looked and sounded horrible. Which reminded me, "The tea…"

I was going to the sink where the kettle was overflowing, when Crow put a hand on my shoulder. "I'll make everyone some tea. I'll even bring you some up. Just go."

"Don't treat me like a little kid," I complained, aware that made me sound exactly like a child. My excuse of being tired and needing a nap didn't help matters.

"I am not treating you like a kid, I am treating you like a friend who has run herself ragged over an emotional few days. You are mostly human. We're not, and even we're worn out. Go get some rest." Crow turned me and lightly pushed me towards the door.

"Okay, but wake me if anything happens," I said, the weariness dragged at me as I trudged forward. It was like thinking about it made it worse.

"We will. Now go. I want to sleep as well, and I won't feel right about it till you go to bed." Sidhe waved me away, his smile fondly exasperated. With that reminder, a little bit of guilt followed me as I asked the kitchen door to please take me to my bedroom. The others chuckled and shuffled off. I'd just take a short nap.

Instead of getting into bed, I fell into the big recliner in front of the TV and kicked it back… Something clinked beside me and I startled awake. Crow was setting a teacup and saucer on the little table next to me.

"Huh? S' up?" I think I was mostly understandable.

"Shh," he whispered. "Nothing is wrong, I just brought you some tea. Go back to sleep. It'll be warm when you wake up, I promise."

I murmured something that was supposed to sound like thank you. Unwilling to wait any longer, slumber dragged me back down. The next time I awoke, it was with surprising clarity, hearing tapping on glass.

I glanced toward the noise and couldn't see anything immediately. It was late enough to be dark and the night pressed against the windows. I hadn't paid them much attention before. They were old-fashioned, opened inward like a door, and had some pretty metal work around the hinges and handles.

There was a teacup sitting on the little table next to me. I brushed the side of it with my fingertips, expecting it to be cold. The touch of my hand did… something, triggering some kind of magic on the porcelain that I could feel like a static shock. Steam started to rise.

Vaguely, I remembered Crow's visit and promise that the tea would still be hot when I woke up. I smiled at the courtesy, but also a little because the pretty rose-patterned china cup made me happy. I took a sip. It was the Earl Gray I picked out, with just a little bit of honey, exactly the way I liked it. Had Crow just guessed, or had I preferred my tea the same way ten years ago?

Again there was a tapping noise. This time, because a breeze was blowing, I noticed the envelope taped to the outside of the glass near the ornate curlicue handles as it flapped. My eyebrows furrowed. How the hell did that get there? Setting down the tea, I opened the window. The paper was unremarkable and unaddressed. The tape left a small smudge on the glass that evaporated like it was water. Points for a self-cleaning house.

I flipped open the unsealed envelope and pulled out a single sheet of paper. It was stationary from the hotel I had stayed at in town. The writing was jagged and the letters long. Reading the words out loud, my throat started to constrict.

"I have the Incubus and will kill him unless you give yourself up. Come out to the hotel alone and wait for me on the roof. If you do not, you'll find the Incubus's body there by dawn."

The note wasn't signed. It didn't need to be. So many thoughts were racing around my head that they were tripping over each other. Was this really my Guardian? How did he get a hold of Ink? It was impossible. He was in the house and Buggy couldn't get inside, so it had to be some kind of trick. I could prove it.

I raced for the bedroom door. "Take me to Ink."

Grinning maniacally at my cleverness, I opened the door and found only my sitting room. I closed the door. I must not have been clear enough. Telling the house to take me to whatever room Ink was in, please, I opened the door again. Nothing had changed. I slammed the door, thinking maybe the house didn't understand nicknames, and asked it to take me to the Incubus. Still nothing.

My heart felt like it was beating in my throat and panic was curdling my stomach. I wanted to scream. So I did.

"Tommy!"

Chapter 32: Hostage

My Champion burst out of his room in his human seeming. His hands were balled into fists and his teeth were bared. He was by my side in an instant, but before he could ask me what was wrong, I shoved the paper at him. Tommy's eyes narrowed as he read and then turned to me.

"You are not going out there." His voice was as deep as it was in his larger form and full of warning.

"Of course not." Tears were streaming down my face, hot enough to burn while the rest of me was so cold. "But if he has Ink, we have to do something. Please, help me!"

Uncertainty chased through Tommy's face. Resignation replaced it as he said, "Very well."

Tommy grabbed my hand and pulled me into his room. Next to the bed, there was a small square nightstand, and Tommy's phone sat on it, plugged into a charger.

Pulling me around him, he motioned me towards the bed. "Sit."

"Why–" I began to ask but was cut short by my Champion's withering glare.

"Because you're a brave, compassionate girl, who I could see running off to try to save that idiot." Tommy had already begun texting while he talked. "For the moment, I am not letting you out of my sight."

"If I wasn't going to wait for your help, I wouldn't have called for you. I would have just gone." My nerves were raw and my temper was in poor shape. "I would have been there before you even knew I was missing."

He snorted. "Tell yourself that if you like, but stay right there."

Sitting on the bed like I'd been told, I took the moment while Tommy was texting to collect myself. Maybe Ink was still in the house and my navigation ability didn't work when I didn't know where I wanted to go. Even if he had left the house, that didn't mean that he'd been caught.

This was a trap, no doubt, but it remained to be seen if the bait was live.

That was an option that I dreaded to consider but had to prepare for. Ink might already be dead. If he was…

I didn't care that Buggy had been my Guardian, once upon a time. He was going to pay. Now, I was sincerely hoping no one asked me how I was going to accomplish that, because if Tommy couldn't beat him, I was pretty sure I didn't have a hope in hell.

A sharp knock on Tommy's door made me squeak, but he seemed to expect it. Holding out a hand to me, he said, "Come on."

I took my Champion's hand, feeling like I was being pulled along like a naughty child, but Tommy kept his pace slow enough for me to follow without rushing. He led me to the sitting room, where Red, Rat, and Crow were all waiting. Sidhe, who was looking a lot better for whatever rest he'd gotten, stalked in waving a piece of paper.

"The idiot did leave." Sidhe slammed the letter down on the coffee table. "He left a note in his room saying he was going to his stupid hotel if Addie didn't want him in her presence."

Many things to say went through my head, starting with raging about Ink leaving the house when I expressly told him not to, to being hurt that he just ran off like that, to being afraid that Buggy had already killed him. Stupidly, what I said out loud was, "I'd forgotten that he owned the hotel."

"Between all of us in the old court, we owned most of the town," Sidhe said, waving off the question as unimportant even as he answered it. He was right, but I wasn't going to hold myself responsible for anything that came out of my mouth at the moment. It had been a rough couple of days.

"I called his cell phone." Crow looked grave. "I got nothing, and he's religious about answering. I'd say it is extremely likely that the Boogieman has the Incubus."

"I checked with all the perimeter guards," Red said. "No one saw the Boogeyman, which isn't unexpected. The skulker can get anywhere but inside the house, so he could have grabbed the idiot at any point between here and the hotel."

"That means our best course of action is still to stay put until we can build up some strength and a plan." Sidhe made that sound so final, and Crow and Red were nodding in agreement.

"Wait." Panic squeezed my heart. "We can't just leave Ink out there. Buggy will kill him."

"There's a very good chance that he's dead already." Red's eyes brimmed with sympathy as he patted my shoulder. "Even for someone as powerful as your former Guardian, keeping one of the fae captive is prohibitively difficult. The message didn't say whether or not the Incubus was still alive, just that if you didn't comply, you would find him dead."

"But if he is alive, we can't just abandon him." I scanned their faces. Not a one of them met my eye. "Right? Tell me that none of you would just desert him?"

"It's not like this is something we want to do." Crow spoke slowly, like he was unsure of each word's reception. "Who would you send after him to die in his place? You saw what he did to Red and Jack. From what I heard, what happened to the Knocker was worse. Would you send Tommy as your Champion? Could you do that to him?"

I started to cry again. I didn't want to, but it was either let the knot in my throat choke me to death, or let out the tears. "No... but, I... Please, there has to be something we can do. Maybe if I gave–"

"Don't even think of giving yourself up." My Champion growled, then the anger faded as he looked thoughtful. "Although, that does give me an idea. Sidhe?"

"Yes?" he asked, warily.

"How good of an illusion could you create right now with what you have on hand?" Tommy asked.

"Serviceable. I stored quite a few supplies here, back when I was Addie's tutor. I never bothered to remove them," Sidhe said.

"Good enough to fool her Guardian at a short distance?" They exchanged looks, a silent conversation happening between them.

"If I could have an hour for preparation and casting, yes. He hasn't seen her in ten years, so shouldn't know how she moves and talks." Sidhe seemed rather intrigued by the idea. "You're setting a trap?"

"Yes. He'll be expecting Addie to come alone, and my people are experts at hiding. The element of surprise and overwhelming numbers is a fine advantage, wouldn't you say?" Tommy's grin was toothy and wide.

"Could you hide that many?" Crow cocked an eyebrow at a skeptical angle.

"Forever? No. For long enough? If you are willing to come with us and do some of that shadow weaving you are so well-known for, I think so. My people may not be good at guarding, but ambush is a specialty of ours." Tommy looked me straight in the eyes. "This isn't without risk, Addie. Some of us will be hurt and possibly die. I want you to understand that before we go, so there are no misunderstandings. I believe this is the best possible choice available to us, even above staying here. Waiting would give us more time to plan, but it would do the same for him, and I've never been in a good siege. Your old Guardian is mad, and he will strike out at my people and anyone else he thinks will hurt you. If we can catch him off guard, we stand a chance. I think this is what we should do, but I can't move without your word. What do you say, Addie?"

I didn't ask why they were looking at me when they all obviously knew better than I did. I understood. This had to be my decision, because I was the one asking for this to be done, and I had to own it. Tommy was right, too. Even if I didn't risk this for Ink, the trouble wouldn't end. It had to be now, and if I wanted to do more than play at being fairy queen, I had to be the one to order it.

Nodding to the boogie, I said, "Do it."

Besides that decision, I was not needed for any part of the assault other than for Sidhe to cut a small piece of my hair. After that, I was banished to my room to sit with various babysitters. Most of the time it was Red, but when the casting was finished and the troops readied, it was Sidhe who stayed behind with me. He was tired from creating all the magic that made Rat look, sound, and smell just like me.

The effect wasn't perfect, because she just didn't move like me. It was unnerving as hell to watch. Now, my old tutor's job was to let the house guard us and make sure that I didn't do anything stupid like go after them.

It was a risk, leaving just us two in the house, but for this to work, it had to be an all-out assault. Everyone but Rat disappeared into the darkness. I watched her from my window, my exact double, walk timidly into the night for the benefit of anyone spying. She was possibly in the most danger of all, and my blood ran like ice out of fear for my friend.

When she was out of sight, I sat down in front of the TV and pretended to watch my show. Sidhe was seated in the high-backed recliner off to the side, reading a book. Against expectations, it wasn't a tome of magic or anything like that, but a contemporary fantasy novel.

"Isn't that a little silly to you?" I asked, pointing to the elven-looking character on the front cover sporting biker gear and a shotgun.

"Yes," he admitted. "But the writing is good and the humor is fantastic. There's nothing wrong with a bit of silliness, especially after the day I've had."

"I'm sorry," I said for the thousandth time in an hour. "I'm sorry you got hurt, and I can't thank you enough for saving Red."

"Please, stop apologizing. I didn't want to leave that idiot to die, and what happened wasn't your fault." Sidhe sighed. "I think I understand part of the problem. You still think we have no choice in this?"

"It's pretty much what you guys said." I drew my knees up to my chest and wrapped my arms around them.

"Yes, but I think you misunderstood. There is a type of compulsion, but it is only irresistible in the same way a favorite meal is irresistible. We could pass it up if we wanted to, but why? We crave that connection so strong and pure that it cannot be denied. A sense of belonging." Sidhe closed his eyes. "So very few of us are able to form meaningful connections by quirk of power, looks, or personality. We are starved for it. The Incubus, for example, who is immersed in humanity more than most of us by necessity of his diet. Because of this, he doesn't interact with the rest of the fae on a regular basis, and doesn't have much in the way of peers. Getting friendly with your food is never a good idea, so he doesn't deal with humans on a personal level. He doesn't have many associates, much less friends. I've heard that even his twin sister can't tolerate his presence, so you are the only real family he has."

That did explain a lot about Ink. I shifted on the couch to more fully face Sidhe. "What about you and Crow? You fight like you're close."

"Only because of our association with you." Sidhe shook his head. "Before we were brought together by the need to take care of you, I doubt the three of us said three non-adversarial sentences to each other. We only gained any semblance of closeness because I had to work with them on a daily basis. After your… disappearance, we started drifting apart again, although whenever per chance we met, there was an element of kinship, I suppose. A bond over our shared grief."

"Did you miss them?" I asked.

For a long moment, Sidhe stared out the window, then looked back at me, face twisted in a grimace. "In all fairness, yes, a little. Or maybe it was more accurate to say I missed the companionship more than the actual men. I have to admit to being a bit of a hermit on my own. I missed teaching, as well. You were a good student. There had been others, but that had always been a reluctant relationship. You were the first I had ever actually made a commitment to, determined to see you outshine even me in your spellcraft."

"Is that why you came when they called you to help me? To get your pupil back? Or maybe an excuse to see your old friends?" I added the last to poke his pride a little, since he didn't want to admit he cared for them.

He laughed, eyes closed while he shook his head. "A bit, maybe. More that I missed you. Not as a student, but as you. You had a talent in those days for drawing me out of my shell and forcing me to enjoy myself. As a child, you were a pain and a delight at the same time. I was eager to see the woman you've become and the queen you are going to be."

"Well, my mother can attest to the fact that I am still a pain." I laughed mirthlessly.

"Your mother was a ninny." Sidhe waved a dismissive hand.

"That's… true," I admitted. "As for what kind of ruler I'll be, I don't know. The idea of being a fairy queen sounds cool, but practically I'm not sure how this works. Tommy seems ready to march an army to conquer worlds for me if I ask, but I don't really feel comfortable making people follow me. And, other than you all, who would want to?"

"More than you think. There are those like me that believe that the fae need a hand at the reins and would back almost any competent contender to the throne. You are the only one fitting that description. Others would come to you because they want someone to rule them. Many of us feel alone. Like me. Like the Incubus. I have a theory." Sidhe's face lit up with intrigue. "Some of our oldest legends speak of a queen and king of the fae. When they ruled, it was a golden time. Perhaps the reason our kind make such bad decisions now is because we were never meant to. We are natural monarchists. I would like very much to see you on the throne, and will work hard to make it happen. It may take you many years to be ready, but we have that time."

"That's right, huh? I haven't dealt with the whole semi-immortal thing yet." I looked out the window beyond Sidhe. "I always figured that if I ate healthy and exercised I'd be lucky to get a hundred years."

"You'll get used to it," Sidhe assured me. "And I wouldn't have it any other way. Now, since neither one of us can concentrate till we get some news, why don't you come with me down to the kitchen? I'll make us some hot cocoa."

Flash

***

Sidhe held out his hand to me, a sympathetic smile on his lips. My teacher confused me. Sometimes he was so mean and strict, never letting me do anything. Then sometimes, like today, he could be so nice. I had come to him because there wasn't anyone else right then. Ink was arguing with my Guardian and parents, and Crow wasn't home.

I'd opened his study door, remembering too late to knock first, and expected an immediate scolding. Sidhe had looked ready to give one too, but when he saw me, he stood from his desk and came to crouch by my side. He asked me what was wrong and stroked my hair. I told him everything, about how Daddy had said mean things to me and how Buggy had threatened to rip his tongue out and then Ink had gotten involved and now everyone was yelling and saying that Daddy should go away.

Sidhe had held me and shushed the tears until they stopped, then he offered to take me to the kitchen. He'd make me some hot chocolate. Now, he was holding his hand out with a smile. Hiccuping a little, I took his hand and felt a little better.

***

The memory made me smile sadly. "Yeah, I'll be there in a minute. I need to hit the bathroom. Let me meet you there."

"No, I'd prefer to wait. My hearing isn't as good as some of the others, so with only me here to stand guard, I'd like to stay close." He seemed apologetic for the necessity.

I nodded and headed into the bathroom. It had faded to white, like the rest of the bedroom. I considered leaving it that way. Repainting was so far down my list of priorities at the moment I doubted it was ever going to happen. There was a tap at the window and my head whipped around to see a black, taloned hand holding a piece of paper against the glass. I had just a moment to read it before the hand snatched it away.

It said, "If you ever want to see the Incubus again, go to the main hall. Do NOT tell the Sidhe."

Chapter 33: Answering for Crimes

My heart stuttered. The ruse hadn't worked. Ink was going to die because our plan didn't work. No. There was still a chance I could salvage this, I just had to go to the main hall. All the gears in my head were turning, trying to figure out what he was up to. He couldn't get in, or he would have snatched me when Tommy and the others left. Not knowing what else to do, and not wanting Sidhe to get hurt again, I whispered as quietly as I could for the house to take me to the front room. Hopefully, my trick wasn't something that Sidhe could see, or sense, or whatever.

I exited through the door beside the stairway that I had used before. The second I stepped through and closed the door behind me, I heard a shrill chime. I dashed out into the hall, trying to pinpoint the sound and followed it to the black princess phone. I nearly knocked it off the desk in my rush to pick up the receiver.

"Hello?"

"Hello, Adeline." I had heard that voice before in my memories over the last few days, but hearing it in real life doused me in more fear than every nightmare I'd ever had combined. The tone was more reedy, more hollow than I remembered, but the sound was still achingly familiar. With recognition came a shower of memory fragments, raining down like broken glass, cutting me a little more with each one.

Flash

***

"Buggy! Buggy!" I called out.

Out of the darkness, two red glowing orbs appeared. "What?"

"I had a nightmare," I mumbled, biting onto Tiger's ear.

"And?" My Guardian slithered up to the side of my bed, his head, kind of like a blackened bird skull, tilted at a disapproving angle. The clouds of shadow that clung to him curled and whipped around. They did that when he got annoyed. "Go back to sleep."

"I'm afraid the monsters will get me," I said around a mouth full of fuzz.

"What monsters? All the worst monsters of the world are wrapped around your little finger." I looked at him with wide eyes and his shoulders drooped, red eyes narrowed. "You want me to guard you till you fall asleep?"

"All night," I whimpered.

He hesitated, then sighed. "Fine then. All night. Just go back to sleep."

"Buggy?"

"What!"

"I love you."

"I… I love you too."

***

Flash

***

Daddy screamed. I ran to the room and it was completely dark. My dad was only visible by the glow of Buggy's eyes. "What are you doing? Stop!"

"I am done listening to this stupid, ungrateful wretch!" Buggy slammed him against the wall. "Time for you to die!"

"No!" I cried, grabbing onto his leg, pulling against his smooth, bug-like skin. "Don't kill Daddy!"

"Why not? He is less than useless to you, and you'd be happier without him." I could barely see the black talon lying against Daddy's throat, but I could smell the blood as the skin split under it.

"No! No! If you hurt Daddy, I'll make you go away. I'll send you away!" I beat my fists against my Guardian's leg so hard they hurt. Making a disgusted noise, he dropped my father to the floor.

***

"Hello, Buggy." That sounded heartbroken, even to my ears.

"Are you ready to come to me now?" His words were bitter and ended in a wet, barking cough.

Closing my eyes didn't stop the tears that ran hot down my face. "Why are you doing this?"

"Because it has to be done," he hissed. The noise was dry, like dead branches rattling against each other. "You were never supposed to return to this world, these people. You were going to be safe. I was protecting you. I can still protect you. No, I will still protect you. We can cast the spell again. You can go back to being just human. Adeline, come to me and I can make it happen!"

"I don't want to go back to just being human." I pressed my empty hand against the desk as I fought to stay still. I still couldn't open my eyes. "You stole my life away from me. You took my friends, my memories, my magic, and... damn it, Buggy, you took my future! Do you have any idea what it was like? Being alone with my parents? Daddy hated me so much that he abandoned me. Mom has been hell-bent on controlling my life, trying to make me into the perfect daughter she always wanted me to be. For ten years, I had to live with the pain of that spell you put on me. Every time I tried to think of the past, every time something reminded me of this life, it felt like my brain was being torn apart. Why would you do that to me, Buggy? Why would you hurt me like that? I thought you loved me. I thought you loved me like I loved you!"

He was quiet for a long moment, then he began, "It was necessary–"

"Necessary? What was so bad, that you think doing this was preferable? What was so horribly dangerous that violating my mind was the better option?" I was so angry my hand shook and the phone tapped my ear.

Again, silence, then he whispered, a sound like dry leaves against concrete, "I did it so you would never know."

We were both silent then, except for my crying and Buggy's faint breathing. There was something wrong. It was like his lungs were phlegmy, or... worse. Maybe a full minute passed before either of us said anything. Dragging myself away from the pain enough to think, I recalled why we were having this conversation.

Trying not to hiccup, I opened my eyes and growled, "Give Ink back to me."

"No." His voice was a little shaky, but the intent was clear. "Come to me and I'll let him go."

"Why should I believe you?" I sneered, picturing Buggy's big, red eyes as I stared at the cream-colored wall. "Is he even still alive?"

"Yes."

"Let me talk to him." That was something hostage negotiators always said on TV, and it sounded like a good idea in my head.

"I can't. He's unconscious." Buggy's voice faded mid-sentence, like his head turned from the phone.

"Why should I believe you then?" I snapped.

"I have never lied to you, Adeline, only tried to protect you." It was my former Guardian's turn to sound sad.

"You lied to me every single time you said you'd protect me." The barb was intended to hurt and the hesitation before he spoke again told me that it had.

"Whatever you may think, I am being honest." It was stupid, but I did believe him. Not that it made things any better. "I have him and will release him if you come to me."

I was so tired. No matter how much I'd slept earlier, I was still exhausted. The rage drained from me, and I hugged an arm across my stomach. I had no ideas, and I'd never felt so helpless. "What exactly do you plan to do, Buggy?"

"I will take you to get your memory locked away again. Without that upstart Tommy to interfere, it will work perfectly this time, I promise." His voice rose with excitement, but he didn't sound good. He sounded old and brittle. Sidhe was right, the fights before had hurt him. "I can put you back in your real life. It will be good this time because I'll be able to watch you and make sure of it."

A plan was starting to form. "So, you just want to take my memories away and then stick me back in my old life again. Is that it?"

"That's it," he agreed eagerly. Buggy thought he was offering something positive. He really had gone mad. "It will be so much less painful this time if you don't resist. You'll see."

Biting my tongue to prevent a pointless comeback, I explored my options. Tommy's plan had failed, and I doubted that Buggy would ever let him or the other boogies get close. If I turned myself over, he would have no reason not to let Ink go. Of course, he would wipe my memory again, but maybe there was a way around that. Tommy had said that he had a way to remove the spell. If I could save my stupid, wayward sheep, I could tolerate a little while of mediocre misery. With our connection, my Champion and Steward could find me, rescue me. It would suck, but it should work.

Exhaling, I forced my spine to straighten and said, "Here's the deal. I give myself over, and you drop Ink somewhere safe where the others can find him. Okay?"

"Yes," he agreed. "Come out to the guest house, and I will leave the Incubus there for them. Is that acceptable?"

It was a risk. Buggy might not keep his end of the bargain or my friend might already be dead. Even if my former Guardian was a hundred percent in earnest, there was a chance I was wrong and he could prevent everyone from finding me. Tommy's fix to the curse might not work. So many points of failure, but what else could I do?

This wasn't my fault. I hadn't made Ink leave the house and I hadn't made Buggy kidnap him. Rationally, I knew that, but not my fault was not the same as not my problem. I couldn't play faerie queen, I had to be the faerie queen, and that meant making decisions, good, bad, stupid, or otherwise.

"If you give your word that Ink is alive, and that you'll leave him at the guest house with no further harm done, I will meet you there and go with you."

"I swear, now come, quickly, while the Sidhe is still not looking for you." The first two words he said had a weight to them, like they were more important than just the syllables spoken. Was that a proper oath, like Crow had mentioned? Would bad things happen if he broke his word? It didn't matter right now, because I had to keep my end of the bargain.

Chapter 34: The Last Straw

Instead of going out the front door when I hung up, I asked the little hall door to take me through the kitchen and out into the night. It was shorter than walking around the outside of the house, and time was an issue. I didn't know how long Sidhe was going to wait for me to come out of the bathroom, but I had to assume that when he finally discovered I was gone, he'd come after me. With my luck, he'd have super speed or something like that.

The air was warm and wet, but the edge of fear kept me feeling cold. I passed through the destroyed rose garden. The rubble had been moved into piles, and Spring-heeled Jack's body had been taken away. It was a stark reminder of what I was going to face. Buggy had been my friend and family once, but that didn't matter. He was a killer. Always had been. I just hadn't understood it as a child.

Half expecting to be snatched up by the Boogieman in the night before I ever reached it, I came upon the guest house all too soon. It was a charming place, bigger than the house Mom and I had shared. I stood at the front door, wondering if it was going to be locked. The others had said that this wasn't part of the main house, so it wouldn't just let me in.

Silly me, I didn't need to worry. The door was open and swung in at a touch. It was disappointing because it meant that I had to go in.

The inside was as nice as the outside. Very modern, for when it was built ten years ago. It could have been a model home. Making myself walk normally, instead of creeping like the final girl in a horror movie, I came to the living room and saw Ink crumpled up in the middle of a white carpet. A red stain beneath him covered a large swath…

Flash

***

The lights were on at the guest house when I got there. Creeping around under the windows, I peeked at the two teenagers. I didn't know what Monica's no-good boyfriend looked like, but I'd bet that this was him.

He had his arms around her, kissing at her neck. She was frowning and weakly pushing at his chest like she wasn't sure if she wanted him to or not. They were talking, but I couldn't hear them.

I ran around to the back of the house. The back door was unlocked like always, so I snuck through the kitchen. Lying flat to the floor, I risked a look around the corner into the living room. Monica was pushing against her boyfriend a little more determinedly, but he didn't let go.

"No." She sounded more like she was begging than telling. "You just said you needed somewhere to crash for a couple of days, then we could leave together."

"If we get some shit from the house to sell, we could go tonight." He tried to nibble her ear, but she turned her head.

"They're family. I can't," she said, but she seemed uncertain.

"They're so rich, they won't miss it." He pulled back, grabbing hold of her hair so she couldn't look away when he met her eyes. "Come on, babe. Please?"

Monica bit her lip, then pushed herself away from him in one big shove. She tried to square up her shoulders, probably trying to look tough. It didn't work, but it was a good try. "No. My aunt and uncle have been good to me. I'm not going to do it."

The boyfriend stared at her for a second, before a snarl of anger passed over his face. "Forget you, then, bitch. I'll get it all myself. You can stay here with them if they treat you so good."

He walked towards the kitchen and Monica ran after him. She grabbed his arm, and he batted her away hard enough to knock her over. She hit the wall and started to cry. That was enough of that.

Monica's boyfriend had just about reached the door when I stepped around the corner and seized a random knickknack. It was a wooden ball about the size of a softball that had been sitting in a bowl. Dropping Tiger, I leaped and swung it at him. Mid jump, he turned and instead of catching him in the back of the head like I'd intended, it connected with his shoulder. The impact knocked the ball from my hand, and I was facing a very angry man who was much bigger than me without a weapon. Still, I wasn't afraid.

I lifted my chin. "Get out of here."

"That hurt, you little bitch!" he bellowed and swiped at me.

Ducking the clumsy attempted grab, I showed my teeth and shouted, "Get out or I'm gonna call my friends and then you're gonna die."

"No, Addie, please just go back to bed!" Monica sobbed. She pushed away from the wall but didn't approach either of us. Her hands fluttered around uselessly, like wounded animals.

I gave her my most reassuring grin. "It's okay. I've got this."

I did not. As I was looking at my cousin, her boyfriend lunged forward and seized me painfully by the shoulder. With a yelp, I tried to twist away, but he grabbed my other arm. I thrashed.

He squeezed hard. "So you're the spoiled brat. Shut up before I smack you."

"No!" I hollered as loud as I could. I wasn't afraid, but I wanted Buggy to hear me. He should be there any second. No matter how grumpy he got, he always came when I needed him.

"Shut up!" Monica's boyfriend yelled, shifting his hold to just above my elbow.

Several things happened so fast, it was like they happened all at once. My arm was twisted so hard something popped. I whipped my head to the side to bite his arm. My teeth clamped down so hard that I tasted blood. Monica screamed and her boyfriend let go of me only to backhand me across the face. I fell to the ground.

I wasn't looking when the door exploded inwards, but I turned in time to see Buggy surge forward, like ink flowing through water. Moving this fast, he was hard to watch, looking more like smoke with claws than any sort of beast. He grabbed the boyfriend, hauling him into the air and slamming his head into the ceiling. The drywall cracked and dust rained down.

While holding still, Buggy was a bit easier to see. He was impossibly tall and lean, but the smokiness around him remained. What Sidhe called a miasma of darkness constantly followed him everywhere. I smirked as the jerk boyfriend's head lolled from the impact.

Monica screamed again. She grabbed a small, spindly end table from next to the couch and rushed my Guardian, swinging it like a baseball bat.

One swipe from Buggy and Monica's screaming stopped. She dropped the little table, clutched her throat, and stumbled back a few steps before falling next to me.

Claw marks from her neck to her forehead made her pretty face unrecognizable. Blood was pouring out all over the floor in a flood. I scrambled to my hands and knees. Red rivers were flowing under Monica's hands and from down the deep gouges. Sobbing, I put my hands over hers, trying to help her stop the bleeding.

I watched my cousin bleed to death, helpless to do anything. Seconds. It took seconds, and I couldn't do anything.

I looked up at the sharp crunching noise and saw Buggy drop the boyfriend, who fell into a heap on the ground. His eyes were blank and his head, while still attached, didn't look like it lined up right with his body anymore. Dead. They were both dead.

"Buggy–" I said, sniffling.

He turned away from me. "Go into the kitchen."

"But Buggy–" I extended a hand painted with my cousin's blood.

"But nothing!" He turned towards me with his dagger teeth bared, and I flinched. "I told you to stay in bed once I put you there. I told you not to go out. You didn't listen. You never listen and this is the consequence."

"Buggy, Monica's dead!" I wailed.

"Yes, she is." There was no trace of compassion or regret in his voice at all. "That's a consequence too. Your actions, your parents, hers, mine... and everyone was warned, so we're equally at fault. Now go to the kitchen, Adeline. Clean yourself up. I'll take care of this mess."

Nodding slowly, I got up. I couldn't stop crying. Tiger was laying off to the side, mostly untouched by the carnage, except the blood was still expanding across the pretty white carpet, heading his direction. Wiping my hands on the couch, I picked up my stuffed friend just as the crimson pool reached him and soaked into his ear.

***

My stomach twisted. The rumors were right. The girl who disappeared, my cousin, had died here. Buggy had murdered her. Monica hadn't been a threat to him. He didn't have to hurt her, much less kill her.

I raced across the room, fell to my knees and slid the last foot to Ink's prone body. Frantically, I felt for a pulse and through skin tacky with blood, I found one. My hands shook as I cradled his face and nearly wept in relief.

The hair on the back of my neck stood up as I felt Buggy's presence behind me before I heard him speak. "I've kept my word, Adeline, now it's time to keep yours."

I slowly rose and hoped my legs didn't give out. A lump caught in my throat as I turned to look at Buggy. He was thin and frail compared to the monster I remembered. The tendrils of darkness that used to ebb and flow around his body had been worn away to tiny wisps. There was the finest of tremors in his claws and his red eyes were dim. What was happening to him? He looked less battered than starved, like he was wasting away.

It hurt my heart and I didn't want it to. He was mad, and a murderer, and a monster, and none of that negated the fact that he was my oldest friend, and more family to me than my mother and father had ever been.

275

I closed my eyes, but couldn't stop seeing his painfully frail form. "Okay Buggy, let's go."

He held a gnarled talon out to me that looked like it had been mangled and healed many times. I took it timidly, and he gently pulled me forward like for a hug. The world melted and blurred. One second the ground under my feet was thick carpet, then not there at all, and then solid ground.

We were in a large, circular room made of pale brown stone, with a balcony that looked over an impossible sunset. It had been dead of night a moment ago. I thought at first that I was in a different time zone, but a part of my mind whispered that I was in the Betwixt. The Earth's rotation didn't figure in anymore.

The room was sparse. A half-moon structure on the floor looked a little like a seat and was big enough for me to lie in. Lots of giant, broken old cobwebs hung from the ceiling and three giant gilt frames lined the wall. Only one of them held an unbroken mirror. My former Guardian stood in the middle of the room, looking around like he was lost. Had he accidentally taken us to the wrong place?

"Where is she? She was supposed to meet me here when the time was up. She was going to renew the spell." Buggy sounded so brittle and betrayed, that I had to fight my pity.

"Who isn't here?" I guessed this confirmed that Tommy was right and Buggy hadn't put the curse on me himself. What would he do, in his madness, if he couldn't get it recast?

"I… she… " He stammered and whipped his head back and forth, red eyes glowing brighter in his panic. Instinct warred between running towards him to calm him and running away. The urge to flee won. There were no doors in the room, so I ran to the edge of the balcony, hoping it wasn't a long way down.

All there was, over the edge, was a deep chasm full of a beige haze. On the other side, about a football field's length away, was a shear wall. Beyond that was a flat, featureless desert that went into infinity until it met a rose and orange sunset with no sun. Looking around more showed me only the smooth surface of a cylindrical tower that disappeared into the mist and ran upward to a dome not far above the ceiling.

Behind me, my old Guardian thrashed and screamed. His great talons struck the floor and left gouges in the stone. The black wisps that enveloped his body snapped and writhed like streamers in a gale-force wind. He was burning power so fast, so hard, that he was going to be dead soon, I knew it. Somehow.

He wasn't going to wipe my memory, he was going to burn himself out. Not knowing what else to do, I called on the greatest weapon I had at my disposal. If Buggy had just come from stone, maybe I could send him back and give Tommy a chance to find me. I could save him.

My Guardian collapsed to the floor, and I went to him. I winced at every sound my shoes made, but he didn't seem to hear me. When I got to his side I placed a hand on his back. He flinched, but didn't move any more than that. I smoothed a hand across his back like I was leaning over to hug him. It was like petting a slightly leathery lobster. When my mouth was even with the bat-like ear on the side of his head, so small it was almost invisible, I reached deep into the magic that I could always feel now, and whispered the words.

"Far too weary, far too old. He's gone to sleep in dark and cold. Forsworn, forsaken, all alone. The dragon now has gone to stone."

Buggy started to calm, his breathing slowing as rock formed over his back like frost. Elation wrestled with my concentration. He jerked upward, sending dust into the air. My magic tangled with his will and it wasn't a battle I knew how to win. Buggy didn't want to go to stone, even if it saved him. Turns out, you can't make someone live if they don't want to. His great black head swung around to look at me and his red eyes narrowed, like he finally remembered that I was there.

Lightning fast, he grabbed my arm. "Nice try, Adeline, but I can't rest just yet. I need to fix this. You'll have to stay here. It should be safe enough. It will take that upstart a while to find this place. I need to go find someone."

"Who?" I asked as he released me and stalked towards the balcony.

"Doesn't matter." He hopped up to the railing like a bird getting ready to fly. "You won't remember any of this soon, anyways."

In one grand leap, he cleared the abyss and was fast disappearing into the desert in a motion more slither than run. I was left standing alone, staring out after him.

My confidence wavered as I wondered if Tommy would be able to find me, or be capable of removing the spell once he did. Maybe I had been foolish in leaving. Then again, Ink was alive and I believed that Buggy would have killed him if I hadn't complied.

Even if I forgot everything, and was shoved back into banal existence, never to return, I couldn't regret it. As stupid and immature as Ink was, he loved me. Once upon a time, I had loved him like a brother. Maybe, in the place in my head where all my memories were hiding, I still did.

Chapter 35: Memory in the Mirror

For a lack of anything else to do, I examined the room. There were no obvious entrances other than the balcony, but that couldn't be the only way in. I inspected everything carefully, looking for the secret door I imagined had to be there somewhere.

The curved stone structure in the middle of the room seemed to be just that, a piece of stone. The mirrors were just as fruitless. I spent a ridiculous amount of time on each inch of frame that I could reach and must have pressed and pried every protrusion at least twice. It was as useless as everything else I had tried. There was nothing behind them.

Frustration lingered like a bad headache as I stared at the one remaining mirror, willing it to give me its secrets. There had to be some reason it and the empty frames were there. Their elaborate design was so out of place with the barren stone of the rest of the room. DeJa'Vu had been itching at the back of my head since Buggy had brought me to this place, but there had been no flashes of recalled events. Harder than ever before, I pushed my memory. I closed my eyes, dragging and clawing at it with that new magical muscle I had found inside my head.

Something gave, and it was a horrible feeling, like a bone slowly bending until it snapped. This wasn't like the other memories, but more like when I was looking out of Crow's eyes, seeing two times at once. In one was the now, where I stood in an empty room, staring at the one remaining mirror. In the other, I was a child. All the mirrors were whole, and my eyes fixated on a figure in front of the unbroken one on the right.

In that earlier time, the room wasn't barren. Drapes of pink, white, and gold hung from every wall. There were people behind me, but I couldn't see them in the reflections because younger me wasn't focused on them. I couldn't see now what I didn't see then. The other two frames were covered with glittery white curtains that looked like the lightest gauze and spider's silk.

A bedraggled creature I didn't know knelt near the wall, shivering and wailing. He was naked, and so scrawny I could count every bone under his blue-gray skin. Even curled up I could tell he was tall. His obscenely large head was all sharp projections and pronounced features, with two small tusks protruding from his lips. The sing-song words of a spell came in a sultry female voice behind me, barely audible over the cries of the pitiful monster.

When the rhyme finished, the creature gave one last scream. Silvery tendrils, glittering things somewhere between tentacles and Christmas tinsel, reached out from the mirror and wrapped around his desiccated frame to pull him in. He whimpered as he hit the surface of the glass, making it ripple. Slowly he sank in, like silver quicksand. The mirror distorted and bulged, giving a fun house view of the room.

I could see one of the figures behind me, sitting on the stone crescent. It was big and black, with long dark hair on a mostly human head, too many legs, and eyes that shone red like Buggy's. Except, Buggy didn't have black hourglasses for pupils and a smile that made my stomach freeze.

When the glass flattened out, the figure behind me fell from focus. The mirror was normal again, except the creature was inside, silently sobbing on the floor. It looked for all the world like he was in the room with us, but he wasn't. Whoever he was, he was stuck in there, separated from the world.

The double vision broke and I collapsed, gagging and fighting not to vomit. That felt wrong and I shouldn't have done it. Was that what happened when I forced a memory before it was ready, or was this something else?

I laid out prone on the floor, absorbing the cool of the stone, letting it soothe me. There was something in the front pocket of my jeans, poking into my hip. With more effort than it should have taken, I rolled to one side, and pulled it out. It was the little wooden casket containing my birthday present from the Knocker.

Laughing in an attempt not to cry, I opened the box and set it on the floor. I asked my lovely little ballerina to dance. She stepped out and began to leap and twirl. It was very soothing to watch. Half in jest, I hummed part of the Nutcracker Suite, the only ballet I knew off-hand, and she obligingly danced along. I started to cough around my despair-swollen throat and trembled at the effort not to just give in.

"I wish you could talk to me," I whispered. "I could really use a friend."

The ballerina stopped dancing and turned to look at me, tiny face puzzled. My eyes narrowed suspiciously as I asked, "Can you understand me?"

Technically, the Knocker had said she could follow rudimentary commands, but I had thought he meant along the lines of instructing her how to dance. On a wild hair, and because I would feel sillier if I didn't ask, I said, "Could you go get help?"

The ballerina gave a single nod and then stood there, not doing anything. I thought that this must be where the rudimentary part comes in. She had to be told.

"Go find Tommy Raw Head and Bloody Bones and bring him back here to me," I urged her.

Pirouetting, the little golem did an about-face and began dancing towards the balcony. She made several elegant leaps before spinning the rest of the way across the room. I followed her out to the edge, wondering if somehow the small figure could make the jump, or if I would have to catch her as she made the leap into the abyss.

I was completely wrong. Instead of going off the balcony, she made an abrupt left turn and stopped at an inch-thick ridge that looked to ring the tower at least as far as I could see. With an almost military briskness, she arched her arms above her head and tiptoed down the ledge that was narrow, even for her.

I tried to squash down hope, because it was silly to put that much stock in a doll. Still, as I watched her disappear from sight, I couldn't help but think that this might just be crazy enough to work. I was stupid. This whole thing happened because I had the gall to think I was clever enough to outsmart the Boogieman, and now I was idiotic enough to think a little doll could get me out of this.

With a frustrated growl, I kicked the wall, then sank to my knees. I was so screwed. I turned to sit against the stone and stared off into the desert. My internal clock wasn't terribly accurate, but I would be willing to bet that a few hours had gone by and the sunset had not moved at all. Maybe it never did.

I was crying again. I was tired of crying but the ache in my chest wouldn't let me stop. Finally, I dozed, exhaustion making the world fade away.

I didn't know how long I nodded there, but I jerked awake to a faint tapping. The sound was quiet. Ordinarily I wouldn't have noticed it, but any noise was jarring in the silence of this desert tower. For a moment, I couldn't pinpoint the origin, but then I saw the ballerina, doing her strange little dancing step towards me across the floor. I rose, stiff and aching, and hobbled over to meet her.

Charmed by her adorable walk, I smiled. "Did you find help?"

I didn't expect anything, thinking maybe it had just taken her that long to tiptoe around the little ledge and circumvent the tower. Poor little thing had done her best. When she nodded slightly and elegantly pointed back towards the balcony, I was stunned. Scooping her and her box off the floor, I carried them both over to the railing. There was nothing new to see, but deep in the swirling mist I could hear the echoes of growls, and they were approaching like a fast-moving storm.

This felt like trouble. Trusting my instincts, I retreated from the balcony to the back of the room. I held my ballerina up next to her box. "Go to sleep, okay my lovely? It's the safest place, I think."

The ballerina stepped delicately across my hand, but before she lay back in her little casket and crossed her arms she touched my thumb. I closed her lid and slid the box back in my pocket and not a moment too soon.

Chapter 36: Into the Fray

Something erupted from the abyss, taking a piece of the balcony with it in an explosion of pale brown stone. I covered my head with my arms as hunks of rubble rained down on me. I flattened against the wall to keep as far from the fight as possible. Dust clouded the room, but I could make out two titanic forms doing battle.

Tommy, in full boogie form, rolled to his feet and roared. Spittle flew from his mouth as he grabbed a chunk of rock, hurling it at Buggy. My Guardian was slithering up the wall like a lizard and it hit him square on the shoulder. The force of it buckled his arm and he fell to the ground with a hiss of pain.

Buggy shrieked like a demon and launched at Tommy. They collided, slamming against the wall before the Boogieman leaped towards the ceiling, only to hurdle back and ram into my Champion again as he rose. This time Tommy caught him and used the momentum to turn and slam him into the floor. Black talons and red fists flew as blood splattered, mixing with the dust on the stone.

When Buggy tore free with a rain of gore, he jumped to the ceiling, then sprang back. And they did it again. And again. And again. Buggy would fly at Tommy with momentum and claws, to be met with blows. Anytime Tommy got a good hold on the Boogeyman I'd hear something snap and Buggy would scream, but my Guardian kept fighting and my Champion kept bleeding. The floor was covered in a slurry of bloody mud. I crouched behind the largest piece of rubble I could find and whimpered at every blow.

Something grabbed my wrist and I tried to break away but it was like trying to break iron. I opened my mouth to scream, but the dust sent me into a fit of coughing. When I was able to focus, there was Red, grinning madly.

"I have never been so happy to see anyone in my life!" I hugged him as tight as I could.

"Glad to hear it," Red said, and gave me a single pat on the back before pulling me towards the balcony. "But I have an order from my king to get you out of here while he deals with the Boogieman, and this is one order I do not intend to disobey."

Tommy roared as Buggy landed on his back and raked a talon down his shoulder. My Champion rolled to the side, managing to dislodge him yet again, barely avoiding a blow to the back of his head. Buggy lit against the wall only to push off like a swimmer diving into a pool. Exploding forward, Tommy took advantage of his opponent's momentum, catching him midair. He wrapped his colossal arms around the frail-looking form of my Guardian and squeezed. There was a horrible, wet cracking noise and Buggy's head snapped straight up, beak-like muzzle pointing to the ceiling.

My heart lurched. I thought for a moment that it was all over, and Tommy had broken the other boogie, but Buggy, faster than I could see, slithered down out of the iron grasp, both his arms flopping uselessly. With a banshee scream, Buggy wrenched his own limbs back into place and sprung up to run along the wall in defiance of gravity, trying to flank Tommy.

A sharp yank on my arm reminded me of Red's presence. "Come on, Addie."

"Can Tommy beat him?" I asked, turning back to the brawling giants.

Red tugged again. "I would rather not have to find out. Move, now! The sooner you are out of danger, the sooner he can retreat."

Snapping out of it, I shook my head and ran across the rubble strewn room. I had no idea what was going to happen when we reached the edge of the balcony, but I trusted Red not to lead me to my death. Behind me, there was a horrible anguished cry.

"No!" The screech hurt my ears and made me flinch.

I had to look, and in the way of all tragedies, time distorted, slowing down. Before I completely turned, a pale brown chunk of rock was flying at my head. Instinct took over and I raised my hand like I was flicking it away. My magic sparked like when I'd forced Sidhe and Tommy apart. The trajectory of the rock changed, but I think I missed because it didn't move much. I realized it hadn't been aimed at me anyway. Something behind me crunched. I had enough time to see Buggy straightening from a throwing posture to face the great red boogie that was lunging to attack his exposed back. Time resumed its normal pace as I whipped around again in time to see my Steward crashing to the floor, the flying rock having just clipped him on the side of the head.

"Red!" I screamed, collapsing to my knees beside him. He didn't respond to my call, so I felt for a heartbeat. It was there, and strong. Unless that was just my own pulse thundering in my fingertips. Anyway, he was breathing.

I brushed the blood away from the cut on his temple. While it was bleeding a lot, it didn't look all that bad. With a head injury on a fae, though, how could I tell? Maybe his brain was jelly, maybe he was fine. Either way, he was out cold and I couldn't desert him. Even if I was willing to leave him behind, undefended, I didn't know how to get out of the damn tower. I had to bet that leaving him in the middle of the floor was riskier than moving him and pulled Red off to the side by his arms. I got as close to the wall as I could and stationed myself protectively in front of him.

The battle between Bloody Bones and Boogieman raged on. Right. I had forgotten about my trick. Maybe I could help Tommy. Yeah. I could do it. I concentrated, muscles so tense they hurt, and waited for Buggy to launch from the ceiling toward my Champion. The power lashed out, and… struck the wall past where Buggy had been, cracking like thunder across the stone. He was too fast, and I had too little control to hit him. The magic inside of me felt strained, like the muscle was pulled. My knees buckled and I fell to the floor next to Red. Useless. I could only cringe as I watched them beat against each other like the ocean against the shore.

Buggy was bleeding less than Tommy, but he wasn't better off. The longer the fight went on the more smoky tendrils grew around him, and the less physical he seemed to be. It was burning him up, fighting like this, using magic like this. My former Guardian, my old friend, might win, but it would be a Pyrrhic victory. He would eat himself alive, and after the battle, there would be nothing left.

My Champion looked like he was pouring out blood by the gallons. He struck at Buggy with as much strength as when he started, but he was slower now, and I didn't think it was my imagination that I could feel his pain and distress like a stone in my gut. If they continued on like this, neither of them would make it.

"No," I said softly, placing a hand on Red's forehead. Maybe he was okay, or maybe he was dying.

Maybe we would all die here. Red and Tommy would fall to the Boogieman. Buggy would be consumed as he burned through the magic that had brought him from stone. I would starve to death here in a tower in the middle of some unknown desert where the sun never set.

"No," I said again, stronger, moving my feet underneath me and slowly pushing myself to stand.

Their battle had led them right in front of the frames. Tommy was crouched with one arm spread wide to strike, but the other hung uselessly at his side, held on with only a bone and a few strands of muscle. Buggy perched on the one intact mirror, almost more shadow than flesh.

The mirror.

Something in my head snapped. My feet started walking towards the fight, and I hadn't asked them to. I didn't think about whether this was going to work, or how much it was going to hurt if it did. I didn't think of Tommy, Red, or Ink, who I had left behind in the guest house. Or Sidhe, who for all I knew was still outside my bathroom door, waiting for me. I didn't think of Loren, who I'd sent far away to protect her. Only one thought crossed my mind in the walk across the floor that took mere moments, but seemed to last forever. Wasn't it ironic that I was going to have to trust my treacherous Guardian one last time?

If Buggy hadn't been slowed down by his injuries, I would have never made it before he hurt my Champion again. I stood between him and Tommy, looking defiantly into his glowing scarlet eyes. He froze and I knew that I was right. The Boogieman wouldn't hurt me, at least not physically. The rock had been meant for Red all along. Moving it had probably saved his life. Tommy was yelling something behind me, but I couldn't hear it.

I laughed, and my voice didn't sound right. I didn't feel okay, but right now, that didn't matter.

Time was malfunctioning again. I was the only thing in the world that moved. Tommy and Buggy froze where they stood. The dust in the air hung like it was suspended in glass. Everything had stopped, but my heart raced. The world tilted like a fun house spinning tunnel.

I remembered the poor, cadaverous fae being dragged into the mirror as I stared at my emaciated Guardian. Watching him disappear into the glass had been horrifying, but I couldn't feel that right now. That was good, because remembering this was going to cost me. I could feel that.

Looking into the past, I focused not on the horror or the fear, but the words. The pain was exquisite, but I threw myself into it without reserve and got what I wanted. Almost crystalline clear through the agony, I heard the words of the woman behind me in the mirror. I whispered them, a child's rhyme of damnation, to my poor old friend's frightened face.

"Wicked beastie, be now bound, away from scent, away from sound. Away from touch, away from taste, in the mirror be encased. In sight alone in this world pass, 'till someone breaks the looking glass." I grinned, and it felt crooked and sickly. Hot tears rolled down my cheek. At that moment, I was just as crazy as my Guardian.

Glittering silver tendrils reached out of the mirror and snatched Buggy by his arms. It took a long time to drag him in. Perhaps because my old Guardian was just so much stronger, and struggled so much more than the other fae. Not that it mattered. No matter how many furrows he dug in the stone wall, no matter how many times he screamed my name, into the mirror the Boogieman went, sinking beneath the surface until only one claw waved helplessly in the air, reaching for me. Soon, even that was gone. When the bulging and rippling glass calmed, he lay on the floor of the room on the other side of the mirror, with our reflections, but not us, and the room was deafeningly quiet.

Time flooded in like water filling a burst bubble.

"What the hell just happened?" Tommy asked, his voice sudden and perplexed.

Giggling, I turned to tell him… I don't know what. I never found out either, because the floor was rushing towards my face at an alarming pace.

Chapter 37: Empty Endings

And… I was in bed again. The pink sheets and canopy of my bed in my house were a welcome, if confusing sight. My house. Huh. I was getting used to that.

Sitting up, I was stiff, but nothing hurt too bad. That was welcome too.

"Oh, thank goodness." Sidhe's voice came from beside me. I looked to see him rising from the chair he had pulled up at some point.

"Well, I'm not dead. That's good." I smiled weakly, wondering how mad Sidhe was going to be about me ditching him. It turned out, pretty mad.

"Not for lack of effort on your part," he hissed, and I lowered my head in shame. I deserved that. "Before we even begin to discuss you leaving me behind to sacrifice yourself to the very monster people were willing to die to protect you from, let us address how the hell you put the Boogieman in a mirror with a spell that has been lost for over a thousand years."

"Um, yeah." I rubbed the back of my neck sheepishly. "I don't really get that one myself. I think I forced a memory, and… I don't know. It wasn't like the other ones. Dragging it out with magic like that hurt. Like a lot."

"That's not surprising." Sidhe leaned over me, looking at my eyes like a doctor would. "You nearly gave yourself a brain hemorrhage."

"Yeah, but at least everyone is alive, right?" When Sidhe didn't answer right away, I grabbed his shirt. "Everyone is alive, right, Sidhe?"

"Yes, everyone is alive, now calm down." He pulled my hand away and I let him. "When you didn't come out of the bathroom, I kicked in the door and realized that you'd given me the slip. I sent a message to the Bloody Bones and tracked you using magic, only to arrive at the guest house too late. You'd already gone. I found that idiot Incubus, though. He was hurt, but not any more than he could heal himself with a little time and… help from a young woman in town."

I felt like I could breathe again. "So how did you find me?"

"Nearly immediately after I got to the guest house, Tommy and his court showed up. I didn't have a spell that could track you into the Betwixt, but that proved to be a non-issue. The bond that you and the Bloody Bones share is as strong as he said it was, and he used it to follow you. He and the Red Cap took off after, leaving everyone else behind." Sidhe didn't even try to hide the bitterness. "A couple of hours later, Tommy showed up, half dead, with you swung over one shoulder and your Steward over the other. That was about six hours ago."

"Huh," I said inelegantly. That explained why I needed to use the bathroom. I eased myself out of bed.

"Where do you think you're going?" Sidhe put a hand on my shoulder to shove me back down. "Get back in bed."

"I need to go to the bathroom," I said. The look on his face was terrifying, then I remembered why that might make him mad. "I promise that I will not go anywhere else and will come right back out the same door I went in through, but you gotta let me go. I really need to pee."

Sidhe hesitated, but finally moved away from the side of the bed. Before he changed his mind and assigned me an escort, I scampered off to the bathroom. After completing my business, I paused in front of the mirror. It felt like something should be different after sending someone through the looking glass, but I looked the same. I, inexplicably, appeared to still be me. Maybe there was a lesson in that.

Anyway, it didn't matter. Looking at my reflection made me uncomfortable, reminding me of twisting silver tentacles and reaching, pleading claws.

Tommy's deep voice sounded from the bedroom, and Sidhe's irritated response conveyed the tone of their conversation, even if I couldn't hear the words. Leaving the bathroom, I found them standing next to my round table, facing each other. In his human guise, Tommy was significantly taller than Sidhe, but his posture was tired and docile. My old tutor looked ready for a fight, and seemed frustrated at Tommy's unwillingness to engage.

"Hi," I said, causing both of their attentions to shift. "Are you okay?"

Tommy gave a crooked smile. "I am fine. After a couple of days more of recovery, you won't be able to tell I was ever hurt. Are you alright? The Sidhe is convinced that there has to be something wrong and that you need to spend more time in bed."

"I mean, I feel okay," I shrugged, "but what do I know? In fact, thinking over the last few days and all the stupid things I've done, I am severely questioning my judgment."

"Well, that at least shows a little wisdom." Sidhe rolled his eyes before sighing heavily. "I suppose there's no harm in getting up and moving around a little. Just don't do anything too strenuous and you do not go anywhere alone. I want you under constant surveillance until we are sure there are no long-reaching effects from your little stunt."

I held up my hands, surrendering to his demands. "Cool, but can I get some food? I'm starving."

"There's stew in the kitchen. Red made it, and he's a decent cook as long as he's making something simple." Tommy's nose wrinkled.

"So Red's back to normal?" I asked, going for some normal clothes. Probably no one would care if I ran around in my jammies, but I did.

"Oh, please." He shook his head and lightly rapped his knuckles across his temple. "With his hard head? There was barely any injury to speak of. I'm surprised that rock phased him. He'll be catching hell years from now for fainting during the battle of the millennia."

"Tommy Raw Head and Bloody Bones versus the Boogieman," I mused, finding my old pair of jeans, dusty and much worse for wear, draped over a chair. Noticing the bulge in the front pocket, I fished for the little ballerina's box. When I pulled it out unharmed, I sighed in relief.

"More the queen of the fae versus the Boogieman." Sidhe scoffed. "You were the one that finished that fight, not the Bloody Bones."

I felt Tommy's presence over my shoulder as I opened the little casket, revealing its small passenger. He murmured, "She's the unsung hero of the day, you know? I had managed to track you through the Betwixt to the Lair of the Fallen Spider Queen. I knew you were in there, but the Lair is an ancient citadel, protected by a maze full of illusions and traps. I couldn't find my way to you. She showed up out of nowhere and gestured for me to follow her. Your little golem here led me through the labyrinth."

"My little hero. She was a gift from the Knocker. A birthday present. You know, Buggy had lied to him. Told him that he would get to serve in my court as a tutor. He made her for me, just an amusing gift for a child. He had been so excited at the idea of getting to serve me now. It broke my heart when I heard that he had died. Turns out, he served me better than he could ever have imagined." I stroked a finger down the side of her face, smiling gently even though my chest ached. "I wonder if he knows that, wherever he is now? Do the fae have an afterlife, Tommy?"

He was silent for a long moment before answering carefully, "If the Knocker had any beliefs along those lines, he never shared them with me. Personally, I believe that we become part of the greater magic. Kind of becoming one with the universe, if you will. If I am right, then he knows and is happy."

I smiled, not caring if he was just saying that to humor me. I had an idea and took the ballerina to the large, ornate dollhouse that sat in the play area and set her casket down in front of it.

"Wake up, my lovely." The ballerina opened her eyes and stepped out of the box with a little curtsy. Half in jest, I said, "You have done me a great service. In honor of your service, and that of the one who created you, I gift you this holding. It is your domain to rule over and do with as you please. I hope you like it, and that you continue to be as good a friend to me in the future, as you were that day."

I bowed my head and after a moment of hesitation the little ballerina curtsied again, then opened the door of the doll house to walk into her new home. I closed the box, intending never to make her go to sleep again.

"What was that about?" Sidhe sounded bemused.

I shrugged defensively. "Closure, I guess. Maybe. I don't know. It seemed like the right thing to say at the moment and made me feel better. Leave me alone."

"Good enough." My tutor chuckled. "Whatever makes you happy, but I hope you know, that was official. That golem is the first landholder under your rule."

"Yeah, well, she's earned it." I sniffed.

"What about me?" Tommy asked in mock distress.

"You don't count. You're contractually obligated to nearly die for me," I said, smirking.

"True enough. Come on. Stew awaits, and we have many things to discuss about what needs to be done in the next few days." My Champion made an ushering gesture to the door. "And you can call Loren. The Crow passably mimicked your voice for your last check-in, but it would be better if he didn't have to do it again. Your friend is surprisingly sharp."

I had to laugh. "Yeah, she is. Alright, let's go."

About The Author

Sharon Gray Sharon is a forty-year-old woman from Texas. She is fighting with MS but currently, the biggest foe to her writing is her two cats, who are too cute for their own good. As always, her greatest help is her loving husband, who she couldn't do this without.

Printed in Great Britain
by Amazon